stories and satires
by
sholom aleichem

Stories and Satires by
Sholom Aleichem

translated by Curt Leviant

Drawings by Arthur Aidenberg

SHOLOM
ALEICHEM
FAMILY
PUBLICATIONS

ROBERT V. WAIFE

R/W New York

PUBLISHED BY
Sholom Aleichem Family Publications
PO Box 411
9 NORTH FERRY ROAD
SHELTER ISLAND, NY 11964

www.Tevye.net

Manufactured in the United States of America

ISBN: 1-929068-19-0

cover by NUMA STUDIOS

for my parents
jacques and fenia leviant
c. l.

contents

INTRODUCTION

In 1959, the literary world celebrated the one-hundredth anniversary of its most beloved Yiddish writer, Sholom Aleichem. Born Sholom Rabinowitz in Pereyeslav (Russian Ukraine) on March 2, 1859, the future writer went through Russian schools and later supported himself by becoming a private tutor. He fell in love with, and eventually married, his pupil, the daughter of a wealthy landowner. Upon his father-in-law's death, he administered the vast estate and came into contact with the upper-class Jews whom he so well satirized. Like his creation, Menakhem-Mendel, Sholom Aleichem played the stock-exchange and lost his entire fortune. But one man's loss proved to be literature's gain. Besides contributing to periodicals, he established and edited, in 1888, an annual called the *Jewish Folk Library*, and was the first publisher to pay high sums to authors writing in Yiddish.

From 1900 on, he devoted all his time to writing. He came to the United States in 1914 (previously, he had visited the United States from October, 1906 to June, 1907), and two years later, on May 13, 1916, he died, mourned by Jews the world over and by the one hundred and fifty thousand people who attended his funeral in New York City. At the time of his death, his completed works totaled forty volumes. Only twenty-eight have been published in Yiddish, and a fraction of this, in English.

A creator of stories and satires, novels and plays, monologues and children's tales, fantasies and sketches—he even wrote a lullaby which almost every Jewish mother sang—Sholom Aleichem endeared himself to the public with his shrewd, loving, and accurate portrayal of the speech, manners, and foibles of the East-European Jew.

There was something unique about Sholom Aleichem's relationship to his people. There was hardly a Jew who had not heard of him. Surely this is a phenomenon of which no other modern literature can boast. Has every American heard of Hemingway or Faulkner, every Englishman of T. S. Eliot, every Frenchman of Albert Camus? Today, television stars and soap, toothpaste, and athletes compete for the average man's attention. Modern society has converted these, instead of the literary man, into the idols of the culture.

But all Jews knew Sholom Aleichem. And this fact compliments both the writer and the people, for in the Yiddish-speaking world there was no great gap between artist and public. Sholom Aleichem worked within a literary tradition which everyone knew. When Tevye the Dairyman misquotes the Talmud or the Bible, or wrongly interprets them, everyone knew the mistake. No footnotes were needed. However, when a modern poet like Eliot writes and quotes from his tradition, he must append footnotes, since he cannot even communicate directly to the intellectuals, much less to the man in the street.

The Bible, the Aramaic translation, the commentaries, the Talmud, Jewish customs, holidays, a basic education in Hebrew—all these were part of the people's lives. That they are enshrined today as college courses with imposing section numbers, shows their final separation from the mainstream of life. But when Sholom Aleichem draws upon tradition—when he uses phrases from the Bible, Mishna, and Talmud, and couched references to holidays and customs in his metaphors, he simply goes to a storehouse of knowledge common to all. And there is no academic or intellectual pretension about it either.

Herein lies the great difference—the entire tradition was the people's daily bread, their very existence. You could not separate what they knew from what they lived.

Aside from the common field of experience and ideas, author and public were one with the Yiddish language, as well. Sholom Aleichem's Yiddish was neither above the folk, nor beneath it. It *was* the folk—the real, the brisk, the pliable, the down-to-earth and vibrant expression of the Jewish people.

In reading him, the oral tradition of story-telling must be remembered. All the accouterments of daily speech—the

pause, the sly glance, the gesture, shrug, or deprecating wave
—all these are inextricable parts of the text. Often, a positive
statement in print turns negative if the ironic twinkle is seen
between the lines.

Sholom Aleichem's characters, unlike Peretz', are more types
than individuals. Having had contact with all classes of Jews—
he had been tutor, crown rabbi for three years, businessman,
insurance agent, and publisher—Sholom Aleichem's penetrat-
ing eye was able to grasp the representative essence of each
group. Since his characters are always talking, there is a measure of self-revelation, but hardly self-penetration or inner
probing of the soul.

Many of his pieces are told in the first person. Taking this
into consideration, the long tales *75,000* and *Three Widows*
are really monologues, as are *Happy New Year* and *Three
Calendars,* despite the story lines in them. In his conversational
tone lies the secret of Sholom Aleichem's charm. Words for
him were not the medium of separation between author and
reader. They were not used to make the reader aware that
he is experiencing literature. Words, rather, for Sholom Aleichem, were the magnet which united reader and writer; it
made them aware that they were experiencing life. He knew
well the distinction between the language of literature and the
language of the people. And his was the language of the people
elevated to literature. That is why so many of his expressions
and metaphors have become a living part of the Yiddish language. His own estimation of himself as a writer is shown in
one line of a letter written to Chekhov. In it he requests a
story from Chekhov for a volume to be issued in benefit of
victims of the Kishinev pogrom. (Previously, Tolstoy had ac-
ceded to the same request.) He guarantees the Russian writer
that: "I myself will translate (it)—I consider myself one of
the best stylists in the Yiddish language . . ." (June, 1903).

Though he started as an imitator of Mendele Mocher Se-
forim, the grandfather of Yiddish literature, and dedicated his
early novel, *Stempenyu,* to him; though there are traces in
his writings of Gogol and Chekhov (in this volume, especially,
in *Birth* and *Someone to Envy*), Sholom Aleichem is uniquely

his own. Each writer, after all, has his own inner vision—and Sholom Aleichem's was his people seen through spectacles of love.

Mendele wrote from a pedestal. He was, to use a current term, alienated from the reader. There was more antipathy than identification in his works; honey hardly touched his acerbic pen. But Sholom Aleichem loved the people, even while he satirized them; among them he felt at home. He laughs along with his characters; he neither approves nor condemns; he observes. An abundant faith in man shines forth from his writings. Although the Jews of his time had reason enough to be depressed and pessimistic—pogroms, social upheaval, the breakup of traditional life were rampant—it does not become a theme in Sholom Aleichem. Optimism reigns. There is nothing lost or beat in the generation of Sholom Aleichem's Jews. For the eternal messianic hope, rooted through centuries into their psyche, had its comrade-in-arms in laughter. Laughter was the balm for here and now—the Messiah was for tomorrow.

Perhaps this is why everyone read Sholom Aleichem—the poor working man, the bourgeois merchant, the assimilated man of wealth. They took his pamphlets wherever they went. Reading Sholom Aleichem aloud in family gatherings became a Sabbath-eve tradition. His writings were translated into scores of languages—among them, Hebrew, French, English, Spanish, Esperanto, and Japanese. In Russian, he was acclaimed by Gorky. Three million copies of his works were sold between 1917 and 1942 in the Soviet Union alone. There he was likened to Gogol; in America to Mark Twain; in England to Dickens. These three, incidentally, in addition to Cervantes and Chekhov, were among Sholom Aleichem's favorite authors.

Through the body of Sholom Aleichem's works, three main characters stand out: Tevye the Dairyman, the down-to-earth Jew, a realist who has misfortunes, but never despairs; Menakhem-Mendel, the man who lives on air and dreams, for none of his get-rich-quick schemes provide him with a livelihood; Motel, the Cantor's son, the picture of free Jewish childhood. Yet there is a fourth personage, unnamed and not as well-

rounded a character as the ones above, who moves like a whir-
ring lens from place to place, recording and observing. This
is the "I" of his satires. Though we usually think of Sholom
Aleichem as a kindly folk humorist, he is also the sly satirist.

In this volume, in four of his longer satires (two each at
polar ends of the book), this first person narrator goes from
town to country, from Kasrilevke abroad, and tenderly excori-
ates the institutions and ways of modern life.

In *Progress in Kasrilevke*, the narrator returns to his old
home town. Plucked out of its torpor, affected by new cur-
rents, Kasrilevke strives to imitate the big city. The new,
modern little village gradually sheds its traditional *shtetl* garb
and tries on a more progressive mode of culture for size. Since
Progress in Kasrilevke was written during 1914-15, while
Sholom Aleichem lived in New York City, it is possible that
many vagaries of American-Jewish life of the period were dis-
guised under a Kasrilevke mask. In fact, many of the things
he satirizes—notably competition among the Yiddish press
and theater—have their real-life parallels in Sholom Aleichem's experiences in the New World.

In *Summer Romances, A Home Away from Home*, and *To
the Hot Springs*, we see both the poor and the *nouveaux riche*
who have succeeded where Menakhem-Mendel, the *luft-
mensch*, has failed. He satirizes the people who have climbed
the social ladder, but do not seem comfortable on the rungs.
In all these pieces, Sholom Aleichem punctures bombast and
reveals the core of provinciality which never has been
sloughed away.

Satire is valid if it can be read anew by every generation.
Names and places change, but people remain the same. Substitute Park Avenue doctor for Vienna professor, ulcers and hay
fever for nervous conditions, Miami Beach and Saratoga
Springs for the European spas, summer bungalows for villas,
the organization man for the club devotee—the list is endless
—and a satire on contemporary life appears.

As a humorist, Sholom Aleichem ranks among the world's
greatest. As a portrayer of his society, he stands unrivaled. To
his generation, to those who spoke Yiddish and lived in its
world, Sholom Aleichem mirrored what was known. For the

succeeding generations, for those who neither speak nor read Yiddish, but have a faint memory of it and long to know its culture, Sholom Aleichem opens the door to a world unknown, and, with laughter and tender pathos, shows us the spirit of our forebears and their heartbeat, which has been the key to our survival.

There are several people to whom I would like to express my thanks: to the prose artist, who continues in the bilingual tradition of Jewish literature, Shlomo Damesek, for patiently listening to some of my translations and offering valuable suggestions; to the lexicographer, who did for Yiddish what Roget did for English, Nahum Stutchkoff, for kindly explaining some rare idioms. Further thanks to Anita DeVivo and to Alfred Ivry for their careful proofreading and comments on parts of the manuscript. But most of all, my heartfelt appreciation to my parents, in whose home I lived Yiddish, and where the laughter of Sholom Aleichem and the oral tradition of humorous story telling preceded my literacy. Whether personally, or via phone and letters, they constantly advised me and helped explain (what seemed to me) difficult words and phrases, especially those of Russian origin.

In commemoration of the one-hundredth anniversary, I have translated these works not only for the public at large, who cannot read them in the original, but for Sholom Aleichem, as well—a posthumous gift of appreciation. He whispered his inimitable Yiddish into my ear, and I, by using as wide a vocabulary range as Sholom Aleichem's Yiddish—from the polysyllabic to the idiomatic, from the colloquial to the slang—have tried to convert the mood and rhythm of Yiddish into American English. I hope this translation will in some measure reciprocate all that Sholom Aleichem has given me. While reading his works, one cannot help but feel that he is still with us. It is hard to imagine that he was born one hundred years ago, for the man and his works have become so integral a part of the people, that so long as the people remain, he remains.

CURT LEVIANT

STORIES AND SATIRES
BY
sholom aleichem

PROGRESS IN KASRILEVKE

1. The Village

It's amazing what can happen to a village! You know, my old home town has undergone such changes I can't even recognize it any more. After being away for ages, I came back to Kasrilevke for a few weeks and wandered around its streets, spoke to the people, and looked for old friends. But how? Where? For whom? Most of them had gone the way of all flesh, a few had gone to America, and the newly-rich weren't the ones I was looking for. It was a topsy-turvy world. Where did the famous little people with their little ideas disappear to? Where were all those know-it-all, bearded Jews who poked fun at everything? Where were those young people with canes who used to wander around the marketplace looking for business in vain, who out of depths of despair ribbed one another and then the whole world?

Now, I saw dandies strolling through the streets, staid people with homburgs and pince-nez. Of the once slovenly women with their white stockings and red garters, and of the girls with their colorful kerchiefs—not a trace remained. Ladies with chapeaus now walked past me. Matrons with parasols. Chic young ladies wearing gloves. New people. A new world. What's more—and this is a good one—the village had even paved its streets and put up lamp-posts. They had phonographs, they had movies. They really enjoyed life!

That's the external picture, so to speak. But, under the surface Kasrilevke had changed even more. I just couldn't believe I was home. As I walked through the village, I looked for at least one of the old clubs. I remember there used to be clubs to the point of excess here. And I'm not talking about the Psalms and Mishna Clubs. I mean societies like the Free-

Loan, the Free-Kitchen, the Visit-the-Sick, the Clothe-the-Poor, the Help-the-Needy, the Medical-Aid, the Relieve-the-Oppressed. It seemed that all these groups had gone the way of their founders. They passed on like most of the little people, like lonely old Rabbi Yozifl, may the fruits of Paradise be his. Thinking of him brought tears to my eyes.

In place of these above-mentioned old groups, there sprang up in the modern Kasrilevke entirely new and forward-looking clubs, organizations, if you will—societies for art, language, and culture. It was impossible to count them all. We could just throw a passing glance at those groups of which there were two of each in the new Kasrilevke. For instance, concerning language, there was a Yiddish Club and a Hebrew Society. One couldn't bear the sight of the other, or stand mention of the other's name. Then there was the Choral Society which had split into two. One group was now called "The Flute," the other, "The Trumpet." They were quite ready to eliminate each other. Then there were two progressive schools—*aggressive*, really—each with murder in its eye. And then the two Yiddish theaters. If not for their fear of God and the Czar, they'd have gladly burned each other's buildings to the ground one night. And two publishing houses, each ready to swallow its rival, boots and all. And moreover, there existed two literary clubs, two dramatic societies, two emigrant associations and many other sorts of groups. Two of each. It was all for the sake of the village's old plague—unbridled competition. It was just impossible to stamp out this ancient Kasrilevke heritage. If one fine morning a person cut his nose off, you could bet your life that on the very next day there would be two noseless faces in town. Does it make sense, you say? Of course it makes sense—if it pays for him to remove his nose, then it will pay for me, too!

2. Newspapers

Just as there were two of everything in Kasrilevke, there were two Yiddish newspapers, the *Skullcap* and the *Bowler Hat*. Naturally, the *Skullcap* was the traditional, old-fashioned daily for the orthodox, and the *Bowler Hat* was the modern, radical gazette of the progressive elements.

Even the mottoes of the competing papers served quick notice of their policies. In large letters, the *Skullcap* devoted itself "To God and the Public." The editor of the *Bowler Hat* placed his own name in equally large print, and boldly asserted: "When I'm here—everything is here."

When were these two organs founded? Which is older? That's hard to say! For each one proclaimed itself the oldest and only Yiddish paper in Kasrilevke, and ignored, disregarded, and never even so much as mentioned, God forbid, the other's name. Like bacon, *traif!*

But if there were no choice and one had to denounce, defame, and damn the other—then the *Skullcap* would call its rival "the battered *Bowler Hat*," and the *Bowler Hat* would call its opponent "the moldy numb*Skullcap*." For the most part, though, they approached the problem under cover, avoiding the mention of their competitor's name.

For example, let us say the *Bowler Hat* wanted to talk about its neighbor without printing its name. Instead of saying *Skullcap*, it would think up an alphabetic acrostic like this:

"That asinine, beggarly, crooked, drunken, envious, feeble, galling, hair-splitting, idiotic, jagged, knee-bending, leprous, mangy, nefarious, ossified, provocating, querulous, rabble-rousing, skimpy, tottering, ugly, venomous, wayward, xenophobic, yellowing, and zig-zagging rag whose name we don't even want to mention."

That was a grand success in Kasrilevke and the copies sold like hotcakes. Everyone repeated this "a-b-c-" until he had it memorized. Naturally, this stung the *Skullcap* to the quick and it came out with its alphabetic answer the next morning.

"We have read the 'a-b-c-' of that ass, bastard, coward, dunce, eel, fool, gyp, hound-dog, inquisitor, jellyfish, knave, liar, miser, nihilist, ox, pagan, quack, reptile, scandalmonger, terrorist, unmentionable, villain, wastrel, Xerxes, yokel, and zoo of a paper, but we're not answering, for we have no desire to defile our pens."

The Kasrilevke reader prefers just this sort of literature to all others. He calls it "criticism," and is in seventh heaven when the editors "criticize" one another. On the days when the pages lack "critiques," circulation lags in Kasrilevke. Then, the editors dig in and wash each other's dirty linen in public so that the people can have something to satisfy their hunger for "criticism."

3. Competition

On New-Years, things start humming at the two local dailies. They blow their own trumpets and outdo each other by issuing blatant prospectuses for the coming year. Like newspapers the world over, the *Skullcap* generously takes stock of its achievements of the past year. Heaven forbid that it speak ill of its competitor. After all, the Bible forbids that sort of talk. But, in passing, it recalls that the battered *Bowler Hat* is: "a stray waif, and its editor a barefoot boy, while the *Skullcap* is already, with the help of God, a fullfledged journal."

The *Bowler Hat* boasts quite modestly in its prospectus that "while the moldy numb*Skullcap* still rolled in mud-puddles, the *Bowler Hat*, in all its magnificence and luster, already had broadened Kasrilevke horizons. If it were not for the *Bowler Hat*, Kasrilevke still would be drowsing in the lethargic torpor of medieval fanaticism."

It's hard to find out which of the two really had the larger circulation. The *Skullcap* bent hell and high heaven, and swore in God's name that no Yiddish paper in the world was so widely read. Whoever wished to take the trouble and come to the editorial offices would be shown proof positive.

The *Bowler Hat* claimed the same, and outdid itself by offering a ten-thousand ruble award to anyone who could show in black and white that there was another Yiddish newspaper on earth with a greater circulation.

In its usual modest manner, it said: "We do not like to make extravagant claims about our paper. We do not believe in bragging. Boastfulness is an indication of inferiority. We leave it up to the reader himself. Compare papers and editors and make your choice."

It goes without saying that, since the competition was great and all for the good, the papers strained every muscle to surpass each other. They published their editions as early as possible, filched as many items as they could from the gentile press, etc. But they carefully watched each other and noted what was cooking in their competitor's pot. As soon as one editorial staff though up something new, the other knew about it to the last detail.

To illustrate the point, I'll tell you a story which I heard while in Kasrilevke.

The *Skullcap* had a long-standing custom. Every Friday afternoon, they came out with a special page called "Sabbath Greetings!" The poor *Bowler Hat*, although it was radical and claimed to be the *Skullcap's* senior, had to follow suit. They started issuing a special Friday afternoon supplement entitled "Sabbath Greetings!" They had no choice. This was competition!

But one Friday, they got sick of that mimicry and explained that, since many of their readers found no interest in the Friday supplement, and the editor only wanted to please his readers—from that day on the *Bowler Hat* would be issued without "Sabbath Greetings!"

Then the *Bowler Hat* speculated: let us see if the *Skullcap* is really monkey see, monkey do. It hit upon the idea of publishing out of curiosity, a Wednesday edition with only three pages. The fourth page was as bare as a barn wall. But the *Skullcap* was no shirker, and on that same Wednesday, it, too, came out with only three pages. Its last page was as bare as a barn wall. This annoyed the *Bowler Hat* no end, and it fired all the "informers" on the editorial staff. But it didn't help much. The *Bowler Hat* was convinced that you couldn't keep a thing from the *Skullcap*.

4. Public Opinion

The Kasrilevke editors hated to boast or raise a storm about themselves publicly. Quite the contrary. In Kasrilevke, there was a special thread which bound the editors to the readers. In Kasrilevke, the editor liked to ask his readers' advice concerning his paper. He was tickled pink if a reader wrote him a letter. This way he was able to start a poll.

It's about these polls that a Kasrilevke *litterateur* told me the following story. But he had to take me way out of town to tell it. Once we were alone, he broke into uncontrollable laughter. When he'd had his fill, he started:

"You know the worst season for newspapers? Summer! Unless, of course, there's a cholera epidemic, with God's help; then it's another matter.

"But one summer, there was no cholera. It was maddening! What could be done? So the *Bowler Hat* suddenly went crazy (I worked for them at the time) and comes up with a new thing. 'It seems that our readers are dissatisfied with our masthead. Some say that the *l* in *Bowler Hat* is much too long, that it looks like a giraffe's neck. Others say, no, that a long *l* is much nicer than a short one. So we turn this problem over to our readers. If a majority of our readers say that they want a new masthead, we'll go to any expense to give them a new one. Whoever wants to join this poll, should write a letter to the editor of the *Bowler Hat*.'

"Having finished that bit of business, our editor was overjoyed. 'Those animals,' he said, 'will have something to chew on.'

"The finale came when we arrived at the office the next morning. We give a look—and there's our editor steaming like a samovar. What happened? We're making him miserable, he says. We're giving away all the editorial secrets! And he shows us the *Skullcap* with our announcement in it:

" 'Not all our readers are satisfied with our masthead. Some find that the *l*'s in *Skullcap* are much too short, that they look like a pair of lame ducks' necks. And some oppose this, saying that the short *l*'s are much nicer than long ones. So we're turning this question over to our readers. If most of the readers ask for another masthead, we'll spare no expense to give them a new one. The readers of the *Skullcap* are asked to post their letters in care of the editor's office.'

"This was a death blow to the *Bowler Hat*. From then on, day in and day out, the *Bowler Hat* never stopped printing the announcement about the masthead. And the *Skullcap* did just the same. The masthead business didn't let up for a single day. And so we were mastheaded for almost a whole summer in Kasrilevke, until one fine morning, the *Bowler Hat* came out with a bulletin:

" 'This is to inform our readers that the *Bowler Hat's* masthead will remain the same. For out of our 20,000 readers, only 187 were against the old masthead, and the remaining 19,813 were in favor of it.'

"Do you think that ended it? Sure enough, that very day the *Skullcap* came out with the same news:

" 'Since, out of our 20,000 readers, only 187 were against our old masthead, and the remaining 19,813 favored it, we are keeping our old masthead.'

"How did the *Skullcap* find out? There's no one here but you and me and God, so I'll tell you. It was a sorcerer! Black magic! The devil only knows! But you want to know how it ended? It was a bloody finish. The editor of our *Bowler Hat* locked himself in his office and cried. How do I know? Leave it to me. If I tell you, I know. Well, after he had a good cry, he fired all his co-workers—me among them—and hired a new staff. But, he's since fired the new ones and rehired the old. But, he hasn't come to me yet. He probably will, though. I still have hopes. The *Bowler Hat* is completely crazy. But, I have to admit, you make a ruble there. At the *Skullcap*, you can't even do that. There, it's much worse!"

5. Sensationalism and Novels

As in the rest of the world, the Kasrilevke press depended upon extraordinary and sensational daily news. However, the press of the rest of the world knows when enough is enough, but Kasrilevke doesn't know when to stop. Anything for competition! For instance, when the *Bowler Hat* reported that a woman in France gave birth to a baby with two heads, the same news was in the *Skullcap* the next morning, only spiced a bit. They said that a mother in France gave birth to a child with *three* heads, that the baby was alive and kicking and eating with all three mouths.

At another time, the *Bowler Hat* succeeded in revealing that there was a terrible wintry snowstorm in Odessa in mid-July. The next morning, the *Skullcap* snatched this same item, but made it a shade stronger; Odessa suffered a three-yard-high, midsummer blizzard and over a score of its citizens were found frozen solid.

But best of all was the fish story. One Friday, the *Skullcap* printed this article:

"A Jewish woman, a reader of the *Skullcap*, bought a pike weighing several pounds for the Sabbath. She brought the fish home, cleaned it, and, in cutting it up, she found a ring and a pair of earrings. Pure gold. Valued at a high price. Whoever wants to see the ring and earrings can do so at the *Skullcap's* editorial office."

This pierced the *Bowler Hat* to the core. All Sabbath long, they were in a dither. Barely enduring till Sunday, they informed their readers about the following:

"A Jewish lady, a reader of the *Bowler Hat*, bought a fish for the Sabbath, a tench weighing ten pounds, and just about managed to drag it home. She cleaned it and cut it up and took out a veritable treasure: a half-dozen tablespoons, a dozen teaspoons, three gold-plated wine-cups, and a pair of silver candlesticks—pure sterling through and through. Whoever wants to see these items can come to the *Bowler Hat's* editorial office."

The most sensational of all was the novel. While I was in Kasrilevke, both the *Skullcap* and the *Bowler Hat* serialized a fascinating and thrilling novel. One called it, *The Stolen Bride's Forbidden Kiss*. The other entitled its work, *The Forbidden Bride's Stolen Kiss*.

The afore-mentioned Kasrilevke *litterateur* told me confidentially that the novel was stolen from an old Russian book by two writers who tried their best to make the action last indefinitely. In order to keep the public in suspense, they thought up new sensations daily. In broad daylight, they put away a hale and hearty hero forever, and just as suddenly brought him back to life. No lazybones, they—they even brought two women back from the other world so long as it fit their plans.

And what's more, all of a sudden they'd start the potboiler all over again—and go fight them! But to be frank, I must say that Kasrilevke read this novel with gusto. They licked their fingers in anticipation of the next installment. Barely enduring until morning, they quickly flipped to *The Forbidden Bride*, all agog to see the outcome.

Truth is that the end was long overdue. The writers themselves were sick and tired of stretching the old story's bones. Its heroes had been put away ages ago—some hanged, some poisoned, some shot. But the vicious competition made the editors call for further padding. Neither paper wanted to end it all until the other did so. Things were in such a state when I was in Kasrilevke, that some of the heroes had been shot for the *third* time, and the forbidden bride had been stolen twice, seduced, and tortured, then sought, found, stolen, and brutally tormented once again! There was no end to the butchery of these two authors. Who knows what they'll think of next!

6. Ads

If the Kasrilevke papers had to depend upon circulation alone, they'd be in a fine pickle. All the hullabaloo was aimed in one direction only—the fourth page, the home of ads and personal announcements, which support the press the world over.

Concerning advertisements, the Kasrilevke papers not only followed the path of the American press, but went a step farther. In Kasrilevke, ads became highly fashionable. There was no merchant, dairyman, or laborer, not even a plain housewife or maid, who didn't use the ad columns. Like it or not—you had to advertise. You marry off a child—an ad. A son is born to you—a public announcement. A daughter—an ad, too. If you tried to outsmart them and didn't advertise—hold on to your hat! This didn't mean, God forbid, that they *did* anything *to* you. They just *printed* things *about* you until they had you begging: "Friends. Here's an ad, two if you please, even three. But for goodness sake hold your tongues!"

Many fine stories are told in Kasrilevke about just this type of high-pressure salesmanship. Here are some of them.

1. *Incident with a Grocer.* Nokhem the Grocer got sick and tired of advertising. When he got up one morning and opened the papers, he almost had a stroke. There, in black and white, front-paged in large letters, it said: "Last night a flock of rats stormed the large grocery of a local villager and completely destroyed his entire stock. Gorged with his groceries, the rats immediately started dropping dead en masse."

Naturally, Nokhem the Grocer was fit to be tied. He swore up and down that he'd teach the papers a lesson. But the outcome was that on the fourth page of both papers the following ad appears daily:

"Fine, fresh merchandise and all sorts of groceries can be bought only at Nokhem's Grocery."

After you pay through the nose, you smarten up.

2. *Incident with a Wine Barrel.* Judah Winepresser had a fight with the papers and decided: "That's the last straw!" He refused to advertise any more. And go do him something! But he soon regretted his move. The next day the papers featured a bulletin saying: "A tragedy occurred at a local winemaker's. A barrel of wine, standing and fermenting, suddenly began to sour. The wine bubbled and the barrel swelled. Finally, it exploded, nearly killing the winemaker."

As soon as Judah Winepresser read this, he ran to both editorial offices with this ad: "Whoever wants a glass of fresh
wine should remember that there's a Jew by the name of Judah
Winepresser in town."

If you can't compete, cooperate!

3. *Incident of the Phenomenon.* A couple gave birth to a
son. The parents, according to tradition, had the baby circumcised. So where's the hitch? They had simply neglected to
order an announcement of congratulations in the papers.

The day after the circumcision, a feature appeared in the
papers headlined: "Phenomenon." It told of a rare occurrence
in Kasrilevke—a once-in-a-millennium event. "A young wife
has given birth to a phenomenon. Only five months after her
wedding, she was safely delivered of a son. The boy, the "phenomenon," is alive, thriving, and remarkably well-formed.
And only yesterday, he was circumcised!"

What the couple went through—I leave to your imagination. The young father of the "phenomenon" scurried around
Kasrilevke like a chicken without a head. He counted on his
fingers for everyone to see that it was exactly nine months
and nine days after his wedding. But go fight the world! The
town heard him out—but choked with laughter. The young
father threatened to bring suit, but, since no names had been
mentioned, what could he do? He couldn't even begin! The
town held its sides from this phenomenal incident. It's just this
sort of thing a Kasrilevke reader likes to see in his newspaper.
A Kasrilevke reader hates boring stories. He adores lively
journalism.

7. Politics

Don't think that Kasrilevke's press is devoted only to what
the Americans call *business*, and that the papers don't dabble
in politics. What sort of press would it be without politics?
What sort of journals would they be if they didn't concern
themselves with the public? When the time came, not only the
editors and reporters, but even the readers were drawn into the
political arena. Parties have wars! Parties fight! The heavens

are split asunder. Brother rises against brother. The word "justice" ceases to exist. The feeling of pity dies away. The end of the world has come! And this situation repeats itself every three years, exactly. They're choosing a new crown rabbi!*

There were as many parties in Kasrilevke as candidates. Two candidates—two parties. One candidate was supported by the *Skullcap* and by its party, the Skullcappers. The other candidate was boosted by the *Bowler Hat* and its party, the Bowler Hatters. Both candidates had already held office. But only for three years. No one lasted any longer. And each candidate, naturally, had his own platform.

For example, the candidate of the Skullcappers, if elected, would come to Sabbath services before anyone else. At home he wore a skullcap (a fanatic Skullcapper, he). He had a habit of bargaining. No matter how much you wanted to give him —it wasn't enough.

In opposition, the candidate of the Bowler Hatters didn't come to the synagogue at all, except occasionally, on a holiday. At home, so the story went, he didn't even wear a hat and, to top it off, ate *traif*, too.

His motto was—"I don't give a damn!" As for bargaining —he didn't bargain like the other candidate. God forbid! He had a fixed fee. And if you couldn't meet it, you could even stretch out and croak, it was still—"I don't give a damn."

The time I voted in Kasrilevke, it was just—as the Americans call it—election eve. And a real hot time it was! Oh my, you can't imagine what those two papers cooked up. It's impossible to describe all they wrote.

As a sample, I can only quote their own words to show how the two editors dealt with each other.

"How much sweat, filth, and dirt has been collected under the Yiddish *Skullcap*. How much distress and mockery have we had from that historic *Skullcap*. The day when we are free of them will be our second independence day. The day we get permanently rid of them will be our second Redemption from Egyptian Bondage. Down with the *Skullcap*. Long live the

---

* One who would represent the community vis-à-vis the state—not the town's spiritual leader.

Bowler Hat. Down with the Skullcappers. Long live the Bowler Hatters. Hurrah!!"

This time, the *Skullcap's* reply to its opponent was short and sweet. It said:

"The dingy *Bowler Hat* has suddenly found its tongue again. Where are these Bowler Hatters crawling with their candidate? Don't they know that Kasrilevke is a Jewish town, a shining light in the community of Israel? What won't such a crown rabbi think of, one who gobbles porkers fried in butter, and who, in these modern times, goes bareheaded and unwashed before his prayers."

How the fight ended, I don't know. I left town.

8. The Tale of the Seven Matchmakers

A newspaper has to adapt itself to its readers and their needs. The first to realize this was the editor of the *Skullcap.* Soon thereafter, he established in his columns a sort of matrimonial bureau known as "Calling Bride and Groom." He announced it to his readers with an ad which read as follows:

"Kasrilevke is growing. Its children are getting older. The matchmakers can't be everywhere at once. We therefore propose a solution for Kasrilevkites who worry about the future of their children. From now on they won't have to depend on the help of matchmakers, but will be able to provide brides and grooms for their sons and daughters by themselves. How? Very easily. Anyone who has a child of marriageable age should not feel shy, but report it to the *Skullcap.* He should inform us that he has a son or daughter with such and such qualities, offers so much dowry, and wants this or that. All the announcements will be printed free of charge, for we are doing it purely as a good deed and as a public service."

Understandably, this was a bombshell to the *Bowler Hat.* The *Skullcap* beat it out in something like that?! At first, the *Bowler Hat* planned to come out with a fiery article against the *Skullcap,* yelling blue murder: The Kasrilevke press had sunk pretty low if that moldy numb*Skullcap* turned into a "Miss Matchmaker" in its old age.

But, finally, the editor changed his mind and came out with the following the next day:

"The world does not stand still. Progress goes on. That era is long gone when fanatic parents forced their own choice on their children. Gone are the days when a shady matchmaker came to congratulate the bride and groom. No more! The children of our modern age are smarter. They can take care of themselves. The sacred feeling of holy love breaks through brick and penetrates iron walls. Hearts meet. Souls join. With this end in mind we are throwing our columns open to our readers. In the section 'Lad to Lassie' anyone can advertise to his heart's desire, be it boy or girl, widow or widower. The *Bowler Hat* is at their service—for our paper's motto is: 'The People's Welfare.' And the slogan of our new section is: 'Liberty and Love.' "

There was a flood of marriage ads in both Kasrilevke gazettes. In the *Skullcap*'s "Calling Bride and Groom" appeared the parents of the prospective couples. In the *Bowler Hat*'s "Lad to Lassie," the prospective brides and grooms introduced themselves. Things were surely popping in Kasrilevke! It was nothing to sneeze at—you wrote what you wanted and didn't pay for it. Everything would have been wonderful if Kasrilevke had had only one paper and not a trace of a matchmaker. But what are you supposed to do when one paper pecks out one match, the second paper butts in, and a marriage broker pokes his nose in too? Then everyone raises hell and they tell you to get out of town.

Shortly before I left Kasrilevke, something happened which is worth telling. Not for the story alone so much as for the moral of it. That the story wasn't concocted, heaven forbid, and was perfectly true was guaranteed by its teller, the very same knowledgeable young man who revealed the secret about the mastheads.

"When you're ready to write this story, call it 'The Tale of the Seven Matchmakers,' " the young man began. He then covered his mouth with both hands and laughed himself sick. I didn't want to interrupt him. If he laughed, then obviously it was pretty funny. So I let him laugh himself dry. When he finally had, he started the story, which we relate here in his own words:

"You realize that those public benefactors of ours, the conservative *Skullcap* and the modern *Bowler Hat*, don't do anything for themselves, God forbid, but only for the general good. Reading them, you'd think their motto is 'What's mine is yours, what's yours is yours.' But you probably won't believe me if I tell you that both editors are professional matchmakers, marriage-brokers from the word go! What if I prove it in black and white?"

Saying this, the young man took a pack of newspapers from his jacket pocket. The first batch were issues of the *Skullcap*, the second, the *Bowler Hat*. He started reading. "This is from 'Calling Bride and Groom.' 'Dear Editor. Since I'm a steady reader of your worthy *Skullcap*, I find it commendable that you have inaugurated "Calling Bride and Groom," and I hereby ask you to print that I am an upstanding Kasrilevke landlord of noble family who has an only daughter. I really shouldn't praise her, for the Proverbs tell us: *Let another praise thee and not thine own mouth*. But I will herewith briefly list her fine points. 1) She's a virgin, 2) a beauty, 3) a genius, 4) expert at everything, 5) cultured to the point of danger, 6) a pianist, 7) has ten thousand for a dowry, 8) dresses like a queen, 9) speaks French, 10) dances, too.

'Whoever has a son with residence rights and a white rejection slip from the army should contact the *Skullcap* and ask for Mendel Landlord.'

"That's number one. The same day, ad number two was printed.

" 'Dear Editor. As a constant reader of your distinguished journal, I too find that you have done a good deed in introducing such a worthwhile column as "Calling Bride and Groom." To show you how excellent it is, I hereby notify you that I myself am a native-born Kasrilevkite. My parents and great-great-grandparents were Kasrilevkites. I have a good name, thank God, and am of noble and of excellent familial lineage and arrange matches with the best families. I have a son to marry off who has plenty of good qualities. And although the verse in Proverbs reads: *Let another man praise thee and not thine own mouth*, I interpret the words *and not* to mean *if not*. In other words, let another man praise you, and *if not*—if there's nobody else around—"thine own mouth"— then you have to praise yourself. Here are my son's qualities. 1) He's a pure, 2) devoted, 3) only son, 4) has a white rejection slip, 5) is brilliant, 6) writes well, 7) plays the violin, 8) speaks Hebrew, 9) is religious, 10) offers dowry. Whoever has a beautiful daughter should turn to "Calling Bride and Groom" and to reader Nisel Noble.'

"Two neat little ads, eh? It just so happened that on that very same day, as you can see here, the *Bowler Hat* also printed two announcements in its column 'Lad to Lassie.' Not from the parents but from the young ones themselves. This is how the young man described himself:

" 'Dear Editor. As a loyal reader of your noted paper, I herewith notify you that I am a tall and handsome young man of twenty-three. And although I have a white rejection slip, I am healthy and strong and hope I stay that way. I finished six terms of high school and have the right to practice pharmacy. I'm looking for a beautiful girl with a good character who has a nice few thousands, for a dowry. It's no drawback if she can play the piano. And it won't hurt if she comes from a fine family. Whoever wants me should write to the *Bowler Hat* and ask for "The Fine Pharmacist." ' "

"That's what the boy in the *Bowler Hat* wrote. Now let's see what the girl had to say.

" 'Dear Editor. Since I never miss an issue of your renowned paper, I'd like to inform you that I am a twenty-one-year-old girl of average height with black hair, fair complexion, dimpled cheeks, and very fine character. In Kasrilevke, I'm considered a beauty. At a ball, all the boys swoon over me. But they can all go to hell for all I care. I want a boy, over twenty-two with a good character, who can earn a living for his wife. If he has a dowry, I don't mind. In any case, he'll find me a loving wife. Write to "The Black-haired Beauty," care of the *Bowler Hat*.'

"You'd think that according to logic, Mendel Landlord,

who was looking for a young man with a white rejection slip, would have contacted Nisel Noble, whose son had just that and played the violin and spoke Hebrew, etc., besides. They would have gone together like peaches and cream. But, look at the way the wheel spins. The father, who usually reads the *Skullcap*, suddenly gets it into his head to scan the last page of the *Bowler Hat* and see what's what in matrimonial offers. Reading the announcements on the fourth page, Mendel Landlord sniffs something worthwhile. What good was that only son from the fine family? So what if he wrote well and spoke Hebrew and fiddled! There was no better groom than 'The Fine Pharmacist' from the *Bowler Hat*, who had the white rejection slip and the right to practice pharmacy to boot.

"Too bad he had to go ahead and read the *Bowler Hat*. But, never mind. There's no law that says all Jews have to read only the *Skullcap*. In fact, there is a written law which says: co-exist with your brother. To make a long story short, Mendel Landlord called a matchmaker and said: 'Find me the address of "The Fine Pharmacist" through the *Bowler Hat*, and if it's God's will, bring him over. He'll meet my daughter and we'll make arrangements and everything will be settled.'

"Now, let's leave Mendel Landlord and his daughter and turn to Nisel Noble, the father of that only son who came of good family, played the violin, and all that. Reading in the *Skullcap*'s 'Calling Bride and Groom' that Mendel Landlord's beauty was available and that she has so many fine qualities and a dowry of ten thousand too, he thought it a fine and proper match. But where was the hitch? The ten thousand dowry stuck like a bone in his throat. A Jew who offered ten thousand dowry, meant six and came across with three. If you were lucky, that is. We know them, these Kasrilevkites! Dogs ought to deal with them. What's more, Nisel had read something better in the *Bowler Hat*—a twenty-one-year-old, black-haired beauty wrote looking for a husband with a fine character. 'There's no better character than my son's,' said that devoted *Skullcap* reader, Nisel Noble. He called in a matchmaker and told him in utmost secrecy: 'In the name of God, find out who that black-haired beauty with the good character is.' He also told him to offer her his only son with the white rejection slip, who played the violin, spoke Hebrew, etc., etc. With the help of God, things would work out and everything would turn out fine. Amen.

"Now, let's go to the young man from the *Bowler Hat*, who finished six semesters of high school and had the right to practice pharmacy. Even a baby would have told you that this young man was fated for the black-haired beauty from the *Bowler Hat*, for whom all the boys swooned. But how did it all end? The boy had a desire to look through the *Skullcap*. All he had to do was read in 'Calling Bride and Groom' about that Mendel Landlord of good family, who had a beautiful only daughter with ten attributes; who sought a husband with a white slip and residence rights, and who threw in ten thousand to top it off—well, that was all he needed. He was walking on air. Well, he *did* have the white rejection slip, and he *did* have residence rights. Without dilly-dallying, he discussed it with a friend who was looking for a quick ruble.

"The latter went to Mendel Landlord and offered him the pharmacist. Mendel was as pleased as punch and said: 'Well, I just now sent a matchmaker to that same young man.'

" 'So what!' said the matchmaker, 'There'll be two marriage brokers. So long as it turns out well.'

" 'From your mouth to God's ears,' said Mendel.

" 'Amen,' said the pharmacist's friend.

"That leaves only the black-haired beauty from the *Bowler Hat*, and then we're through with all the matches. Reading in the *Bowler Hat* about the man with a white slip and the right to practice pharmacy, the beauty thought him just the thing for her. But there was one flaw. He was looking for a bride with a dowry, and a fat one to boot—a fat plague on him!

"Our Bowler Hatters, begging their pardon, are really modern and liberal and all that. But when it comes to money, the devil himself takes over. For money, they'd sell their own mothers. In money matters, the Skullcappers are much finer. For proof, look at the *Skullcap's* marriage column. There, the rich Nisel Noble announced that his fine son sought a Venus, a Helen of Troy, and he never so much as mentioned a dowry.

He'd be an excellent stand-in for that pharmacist. But there was one drawback to the rich man's son. He was religious and spoke Hebrew. But it didn't matter much. Religion was a private thing and his speaking Hebrew, well that was a passing sickness. Just let them marry and he'd stop that Hebrew-speaking. He'd start talking like a human being!

"The black-haired beauty also made her choice, and worked through her poor uncle, a poor man. She asked him to go to Nisel Noble, the one who was looking for a poor beauty. When her uncle would show Nisel her picture, he would be struck dumb. And that's exactly what happened. As soon as the rich man saw the picture, he exclaimed, 'That's the one I'm looking for! I just sent a matchmaker to her today.'

" 'That should be the least of your worries,' said the girl's uncle. 'So we'll split the fees in half. So what?'

" 'I hope so. From your mouth to God's ear.'

" 'Amen.'

"Do you think that's the last of the matchmakers? Hold your horses! Don't forget that Kasrilevke, thank God, is a town with plenty of poor folk. A Jew stood outside with nothing to do, reading both papers, the *Skullcap* and the *Bowler Hat*, from beginning to end. He didn't miss a word. He noticed the prospective brides and grooms in both papers and jumped up excitedly. 'It's God's will. This girl, the black-haired beauty from the *Bowler Hat*, is made for Nisel Noble's only son from the *Skullcap*, because he's looking for a beauty without a dowry. And Mendel Landlord's virgin from the *Skullcap*, the culture-lover who plays the piano and has a dowry of ten thousand, well, she's looking for a boy with residence rights and that pharmacist from the *Bowler Hat*, he's got it!'

"This smart cookie didn't wait too long. Why should someone else beat him to the draw? In one hour, he saw all four of them—Mendel, Nisel, the pharmacist, and the black-haired beauty. But, wherever he went, he was told: 'You're a bit late to come scratching at the door, old man. A matchmaker has just been here with the same idea.'

" 'What's that got to do with me, if there was or wasn't a

matchmaker? So long as what I say is right. And if not, just say the word and I'll spoil everything, because when it comes to spoiling, I'm an expert.'

"Hearing these words, their hearts flew into their mouths. They saw that they were dealing with a scoundrel, an impudent lout. So they begged the man not to spoil it all, and in return, if everything worked out, and it came to the matchmakers' fees, they'd see to it that he wouldn't be left out.

"God helped—both matches worked, and both engagement parties were celebrated the same evening. Matchmakers sprouted from all over. First Mendel Landlord's, then Nisel Noble's. Next the pharmacist's, then the black-haired beauty's. That makes four. Finally, the one who was an expert at spoiling things. Add them up, and we have a grand total of five. Then, what about the editors of the two papers? The *Skullcap* and the *Bowler Hat* both came dressed to kill, like in-laws, although no one had invited them. But since they had come, they were welcomed. Each one separately. Why not? The hosts served them whiskey and honey cakes and home-made jam. The editors thanked them, but let it be known that it wasn't *that* they came for.

" 'For what then?'

" 'For the matchmaker's commission.'

" 'What do you mean, commission?'

" 'What we mean is, we're not demanding a thing, but it goes without saying.' If it weren't for them, they continued, and their papers, would the matches have come about? Of course they didn't demand a thing, but it went without saying.

"So argued our editors. The in-laws probably would have agreed, for what did they care? They wouldn't pay two matchmakers' fees anyway. But the other five stood up and shouted stormily.

" 'Where do editors come off with being marriage brokers? And since when are there seven matchmakers for two matches, three and a half matchmakers per match?'

"The one who made the biggest noise was the man who had threatened to spoil it all. He promised both editors that he would fix their wagons. And he would have done it, too, for he started to roll up his sleeves. But the in-laws from both sides stepped in and separated them—and our editors, thank God, escaped without a scratch."

Here again the young man put his hands to his face and shook with quiet laughter. When he had giggled himself dry, he asked me when I was free. He said, since I was about to leave town, he wanted to come and interview me. "Stop by tomorrow," I said.

9. Interviews

The next morning, my giggling friend came to see me. He had such a large briefcase with him, he nearly scared me out of my wits.

"I'd like to interview you," he began, taking an oblong notebook out of his side pocket and promptly starting to tell me stories. I couldn't even get a word in edgewise.

"Don't ask me where my interview with you will be printed —I myself don't know! Maybe in the *Bowler Hat*. Maybe in the *Skullcap*. Even chances. The *Bowler Hat* ought to take me first. After all, it's a pretty progressive paper. Although its entire progressiveness is made up of sneering at Jewish laws and jeering at Jewish customs. For instance—it doesn't like the custom of fasting. Comes the eve of *Yom Kippur*, or the Ninth day of Ab, or any other fast day—the *Bowler Hat* goes on a rampage with an article by a doctor. He's as much a doctor as you're governor. Actually, the editor, in all his glory, writes it himself and signs it, 'Dr. Raspberus Marmaladus.'

"In his article, 'Doctor Marmaladus' runs on about how harmful fasting and self-affliction are. He brings proof positive from books and treatises which no one ever laid eyes on, introduces names of famed authorities like Professor Garlic, Doctor Luigi Ravioli, and similar pseudonyms. As if these were not enough, he pounces upon statistics and shows how many people died of emaciation owing to fasting. His conclusion is that the number of people dying from fasting in Kasrilevke is three times as high as the birth rate. In a scientifically mathematical account, he concludes that if Jews were to continue fasting every fast day, in exactly one thousand years and three months, there would be no Jews left in Kasrilevke.

"So much for fast days," my interviewer said. "They then rant and rave about how today's Jews get all worked up about the sacrificial ceremony before the Day of Atonement. It's pagan. And the custom of casting sins into the water before the Jewish New Year—it's wild, they say. The *Bowler Hat*'s editor tells an ancient story, historic, I mean, which happened right here in Kasrilevke. One day, Jews went to cast their sins in the river. A coach drawn by four horses in tandem came toward them. In it were the count's daughter and her adjutant. The horses, seeing so many Jews, bolted and ran amuck with the coach, throwing the count's daughter and her adjutant. Since the count was the boss of Kasrilevke, that is, he owned it down to the last nail, he punished the whole village by whipping and fining the Jews so heavily that it took them more than a hundred years to pay their debt.

"Now, as to why the *Bowler Hat*'s angry with me—you'd probably think it grew out of the masthead incident which I told you about. But as God is my witness, I'm as guilty in that affair as you are. But, never mind. The editor thinks I told the *Skullcap* all the editorial secrets. If so, then you'd think the *Skullcap* would be friendly to me, right? But it turns out that I don't dare set foot in there either. How come? It's a long story, but listen."

Here, my interviewer again went into his silly convulsions. Then, he started:

"This happened long ago, even before the masthead business. At that time, I was jack of all trades for the editor of the *Bowler Hat*. I thought myself practically a secretary of the editorial department. I knew all its secrets. Nothing was hidden from me. The *Skullcap* also had a secretary, the editor's brother-in-law, in fact, and a buddy of mine, too, a true-blue pal. I knew what was cooking in their pots, and he knew what was happening over at our place. What I mean is, we

told each other all the business secrets, exchanged telegrams secretly, showed each other private letters. If something special came up, we phoned each other.

"Once, way after midnight, I was all alone in the office, grabbing forty winks on the sofa. The phone rang, once, twice, three times. I was smack in the middle of sweet dreams and he was pestering me with his ringing. Ring until you burst, I thought. I'm not budging. But the fellow at the other end didn't want to stop. To make a long story short—it was no use. I got up and answered it.

" 'Who is it,' I said.

" 'What're you doing?' my pal from the *Skullcap* asked me, 'sleeping?'

" 'You crazy?' I said. 'What do you mean *sleeping?*'

" 'Then what're you doing?'

" 'Working.'

" 'At what. What's up?'

" 'Well—it's nothing much—back-page stuff.'

" 'What sort?'

" 'What sort?' I said. 'A pogrom.'

" 'A pogrom? Where?'

" 'What do you mean where?' I said. 'I'll give you three guesses where pogroms take place.'

" 'Kishinev, of course,' he said.

" 'Of course,' I said. 'As I live and breathe, you're a genius.'

" 'Is it a real pogrom?'

" 'With all the trimmings.'

" 'Any killed?'

" 'Two hundred.'

" 'Any women raped?' he asked.

" 'Three dozen.'

" 'Any children torn to pieces?'

" 'Can't even count them.'

"I didn't hear any more from him, because he rushed to print with the Kishinev flash. I don't have to tell you what happened the next morning when the *Skullcap* came out with a foot-long headline—"NEW POGROM IN KISHINEV" (by our special correspondent). Our editor blew his stack. Not be-

cause of the pogrom, God forbid. But because the *Skullcap*
had such a fat piece of news and the *Bowler Hat* didn't. He
made mincemeat out of us, nagged and ate his heart out all day
long until he found out that the whole thing was an out-and-
out lie. The *Skullcap*'s editor then went to work trying to get
to the bottom of the matter—the source of that off-beam
newsflash. Things got to the point where their secretary, despite his being brother-in-law, was supposed to get out and
receive a sound thrashing, too. The pressure was on until he
finally admitted where the news originated. It was then that
the *Skullcap*'s editor decreed that if I ever showed my face
around his office, I'd be as good as dead."

Just then there was a knock at the door. "Come in," I said,
and in came a young man with a splotchy red face. He too
carried a huge briefcase. Seeing the newcomer, my giggling
young friend looked as if he had seen a ghost. His eyes popping, he grabbed his briefcase, said a hasty goodbye, and disappeared.

I asked the new man to take a seat. He thanked me, took a
sheet of paper out of his briefcase, a pen from his side pocket,
and sat down, ready to work.

"I hope you'll excuse me," he began, "but ever since I heard
you were back, I wanted to interview you. What was that
slob doing here?"

"What slob?"

"That one. With the briefcase. The one who just grabbed
his hat and ran as if his pants were on fire. Did he tell you lots
of cock-and-bull stories? May he only drown. Great God!
Just as I didn't hear his stories, so may they not harm me."

"What's the matter? Is he a . . . ?"

"You wanted to say a liar, right?" he laughed. "But you
can't compare one liar to another. *Everything* that comes out
of his mouth is a damn lie. I once wrote about his type in an
article. There are two sorts of liars, I said. There are liars who
call black white and sour sweet. But, I tell you, he's the sort
of liar who says that black is sour and that sweet is stale. Ha,
ha, ha. Well put, huh? He has another fine quality. Before he

tells a joke, he laughs himself sick and then comes out with something foolish. About a type like him, I once wrote an article. There are three sorts of wits, I said. One tells a joke, and laughs himself. The second tells a joke, and makes another laugh. The third tells a joke, and no one laughs. Ha, ha, ha. How do you like *that* one? Wait! You're not through, yet. He's deaf to boot. Deaf as a stone. I once told him to his face that I was jealous of him. But, he didn't hear a word. And that thing has got the nerve to call himself a writer. He's a writer like I'm the Queen's maid. Ha, ha, ha. You're wondering what I'm so jolly about? That's the secret of my talent. I'm from your school, you see. I mean, I'm a humorist, too, and write only satires. Nothing but. I once wrote a satire about a young couple, but I had to burn it. Yes, I had to burn the manuscript. Why? Because that's the sort of town we have. There are no secrets in Kasrilevke. I read my satire to some people in Kasrilevke, and swore them to strictest secrecy. Mum's the word, I said. Not a soul was to know. So they thought it over, and promptly spread it all over town. Well, that couple sure gave me a hard time. The wife said she'd do herself some harm, and the husband swore to God that he'd cut my heart out. What do you think of a rogue like that? Go write satires about their kind! Do you need more proof? I'll tell you a better story."

Again, there was a knocking at the door. I asked the man in. As soon as he appeared on the threshold, the satirist jumped up, took his briefcase and sheet of paper, said a quick goodbye, promised to come later, and dove out of the room. In his place stood a tall, thin, insipid-looking young man. He had a wispy beard and tragic eyes under his silver-framed glasses. A sort of modern Don Quixote. He, too, came in with a huge briefcase and inspected the room thoroughly. I asked him to sit down. But he continued staring about him, as if he were looking for something.

"What are you looking for?"

"I'm not looking *for* anything. I'm just looking. What was that sharpie doing here?"

"What sharpie?"

"The one who just left. I'm just looking to see if he made off with anything."

"What's the matter? Is he a . . . ?"

"Exactly. A thief! A pick-pocket. Everything goes with him. After all—a watch is a watch, a spoon, a spoon. He never wrote a line that was his own. Ask anyone! Once I wrote a poem. I'm a poet, you see, and with the good Lord's help, write lyrics—poetry, that is. Here's my card. I came to interview you because I heard that you're here and that you'll tell us something. But if you'll pardon me, since I started telling you the story about my poems, I'll have to finish it. Well then, I wrote a poem. An excellent one. If you wish, I'll leave it with you—if not, I'll read it to you from beginning to end, and then you'll see for yourself the stuff it's made of. You'll admit that a poet has to be made of iron to keep himself in a place like this, may hell-fire burn it to a crisp. Imagine! I bring my poem to the *Skullcap,* and ask them to read it. Only *read* it, mind you. They tell me that they don't appreciate poetry. So I go to the *Bowler Hat,* for all intents and purposes, a radical organ, an independent paper.

" 'There's no room,' they say.

" 'But read it at least,' I say.

" 'We have no time,' they say.

"That's how they all are. This one has no time, that one, no space. Go and write poetry. Who tells you to write, you'll ask. But what can I do if I can't help it? I must write every day. I finish one poem, sometimes two, every week. . . . Oh, yes, since I started telling you about that sharpie, I'll have to finish *that* story. I read my poem to a few friends and they went *meshugge* over it. They said it had been years since they had come across such a gem. Fine and dandy! So then that swindler decides to write a poem with the very same title and content. Word for word. He carried it around town with him and read it to everyone and passed it off as his. Am I supposed to take this sitting down? So, I yelled blue murder. Let's mediate! He refused. I asked some good friends to force him. To make a long story short, they brought that shrewdie to mediation and they—all of them literary men—heard us out and listened to witnesses from both sides. Then they compared both poems, and the outcome was that his was really word for word like mine. You'd probably think that they fined him God knows how much. Then you don't know Kasrilevke's literary men. According to them, the two poems were allegedly written in the same manner as Pushkin—meaning that Pushkin, so they said, covered that same theme much earlier and therefore . . . Hey, Mr. Sholem Aleichem, wait a minute! Where are you rushing off to? What about our interview?"

10. An Anniversary Tale

> Your presence is hereby requested this evening at the dinner in honor of the great writer and dramatist, Kopel Beggarman. The affair, celebrating his twenty-five years of writing, will take place in Alter's restaurant in Kasrilevke. (Formerly Yankel's.)

That's the invitation I got in the morning mail. It was signed by none other than—The Committee.

The day dragged on and on. I thought evening would never come. Finally, it did, and I changed clothing, hired a horse and buggy, and told the driver to take me to Alter's roomy restaurant, formerly Yankel's.

It's a universal custom, if you're telling a story and come to a house, to stop and describe the house, first from without, then from within. But, just because that's the way it's usually done, I'm going to do just the opposite and start the story.

It turned out that I had been a bit hasty, for the hall was almost empty. Some waiters roamed around in faded frock coats and none-too-white paper dickies, setting the dishes on the long table and clanging the silverware. Chopped herring and onions made their tangy presence known all over the rooms.

Aside from the busy waiters, there were some young people around. Judging by their long hair and glasses, I was almost positive that they were writers and *literati* who also had come to the anniversary party. One thing puzzled me, though. These young folk ignored one another. Not only didn't they talk at all, they didn't even *look* at one another. Hands in pocket, they roamed around, completely at ease; they stared through the windows, whistling, as if each were alone in the hall. Then fate stepped in, and more people entered. Among them was my friend, the giggly interviewer. He whispered that all these people were not only colleagues, but some had been working together on the same paper since God knows when.

"If they're colleagues, why don't they talk to one another?" I asked.

"That's just the reason why. *Because* they're colleagues. See that one with the black hair? He's a poet. Once in a great while he writes prose. But when it comes to talking—he clams up completely, doesn't even talk to his wife. It's beneath his dignity. He thinks he's tops. No one beats him. Pushkin is a dog. Lermentov—a tot. He was once compared to Heine, and flew into a rage. Who was Heine? A clown, a wag! There's a fine tale they tell about him: he doesn't go to the public baths any more. Once at the bath, he saw himself in the nude and got all riled up. Such a great poet as he shouldn't be seen stark naked!"

My friend covered his face, giggled softly and, when he quieted down, proceeded.

"See *that* one? With the blue specs and the short jacket? He's a playwright who churns out plays like you churn out butter. A play a week. Do you think it pays off? Surely, in headaches. You see, he's got a wife and she gets pregnant every year. This he can't stand. 'Every year a kid,' he complains. 'You know what,' she says, 'let's switch. You have the babies, and I'll write the plays.'"

My friend tittered for a while, then continued in his soft, soporific voice.

"Now you see *that* one? With the bad eyes? He's a novelist. Writes novels. Day and night, he writes them. It's not for nothing he's ruined his eyes. Why he writes novels, no one knows. All told, he's written only one story, and the *Skullcap* printed it. Since then, he just keeps on writing novels. No one publishes them. No one reads them. But what does he care? He just writes. In return, he's been blessed with a wife. She operates a little stationery shop, so he lets her earn the money. That is . . ."

Suddenly, my friend snapped to silent attention, like a soldier who sees an officer. Two new people entered. One was tall and wore a bowler hat. The other was a pygmy with a pot belly. Both came through one door, mad as hell at each other. One looked this way, the other that. The tall one removed his bowler hat, winked at the assembly, and looked for a spot to sit. The other one, the shorty with the paunch, took off his hat, donned a silk skullcap, and also looked for a seat. Meanwhile, my laughing boy told me a secret. The two newcomers were the editors of the Kasrilevke papers, the *Bowler Hat* and the *Skullcap*, respectively.

"You ought to meet them," he said. "But it's impossible now."

"Why?" I asked.

"Because if you meet one first, the other'll be angry with you."

"What's to be done then?"

"Nothing. Suppose you were dead?"

"Thanks."

"Don't mention it."

The people kept streaming in. The hall was tightly packed. Finally, the affair began. All this time, the guest of honor himself, a pale and hungry-looking man well along in years, wearing a Sabbath jacket, had been sitting modestly on the side. No one even knew he was there. When the time came, he was called up to the dais. There he looked like a victim before the gallows.

One thing, though. His jacket was brand new. There was only one flaw. It didn't fit. As if it weren't his at all. Seemingly reading my thoughts, my friend whispered:

"It's not his. It's hired. Because he's such a pauper, God save us. This party we're giving—well, it's because we feel sorry for him."

"What do you mean, sorry?"

"Just what I said. A man struggles for a lifetime. He never made much money out of his writings. As for honor—even less than that. So, in his old age, why shouldn't he have some pleasure, a little anniversary dinner?"

A yellowish young man with gold-rimmed glasses and a mouth which belied his years, stood up and said: "Gentlemen! Please take your seats!"

He was the president of the committee, and swiftly showed each person his place. When it came to the guest of honor, the president took him by the hand and seated him at the speaker's table. Then, he very cleverly seated the two editors at one and the same time. They immediately turned their backs on each other, looking like two feuding in-laws with murder in their eyes.

"Gentlemen," the jaundiced-looking president began. "Gentlemen. We've assembled tonight to celebrate the anniversary of our oldest and greatest writer."

"The greatest?" the black-haired poet shot out of his seat. "I won't argue the point that he's the oldest. But the greatest?"

"A slight exaggeration," the blue-spectacled playwright backed him up.

"It's one hell of a nerve," the poet continued, "it's nervy and idiotic, too."

"You're one hell of an idiot yourself," the president couldn't take it any more.

The poet started shaking with anger. I looked at the poor guest of honor in his rented dinner jacket. His pale face became white as chalk. His eyes seemed to plead: friends! Have pity. Don't ruin my party.

But it was too late. The free-for-all was beginning. After all, they'd taken the greatest poet of them all (compared to whom Pushkin was a dog, Lermontov a tot, and Heine a clown and a wag), and called him an idiot. If that was the case, well then, he'd show them a thing or two.

"It's best to beat it now," my good friend whispered.

And that's just what we did.

Epilogue

The next morning, my pal told me that we had got away just in the nick of time!

11. The Story of a Funeral

One morning, I opened both Kasrilevke papers and saw the following announcement first-paged in heavy, black borders:

Last night, Kasrilevke suffered a colossal loss. A. Y. Pauperman, the famous writer, passed away in his fifty-second year. The funeral will take place at twelve noon. All writers and *litterateurs* are asked to come to the New Synagogue for the funeral oration. There, the burial arrangements will be made and means of support for the poor widow and her unfortunate orphans will be decided upon.

Well, in that case, one must dress and go to the New Synagogue, called that not because it's so new, but because the old one was too decrepit, big-bellied, and bent. One of these days, it'll just collapse, I'm sure, and there'll be a catastrophe, God forbid.

If I were a Kasrilevke resident, and not the sort of guest who stays for a while and sees for a mile, I'd suggest that the synagogue be torn down. But since synagogues aren't torn down, I would just order them to re-do the walls and put up a new roof. That would be it! But there's one problem—you need cash. And there's none of that around. The old Kasrilevke problem. Modern Kasrilevke has everything. Still, there's only one thing missing—money. Oh, if Kasrilevke only had money in addition to brains and progress!

First of all, there wouldn't be so many poor people, and that alone would be a boon to the village. I think it's better to have one rich man than fifty paupers. That's number one. Secondly, if they were rich, where would they get their supply of assorted sluggards, dilly-dallyers, loafers, and dawdlers, who only know how to die of hunger and exposure. Hunger and cold, I said to myself. When would those two plagues stop tormenting hapless humanity in general and our poor brethren in Israel, the Kasrilevkites, in particular.

Deep in such altruistic and humanitarian thought, I came late to the memorial meeting in the synagogue. When I arrived, the place was fully packed and someone—a writer, naturally, was delivering a sermon. It was a fine, heart-stirring speech. Moving to the point of tears. The speaker talked only of the deceased and how he lived. That is, he spoke of how he died, because, actually, you couldn't call what he did, living.

"Gentlemen," the speaker was finishing, "gentlemen. He died for fifty-two years in a row. Our late friend continually dreamed of a Paradise which he well-deserved, but never had. But all through his fifty-two years, he found himself perpetually in hell. I'm sure that he'll head straight for Paradise. That's why we have to pay him his last respects. It's only fitting for a man who's on his way to the Garden of Eden. That's why we have to immortalize his name. It's only fitting for a man on his way to Paradise. And since he's on his way, it's only fitting that we provide for his poor stranded widow and orphans."

It seemed that the speech was well-received. The listeners gave him an ovation. The speaker came down from the pulpit perspiring, and a second speaker immediately followed him. He repeated almost everything the first speaker had said. Only he said it a little differently and a lot worse, and ruined the good impression left by the first speaker. But the applause for him wasn't too bad, either. A third speaker got up and re-hashed the second speaker's words. Only, he too said it a little differently, and killed the impression left by the second speaker. He got a round of applause anyway, but it was nothing compared to what the first two got. Then a fourth speaker got up and re-echoed the previous speech. And so it went, and the crowd kept applauding them, rather feebly, but still they clapped. Then a discussion began: what was to be done with the poor widow and the unfortunate orphans?

This kicked off a round of hot debates. One excellent speaker suggested that a fund be started through the papers.

From the money collected, some sort of business would be bought for the widow and she would earn her living. The crowd really liked that and applauded the speaker's project wildly.

But another man, an orator too, stood up and said: "No! A business is no good. She's a housewife and not suited for business. She'll eat up the money in two years and what'll happen then? That's not the way. I think that we should publish an edition of Pauperman's collected works with the collected money."

This plan was even better received. The second speaker was given an ear-splitting hand. But a third stood up and said that the previous idea wouldn't do either. As is, there were plenty of books rotting in Kasrilevke's bookstores which no one was buying.

"We have a custom here in Kasrilevke," he argued, "an ancient, sacred custom. Books aren't bought. They're borrowed. That's how they're read. Kasrilevke doesn't know beans about book-buying. They only know how to borrow."

This argument won a storm of applause. They clapped on and on until the chairman had to silence the crowd with a few smart raps on the table. With his booming voice, he called out:

"Gentlemen. Let's end this discussion. The chair recognizes the debate as over. In other words, we're through with the widow and the orphans. And now let's finally turn to the deceased. How can we perpetuate the memory of our departed colleague? Whoever has anything to say, speak up."

Almost all those present asked to speak, and the first to get the floor cleared his throat and spoke at great length. But he talked quite well. He noted the sad situation of writers in general and of Yiddish writers in Kasrilevke in particular. He explained how bitter a lot it was to write for the Jews of Kasrilevke, and have neither honor nor means. So, at least, the writer deserved to be honored after his death, he said. Therefore, he thought it would be best to use a part of the collected funds to put up a monument which would be placed in the synagogue courtyard. On the top of the monument, there should be a marble or bronze bust of the late writer. Carved in golden letters under the bust should be these words: "To our unforgettable colleague, A. Y. Pauperman, from his devoted friends."

This really captured the crowd's imagination, and they thundered their applause in approval. But there was someone who didn't like this idea. He hated it, in fact. It was the black-haired poet. He rose and analyzed the monument proposal. He lambasted the first speaker; he gave him a piece of his mind; he tore his project to shreds.

"First of all," he argued, "Where will we collect so much money in Kasrilevke? Money, money. That's all I hear. Money for the widow, money for the orphans. Money for a monument. That's number one. Number two: since when do Jews suddenly put up monuments? We've had greater personalities who didn't get statues put up for them. Do you find many monuments in Jewish history? So much for number two. Now, three: who'll permit you to put up a statue in Kasrilevke? They'll give you statues until you turn blue in the face."

Someone else jumped up.

It happened to be a freckle-faced young writer, wearing an old jacket. "Our poet is right. I even know why he's so against a statue." He stopped and spoke slowly. "It's because he figures that *he's* first in line, and that the first monument belongs to *him* and no one else."

That's all they needed. The black-haired poet turned purple with rage and hollered: "Lout . . . beggar . . . tramp," and immediately flew at the freckled writer with both hands flailing. Luckily, the chairman held him back, preventing a scandal. The chairman said:

"Honored guests. I'd like to say that since it's late, and since we've set the funeral for twelve sharp, let's postpone the discussion about a monument or any other thing to keep the memory of our late friend alive, for another time. It'd be better if we turn now to the question of the funeral procession. Who will be the pallbearers? Who will be the first to carry out the coffin? Who will be in front, who in back, and so on. Whoever wants to participate, let me know."

A hubbub started which raised the roof. Everyone crowded around. Everyone wanted to be the first pallbearer, no one the last. The chairman asked for order in vain. In vain, he rapped for silence, threatening that if it didn't get any quieter he'd close the meeting. But the longer it lasted, the louder it became. They got feverishly excited and insulted one another. Tension was at a high pitch. Suddenly, I felt someone tugging at my sleeve. I turned around and saw my friend, the giggler. He looked at me seriously, with eyes that were a bit frightened, and whispered: "The time's ripe to get up and slip out of here."

I listened to him. I got up and slipped out of there.

I understand that the move turned out to be a wise one.

Epilogue

The custom of burying a person as soon as he dies, without waiting a day or two, was in force in modern Kasrilevke, and has been since ancient times. The local burial society saw that the deceased was just lying around while his friends gathered in the New Synagogue and raised a rumpus without getting anywhere. Meanwhile, the sextons brought the corpse to the new cemetery, paid their respects, and buried him. The orphans recited the mourner's prayer, and the widow, as was fitting and proper, fainted a couple of times. Well, may he rest in peace.

12. Yiddishists and Hebraists

When new winds blew through Kasrilevke, and the people started moving ahead and demanding modernism just like the big city's, the only thing left to do was to found an association (a club, I mean) called "The Choral Society." Why? Because every civilized town had a group like that. The people liked it. Especially the name—"Choral." It was a fine word, with a pleasing sound. So poetic. They worked out a plan and put up a constitution with all the necessary by-laws. All that was needed was the first meeting. That was a cinch in Kasrilevke. All you had to do was put an ad in both papers saying: "To-

night, at 8 P.M. sharp, there will be a meeting in such and such
a place. You are cordially invited to attend." And they do.
Not only the big wheels and the cream of the crop, but the
entire Kasrilevke intelligentsia shows up, with the editors of
both papers leading them all.

You realize, of course, they all didn't come at once. Their
timing was poor. Everyone came when he could. Some at
eight, some at nine, some at ten, and some at eleven, as well.
Although you wanted to come on time, there were various
reasons and circumstances which prevented it. For instance—
you had a store, and there was a wave of customers just when
you were closing up. Or—you came home and found your
wife out, the kids screaming for supper, and not a pressed
shirt anywhere in sight. Or—you could only find one blue and
one brown sock. Or—you had such a toothache that you
found yourself clawing at the walls. Who can list all the things
that can happen just when you're about to go to a meeting?

But, nevertheless, everyone did come, and the meeting
(however late) was opened by Noah, the son of Reb Yosel.
Although he was not a young man, despite the fact that
there were more gray hairs on his head than black ones, and
although he was a grandfather (oh my, how time flies—I remember Noah first as a young bachelor, then as a married
man, freeloading in his father-in-law's house, studying the
Talmud), he still remained the same old Noah. He didn't
change a bit. Young at heart and idealistic. An honest, kind-
hearted man without a fault—you could do anything you
wanted with him. You see, he trusted everyone. He was devoted to Kasrilevke and its clubs and societies heart and soul.
As usual, he didn't consider himself, his wife, or children, but
only the village, its organizations, and the public good. His
biography is worth knowing. He was, at one time, the only
journalist in Kasrilevke, the leader of both the old "Lovers of
Zion" group, and of the latter-day Zionists, and the founder
of many old and new organizations. He was also a bottle
dealer. Bottles were a good business, but he couldn't make a
go of it. All the bottle dealers in Kasrilevke made money. He
lost. He couldn't make a go of it with women, either. As for

his first wife, his in-laws divorced him. The second one divorced him herself. Things were pretty close to a divorce with
the third—but it was too late. She dropped dead. All this because he was such a public do-gooder and gave all of his time
to the community. People said that the three dowries he got
from his three wives went into the societies' funds. An inheritance from his childless uncle (the only childless man in
Kasrilevke) was fizzled away into his community affairs. In
short, Noah lived for the other fellow: he didn't take care of
himself.

When these modern winds breezed into Kasrilevke, the bug
bit Noah stronger than anyone else. It really made him
crazy; he didn't know whether he was coming or going.
He went to work with such zest, as if his life depended on it.
Or his happiness, at least.

Hearing that the town wanted a "Choral Society," Noah
rolled up his sleeves and got down to business. Single-hand-
edly, he wrote the constitution and all its by-laws in one night,
ordered a meeting place, wrote letters to the editor, and even
delivered them himself. He wasn't fussy, and certainly not
lazy.

When they all gathered, Noah opened the meeting and suggested they pick a chairman. Noah didn't fancy that seat of
honor at all. In fact, he hated it. He was no glory-seeker, as
they say. It's a well-known fact that if you're set upon honor,
honor slips around you and heads for where the daisies grow.
And the reverse holds true. If you avoid honor, honor tails
after you, begging: "Dopey! What are you running away
for? Take a little bit, at least."

It's no news, then, that Noah was honored more than anyone else. Whenever there was some communal job to be done,
whenever someone had to be sent scurrying here and there—
Noah was picked. He accepted the call and worked like three
men. He never even questioned why it was he and no one else.
He knew very well that it was his to do and no one else's.
And the rest of the club members were pleased with him. If
at times they weren't, they told him straight off. Often they
said it with a hint, a verbal dig, a joke, or just a plain story—

the old-fashioned Kasrilevke way of driving someone *me-shugge*. Sometimes, they really gave it to him and annoyed him. Unfortunately, there were some people in Kasrilevke who didn't care a straw about another person's gray hairs at the community's expense. But who's talking about scoundrels and boors? Let's return to the initial meeting of the first "Choral Society."

Hearing Noah's suggestion about choosing a president, the people started dickering. There were a host of eager candidates. But none were suitable. When there was a job to be done, no one was at home. Go see Noah. But when it came to an appointment or any honor there was a whole hullabaloo:

"Who are you?"

"Why him?"

"Why the other guy, and not me?"

They begrudged the next fellow the office, you see. Often, the entire affair ended up in harsh words, frequently, with scandal. Sometimes, they even came to blows. But this time things didn't get that far out of hand. There was a shrewdie who hit upon a good idea.

"Men," he said, "do you have to bicker and brawl as to who I am? Why here I am already in the chairman's seat. Any objections?"

Who was he? None other than the famous black-haired poet whom we've previously met. This poet took the chair with military stature and smacked the table with his hand with an executive air.

"Friends," he said in Yiddish.

But he didn't get another word in. They didn't let him. Who, you ask. Why the anti-Yiddish bloc. They hated Yiddish, because they said Yiddish was a jargon and a jargon was sickening. So they protested:

"Hebrew, Hebrew."

The black-haired poet wasn't one to let a protest scare him. But it left him a bit off-balance. He patted his belly, straightened his vest, and repeated in a slightly higher tone: "Friends," as if all the tumult wasn't aimed at him at all.

Pandemonium broke loose. They banged, they whistled. They made all sorts of noises you could hear for a mile.

"Hebrew, Hebrew, Hebrew!"

Evidently, the Kasrilevke Hebraists had pre-planned a demonstration against Yiddish. Nothing helped. But nothing! The poor poet had to leave the chair, humiliated, and his place was taken by the freckle-faced writer with the tattered jacket. He, too, didn't stand on such formalities as an election, but thumped his hand on the table and began in Hebrew:

"Gentlemen."

He pronounced it with the proper Sephardic accent, just like they did in Palestine. The new chairman had some lungs. His first word rang out like a bell. But, he didn't get to the second. They didn't let him.

Now the Kasrilevke Yiddishists demonstrated against Hebrew. This little riot, too, was prepared in advance, and with the same weapons. In other words, they hooted and tooted, whooped and howled. They stamped their feet and yelled to high heaven. The walls shook. The rafters rang. It was a first class snag.

"Yiddish. Yiddish. Yiddish!"

Then, one Hebraist decided to throw a bombshell into the proceedings. Above the general caterwauling, he shouted:

"Tshernovitz."

You'd wonder what was so terrible about that word. It was only a town in the Bukovine section of Austria. Two countries were currently fighting over it—each chasing the other out. Today it belonged to one, tomorrow, the other. But if you reminded a Yiddishist of Tshernovitz*—well, that was a thousand times worse than cursing his father.

You could accuse him of the worst. You could say he did anything—just so long as it wasn't Tshernovitz. That's the way the Yiddishists are.

The same goes for the local Hebraist. If you want to get

* At the first Yiddish Conference held in Tshernovitz (now Soviet Union) in 1908, Yiddish, rather than Hebrew, was proposed as the national language of the Jews.

his goat, just make fun of his pronunciation. But you have to watch out for him, for he's liable to break your head open, too. Folks of the new Kasrilevke generation are a strange bunch. Terribly touchy. They act on the spur of the moment. They fly off the handle. They've got excitable natures.

Anyway, hearing the word Tshernovitz, one of the Yiddishists (a weak and consumptive one at that, but a hot-head) didn't dilly-dally, but removed his left boot and heaved it right at the face of one of the Hebraists. He got him smack where his eye left off and his nose began. Lucky for him, he didn't wear glasses. He would have ended up with one eye less!

As you'd expect, some of the Hebraists then stood up to take the part of their insulted friend. They fell on that weak, consumptive Yiddishist with elbows flying, and let him have it with such gusto that if it weren't for the rest of the Yiddishists, they would've had to carry him out on a stretcher.

Obviously, the Yiddishist's boot triggered a conflict. Better yet—a total war, which neither the Yiddishists nor the Hebraists underestimated. But Noah, our loyal community-man and congenial founder of clubs and societies, suffered more than anyone else. Undeservedly, he got it royally in the back. And all because of the saying: if you run from honor, honor chases after you. That is, it follows you so closely, it steps on your ankles.

Epilogue

You have to look pretty hard to find a secretary like Noah from Kasrilevke. Everything was conducted according to protocol. Everything was recorded. He didn't miss a thing. If a future historian would like to know what happened in Kasrilevke, all he'd have to do is look into Noah's minutes. He'd find a treasure-house of information.

From his notes on the historic assembly of the Yiddishists and Hebraists we'll just quote the most pertinent facts:

"After very brief speeches by the orators of the day, there ensued lively and heated debates which could not resolve into common agreement the differences of opinion and friction current between the two parties. Owing to the dissension over language, and owing to the unavoidability of the language question, a single way out was found. Instead of organizing one 'Choral Society'—two were to be established: one, a Yiddish 'Choral Society' for the Yiddishists; the other, a Hebrew one for the Hebraists."

13. Lecturers and Dramatic Readers

Kasrilevke likes literature, art, and music. There's something doing in town every night. Especially during the winter. The nights are long, there are some who don't play cards, and the people ache for something different. If it isn't a theater, it's a concert. If it isn't a meeting or a reading recital, it's a lecture with discussion or without.

But above all else, they fancy lectures *with* discussion. A lecture alone, where someone else does the gabbing, is boring. The man just rants on and on and you sit there staring him in the face. But as soon as there's a lecture with a discussion following, you can throw in your two cents' worth and show them all that you're no dummy. Since there's a shortage of lecturers and dramatic readers in Kasrilevke, and since they don't think much of local talent, anyway, they always import the goods. That's why lecturers, dramatic readers, and artists are hired out of town.

When it comes to concerts, lectures, and reading recitals, cut-throat competition reigns between the two Kasrilevke choral groups. If the Yiddishists sign up a world-famous lecturer, the Hebraists bring in an internationally known dramatic reader. The sky's the limit. Often, there are two events in Kasrilevke in one and the same night. A lecturer *and* a dramatic reader, and although you rip them in two, the poor people don't know where to go first. The fact that the Yiddishists and the Hebraists are at odds with each other doesn't make the slightest difference. You never cut your nose to spite your face. And anyway, Kasrilevke is always dying for something new. So you do whatever's humanly possible. You listen for a while to one, then hurry over to listen to the other. You snatch a part of the lecture and then dash over for a bit of the dramatic reading. Kasrilevkites hate to miss a thing. Life is so short, you have to sample everything. That's why a speaker in Kasrilevke, no matter who he is, can be sure of a full house, an over-crowded one, in fact. He can also be sure of leaving the place feeling like he'd just been in a Turkish bath.

Kasrilevke looks to the big city and follows the latest trends to a *t*. In the big town, it's the latest fashion to throw a banquet after a lecture or a reading. Kasrilevkites, too! As soon as the lecture and discussion period are over, even if it's after midnight, they take the lecturer to an eatery, put him up on the dais, and have a meal in his honor.

You can almost say that this party is more important in Kasrilevke than the lecture or the reading itself. The meal's the main thing. When it comes to arranging dinners, there's no beating the Kasrilevke intellectuals. As soon as they get together after the lecture or reading, a herring is cut up and beer is served. Glasses are filled, and the toasts in honor of the guest begin. These can drag on until daybreak. Actually, these toasts reactivate all the previous discussions from scratch. The poor guest speaker has to listen to them all, and has to answer them again, one by one. At times, they lionize the visitor to high heaven, say he's smarter than King Solomon, and (forgive the proximity) is greater than Shakespeare. They make his head spin until he's ready to pass out. Then again, sometimes they pull the speaker's lecture to pieces, favor him with such critiques and analyses and hair-splitting until he's blue in the face and groping for the door.

Sometimes those who throw the party wrangle among themselves and stray away into new discussions and debates. They start a battle royal and the guest of honor can thank his lucky stars if he gets away in one piece. I don't mean that anyone would hit him, or insult him. God forbid! Not that. But because of the local competition between the Hebraists and the Yiddishists, the guest sometimes has been roughed-up a bit. Which means he's likely to fall willy-nilly into the sort of mud-puddle from which no soap will cleanse him.

To illustrate this, here's an incident which happened in Kasrilevke to a learned Hebraist, a doctor of philosophy. Because of the local parties' competition, and an intrigue involving the two gazettes, this innocent man was drawn into a sad situation.

The Kasrilevke press gave him a good raking over. Out of thin air, they whipped up lies and libel about him. They pestered and badgered him until the whole village was gossiping. As it turned out later, there was absolutely no foundation to all this mud-slinging. It was perfectly disgraceful!

This is how it happened.

One fine day, the Hebraists imported a famous Ph.D. from the big city for a lecture and discussion period. He came into Kasrilevke, delivered his discourse, conducted the discussion part of the program, managed to survive the banquet, and went on his way. All right. But what happened? The two Kasrilevke papers took the Ph.D's lecture apart and aired their opinions about it. What one said, naturally, the other had to contradict. The *Skullcap*, the organ of the Hebraists, praised him to the skies, said his delivery was spellbinding, called him a sensitive artist, and said that his ideas were akin to Kant's and Spinoza's.

The *Bowler Hat*, of course, as the Yiddishists' organ, had to say just the reverse. They ripped him apart and tagged him with such fine labels as "loafer," "stutterer," "prattler," "seat-warmer," and "hypocrite." They called him a hypocrite because he preached to the audience. He asked why weren't they more Jewish, why the Kasrilevke youths sat bareheaded in the movies, and why the Kasrilevke girls publicly carried parasols, kerchiefs, and gloves on the Sabbath.

Naturally, this write-up galled the Hebraists. In the *Skullcap*, they came out with a rebuttal against the Yiddishists and asked a foolish question: "Where do such ignoramuses, boors, idlers, shoe-shine boys, and butchers' assistants, who can't even cross a *t*, come off passing judgment on such a great scholar, sensitive artist, and renowned Ph.D.?"

The next morning, the Yiddishists' progressive *Bowler Hat* snapped right back and answered their Orthodox competitor with an editorial. In it, they posed a question to the great lecturer:

"Why is it that a Jew—although he be scholar, artist, and Ph.D.—preaches to an audience about sitting in the movies without hats, and girls carrying parasols, kerchiefs, and gloves on the Sabbath, when he himself, that great scholar, that famous doctor of philosophy, that sensitive soul, has a grand total of two sisters, one baptized and the other a common thief?"

This sneak attack by the *Bowler Hat* was a bolt out of the blue for the Hebraists. It shocked them at first. But then they called a meeting, chaired by the *Skullcap*'s editor. They decided to wire the lecturer and ask him quite openly what was what with his sisters. But how do you go about asking? For, if the whole thing was true, if he really had two sisters, one a convert, the other a thief—well, it would be like a slap in the face. The only alternative was to send a non-committal telegram with a pre-paid reply:

"How are your sisters doing?"

A couple of days passed without an answer. On the third day, a two word statement came:

"What sisters?"

The Hebraists again telegraphed with a pre-paid reply:

"Your two sisters."

The answer came a few days later:

"I have no sisters."

The Hebraists didn't give up and sent a third telegram:

"Perhaps your sisters are dead?"

The return wire had an angrier tone:

"What do you want from me? I never had any sisters. I'm an only child."

Like a refreshing shower on a summer day, this gave new life to the Hebraists. A weight rolled from their hearts. The first thing they did was to publish all the telegrams in the *Skullcap* and comment on each one of them. Let the world know what the Yiddishists were capable of doing. In addition, they collected all the copies containing the story of the sisters and sent them to the lecturer. The Ph.D., a high-strung fellow, quick to defend his honor, was angered, packed bag and baggage, and came to Kasrilevke. He started an action against the *Bowler Hat* and the Yiddishists, and called a mob of witnesses into court. He wanted to send the whole staff to jail for libel and slander and defamation of character. In order to clear himself and show that he had neither a convert nor a thief for a sister, that he had never had any sisters at all, he subpoenaed the birth certificates of his entire family from his village archives. They proved that not only was he an only child, but that even his father had never had any sisters.

That didn't help the case much, though. The Hebraists—well, listen to the judge's decision:

"Had the plaintiff had any sisters and had others libeled them, and had the libel been proved false, then the defendant would have been punished according to law. But whereas the plaintiff himself has shown and whereas the exhibited documents testify that he has never had any sisters—it follows, therefore, that the defendants have allegedly libeled those who have never even existed. Therefore, the court finds that there is no insulted party, and since there is no insulted party there can be no insulter. The plaintiff's charge is null and void. Case dismissed!"

Epilogue

The other day, the Hebraists and the *Skullcap* called an emergency meeting. At the same time, the Yiddishists and the *Bowler Hat* had a party. They made speeches and caroused all night long. They drank and sang and danced until dawn, and had a wonderful time.

14. Amateur Actors

There were two theaters in Kasrilevke, the Yiddishists' and the Hebraists'—but no actors, unless a troupe or two came down from Yehupetz and performed for a couple of weeks. If they had the means, they went back where they came from. If not, they pawned their watches, clothes, and scenery, lock, stock, and barrel. If they didn't even have that, they went

from house to house with an outspread shawl and everybody
chipped in. What could you do? You couldn't let them starve.
After all, you're still a Jew!

When the troupe left town, they swore that neither they,
their children, nor their grandchildren would ever set foot in
Kasrilevke again, no matter what happened to it—be it fire,
plague, or whatever. You'd think this some insult, eh? But next
year rolls around and guess what? They're back. That's how
the Yiddish actors are. They're drawn to Kasrilevke. But you
might well ask, what would happen if the next season's loss
were greater?

"You don't know the theater business," a foxy old Yiddish
actor once told me. "Today's it's bad. But tomorrow can be
even worse."

Since the Yiddish theater came to Kasrilevke only for guest
performances, and you just can't get along without a theater,
there were many amateur actors and enthusiasts of the Yiddish
drama in the village. I'm afraid to mention this for fear of ex-
aggerating and blowing it out of proportion—but it's a fact
that almost all of the Kasrilevke youth were amateur actors.
Wherever there was a grown boy or undergrown girl, a prospective bride or groom—they were in show business. And
not only the unmarried ones. There were bearded young men
and mothers with children who were amateurs and acted on
the stage. What do you think? Pity the poor wife whose husband was an amateur; and it was a sad life for a young man
whose wife acted for the fun of it. The poor man came home
from the store tired and hungry and found neither supper
nor samovar, but the baby tearing his lungs out crying. What's
the matter? His wife was at rehearsal.

Or just the opposite. The man was the player, up to his
neck in the theater, having a gay time for himself. If it wasn't
an extravaganza, it was a rehearsal. If not a rehearsal, then it
was just a plain get-together of theater-lovers: they were
reading a new piece by a Kasrilevke playwright and were
assigning the roles. Then they all ate supper together, drank
beer, smoked, and had an all around jolly good time. And the

poor wife had to sit at home, rock the baby, or pine away in bed through the night wondering when her faithful thespian would return.

Worst of all was when both husband and wife were actors. And worse than that was when husband and wife were at loggerheads (then it was really a plague!)—that is, when the husband was an amateur with the Hebraists and the wife an actress for the Yiddishists. Or vice-versa. Squabbles came up which ended in scandal and insult.

Not long ago, an incident happened with a young couple— both of them amateurs. He was a fiery Yiddishist, a Bowler Hatter, she—an impassioned Hebraist, a Skullcapper.

As a couple they were fine. They lived peacefully for almost a full year after their wedding and already had a baby boy. But, suddenly, fights broke out between them. What caused it? He didn't want her to act in the playhouse of those pudding-headed Hebraists.

"If you want to act, I don't mind. But come act with me at the Yiddishists' theater."

She looked at him as if he had gone mad. "Why all of a sudden? I've been a Hebraist all this time and it hasn't killed you. All at once, you can't take it. Where's the logic?"

As it turned out, the logic was quite elementary. The husband miraculously found out, through a note from a Hebraist, that his wife was carrying a torch for another Hebraist from her pre-wedding days. The husband was angry and raised a rumpus. The story shook the village to the core. All sorts of gossip and slander sprouted wings. They went out into the streets, the marketplace, and finally made the papers—the Kasrilevke dailies that is, the *Bowler Hat* and the *Skullcap*. There was no envying the victims when Kasrilevke journalism stepped in.

What sort of role did the press play, for instance? Very simple. Since the Yiddishist *Bowler Hat* wanted to right the wrong done to the Yiddishist husband, one fine morning the editor came out with an embittered article blatantly entitled: "To Hell with Darwin!"

Following is an extract from this juicy morsel, word for word as it appeared in the progressive *Bowler Hat:*

Those scholars, those so-called Darwinists, just want to talk us into something. They would have us believe that for appearance's sake there is a force in nature known as heredity, and owing to this force a child must resemble his parents. But this theory hasn't got a leg to stand on. We shall prove it with facts. We do not support empty hypotheses. We like facts. For example, here is a case that happened not so long ago, not in our own Kasrilevke, heaven forbid, but in Yehupetz. A couple lived there, both of whom were amateurs in the Yiddish theater. He was a fiery Yiddishist, she, a rabid Hebraist. One day, a baby boy was born to them. Within a year they discovered something about the baby. Not only did he not look a bit like his Yiddishist father, but on the contrary, he was the spitting image of a stranger, also an amateur, but a Hebraist. Although this Hebraist amateur was anti-Yiddish on principle, he did visit the Yiddishist's wife quite often. It's quite possible then—almost a sure thing—that the baby's resemblance to the amateur Hebraist stems from the fact that the two had simply stared at each other so long.

If so, then it is further proof that the learned Darwinists who talk about inheritance haven't got the faintest notion of who's pulling the wool over their eyes. They only babble on at random about their silly theory and don't even bother finding out what's happening under their very noses.

The whole thing might have passed over smoothly. For who cares what an editor hatches up. This sort of rampage doesn't impress a Kasrilevke reader. He knows that all that ferment is just so much hot air.

But there's another daily in Kasrilevke called the *Skullcap,* and you can bet your last ruble that it won't let a word of the *Bowler Hat* slip by unnoticed. The *Skullcap* needs but the slightest excuse to catch the *Bowler Hat* at something, and the fur will start to fly.

And that's exactly what happened.

No later than the next morning, the Orthodox editor of the Orthodox *Skullcap* came out with a fiery lead editorial topped with a screaming large-lettered headline: "Canine Politics."

In this article, the *Skullcap* really laid into its bitter rival. It showed that two times two was four, that the whole meaning of that quasi-scholarly stew was to throw suspicion on a couple, a local one at that, right here from Kasrilevke. Despite the fact that that Jesuit from the radical sheet made as if it happened not in Kasrilevke, but in Yehupetz.

"Even a baby," said the *Skullcap*, "even the tiniest baby knows who that couple is, and only an ass couldn't guess that it was meant to compromise a poor innocent woman, a pure soul and loyal amateur, just because she isn't a Yiddishist."

Understandably, the polemics didn't end with that. The fireworks had just begun. What the Kasrilevke reader called "criticism" was just starting. A Kasrilevke reader adored that. In the meantime, the poor couple had their hands full. Friends and strangers stopped and asked them what was going on. Neighbors came in to inspect the child and see whom it resembled. Good friends advised them to sue the *Bowler Hat* for libel, slander, and defamation of character. Others felt sorry for them. Still others felt sorrier for the child. "What do they have against the baby?" they said. "Poor little creature of God. Poor little thing."

Epilogue

The couple were divorced and in a short time the woman Hebraist married the very same young man, the amateur actor and Hebraist, of whom her baby was the spitting image!

SUMMER ROMANCES

1. *Israel* and *Palestine*

As far back as I can remember, Kasrilevke has been like any other village. In the winter, the people lived behind boarded windows, and summer, behind drawn shades and closed shutters. If the sun got too hot for them, they took to the cellars during the day and slept outdoors at night, gasping for breath. It wasn't that terrible, though. They didn't die from it. That is, they *did* die, but not from the heat. The sun had nothing to do with it.

You ought to see the Kasrilevkites now. When summer rolls around, they go into a panic. The village gets too stifling and sticky and they start talking about the country air and about renting a summer villa. And they need not travel to God knows where, either. The Kasrilevke folk, thank heaven, have the country right under their very noses. Right in Kasrilevke, in fact. That is, not right in Kasrilevke itself, but at any rate, in the outskirts, at a place called Slobodke. When we were school children, we used to celebrate *Lag B'Omer* in Slobodke, and play at war armed with wooden swords and painted guns. Today, you wouldn't recognize the place. Once upon a time, it belonged to the gentiles. Now the Jews own it. That is, it is *still* owned by the gentiles. For it's considered outside the town limits, you see, and no Jews are allowed entry there. But renting a gentile's summer villa—that's permitted. Actually, it *isn't*, but if you pay off the police inspector and get a doctor's note saying you're sick and need country air, they'll let you into that forbidden Paradise.

One summer, I remained behind in Kasrilevke and saw everyone preparing for the big trip. Carts and wagons dragged along the road, entire caravans laden with necessary sundries:

68

tables and benches, beds and cots, covers and pots, exhaust pipes for samovars, mortar and pestle, pillows and quilts, old women and babies—in a nutshell, the works. Seeing all this tempted me so much that I too wanted a summer villa. So I hired a wagon and went to Slobodke.

My wagoner, Ephraim, the grandson of Yankel Bulgatsh, was clad in a white dicky and spats. As we clomped along, he asked: "Where are you headed to? *Israel* or *Palestine?*"

"First *Israel*, then *Palestine*," I said.

At this point, we'll interrupt the narrative for a moment to tell the reader what sort of birds are *Israel* and *Palestine*. It's really so simple that later, when you have it down pat, you'll agree that they couldn't have been called anything else. Here's the story.

At first, the well-to-do, the upper-crust, the so-called Kasrilevke aristocrats started going to Slobodke for the summer. The middle-class villagers were next. And, finally, came the bottom of the barrel, the paupers. That put an end to the gentile Slobodke. Now it was a Jewish community right and proper and was given the name of *Israel*. As time passed, the Kasrilevke Jews started flooding *Israel*. Soon there was no elbow room. This caused the blue-bloods to start moving further and further away from Slobodke, deeper into the village, up the mountain to the other side. Soon, Slobodke became two. The old section where the paupers stayed was called *Israel*. But the new Slobodke, where the elite gathered, was called *Palestine*. In other words, a classier and more modern *Israel*.

It goes without saying that *Palestine* was much nicer than *Israel*. In *Palestine*, new houses with painted fences, lush orchards, and green gardens with sweet-smelling flowers could be seen. The last word in summer villas. But you didn't find this in *Israel*. A gentile's thatched-roof hut covered with gray clay from within and without, the combined smells of the cow, the garbage, and the sour-dough, a courtyard no bigger than the palm of your hand, a pig-sty, a rooster strutting around with his harem, nettles, thorns, high grass—that was the Taj Mahal of the summer boarder in *Israel*. But they enjoyed it. So long as—with God's help—they could pay the rent and had a bit to spare for food, they were in seventh heaven. The women prepared a cold sorrel borscht, heated the samovar with sticks and twigs and dried cones. It saved coal. Then men threw off their long jackets, sat down comfortably on the bare earth, looked up at the hot, glowing sky, and felt something new in the air which they'd never noticed in the village. And the children! They had the time of their lives. In the summer, a new world opened up for the Jewish children. Not only a world—an entire cosmos. Speak of grass, nettles, crackling leaves, shrubs, pine cones, green currants, red gooseberries, yellow sunflowers, and white buds. Speak of the thrill of seeing tiny chicks hatching. And the young ducks who waddled like Kasrilevke matrons out for a Sabbath stroll. Being able to pick up a handful of dust and blacken the air with it was nothing to sneeze at, either. And how about the joy of running after a cart filled with freshly cut corn and nabbing a stalk or two. A plague on the peasant—he'll never know! And on top of that, the pond where you could do so many things at once—catch fish, wade, and swim. Swimming there was best of all. You could swim and splash and splash for days on end, if it weren't for the little gentile boys, the devil take them, who showed up just when the Jewish children were removing their ritual fringes and were about to take off their pants. The peasant lads then started to jeer and throw stones and hoot and whoop and shout, "Hey, Jew-boys, Yids, fringy, hey!"

The Jewish children rushed to get dressed, shaking like scared lambs, their mothers' milk curdling in their stomachs.

Besides the pure joy of it, renting a summer villa had prestige value, too.

"God willing, where do you plan to go this summer, if all goes well, Sore-Brokhe, honey?"

"If all goes well, God willing, and we're all in good health, I plan to rent a room at Mikole the Swine's in *Israel*. And you Khane-Mirel, dear, live and be well, where do you plan to go this summer, if everything is all right, God willing."

"If God grants health, I too plan to go to *Israel*, Sore-

Brokhe, honey, and stay at Maria the Drunk's. She has a lovely
summer villa."

That's how two Kasrilevke housewives converse as they
tap their double chins, one more stuck up than the other.
You'd think they were highfalutin Yehupetz matrons who
have everything under the sun and haven't a care in the world
besides a summer villa.

2. Who's Who?

It happened on a Friday, during the height of the summer
season. The heat was terrible. The Kasrilevke Jews were hurrying to *Israel* for the Sabbath, pushing and shoving and
crowding and tearing themselves over to Avremel the Trolleyman's oversized wagon. They climbed over each others'
backs and literally fought for the seats. Avremel's "Trolley"
was a product of Kasrilevke's progressiveness and modernism.
Actually, it was a plain cart, formerly a covered wagon. He
had simply torn away the covering and installed two long
benches on each side of its interior. This was dubbed the
"Trolley." He came up with his bright idea one fine day and
has been working with it ever since.

During the mad rush, Avremel, the conductor and owner
of the "Trolley," stood calmly on the side, cigarette in mouth,
watching the crowd fighting for the seats, having the time of
his life. Beneath his pushed-back hat was seen his broad and
wrinkled, red and heavily perspiring forehead. He held one
hand behind his back, shut one eye and half-smiled with the
other, as if in drayman's language he wanted to say:

"That's right, folks, bang each other around, push and pull,
bite, too. Just let me finish my smoke and I'll show you all a
thing or two—the devil take every last one of you."

That's just what happened. Spitting out the cigarette, he
rolled up his sleeves and turned to the passengers, setting
things aright in the Trolley. Quietly, without any big to-do,
he started dragging this one by the hand, that one by the leg,
pulling them from the benches and chucking them out of the
Trolley as if they were sacks of potatoes instead of living

creatures. Curse him, insult him—he didn't give a damn. He didn't pay you the slightest attention. Here, he was the boss. Not only boss, but king. Not only king, but autocrat. For he was the only one of his kind. The Trolley was his brain-child. He thought it up and put it into operation and wasn't afraid of any competition. Just let anyone copy the idea. No one would dare start up with a roughneck like Avremel. That was the first thing. Then, secondly, what would two Trolleys do if, as it is, the one doesn't even do any business the entire week, just Friday afternoons. That's why Avremel's enterprise was a sure thing. He feared no one, except God.

A moment later, Avremel was up on the driver's seat. He pulled the reins, cracked the whip, clicked his tongue, and the crowded Trolley was on its way. Too late. Any poor souls left behind would have to wait until his return trip from *Israel*. Those who had no patience could always pick up their feet and march to *Israel* for the Sabbath.

The very moment when the packed Trolley started moving, two more passengers, a mother and daughter, sprouted up, as if out of nowhere. The mother was weighed down with packages from head to toe. The girl was outfitted in a parasol, a little hat, and blue gloves. The red-faced, sunburned mother was completely in a dither, perspiring, and disheveled. She didn't know if she was coming or going. The daughter, a smartly dressed young miss, walked with tiny, mincing steps. Her lacquered pumps had heels so high it was a wonder that she kept her balance.

Paying no mind to the fact that the Trolley was moving, the rattled-brained woman grabbed hold of the wagon. As if it weren't enough that she could have lost her life, she also shouted to her well-dressed daughter:

"Hurry up, Esterel, hurry. Grab hold of the Trolley. We'll be late. Reb Avremel, God be with you," she called to the driver. "What's the big rush? The Sabbath is a long way off. You'll make it."

Not only didn't Avremel the Trolleyman want to stop the wagon—on the contrary—he decided (wagoner's decisions are

dangerous) to pull the reins and give the woman a royal welcome. He then poured all his wrath out at her:

"First of all, comes Friday and they all go crazy. All
week long you don't see a soul. What a village. To the blazes
with it. Giddyap, my little sparrows, plagues upon you."

With the very same vehemence with which he urged on
the "sparrows," he turned and smacked the hanger-on's hand,
telling the woman in so many words to let go of the wagon.

The incident might have ended with that. But a cavalier
happened to be riding on the Trolley. He was a young man
with a little straw hat, white shoes, white trousers, and a wide
yellow belt from which dangled a little steel horseshoe on a
leather chain. He was clean-shaven and was perspiring to beat
the band. In a flash, he nimbly jumped out of the wagon, devotedly pushed first the woman and then her daughter onto
the other passengers' feet. Then he wanted to squirm in, too—
but Avremel the Trolleyman stopped him. He was so infuriated at that clean-shaven, white-trousered, yellow-belted,
steel-horseshoed cavalier, that he couldn't sit on the coachbox
any longer. With a sharp "whoa," he stopped the horses,
jumped quickly off the wagon, and walked over to the young
man. His eyes shot sparks, and his face became red as fire.
More perspiration covered his already wet forehead.

Our young hero, evidently realizing that he wouldn't get
off lightly, boldly stood up to the drayman, all set for a bawling out. The people in the wagon, seeing that the fun would
begin, also prepared themselves for the worst and considered
the two heroes: the drayman with his whip and the young
man with his horseshoe. They stood face to face, stirred up
like a pair of fighting cocks, throwing short, but sharp words
at one another.

Their conversation was so interesting and apropos, that it is
included, word for word:

AVREMEL: Tell me, you son of a goat, who the hell are you?
I've never seen you around.

THE YOUNG MAN WITH THE HORSESHOE: What's it to you
who I am?

AVREMEL: What do you mean, what's it to me? You know who you're talking to?

YOUNG MAN: I sure do!

AVREMEL: Since you know who I am, the question is how come you're such a wise-guy, and put people on my wagon without me knowing it? Who are these women to you anyway?

YOUNG MAN: None of your business who they are to me. Just sit down where you belong, whip up your sparrows and drive to *Israel.*

AVREMEL: Says you! And I say I won't budge until this woman and her daughter get off the wagon.

YOUNG MAN: What did you say?

AVREMEL: You heard me. I should drop dead right now if I move from this spot and a pox on your father besides.

YOUNG MAN: You say you won't move no matter what happens?

AVREMEL: Nope!

YOUNG MAN: For no money in the world?

AVREMEL: Not even a million.

YOUNG MAN: How about two millions?

AVREMEL: Not even ten million!

YOUNG MAN: Not even for ten million, either? All right, then, lots of luck and twiddle your thumbs!

Before the wagoner could say boo, the young man was already sitting in the driver's seat, holding the reins. With a whoop and a whistle, he shouted: "Giddyap, my sparrows, get on with you." The Trolley flew to *Israel.* It sped with such a rattling and a clattering that the women screamed and giggled, and everyone held on to the railing for dear life.

They screamed out of fright, worrying lest they fall out of the wagon, God forbid, and they laughed at Avremel the Trolleyman, who ran after his wagon, snapping his whip, yelling: "Stop the horses," and wishing a healthy dose of the cholera on someone's father. But no one paid any attention to him. It was pure comedy. All the people in *Israel* crammed the verandas, watching the farce—the Trolley bouncing, and a young stranger sitting in the driver's seat beating the horses, the men holding on, the women screaming, and Avremel, the owner of the Trolley, running way behind, waving his hands like a madman. What did it all mean, they wondered.

The question now is—who were the mother and her daughter. Who was the young man with the horseshoe? And what business did he have risking his life for them?

Unfortunately, the limited size of a chapter cannot contain all the details. So the reader must patiently wait and read the coming chapters. They'll clear everything up.

3. Purim and the Fast Day

Who would have guessed that the persecutions which sent Jews fleeing from the villages would result in Kasrilevke becoming a city whose summer villas in *Israel* and *Palestine* would overflow with Jews and win world-wide fame?

It's always that way. One man's downfall is another man's rise. One man's loss is another's gain. Your misfortune helps me. It's all in the hands of God, and it's no one's fault. Certainly not Kasrilevke's. Kasrilevke didn't ask them to chase the Jews out of Yehupetz. But, as soon as the expulsion began, the rents for apartments and stores shot up, and the summer villas were worth their weight in gold. The prices of cottages skyrocketed, especially on the Jewish side of the mountain known as *Israel*. People from Yehupetz, Boyberik, and the rest of the world, started spending their summers there. The Kasrilevke Jews, those world-renowned exploiters, saw the writing on the wall and took advantage of it. Apartments were rented from the gentiles and turned into grocery stores, soda stands, buffets, inns, hotels, and boarding-houses. Mostly boarding-houses. Kasrilevke Jews swooped down on the boarding-house business like a swarm of locusts, and started some terrific competition. In the meantime, *Israel* still had only two boarding-houses. But there was talk of a third, fourth, and fifth. It was the old Kasrilevke plague. If it pays for him

to cut his nose off—it pays for me, too. It's impossible to pre-
dict how many boarding-houses Kasrilevke will eventually
have. But the two boarding-houses which it does have are
certainly worth a book. If it's fated, perhaps they'll even be
immortalized.

The first boarding-house was at the edge of town, close to
the Jewish cemetery, on the other side of the bridge, right
where the gentile section began. It was given the romantic
name of "The House of Recreation." Its landlady's name was
really Alte, but everyone called her Mrs. Recreation. In Kasrilevke, if a woman asked her friend, "Where are you staying,
Perl, honey?" she answered sweetly, "What do you mean
where? At Mrs. Recreation's, of course."

The name was a bit long, and didn't have a pleasing sound.
Some even had trouble pronouncing it. See for yourself. Just
try and say it in one breath. "Mrs. Recreation's House of
Recreation." You'll get all tongue-tied. But there was one excellent thing about the place. The veranda. It was big and
wide. A yard, literally, not a veranda. Taking a samovar out
there and drinking Wisotsky's tea put you in seventh heaven.
It could accommodate three dozen tea-drinkers with ease. Not
all at once, of course. One at a time.

Now that boarding-house just across the way, with the famous name—"Garden of Eden"—well, it had a peanut of a
veranda. But to make up for it, the "Garden of Eden" sported
a garden as big as ten verandas. All sorts of good things grew
there. Onions and radishes and garlic and horseradish, nettles,
tall grass, and sunflowers which provided seeds to last through
the entire winter, until Passover. And if, with God's help,
there was a good crop, the tall grass came up to a man's head,
and the sunflowers grew even higher.

Of course, for the sake of competition, there was a bitter
battle raging between the boarding-houses. What one said
about the other was like water over a dam.

For instance, Mrs. Recreation said that the "Garden of
Eden" reared its guests on air alone. The "Garden of Eden"
said of the "House of Recreation," that their guests had to

sleep outside through the summer because of the bedbugs. But it wasn't true. Neither place had fresh air, and in both you could get bitten up so quickly that you found yourself cursing the day you were born.

No one was at fault, though. It was all up to God. Fated! Sometimes you could spend a night in a deluxe hotel without a bit of trouble. Then, again, you stop at an off-beat rattle-trap of an inn and get a room no bigger than a yawn—*there* you'll get attacked from all corners and wonder where *did* they all come from?

The rooms in the two boarding-houses were neither overly roomy nor overly bright. But, because of that, they weren't expensive. You could well say—cheap as dirt. For three rubles a week you had everything. A summer villa, a veranda, country air, and food. That is, you'd be better off not eating there, unless you wanted to encounter the Kasrilevke doctors. Like bedbugs, they also had the habit of putting the bite on. They'd fill you with drugs and herbs and powders and pills and then they'd send you to Carlsbad or the Riviera, anyway. Sometimes, they'd send you even further, to a place where there are no border guards and where no passports are needed.

That's it for the Kasrilevke boarding-houses in *Israel.* Now let's turn to the heroes of our summer romances.

Do you remember the confused, rattle-brained woman who was so heroically placed on Avremel's Trolley by the horse-shoed young man? Well, she was none other than the owner of the above-mentioned boarding-house, the "Garden of Eden." The pretty girl named Esterel was her daughter. As for the hero himself—he was their boarder. The owner of the boarding-house, also a Kasrilevkite, had an odd name. Her real name was Sore. But everyone called her Sore-Moyshe-Purim's. Why? Because she was Moyshe-Purim's wife, in other words, married to Moyshe-Purim. Behind her back, they called the daughter, Esterel-Sore-Moyshe-Purim's. Not a very poetic name, right? But it's nothing new. There are worse names in Kasrilevke. Here, for example, is a list of villagers taken out of a Zionist roster: Yenkel the Tattered, Dovid-Leyb Gooseberries, Khaim the Bluffer, Benny the Slugger, Zalman the Cliffhanger, Naftoli Hop-n-skip, and many more odd names whose origins are beyond comprehension.

This same Sore-Moyshe-Purim's husband, that is Mr. Purim himself, was a tailor by trade, but he didn't make a living. Since his wife was a great expert at cooking fish, baking honeycake, and preparing home-made jam, and since they had already spent one summer in a villa in *Israel*, they had a brilliant idea. They heard of something good from a gentile friend of theirs —a lot and garden right opposite the "House of Recreation." They leased the property, white-washed the house inside and out, and hung out a wooden sign written in large Yiddish letters:

SORE-MOYSHE-PURIM'S GARDEN OF EDEN
KOSHER

Of course, this peeved the owners of the first boarding-house, "The House of Recreation." They took Sore-Moyshe-Purim's to the rabbi for mediation. They argued that as is they didn't make a living. And now Mrs. Sore-Moyshe-Purim's came along and opened a "Garden of Eden" right opposite their "House of Recreation." What did they want to do— drive them into poverty? Moyshe-Purim's story was that he too was a human being trying to make a living, and who's to tell him how and where to earn his bread.

Had Reb Yozifl, the rabbi, may he rest in peace, been alive, he would have found a way to make both sides happy. Oh, for those that are gone and cannot be replaced. There is no rabbi like Reb Yozifl nowadays. Now there are *two* rabbis in Kasrilevke, and they can't get along with each other. No harm intended, but two cats in a bag get along better than those two rabbis. The villagers haven't the slightest respect for them.

But look, we've neglected the heroes of the romance and got tangled up with the rabbis. In all likelihood, the reader will be a good friend and forgive us.

In brief, both women, Sore-Moyshe-Purim's and Mrs. Alte Recreation, met on a Kasrilevke sidestreet one spring day before the start of the season and triggered, folks say, a royal scandal.

But it didn't do much good, for one fine morning at the very beginning of the season, the police commissioner and two soldiers showed up at the "Garden of Eden." They ripped off the wooden sign and fined the landlady on top of it for daring to display a sign in Yiddish.

Sore-Moyshe-Purim's understood very well that this was all Mrs. Recreation's doings. So she paid the fine, slipped Mr. Police Commissioner a little extra, and went her own sweet way. She promptly hung up the sign again, and it's been hanging there ever since.

The whole world can yell on top of its lungs, but if it's fated that a man make a living, nothing under the sun will help them.

Poor Mrs. Recreation had to look on and see the "Garden of Eden" across the way always packed to capacity with boarders and tourists. And what boarders, too! Take the man with the white pants and horseshoe, for instance.

"Money doesn't mean a thing to that guy. There's a man you can make a penny on. May she choke on it—great God."

That's what Mrs. Recreation wished for her competitor. And she was right. Imagine, previously the young man had been *her* guest—which means he had boarded at the "House of Recreation." But the devil himself had transported him over to the "Garden of Eden." Why?

"Because of Sore-Moyshe-Purim's daughter, the little slut, may she fry in hell." This is how Mrs. Recreation expressed herself. But it was competition speaking. It wasn't the truth, really. Our heroine, Sore-Moyshe-Purim's daughter, was truly a charming young lady who finished four terms of high-school, read Artsibashev, spoke Russian and not a word of Yiddish, mind you, and never so much as lifted a finger. The entire responsibility for the "Garden of Eden" lay on the shoulders of Sore herself. She alone cooked, baked, and cleaned the rooms, and Moyshe, that is, Sore-Moyshe-Purim's husband, served the guests and boarders and catered to their whims. But God forbid that their daugher do a stitch of work! Esterel would be dressed in the latest fashions, outfitted like a bride, read Artsibashev, dance the fox-trot, the tango, and other modern dance steps. Not to mention Russian! With her Russian, she drove all the Kasrilevke boys out of their minds and led them by their noses. But more than anyone else, she drove the young boarder out of his wits and twisted him around her little finger.

Getting all the facts on the young man—he was an agent for a sewing-machine firm, and had the odd name of Aron Solomonovitsh Fastday—the people around *Israel* unanimously decided that it was an excellent match for the owner of the "Garden of Eden." It was made in heaven, arranged by God. Fated! A Purim with a Fastday, they laughed. Since time began, there had been no more brilliant a match. Since that Friday when he had blown into town with Avremel's Trolley, Purim and Fastday had been continually on the people's tongues. Had the young agent saved Esterel from dire misfortune—like preventing her from drowning, snatching her from the gallows, rescuing her from thieves, or simply saving her from certain death—it couldn't have had the same charm and effect as putting the two women on Avremel's Trolley, entering town that Friday with a bang, sitting in the driver's seat, with Avremel running after his Trolley. All this made such a to-do in *Israel*, and got so many laughs, that the young man unwittingly became a hero and Esterel a heroine. Talk and gossip started. People winked knowingly and crinkled their noses. It spread from Israel to Kasrilevke and almost made the Kasrilevke papers.

The *Bowler Hat* and the *Skullcap* would have had some lively copy and would have written it up with their own inimitable commentary. But the couple prevented this in the nick of time by placing a front-page announcement in both gazettes:

```
┌─────────────────────────────────────┐
│  ┌───────────────────────────────┐  │
│  │                               │  │
│  │     Ester  Moysevno Purim     │  │
│  │                               │  │
│  │  Aron Solomonovitsh Fastday   │  │
│  │                               │  │
│  │          ENGAGED              │  │
│  │                               │  │
│  └───────────────────────────────┘  │
└─────────────────────────────────────┘
```

Here our romance truly begins—and ends.

4. The Wedding in the "Garden of Eden"

The jolliest time Kasrilevke and *Israel* had ever seen was on the day when Sore-Moyshe-Purim's married her daughter Esterel to the boarder Aron.

It was an excellent day. One of those choice summer days when everything is quiet and seems to doze. The sun shone and poured forth its fire, and a slight breeze of unknown origins blew by, cooling the fiery rays, making them pleasant and gentle. Like soldiers with colored helmets, the tall sunflowers stood in a line, hardly moving in a breeze which lovingly caressed their yellow, satiny leaves. Everything was still. Everything asleep. Once in a while, a wagon loaded down with a high pile of ears of corn passed by. The wheels groaned silently.

A barefoot, open-shirted peasant with a deeply sunburned face led a team of oxen. He twirled his whip in front of them and addressed them in their own language. "Move on there, nightingales, move on." The oxen, deep in thought, followed him. A few barefoot Jewish lads ran behind the wagon. They tore away some corn stalks and wanted more. But, suddenly, they stood still, as if enchanted. What had happened? Opposite them was Avremel's Trolley, fully packed with a load of strange people holding odd-looking instruments. These were the Kasrilevke musicians coming to Sore-Moyshe-Purim's place for the wedding.

"The musicians are coming. The musicians are coming," they shouted.

The barefoot boys ran ahead of the wagon, rushing to bring
the news that the band was on the way. "The musicians are
coming. The musicians!"

At Sore's place, everything was ready. The whole area was
transformed into a hall in honor of the guests from *Israel*. In
their famed garden, stood long tables decked with all sorts of
delicacies—brandies, cakes, and home-made jams. The family
and friends of the bride came in dribs and drabs, all dressed
up. Then came the rest of the guests—the summer residents
of *Israel*. The men wore their Sabbath cloaks and hats, the
women, their silk dresses with all the accessories. The young
women and girls, outfitted in the latest fashion, their faces red
and damp, were waiting to dance. Just let those musciains stop
scraping and tuning up and start the music. The bride and
groom sat in full regalia. He in a shiny top hat, she in a white
veil. A prince and a princess. Fastday and Purim. The in-laws,
Moyshe-Purim and his wife, Sore-Moyshe-Purim's, ran around
helter-skelter, in a complete daze, like poisoned rats—a normal
state for parents who have lived to marry off a daughter.

Most extraordinarily, the owners of the Recreation House
were mingling with the wedding guests. What were they doing here? They were such bitter competitors, such blood enemies. But it was quite simple. A couple of days before the
wedding, Sore-Moyshe-Purim's decided—why have enemies?
Like they say: ten friends are better than one enemy.

So she went to Mrs. Recreation's home and, as if they had
never fought or exchanged insults and harsh words, Sore
started by saying:

"Good morning, Alte, honey, I have a favor to ask of you."

"What sort of favor, Sore, dearie?"

"You know, Alte, honey, that I'm marrying off my daughter, Esterel."

"Lots of luck and all the best on your happy occasion. You
know, Sore, dearie, what a good friend of yours I am. What
I wish for myself, I wish for you."

"Amen. I wanted to ask you, Alte, honey, to do me the
honor and come to the wedding with your husband and the
kids."

"With pleasure, Sore, dearie. Did we ever fight? God forbid! Tomorrow, God willing, we'll all have fun together. God bless them both. May they be happy and healthy. As I live and breathe, you sure got yourself some son-in-law."

"Amen. May your own children do no worse. The sky's the limit."

Out of depths of affection, the two women kissed each other on the lips and looked forward to the moment when they'd take each other by the hand and dance around after the ceremony. Back in the wedding hall, the tumult was still going on. Someone was shouting that the sun was setting and that it was time for the ceremony to begin. The truth was that, since the bride and groom were not fasting, there was no need to rush. They weren't the sort that believed in those Jewish superstitions. Fasting indeed! But anyway, soon it would be dark.

The entire yard was full of guests. All of *Israel* had gathered for the wedding. The whole street was invaded by gentile boys and girls who had come to see the Jewish wedding. The boys cracked jokes, and the girls broke into shrill laughter every minute, screaming loudly. What a to-do! What a celebration in *Israel*. They had already set up the four poles with the red canopy and its golden tassels on all four sides.

The musicians with the bass-drum suddenly interrupted their bitter-sweet melody, and the in-laws and those accompanying them, dressed in formal clothes and holding candles, took the bride and groom and the ancient and beautiful Jewish ceremony began.

Seeing the Jews and the bride in pure white walking around the groom with the shiny black top-hat—the gathered peasant lads jeered: "Hey, hey. Look at the Yids turning."

But this didn't matter. The rabbi was ready to take the cup of wine in his right hand. The cantor had cleared his throat, ready to sing. The sexton was ready to give the ring to the groom so that he could recite the well-known phrase —"Behold, thou are consecrated to me."

Suddenly, a loud "Whoa" was heard outside. Furiously, Avremel's Trolley pulled up, and two young women dashed out of it, pointing right to the bridal canopy. In the dark, it was impossible to see their faces. Only their high-pitched voices were heard, both of them screaming and whimpering and cursing, one outdoing the other.

"Hold everything!"

"Don't marry him!"

"The deuce take him!"

"A pox on him!"

"That scoundrel! That hoodlum! That blackguard!"

"Look at him with the hat on. He's my husband!"

"He's the father of my baby, may he come to a foul and filthy end."

"He married me just after Passover this year. He took eight hundred rubles from me as if they were a kopek. Dear God, may eight hundred plagues break out on his face and tongue and all over his body. May he not live to roam around and ruin Jewish daughters and make their lives miserable!"

"Hand that gangster over to me! I'll scratch his eyes out!"

"He should be put in irons. In iron chains. My eight hundred rubles. Eight hundred plagues on him! Sweet God!"

Epilogue

The two Kasrilevke newspapers, the *Bowler Hat* and the *Skullcap*, had a field day with that awful incident at the "Garden of Eden." They wrote on and on about it for days. Earnest publicists and moralizers that they were—there was no end to their stuffing the public with their preachings and sermons. They said that nowadays you had to be careful in marrying a daughter to a man with a name like Fastday. This appealed to the punsters and wags.

"How could anything good come of a Purim with a Fastday," they kept punning and wagging.

It ended up with both papers announcing in screaming headlines that their readers would be given a present soon: a new and modern, highly suspenseful, and morally instructive novel drawn from contemporary Jewish life.

The *Bowler Hat* planned to call it: "*The Man with the Three Wives*—a highly interesting novel in four sections, with an epilogue."

The *Skullcap* entitled it: "*The Three-Wived Husband*—a notable novel in four sections, with a prologue and post-script."

Well, it was too bad. Such fine material would be smeared over three hundred pages, and everything would be ruined. One could only pity the heroine, Sore-Moyshe-Purim's daughter Esterel. Once the Kasrilevke papers got through with her, she might as well say goodbye. She'd never get a husband in Kasrilevke as long as she lived. Unless she left *Israel* and Kasrilevke and packed for America.

I hope she does, for we wish her luck. Amen!

5. Our Brodskys and Our Rothschilds

One hot summer day, in the height of the season, our well-known Trolley was clomping along from Kasrilevke to *Palestine*, via *Israel*. It was quite empty, for it wasn't Friday but a regular weekday, a day on which the Kasrilevke summer residents of *Israel* were eager enough to take a stroll. As soon as the conductor is good enough to stop, we'll see who's in it. One old woman and one young one, both ready to pass out from the heat; Avremel is dozing, the horses faking a trot, and the Trolley hardly budging. Suddenly, a strange young dandy sprang out of the blue. He wore an elite white cap and had an aristocratic black mustache. He motioned with his aristocratic cane to the conductor. Excusing himself, he asked him to be kind enough to stop his horses. Then he jumped into the Trolley. But he did it with such class—he was so nimble and skillful, that it was charming to the nth degree. Then, he seated himself on the other bench, right opposite the matron and her young daughter. (The matron—it goes without saying—was the daughter's mother.) He put his left hand into his left pocket and, with his right, he twisted the right part of his aristocratic mustache. Doing so, he sent an upper-classy glance at the beautiful mademoiselle. A girl not yet deeply in love with anyone had to be stronger than steel not to fall head over heels in love with such a gallant blade at first sight. To the matron, this unexpected meeting was a heavenly omen, a

fated encounter. Her motherly heart immediately started
pounding prophetically. It wasn't in vain—it was all from
God. And, despite the fact that her daughter was almost engaged, and with her own second cousin's son to boot (as we
shall soon find out), she was mighty pleased that the aristocratic young man was making eyes at her daughter, hypnotiz-
ing her. But how was she to introduce him to her, if she herself
didn't know him. Then, she had a brainstorm (good old de-
pendable mother). She starting fanning herself and said (in
good old, world-renowned Kasrilevke Russian): "Oh what a
heated day is it."

The daughter looked at the aristocratic young man and
corrected her mother's grammar. "Yes. What a *hot* day it *is*."

Now the young man had the opportunity to break in. So he
turned to the young lady and said in Russian: "Is the air at
your place good, too?"

But, nevertheless, the matron did not let her daughter answer. She had a mind to answer herself (that's a mother for
you), and turned melodiously to the young man and said in
Russian: "What do we need the air for? We have money!"

With this, she wanted to clip his wings and slow his progress. But the result was quite the opposite. The two young people looked at each other and burst into such loud giggles that
Avremel the Trolleyman had to turn around and see what
the blue-bloods were laughing at, a pack of plagues on them.
They soon arrived at one of the must luxurious summer villas
in *Palestine*. They said warm goodbyes and shook hands heart-
ily. The mother informally invited the young man over.
"Please, without any formality," she said.

The pretty girl looked at him so warmly with her charming
eyes and smiled so sweetly, that even if the young cavalier
were made of steel and had a heart of stone, he would have
melted then and there, like wax.

Now we have to tell you who the young aristocrat was and
why it was so important for the matron's daughter to meet
him.

Yehupetz was under a false impression. It thought that only
it had aristocratic millionaires. The great city of Paris also

thought that only it had aristocratic billionaires. People say that Kasrilevke has its own aristocrats, its own Brodskys and its own Rothschilds.

So what? Kasrilevke has what any other town has, only on a smaller scale. That's why our Brodskys and our Rothschilds are just pocket-editions of the real Brodskys and the real Rothschilds. But like millionaires and billionaires the world over, their biographies are worth mention.

It goes without saying, all the big wheels of the world were little wheels at one time—first they grew up and then became famous. The American billionaires, for example, brag all day long about their former sorry state. For an American of high society it's an honor, a source of pride, for him to be able to tell every interviewer that, when he was young, he carried sacks of potatoes on his shoulders, or that he sold papers or matches. Our Kasrilevke elite don't give a hang for any of this. On the contrary, if you ask a Kasrilevke billionaire about his familial lineage, he'll tell you all sorts of tall tales and say that his grandfather was a rabbi and great-grandfather a genius—that their whole family was chock-full of rabbis, geniuses, and well-known millionaires. They'll drive you *meshugge* with their talk of family trees and scare the wits out of you with their aristocracy. You get frightened and think: in the name of heaven, maybe they do stem from the devil knows who.

Our elite, our millionaires and billionaires, I mean our Kasrilevke Brodskys and Rothschilds, were also riff-raff at one time, and their praises must be sung. They pulled themselves up by their boot-straps and in due time worked themselves up the ladder. They flourished and grew, surpassed and outdid one another in wealth, charity, and fine marriages. God knows what else can be expected of them. Everyone and his brother, for instance, knows the familial lineage of the real Rothschilds. They come from Frankfurt and their great-grandfather was first a money-changer, then a money-lender, then, finally, a banker. Our Kasrilevke Rothschilds do not come from Frankfurt. They come from Kasrilevke itself. But, since their great-grandfather was a money-changer all his life and had a little booth in the Kasrilevke marketplace, changing bills to silver and silver to coins—he and his children after him were nicknamed the "Rothschilds." The children were not money-changers. They had no coin-booth in the marketplace. They were money-lenders. In fact, they still are money-lenders, and their children's children will continue to be money-lenders so long as we have that messy thing called money and so long as we have people who will (if you'll pardon the expression) pawn their own pants off to get a loan. If you happen to come to the new and modern Kasrilevke, you'll see a two-story building on the cobble-stoned streets with a huge golden-lettered sign covering the entire wall: "Yefim and Boris Gingold—Banking Office."

Know, then, that these are our Kasrilevke Rothschilds. But up pops the question—why call them Rothschilds if their name is Gingold? I have a good answer for that one, too.

What do you say to this? Right opposite the Rothschilds, there stood an even finer building with a nicer, larger, golden-lettered sign in Russian: "The Dumbo Brothers—Lumber Dealers." Ask a baby who's place it is and he'll say: "This place? It's Brodsky's!"

If you're interested in the biography of the Dumbo brothers, or in the family tree of the Dumbo Brothers called Brodsky, here it is in a nutshell: In Sukholyesye, a village not far from Kasrilevke which once belonged to Count Shtrembo-Rudnyitski, there lived a Jewish manager, an overseer of the ducal forests, whose name was Aron. But he was called Dumbo because he was, to put it plainly, a boor, a country bumpkin, a tall and powerful hick. He wore a coarse, peasant-like coat girded with a piece of rope and a pair of high boots. He knew the trees like the palm of his hand, watched over the count's domain like a faithful dog, and was so important to the count that the count willed the Jew Aron and his children to be the managers so long as the forests and the name Shtrembo-Rudnyitski remained in existence. And, as is customary, the count's heirs gambled at cards and lost, sold the forests, and ruined the Dumbos completely. Aron's children had to pack up and move from the forests to the village and settle in Kasrilevke.

Since neither they nor their children knew anything besides forestry and lumber, their business became forestry and lumber, and has remained so ever since. Theirs was a successful and continually growing firm. As their fame spread, their name spread. At first they were called the Forest-folk, then the wooden Jews, then the Oakies, then the Dumbo Brothers, and then the *nouveaux riches*, the millionaires.

When they began to show off, give big donations, arrange fine matches, and try to outdo the Rothschilds, the town called them, our "Brodskys." But who was richer? Our Brodskys or our Rothschilds? That's a tough one. No one has counted their money yet. I think, however, that the difference between their riches and that of the real Brodskys and Rothschilds would be helpful to all of us. The wealth of local magnates was not stable. Sometimes our Rothschilds were richer, sometimes, our Brodskys. It depended on who made the biggest splash in the town. Since each wanted to step into upper-class life and outdo the other, our Kasrilevke millionaires and billionaires competed—the sky was the limit. For instance if a Rothschild said he had difficulty with Yiddish, a Brodsky would say that he didn't even know a single word of Yiddish. In Kasrilevke, that was a yardstick of aristocracy.

If the Rothschilds reported that one of their sons had lost a hundred at cards, the Brodskys announced that their son had lost two hundred. Here's another story. While abroad, at the spa, the Rothschild's daughter-in-law flirted publicly with a young man, a total stranger. It created a big to-do. As a result, the daughter-in-law of the newly-elite Brodskys flirted with *two* complete strangers while abroad, at the hot springs.

There was a big ballyhoo in town when the rich vied with each other. For once they started, there was no end to the rivalry. For instance, Kasrilevke will never forget the icy winter when the poor people were dropping like flies. Everyone started to squawk:

"Well, where are our rich men hiding? Why are our Brodskys and Rothschilds silent?"

Then the Rothschilds felt sorry for the frozen people, and had some wagon-loads of straw sent from the marketplace as fuel for the poor.

What do you think the Brodskys did? They sent a few wagon-loads of wood from their own forests and gave it to the poor free of charge, here a pound, there a pound.

Then, again, there was nothing lacking that Passover when the Rothschilds went wild and provided fifty sacks of potatoes for the village poor, in addition to money for matzohs.

The Brodskys decided: since you're sending potatoes, we'll donate the chicken-fat for the potatoes. They opened up huge jars of chicken-fat and doled it out to the poor. All you had to do was ask and you got a portion—a teaspoonful per family. For a large family, there was a tablespoonful, that is, if you brought a note from the rabbi saying that there were more than five in the family.

From the village, the rivalry spread to the summer resorts. *Palestine* opened its door to the residents of *Israel*, and the down-and-out guests had themselves a time. How did that happen? Like this. One summer, our Rothschilds built their own summer villa in *Palestine*—under a gentile's name, of course. And what a villa it was! With a veranda and a green picket-fence, a garden filled with gooseberries, currants, and cherries. They opened this garden for all the Kasrilevke vacationers on this side of the mountain—free of charge. Anyone in *Israel* was welcome to stroll there on Sabbath afternoons. But only on the Sabbath. Weekdays—beware!

The next summer, the Brodskys decided to put up an even nicer villa, with a bigger veranda and larger garden, also under a gentile's name, and also with gooseberries, currants, and cherries. They announced specifically in all the little synagogues that their garden was open to the public, not only on Sabbath afternoons, but every day of the week. The only condition was that they were not to come near the trees nor pick fruit nor sleep on the grass. But once a summer resident of *Israel* set foot into a garden and saw grass, don't you think he'd sit right down and remove his jacket? And if Jewish children saw green gooseberries and red currants or sniffed cherries, do you think they'd just look and not touch? So the Brodskys put a fence around the garden, strung barb-wire across it, and locked the gate. An order was issued that from that day on if anyone from *Israel* dared set foot in their villa, they'd have a), their bones broken; b), their teeth knocked out; and, c), the dogs set on them. Actually, the dogs were just a bluff, a phony threat to frighten the public. But it worked. The Jews of Kasrilevke hated to have anything to do with dogs.

6. Every Dog Has His Day

You probably know that the Rothschilds of Frankfurt, the real ones I mean, had an ancient custom, which they followed to the letter. Marriages were arranged among their own, so that the family strain would not be watered down, heaven forbid. Unless, of course, a count or a marquis or a prince happened to fall in love with one of their daughters—well, that's a horse of a different color. Then, temptation was too great, and you couldn't resist it.

The Kasrilevke Rothschilds had the same tradition. Not that they got it from their grandfather, but simply because they thought they were better than anyone else and were convinced that their family tree was noblest of all. There was good reason for the Kasrilevke Rothschilds saying that their family was so august they wouldn't even have *themselves* for in-laws.

There was a time when the *nouveaux riches* Kasrilevke blue-bloods—our Brodskys—never even dared dream of the honor of marrying into the old and aristocratic Rothschild family of Kasrilevke. But when our Brodskys struck it rich and started their way up the ladder, becoming almost as rich as the Rothschilds, one deep-seated wish took hold of them: a match with the Rothschilds. But they never dared say so.

Once, and only once, did these aristocrats-come-lately send a matchmaker to the Rothschilds—the famous matchmaker, Soloveytshik of Kasrilevke. He, I must tell you, wasn't one of the old-time marriage-brokers. He wasn't even called "match-maker," but "marriage-mediator." Soloveytshik was not so well-known for the big matches he arranged as for his smooth talk. He could out-twaddle anyone. There was no man alive who could stand up to Soloveytshik the Marriage-mediator when he got going. It was like a four-alarm fire! Soloveytshik the Marriage-mediator was none other than Reb Sholem the

Matchmaker's son. But Soloveytshik was a modern Jew. He already wore a derby, a white shirt-front, and a tie. The hat was a bit tattered, the shirt-front none too white and the tie —no offense meant—well, a sort of shiny rag. But after all, it *was* a derby, a shirt-front, a tie. Add to these a well-worn undersized jacket, a pair of ill-fitting, loudly-checked trousers which had seen better days. Take all these and you'll see the difference between him and his father, may he rest in peace.

But all that was nothing compared to the beard and earlocks! What beard? What earlocks? The beard, at least, wasn't that bad. If it wasn't a full-fledged beard, it was a tiny Van-dyke. Who says that a man must sport a broom on his face? But earlocks? Not a hint of them! Cut off and rooted out to the last hair. Not to mention his way of speaking! He never came out with a good old Yiddish "Good morning." It was always "hello" and "good-bye" in Russian. He'd never use homey Yiddish to say, "I have a good match for you." He always said it in a hodge-podge of German, French, and Russian phrases. *"Ich habe vier sie dyevushkoo magnifique."*

Want more? His father, God rest his soul, used to carry a huge red parasol. But that wasn't good enough for Soloveyt-shik. He was an aristocrat with a cane and his name was Solo-veytshik the Marriage-mediator. If Reb Sholem the Match-maker would get up and take a look at his son the mediator, he'd turn over in his grave.

Having received the high-level assignment of arranging a match between two such distinguished houses as our Brodskys and our Rothschilds, Soloveytshik dressed himself in his white shirt-front, combed his Van-dyke, carefully trimmed the spot where his earlocks used to be—and was off to the Rothschilds. Before he had time to complete his multi-lingual introduction, they asked him:

"Who's the party you're referring to?"

When they heard the word "Brodsky," they gave him such a bawling out that his ears rang for a week. It was something he'd pass on to his grandchildren. The Rothschilds promised him that the next time he offered them a match like that, he'd fly through the door headfirst. And the door wouldn't be open either. In short—they showed him the way home. Bet-

ter yet—they kicked him out. But, while standing downstairs, Soloveytshik displayed the stuff he was made of:

"Remember Soloveytshik's words. Every dog has his day!"

And that's just how it was. It looked like his prediction came true. The villains were defeated. The very same Rothschilds who previously had shown him the door, now sent for Soloveytshik the Marriage-mediator and asked him to arrange a match for them with the new millionaires, those recent additions to the smart set—the Brodskys.

This was the proof of an old saying: If a thief can be of service, you parole him. Soloveytshik didn't have to be asked twice. When he came to the Rothschilds, he was asked to make himself at home. This time they didn't wait for him to help himself to a chair. They offered him a cigarette and even lit it for him. That's a Kasrilevke grandee for you! Normally, he's all puffed up like a turkey. You can't even get near him. But if he needs you for the slightest favor, he'll come crawling on his hands and knees and will be so butter-soft, you could apply him to a third-degree burn. The Rothschilds didn't beat around the bush, but apologized to Soloveytshik first thing, then told him that under no circumstances would they make a match with anyone beneath them. They swore on the Talmud, Midrash, and (forgive the proximity) the peasant's folksaying, that Soloveytshik pick himself up and go to that newly-rich family named Brodsky and tell them such and such—but they didn't have to put the words into his mouth. He knew his business. Their attitude and their compliments sent the marriage-mediator to seventh heaven. "What do you mean, can I? Of course, I can."

"But Mr. Soloveytshik. Don't come right out with it. Just drop hints."

"Talk about hinting! Of course, I'll hint."

"But Mr. Soloveytshik. Don't tell them that we sent you. Let them think it's your own idea. Right out of your own head. You understand?"

"Of course I understand. If I don't, who does?"

Soloveytshik the Marriage-mediator steeled himself to the task. That same day, he went to the Brodskys armed to the hilt and ready to fire. He had so much to say, he didn't know where to start. No matter how much he'd say, it wouldn't be enough, he thought, and whatever he'd say, wouldn't be right. Since time immemorial, it had been that way. When you come into a big shot's house, you get all flustered, and instead of saying what you're supposed to, you get tongue-tied and babble the devil knows what. Before Soloveytshik came to the new millionaire's doorstep, he had a trunkful of talk—no end of biblical verses and proverbs and Talmudic quotes.

But as soon as the Brodskys looked at him and asked: "What do you want?" all his thoughts topsy-turveyed, and a hodge-podge was made of his bundle of quotes. His talk made no sense at all. At least he got off to a good start:

"The biblical commentator, Rashi, says that when the time comes and you need a fox . . ."

They looked down their noses at him and interrupted with:

"Just what do you mean by all this?"

"What I mean is that you never know when a dog will have his day. Not long ago, if I remember correctly, you were willing, but *they* weren't. But now they're willing. What am I saying, *willing*? They're drooling, they're fainting, they're dying to make a deal with you. They're going stark, raving mad. They'll do anything, so long as . . ."

"Just who are you talking about?"

"Who am I talking about? Who do you think? About *them*, that is, the elite, the blue-bloods, the best, the greatest—I'm talking about the Rothschilds!"

That's all he needed. They would have preferred his throwing acid at them. The Brodskys, it seemed, hadn't forgotten the awful snub they'd received from the Rothschilds—may it never happen again. But they cooled off by releasing all their anger on the poor matchmaker's head.

"*Who* are you offering us? Those Rothschilds?! Those money-lenders, those usurers, those Shylocks! They don't make in a week what we throw out in a day! How does a matchmaker like you have the gall to come and ask us to have anything to do with such people of low birth? Who are these Rothschilds of yours? It seems like only yesterday their grandpa with his bag of coins was freezing like a dog in the marketplace! Now they've become pseudo-bankers! They

take iou's. They fleece you! No sir! Not on your life. Don't
even try to talk back—understand? And if you don't beat it
right now, quietly, then we'll take you—are you listening—
and kick you down the stairs."

Standing down below, the matchmaker could only repeat
his famous words: "You can never tell! Every dog has his
day!"

Neither Soloveytshik the Marriage-mediator, himself, nor
anyone else expected his words to come true in such grand
style. This time Cupid took up the matchmaker's cause. Into
the picture stepped the little god of Love; you know, the one
who shoots poisoned arrows into boys' and girls' hearts alike.
And it happened on that hot summer day in Avremel's Trolley. Riding to Kasrilevke then (if the reader recalls), were
an aristocratic lady with her beautiful daughter. A strange
young dandy wearing a white hat and carrying an aristocratic
cane joined them on the Trolley. He stupefied them both with
his glance and with the very first twist he gave his distinguished black mustache. Now the identities of the aristocratic
Russian-speaking lady and the dignified dandy can be revealed.
It's no longer a secret.

The lady was none other than Mrs. Rothschild. And the
young man—none other than a son of the recently-arrived
aristocrats—the Brodskys. Taking into consideration all that's
been said up to this point, the reader will easily guess whom
Soloveytshik the Marriage-mediator came to help. But one
question remains. Did Cupid play any role here? And did
Soloveytshik have any luck with the match? If so, what did
he get out of it? And where did this great, high-class wedding
take place? In Kasrilevke or at a summer villa in *Palestine?*
All these important questions will be cleared up, dear reader,
in the coming chapter of this summer romance.

7. Soloveytshik the Marriage-mediator at Full Speed

We sort of think that the reader likes the fact that the hero
and heroine of this summer romance are not run-of-the-mill
folk like us, but are true aristocrats, minglers with the four

hundred, members of the league of Kasrilevke millionaires and billionaires. The hero is a Brodsky of our Brodskys, and the heroine is a Rothschild of our Rothschilds. And you can't deny the fact that we peasants are always nosy about what's cooking in the upper-set. We want to know how the upper-crust lives, what they eat, what they drink. Therefore, a millionaire blue-blood's wedding is of special interest, although, when you get down to it, what good does it do us? None whatsoever! But that's the way God made us. Too late to do anything about it. So now we can continue our story with a clean conscience. But let's recall for a moment the first meeting of "The Boy" and "The Girl" on Avremel's Trolley.

Everything clicked for our young hero. Not only did the Rothschild's beautiful daughter fall head over heels in love with him, but her mother, God bless her, Madame Rothschild herself, was also enchanted. She went overboard with her friendliness and invited him over to her villa: "Please, without any formality." Not every man is worthy of such honor and success. For we know that ever since the world began, and ever since people started falling in love, the results have been just the opposite.

When a couple falls in love, either the girl's father or mother, or both, become terribly stubborn and won't give an inch. The nicest thing about it is, begging their pardon, the parents themselves were once in love and fought with *their* parents and then eloped. You'd think they'd remember this fact. But no! Now that they, thank goodness, have become parents, they fight with their children. But their children will be no better. They'll do the same thing all over again when they become parents. It's a strange blight, heaven-sent. Actually, there was only one lucky man in history—Adam. He had no in-laws. Ever since then, there's been trouble. There are misfortunes and grief, heartaches, and all sorts of tragedies. Oh, my. If you really thought of the many tears that have been shed in vain and how many young lives have been ruined —your hair would stand on end. But we're going to steer clear of this whole subject because it's summer in the country and everything is blossoming and blooming and growing in full color, and it's so hot you want to go swimming. Anyway, we're neither tragedians nor dispensers of melancholy.

Luckily, however, everything worked out so smoothly and so well in this summer romance of ours, you might think the only thing left to do was get engaged, call the rabbi, and shout "congratulations!" But what's the hitch? Just as things were about to be settled, the whole thing was called off. What happened? You know, something always has to go wrong at the last minute. Actually, that's a good thing for us writers. For if it weren't for those last-minute snags—if everything always clicked—where would we writers be?

The fence that separated our hero and heroine was not that he is a Brodsky and she, a Rothschild. There was another skeleton in the closet. The fact was that our beauty, as you'll remember, was almost engaged—and to one of her own breed, to boot—a Rothschild. It was a match made in heaven. Both were from noble families, both were born with silver spoons in their mouths. Both summered next to each other in *Palestine*. Their dowries were equal—ten thousand each—and they both knew each other very well. We know her already, having had the pleasure of seeing this sweet, young beauty in Avremel's Trolley. But we have to introduce you to her boyfriend. Here he is in a few short strokes of the pen.

He was one of the boys—a graduate of a commercial school, liked cards, knew everyone of the night club set, had all the operettas down pat, and could whistle the most popular melodies to the last bar. He was sleepy during the day, but by night, he was wide awake. His hat was tilted rakishly, his jacket flared at the bottom and looked as if it were poured onto him. His slim cane was constantly on the move. When he entered a theater, a circus, a movie-house, he walked with a swagger, as if he owned the place. There, you have a portrait of an aristocratic fiancé of the true Kasrilevke Rothschilds. His sort is cool and well-mannered to his girlfriend; he watches his step, doesn't show the slightest affection—for that sort of thing was all right for a lad from *Israel*, but not for a *Palestinian* blue-blood. But this Rothschild began to show signs of love and to make claims on the girl when he met our hero,

Brodsky's son, at his future in-law's house in *Palestine*. He saw the Brodsky boy making eyes at Mademoiselle Rothschild and noticed her mother encouraging him, flattering him outrageously, and babbling away in such fractured Russian that you could have split your sides from laughing.

The Rothschild fiancé, that is, the pseudo-fiancé, didn't appreciate his future mother-in-law's transformation into such a chatterbox. A hellish fire burned in our new hero's heart, and he fumed at the young Brodsky. His love suddenly sparked and blazed up, dangerously. Not so much his love for the girl, but his hatred for this aristocrat-come-lately. What right did Brodsky have to come to a house where he, Rothschild, was about to become a fiancé? So, in order to put an end to the unpleasant business, he asked his parents to speed up the formal engagement. But his parents got the shock of their lives when they were told that there was no point in talking about an engagement. The reasons were three: One, it was summer. During the summer there were no engagements. Two, the girl was too young and they weren't even *thinking* of a match. Three, there was a possibility that she would be engaged to one of the local *Palestine* aristocrats in a few days.

Of course, they didn't mention that the "*Palestine* aristocrat" was the young Brodsky. That was self-evident. This was a two-fold scandal for the Rothschilds. First, their boy was left high and dry without a bride, and, second, some sort of a Brodsky had managed to worm his way into the golden circle of true Rothschilds. The second reason was, perhaps, more important. This came as such a blow to our deceived hero, the semi-fiancé Rothschild, that he was ready to do anything, just like those heroes in the French novels he had read. Even a duel. But meanwhile, he sent no seconds to his rival Brodsky. He did something better. He sent a message to his ex-girl's mother saying that he knew it was all her fault; he wouldn't keep it quiet; he would submit his entire collection of her daughter's love-letters for publication in both Kasrilevke newspapers. Then her *new* son-in-law would well know to whom he was getting engaged.

Evidently there was *something* in those letters, and it could have been hot material for the *Skullcap* and the *Bowler Hat*. They would have worked it up into a good and proper stew and dished it out neatly. And the worthy Kasrilevke readers eat up stuff like that as quickly as they do chopped livers with chicken-fat, stuffed derma, *kugels*, or ice-cold cider on a hot summer day. But, as we shall soon find out, fate had it that the Kasrilevke papers didn't get to print them, nor did the worthy Kasrilevke public get to read them.

Our other hero, the lucky Brodsky, went along his own merry way. He was a steady visitor of the Rothschilds at their summer villa, brought them a fresh bouquet of flowers and half a pound of chocolate every day, and took trips with Mademoiselle Rothschild. They walked, rode on horseback, and, sometimes, took the car for a drive deep into the woods. This happened so often that all of *Israel* became aware of what was going on in *Palestine*. Well, they became the talk of the town. To make a long story short, it got to the Brodsky family and there was a sham uproar. They said the match was off! This annoyed the Rothschild family. "So long as *you* don't want it, we *certainly* don't," they said. Then the young couple upped and said—but *we* do. An upper-class tragicomedy followed. The parties concerned really wanted the match, but they all grumbled and threw snags into the works. Finally, they were forced to come to Soloveytshik the Marriage-mediator to straighten things out. Here, Soloveytshik showed the stuff he was made of. He used all the means at his command, ate his heart out for three days, and smoothed everything out. First of all, he did a neat bit of business with the one-time fiancé. He hinted that Rothschild could turn his ex-girl's letters into cash. By no means should he sell them to the papers. Heaven forbid! Only to the bride's parents! The Rothschilds could afford to pay more for that bundle of merchandise than twenty down-at-the-heel gazettes. And now, just before the wedding, was the perfect time for a deal with the letters. If he put it off until later, the letters' value would decrease and they wouldn't be worth a red kopek.

The Rothschild boy took these words to heart, and the two
sides began bargaining for the letters as if they were a piece
of goods. Finally, they were sold. For how much? That's top
secret. Soloveytshik wished that he had earned the price of
those letters every year. Even, if times were bad, every three
years would do. If you really pressed him—he'd say every five
years.

Then, he started working on the Brodskys. He told them
that although they outshone and were richer than the Rothschilds, and although their lineage was nobler, they were first
to come to the Rothschilds in *Palestine*. So the word was
given then and there. Next came the engagement party and
the wedding was to have followed.

But something turned up, a coincidence, which happens
only once in a century, and it came quite close to upsetting
Soloveytshik's plan.

This coincidence snuck in through the back door, so to
speak. It was no one's fault. Neither Soloveytshik, the Rothschilds, nor the Brodskys were to blame. Imagine—it happened
at the very last minute. All the Kasrilevke swells, wearing short
frocks and white gloves, were gathered in *Palestine* for the
Rothschild's wedding. The affair cost an arm and a leg. Two
orchestras performed, not counting the Kasrilevke band.
Everything was all set for the big wedding. Suddenly, there
appeared—and no one knew where from—a magnificent-
looking woman, tall and lithe and heavily veiled. Whether she
was ugly or not, no one knew. Only one thing was certain—
she was female. As soon as this figure appeared, the aristocratic groom became pale and the bride was about to faint.
The bride's mother went into a dither, wrung her hands, and
stopped speaking Russian. The groom's parents went into
hushed conference. Panic swooped down on the guests. It
caused such a hubbub that we have to stop right here. We'll
leave the veiled woman for the next chapter which, with an
epilogue and a postscript—as is fitting for an aristocratic
novel—will conclude this summer romance.

8. The Woman Behind the Veil

We've always said that it's good to be one of the gentry.
When a problem comes up, things go so easily. Their way
out is—how much do you want and mum's the word. If a
plain Jew from *Israel* had to face the situation which the
Brodskys and Rothschilds faced, the roof would have caved
in on him. But the blue-bloods didn't bat an eyelash. When
the veiled woman made her entrance just as the ceremony was
about to begin, there was a general uproar and hullabaloo.
But it only lasted a moment. The Brodskys took the veiled
woman into another room.

"What do you want?" they asked her.

They didn't ask her *who* she was and *what* she was. They
figured she was probably an old girlfriend, and as they called
it, a passing romance of his from his pre-marital days. For
who didn't flirt nowadays among the aristocrats? That's why
they only asked her *what* she wanted. When she told them,
they weren't a bit surprised. They just had to come to terms,
for the woman's demands were a bit high. She wanted one
of two things:

1. Either the wedding was to be called off and the groom
marry her instead, or,

2. She was to get monthly payments as befitted an aristocrat
like our Brodsky. Also, a sum of money was to be set aside for
the baby.

Baby?! Where did a baby come from? Nevertheless, they
didn't even ask her. It was nothing new among the upper class
for a young man to have a mistress before he was married,
and that this mistress have a baby or two. Our aristocrats-
come-lately, the Brodskys, thanked heaven that she only had
one baby. Would it have improved matters any if she had
had two or three?

But they were a bit peeved at their son. He really should
have let his old folks know that he already had an heir. But
now was no time for anger. The wedding canopy was all prepared. Everything was ready. Little by little, the guests might

even start drifting away and head for home. The high-society wedding might even end with a scandal. But blue-bloods hated scandals! So they started haggling with the veiled woman. A ruble more, a ruble less—finally, they came to terms. They even paid her cash on the spot and gave her a promissory note, and the old Brodsky signed it with his full true name—"Kupetz Perve Gildye Isak Aranovitsh Dumbo." The note said that the mother had to support the child until his eighteenth birthday. For that, the mother would get a certain amount each year. Once the boy was eighteen, Dumbo's son, Aron, the groom, would give a fixed sum. The note further stated that all this would remain top-secret and that both sides were satisfied with the arrangements. None should have any complaints or claims against the other, and then everything would be hunky-dory.

With that, the veiled woman disappeared from the scene. The ceremony continued and concluded in a most grand manner. The rabbi delivered a fine sermon. In Russian, naturally. He talked about the young couple's innocence and pure love and how they would build their house according to the wishes of God. He even quoted a verse from the Scriptures. At this, the blue-bloods sniffled a bit and dabbed white handkerchiefs to dry eyes. They wanted to show that although they didn't catch the meaning of the verse, they knew what he was driving at. The bride and groom then kissed their in-laws and all the guests. Right after the ceremony, without even taking a bite, but just drinking a glass of champagne, the couple got into a beautiful car and drove to the railroad station. They were on their way to their honeymoon, just like the elite the world over. And, of course, our Kasrilevke aristocrats had to be copycats, too.

Epilogue

The morning after the wedding feast, the two Kasrilevke gazettes carried a story about the grand aristocratic wedding in *Palestine*.

The story told everything. Except the incident concerning

the veiled woman. Of that, not a word. Both the progressive
and modern *Bowler Hat* and the Orthodox *Skullcap* went wild
over the wedding. They couldn't praise the majestic fete
enough. All the Kasrilevke big-wigs who graced the wedding
were mentioned by name. Each nabob was singled out for an
outstanding quality—one for his open heart, another for his
wisdom, a third for his philanthropy. The dishes served
weren't forgotten either, and neither were the drinks.

The *Bowler Hat*, for instance, worked itself into a frenzy
about how much slaughtering the slaughterers had to do. All
three slaughterers, they said, had been killing chickens for
three days in a row.

And the *Skullcap* flew into a dither about something else.
The *Skullcap* devoted itself more to liquids than to solids.
When it came to reckoning how much wine was drunk at
the wedding-meal, they said ecstatically that if a Kasrilevkite
were to possess all the empty bottles, he would have been able
to marry off three daughters liberally and have enough left
over to support himself for a year.

The Kasrilevke reader who was used to the newspapers'
habit of exaggeration, wasn't much impressed by either the
slaughterers or the bottles. But, there was such a thing as unbridled competition. The very next morning, the radical
Bowler Hat came out with a sharp critique against the *Skullcap*. A screaming headline announced: THE JEWS ARE THE
BIGGEST DRUNKARDS IN THE WORLD!

The radical *Bowler Hat*'s reasoning went this way: "Whoa,
there. Let's slow up. Let's not rush. Marry off three daughters?
Let's be less 'liberal' than the sinister editor of the snooty
Skullcap in our assumption. With today's prices, it still would
have to cost, at the very least, about five or six hundred per
daughter. We have, then, a grand total of 1,800 rubles. Now
let's figure out the worth of an empty wine bottle. Let's say,
three kopeks. The upshot is that no more and no less than
60,000 bottles of wine were consumed at the wedding! Next!
How many people could have been at the villa? Let's say 30.
Now divide 60,000 by 30. Doesn't that come to 2,000 bottles
per person? The conclusion we therefore draw is that the

greatest drunkards in the world are Jews. And that's surprising news to us!"

But the *Skullcap* didn't let such a critique faze them. The following morning they came out with a critique on the critique. The *Skullcap* went ahead and asked a foolish question:

"Pray tell, oh you wizards of the enlightened *Bowler Hat,* you men of integrity—if you're such big-shots and fault-finders and can catch someone else with their exaggerations down and can doctor up such grand totals and dandy statistics, why can't you get hold of a three-kopek pencil and figure out your own fowled-up facts. Your enlightened sheet reports that so many chickens were massacred for the wedding that three Kasrilevke slaughterers did nothing for three days but kill fowl. Let us not be so lazy, but make a fair account. How long does it take a slaughterer to put away a bird? A minute at the most. That means that in an hour, he can do in at least 60 chickens. In a day (if he sleeps at night), 12 times 60. And that's 720 birds. In three days—2,160. Which means that the three slaughterers together butchered a grand total of 6,480 birds. We'll go easy now and grant that out of such a host of poultry, 480 weren't slaughtered properly and ritually and couldn't be eaten. That leaves a sum of 6,000 defunct chickens. Divided by 30 blue-bloods, as you yourselves say, it leaves 200 chickens per guest. If so, a question comes up—blast you a hundred times over—what person, even if he be the biggest aristocrat and glutton in the world, can pack away 200 chickens in a day?"

But, after all, this is Kasrilevke! Some wags appeared and offered to straighten things out between the parties. "You come down a bit with the wine," they said, "and we'll come down a bit with the birds."

P.S. When the young couple returned from their honeymoon, they said they had been in Italy. But the Kasrilevke jokesters insisted that this was an out-and-out lie. They had really been in Yehupetz. But, in any case, when they came back and Aron, that is the young Brodsky, found out that his father gave the veiled woman a note (he never knew about this during the commotion at the wedding; his parents didn't want to make him nervous), he threw a fit. He swore up and down that for the life of him he couldn't remember the tall, veiled woman as ever having been his mistress. And, as far as he remembered, his mistress had never had a baby of his. That is, he meant to say, he never had a mistress who had a baby. But if the veiled woman was the one he thought she was, it was certainly a job put up by his rival, the Rothschild boy. But no use crying over spilled milk. Once signed, nothing could be done. A Brodsky never broke his promise. Unless, of course, the father passed on and the young Brodsky took over the estate—well, then, they would think about it.

As far as the jilted rival, the young Rothschild, was concerned—don't spend any sleepless nights worrying about him. Soloveytshik got a bride for him. And what a bride! It so happened she came from the newly-rich, the highfalutin Brodskys! Imagine—she wasn't as beautiful as the Rothschild girl. Not only wasn't she as beautiful, but when you really came down to it, she was an outright monster. As compensation, though, they gave the Rothschild boy a large dowry. But what difference should it make to you, dear reader? You didn't chip in!

Another thing should be mentioned here and now to make the reader completely happy. How much of a commission did Soloveytshik get from all concerned? Don't ask! Soloveytshik said that he fetched such a fat sum that he wished his best friend such luck.

"Since Kasrilevke was founded and since Soloveytshik has been a mediator of marriages, no Jew in his wildest dreams has ever seen such a commission."

He concluded with this: "Moreover, old man, what good does it do you to peek into your friend's pockets? By the way, can you find something to tide me over for a few days? Right now I'm on the threshold of a fine match, and, God willing, I'll pay you back with a load of thanks."

BIRTH

"Bungler! When are you going to give birth? Next year?"
"We've been waiting so long for this prize package!"
"If God thinks us worthy, maybe we'll even have a boy!"
"She's probably carrying the Messiah. None other!"

Phrases like these echoed through Henikh the Joiner's house all day long. Meanwhile, the mother-to-be, Reyzl, writhed and moaned and couldn't make herself comfortable. There were moments when she hid in a corner of the room, pinched her face, and clawed her body, wishing she were dead.

"Dear God! Sweet, loving Father in heaven! Help me die!" Reyzl had been due to give birth since early that morning, but she hid so that no one would know. Toward evening, when the labor pains became strong, she fell into bed, wrung her hands, gritted her teeth, turned blue in the face, and screamed in a strange voice:

"Oh, Mama! Give me strength to die!"

Sore-Rokhel, her grandmother, watched over her. Childbirth didn't faze her, having seen it many times before. With her sleeves rolled up to her pointy, grayish elbows, she bent over Reyzl and consoled her by saying:

"Scream, scream, my child. A woman in childbirth must scream. Scream just once more and with God's help you'll come through fine. Your mother is doing her best for you now, up in heaven. Your father is standing before the Heavenly Court praying for you. God willing, you'll come through all right and you'll have a son, a consolation for all your troubles."

The pains came and went and Reyzl lay in a daze, like one drunk. Her ears rang. She wasn't asleep, yet she felt stupefied. She didn't know where she was. Something was happening to her. That she knew. Something was *about* to happen. Perhaps this was the end of her troubles. Perhaps she was dying. But Reyzl didn't want to die. Not at all! She still had faith in the Eternal One that soon her dear husband, Zetl, would come from far-off America, and she would once again know the joy of their being together.

Where was Zetl?

A few months after the wedding, Zetl the Tailor went looking for work. He ended up in America. Everyone was going to America. But once he went away, no more was heard from him. The ocean had swallowed him up.

"He surely got married there and took himself another dowry, may he come to a foul end—dear God!"

That's what they all said about him in Kasrilevke and in Henikh's house. All—except Reyzl. She had a different opinion of Zetl. She knew him better than anyone else, although she lived with him for only four months. She expected him any day, any minute. If he were alive and healthy, he would surely return, or at least write a letter and enclose a snapshot. Oh, if only a letter would come with a picture—there would be no one as happy as she!

That expectation was with her for many days. Many nights she did not sleep. She always pressed her face down into the pillow so that the others would not hear her frequent crying. She neither wanted to trouble her friends, nor give her enemies the opportunity to gloat over her misery. And there was much misery, because she knew that she would soon be a mother. Oh, what would she do then? Where would she turn to? Were it not for her fear of God and hell, she would have done herself some harm.

People said that once when she was doing the laundry at the lake, she was ready to throw herself in. But thinking of the next world, she quickly grabbed the bundle of laundry, neither dead nor alive, and ran home. While running, she met her grandmother, Sore-Rokhel.

"Why are you running, my child?" she asked.

Reyzl began to cry like a baby. Sore-Rokhel, who had an

experienced eye, understood what was wrong and tried her best to console her.

"It's all from God," Sore-Rokhel said. "Perhaps because of this, Zetl will come."

Hearing the name Zetl, Reyzl felt the blood rushing to her face. The two women sat on a stone fence, whispering to each other, reckoning with their fingers. Then, they separated.

Reyzl kept her secret as long as she could. But one fine morning, it was suddenly no longer a secret. From then on, Henikh's house became hell on earth for her. She thought that everyone stared at her and spoke about her. But more than anything else, she couldn't stand their cursing Zetl. Every single one of them laid into him tooth and nail. But Leya the Bakery-woman annoyed her most of all. Leya felt sorry for Reyzl and always brought her some rolls or a loaf of bread, saying: "Here, Reyzl. Have some of this, may your scoundrel in America choke on the first bite—sweet God!"

And Frume, the teacher's wife, added: "May he know at least that he's about to become a father—blast him!"

"So what if he does find out! The most he'd do is absently scratch himself—the devil take him!" Osne the Poultry-woman added another dig.

All the above-mentioned women lived together under Henikh's roof. Each one had her own little alcove, her household goods, her bedding, her husband and children. And they had plenty of children, thank God. There was always a hullabaloo, a racket, an uproar in the house. The children fought constantly. All the women cooked and baked at one oven, spread gossip and slandered one another, fought and made up, lent one another various items if they had them, rejoiced together at happy occasions, and lived, for all intents and purposes, like one big family.

Reyzl, woke from her sleep, screaming with a strange voice: "God! . . . God! . . . God!"

"That's the way, my child," Sore-Rokhel consoled her.

"Now the real pains are starting. A few more healthy screams like that and you'll pull through, God willing. That's the way . . . that's it. Congratulations, daughter, you have a son!"

When Reyzl gave birth to the boy, the first thing they did was bathe and swaddle it and see whom it resembled. All three women said in one voice:

"May he shrivel up! It's the spitting image of *him*."

Then they started talking about cooking a broth for the new mother. Each one reproached the other as to why a chicken wasn't provided for Reyzl. Naturally, the entire blame was laid on Osne the Poultry-woman.

"You're in the chicken business, right? Why didn't you think of putting a chicken away for her two weeks ago? We would have bought the feed and would have paid for the slaughtering, too."

Leya the Bakery-woman rolled up her sleeves and started making butter cookies for Reyzl. Frume ran to her husband, Reb Khaim-Khone the Teacher, and got him to copy some Psalms for the sake of the newborn boy. He too rolled up his sleeves and did work the likes of which wasn't even found in the richest home. In the middle of the page appeared an ornamented pyramid:

On the sides of the charm were written the biblical verse:

A witch shall not live.
Not live shall a witch.
Live a witch shall not.

At the bottom of the page was the famous formula which warded off the evil eye and other troubles: "Sini and Sansini and Semenglaf."

In other words, all the necessary precautions were taken.

Reyzl lay in bed looking at the other women. "May God bless them. Do I deserve all this? What did I do?"

The men, having finished all their work, started speaking of the circumcision party. Henikh the Joiner was not a rich man and had many sons of his own. But he said he would pay for the affair since the event had happened in his house. The credit for the good deed would be his.

But the rest of the crowd was insulted.

"Why should he have all the credit? Why does he deserve all this? The circumcision party belongs to us all."

When it came to giving out the honors, a squabble arose. Henikh thought that since it was his house, he ought to hold the baby during the circumcision rites. But, he was sadly mistaken. Everyone said that Reb Khaim-Khone should hold him, since he was a scholar. So Henikh had to jump on the bandwagon and say that he agreed. He was therefore given the honor of being godfather. The honor of helping the circumciser was given to Osne's husband, since he was a grouch and was likely to make a scandal if he were overlooked. To make a long story short, they divided up the honors. Only one thing remained—the best of them all. Who would provide the drinks?

"Drinks?" Sore-Rokhel said, "that should be the least of your worries!"

She threw the cat-fur stole over her shoulders and ran to her son-in-law, Yehuda, a winemaker who also made sweet liqueurs. He brought two bottles of red liqueur to the circumcision party. When the crowd started sampling it after the fish course, they became lively and toasts started flying through the air.

"To long life," said Reb Khaim-Khone the Teacher. He had a wispy beard and wore a shiny black shawl around his neck. "Here's to you! With the help of God let us all live to drink at his Bar-Mizvah."

"Here's to good health," Henikh the Joiner said, "God grant that we live to drink at his wedding."

Osne's husband, the thick-lipped, scrawny, ex-soldier,

downed three full glasses at one time and outdid the others' good wishes.

"Here's to long life! God grant that we live to drink at his circumcisions and Bar-Mizvahs and weddings. Not only his, but his children's, grandchildren's, and great-grandchildren's."

The women also took a few drops. It made them red and talkative. They all spoke at once, like a bunch of geese. Later, the men removed the tables and chairs, threw off their jackets, and started dancing (begging their pardon) in their undershirts, just like during *Simkhas-Torah*.

On the bed, surrounded by an old, torn sheet, which had been covered with Psalms, the new mother Reyzl sat holding her baby. The tiny, rag-swaddled creature clung to her breast. Reyzl looked at these people who for no good reason wished her well, then looked down at her baby, her consolation.

"It's Zetl to a *t*. It's the spitting image of him," she said. Two tears trickled from her beautiful deep-blue eyes, rolled over her pale, worn face, and fell onto her white, young breast.

GEESE

I don't wish this on anyone, but a year ago *Hanuka* time, I had a stroke of good and bad luck at one and the same time. Just listen to this story! You run across a gem like this only once in a thousand years. I've been selling geese, you see, and kosher-for-Passover goose-fat for these past twenty years, and in all that time, a thing like that's never happened to me.

Geese is my business . . . but you think it's as easy as all that? The first thing you got to do is this: you start buying geese right after *Sukkoth*, in the autumn. You throw them into a coop and keep them there all winter, until December. You feed them and take good care of them. Comes *Hanuka*, you start killing them, and you turn geese into cash. If you think it's so easy to buy them, feed them, kill them, and turn them into cash, you're wrong. First of all—buying the geese. You have to have something to buy them with! And I don't have any reserve money salted away, you know. So I'm forced to go and take a loan from Reb Alter. You know him, don't you? He enjoys squeezing the blood out of you, drop by drop. That is, he doesn't say no right off the bat. But, with his telling you to come tomorrow, the next day, the day after that, he drives you to the breaking point. Then he gets down to work, dragging the interest out of you, adding on extra days. He's some Reb Alter! It's not for nothing he's got such a pot belly and his wife's got a face I wouldn't wish on my enemies and a pair of jowls you could sharpen knives on. Talk of her pearls! Just recently, she had an engagement party for her daughter. Great God! May you and I have a third of what that party cost her. Then I wouldn't have to bother with geese any more. But you ought to see the fellow she got! May God strike me if I'd take the likes of him for *my* daughter. First of all, he was as bald as an egg. But, anyway, the whole affair is none of my business. I don't like to talk ill of anyone, God forbid, and I like to stay away from backbiting. I'm getting off the track. I'm sorry, but that's a habit of mine. You know what they say: a woman was made with nine measures of talk.

Buying geese. . . . Where do you buy them? You'd think, at the marketplace, naturally! Surely! If we'd be able to buy all our geese at the marketplace, we'd be rolling in gold. If you want to buy geese for business, you have to put yourself out and get up early, at an hour when God himself is still asleep, and traipse way over to the other side of town, behind the mill. But there you'll find another woman, just as smart as you, who's gotten up earlier and made her way over to the same spot. Then there's a third one who got up earlier than both of you—and that's the way it goes. The whole thing turns into a fish-market. Everyone stands around waiting, hoping that God'll have some pity and send along a peasant with some geese. And as soon as he shows up, the women close in on him and his birds.

"How much for a goose?" they yell.

If the peasant is the sort of businessman you can talk to, why then you can bargain with him. But if, with the help of God, he's a nervous wreck, you can't even come near him.

"Beat it," he says. "Scat. I don't have any geese."

Well, what can you do. Sue him? You can only mumble, half in Yiddish, half in Russian. "How so, you hick peasant? We see with our own eyes—may your eyes ooze out—that you're carrying a goose—may devils and plagues carry you to blazes."

And he says: "I don't have any geese for sale."

But, if God is merciful and the peasant has let go of the goose, then you have to inspect it. And you have to know how to inspect it, too. People say that you have to be as much a connoisseur of geese as of diamonds. You probably think all geese are alike. Do you happen to know that there's such a thing as a goose and a gander? And that a goose *isn't* a gander. A goose'll give fat, a gander—plagues! But how can you tell the difference between them? Easy. First of all, by the comb. A gander has a little comb on the top of his head and a long neck. You can also tell by his voice. He has a gruff voice, just like a man. When he walks, he always struts ahead of the geese. Forgive the comparison—just like a man. Our husbands —it makes no difference who they are, even the worst bunglers among them—always walk ahead of their wives, as if to say: "Lookee here! It's me!" Need more proof? Take my husband, for instance. There's no greater bungler than my Nachman-Ber. Ever since I've known him, he hasn't earned two broken kopeks. Then what's he good for? He's a scholar and a distant relative of a very rich man. His granduncle's second cousin twice removed! But what do I get out of that? May my enemies choke on it in one bite! Trouble, heartache, and shame is what I get out of it. This rich relative's daughter-in-law doesn't wear a marriage-wig, so they throw it up to me. Can you beat that? And it's no lie either! They hit the nail right on the head! But I don't want to gossip about her or talk behind her back. I'm getting sidetracked. Sorry, but that's the way I am. You know what they say: a woman was made with nine measures of talk.

Buying geese. . . . Once you've bought them you put them into the coop for the winter. If you think that's an easy job, you're sadly mistaken. It's easy to coop them up if you've got a private apartment. But what're you supposed to do if— and I hope it never happens to me or you or any other Jew— you're sharing a place with Yente: that is, if you don't have a little room you can call your own and your landlady, who's called Yente, is also selling geese and kosher-for-Passover goose-fat. Well, I'd like to see you try and keep your geese and her geese in one room and not come to blows three times a day. That's the first thing. Next, try and be the smarty and tell which geese are your geese and which geese are her geese. Listen to what happened some time ago. And I don't wish this on anyone. I was sitting in the room when, suddenly, the door of her coop flew open and her whole pack of geese ran out and made a bee-line for my sacks of oat- and barley-feed. Who do you think suffered? Who was supposed to raise a storm? Me or her? Don't you think she let *me* have it?

"If I would have known," she said, "that you *too* keep

geese," she said, "I'd never have rented you this room," she said, "for a hundred million rubles."

"What'd you think was my business," I told her, "selling jewelry?"

"You're a jewel yourself and you got yourself a gem of a husband and diamonds for kids."

Expect me to take that sitting down? She's a queer one, that Yente! Usually, she'll do anything in the world for you. If you're sick, God forbid, she'll drop everything just to take care of you. But she's a hot-head. You really have to watch out for her. One *Hanuka*—wait, just listen to this story and your hair will stand on end. The only trouble is that I don't go poking my nose into other people's business. I don't like to gossip or talk behind other people's backs . . . But I've lost the thread of the story. You'll have to forgive me, that's the way I am. You know what they say: a woman was made with nine measures of talk.

Let's continue. Putting the geese away. . . . If you want the geese to grow good and fat you have to put them into the coop just before the beginning of the month. Don't you dare come near any geese just *after* the new moon! May God save you from misfortune like that. The geese will be ruined. Their bones will be heavy, their skin scraggly. Don't expect any fat at all! Just forget about it. Don't cage them during the day either, when everyone is around. It's much better toward evening, with candlelight, or better yet, in complete darkness. And when you do do it, pinch yourself and say three times: "I hope you get as fat as me." My husband makes fun of me and says that my hocus-pocus isn't worth a snap. If I'd listen to everything he says, I'd be in some pickle. All he does is sit and study, day and night. I'll never understand why he likes to say that twirling a chicken around your head on the eve of *Yom Kippur* is a silly custom. How do you like that for nerve? Don't worry, he didn't get off lightly for that, either.

"Did you come to that grand conclusion all by your little self?"

"That's what the books say," he says.

"Then the upshot is," I say, "that I and my mother and

Aunt Dvorah, and Nekhama-Breyne, Sosi, Dvosi, Tsipora, and all the rest of us are a bunch of asses!"

My genius doesn't answer, and he can thank his lucky stars he doesn't, because I'd let him have it so that his ears would be ringing for three days in a row. But don't think, God forbid, that I'm such a shrew and spitfire. Believe me, I know how to respect a man of learning, a man who sits and studies Torah, despite the fact that he doesn't so much as put his finger into cold water. You think he's lazy? He'd do anything, poor fellow—but there's nothing to do. So he sits and studies. Let him keep studying. Why should he work if I can take care of everything myself? I can manage, if not to cover expenses, then at least not to go begging. I do everything by myself. Shop, keep house, cook, put up the potatoes, dress the kids, and what's most important—send them off to Hebrew school. As you can see, there's bread in the house—but sometimes there's no white-loaf for the Sabbath. But although stones fall from heaven, there must always be money for the kids' Hebrew lessons. I got four boys, you see, may they live and be well, not counting the girls. I'm not like these modern folk who push their kids to gentile schools. Take Berel the Cantor's boy, for instance. He's become a complete heathen, sausages and all, the devil take him. But after all, I'm not God's lawyer. I'm not doing any backbiting, God forbid, and I can't stand the evil tongue. . . . There I go, mixing one story with the next. I can't help it; that's one of my bad habits. You know what they say: a woman was made with nine measures of talk.

You've put the geese away. . . . Now, you just have to see to it that the geese get their feed and water in time. That's all there is to it. For geese aren't ducks and chickens, you know. Ducks are scared of the pox. Chickens of polecats. But geese just glut. When it comes to eating, anything goes. Oats, millet, groats, and, begging your pardon, they peck at worse things, too. A goose isn't choosy. Everything goes down the hatch. A goose is always hungry, just like—and no comparison meant—a poor man's children. A poor man's children eat anything you give them with gusto. And they're never full. I know it from experience. Let them live and be well, my child-

ren, God bless 'em, come home from school and—well, before
you turn around, they've killed a full loaf of bread and licked
a whole pot of potatoes clean. They don't even leave a crumb.
Comes the Sabbath, you have to portion out the white-loaf
like cake and lock up the rest; for if you don't there won't
be a trace of it left by morning. But it's nice having children.
It wouldn't faze me at all having ten, fifteen, even seventy-five
children. There's only one drawback. They got mouths! The
rich are as lucky as anything knowing that their kids go to
sleep with full bellies and don't dream about beggars and don't
wake up crying, "Mama, I'm hu-un-gry." You feel sorry for
them, you understand, and you practically go out of your
mind. Can you imagine having to tell them: "Get back to
sleep, you little devils. Who's heard of eating in the middle of
the night? Back to sleep!" On the other hand, you ought to
see the storm the rich raise when, God forbid, an extra baby
is born to them. Tsk, tsk, tsk. Just recently, one of their young
mothers died. She was a fine, good-hearted, beautiful girl—
the picture of health. Do you know what she died from? I'd
rather not talk about it, for she's in the other world now,
may she have a bright Paradise. I don't want to slander anyone,
and I like to put distance between myself and the evil
tongue. . . . But, you see, I'm forgetting about the story.
That's the way I am, so pardon me! You know what they say:
a woman was made with nine measures of talk.

Oh, me, what a business geese is! That is to say, it isn't such
a bad business, and if God blesses the geese you can make a
pretty ruble out of them. But what's the rub? That only happens once in ten years. More often you don't make a kopek
from the geese. In fact, you end up in the red. You put so
much work into the whole mess, that I swear it isn't worth the
tumult. If so, you're liable to ask, if there's no profit in geese,
why bother? Here's my answer—what else do you want me
to do after working with geese all these years? Think of it!
Tying up thirty geese, carrying them over to the slaughterer,
coming home with thirty of them, plucking their feathers.
Then salting, rinsing, and scalding them. Then separating the
skin, the fat, the giblets, and the meat, turning everything into

money, not letting a speck go to waste. And I do it all by my-self. First of all, I fry the skin and the fat and make goose-fat out of it. I make Passover-fat every year, for my Passover-fat is considered the best and most kosher fat in the village. When I make kosher-for-Passover goose-fat, Passover steps into the house smack in the middle of *Hanuka*. I make the oven kosher-for-Passover. I send my husband to the synagogue. Let him study there. I chase the kids out of the house. Let them go play with their *Hanuka dredle* somewhere. Goose-fat hates extra company. Especially Passover goose-fat. Once, when I lived with Yente, I got myself into the sort of fix I wouldn't wish on anyone. There were other people living there at the time. One of the women, Genesi it was, suddenly got it into her head to start making buckwheat *latkes*. Just on the day I was killing my geese and had the house kosher-for-Passover. I begged her, "Genesi, darling, honey, sweetheart! Put off temptation just one more day. God willing, you'll make your *latkes* tomor-row."

"It's all right with me," she said, "but the children'll find out. My little gluttons enjoy eating. As soon as they find out there's no *latkes*, the little cannibals will start eating me."

She hit the nail right on the head. The little children, lying on the shelf atop the oven, heard that the *latkes* would be post-poned for the next day. One of them, a little cross-eyed boy named Zelig, screamed: "Mama, if you don't make *latkes*, I'm going to throw myself off the shelf." We looked up, and oh, me! The boy was leaning over—in another minute he'd fall off and be broken to bits. Seeing a performance like this, I shouted, "Genesi, darling, honey, sweetheart! Make your *latkes*, quick!"

They say that a pauper has a bottomless stomach. That's true as the Bible. You ought to take a look at Genesi's children. May God spare me! But I'm not talking ill of anyone, God forbid. And I can't stand backbiting either. There I go—I've lost the thread of the story. Forgive me, but that's my nature. You know what they say: a woman was made with nine meas-ures of talk.

Geese to goose-fat. . . . You can't expect goose-fat and

goose-fat alone from the geese. If you do get some fat out of them, it only covers the investment. The profit comes from the left-overs. First of all, goose-meat. If the geese turn out well and the price of meat in town is high, well, then, you're the boss. But what happens when the butchers have a price war and meat is as cheap as dirt, and to top it off the town has imported a new slaughterer and the old slaughterer slanders him and says that he's one of those modern smart-alecks, a Zionist who piddles with Hebrew Schools and Zionist dues and our town's rich man doesn't think much of these Zionists anyway and says that they're a bunch of sots and since the new slaughterer's slaughtering isn't any good and not everyone is eager for goose-meat—what happens then?

"You can buy the goose-meat from me without thinking twice," I argue with my customers. "They're perfectly kosher. The old slaughterer killed them."

"You're absolutely right," they say, "but the point is there's no tag on them saying who killed them. It could be any one."

"What do you mean there's no tag?" I say. "If I tell you the old slaughterer killed them, the old slaughterer killed them. On the other hand, it's a sad state of affairs if it's come to the point where you don't trust me."

"You're a queer one," they say. "We trust you to a t. But if we can have our own geese sent to the old slaughterer ourselves, why do we have to buy your goose-meat, if we don't know who the slaughterer was!"

"Blast it," I say, "you're starting from scratch again. They're kosher! I swear it by the life of my husband and children. And you know that that's a good oath."

"Why swear?" they say, "we believe you anyway."

"Then why don't you take a few pieces of goose-meat off my hands and lighten my load?"

"We can't take them because we don't know who slaughtered the geese."

Well, go talk to the wall! Try to put yourself into someone else's shoes—that, they'll never do. Have some pity! A woman breaks her neck over the geese, hoping that she'll make a little something out of it. We had some winter! There was no wood and straw was so high you had to pay a ruble for each wagon-load. The poor children went to school barefoot. They came home blue with cold and clambered up on top of the oven and snuggled in like little rabbits, waiting for hot potatoes, and you couldn't buy potatoes with gold. Part of the crop failed, and part of it rotted underground. What a town! You'd think someone would care. Poor people were dying of cold, they were swelling up with hunger. The children were falling like flies. But it wasn't so terrible, because only the poor were dying. May God not punish me. I'm not talking ill of anyone. I don't want to gossip. But, I seem to have lost the thread of the story. Sorry—but that's a bad habit of mine. You know what they say: a woman was made with nine measures of talk.

Goose-meat. You'd be in some pickle if you only depended on the goose-meat. Besides that, there were fried scraps and livers and gizzards and heads and feet. Then there were gullets and wings and tongues and hearts and kidneys. Not to mention necks. There's one woman I know who buys up every single neck I have. Even if there's four dozen, she takes them all. It's her husband, she says. He goes wild for necks and white meat. He eats the white meat cold and peppered. He prefers the necks stuffed either with flour and groats, or with chopped liver and crisp *grieven*. And it makes no difference to him if it's roasted separately or cooked with carrots. Well, what do you say to that? Like the saying goes: the dead look the way they eat! And you ought to see that woman's husband! Compared to my husband, he looks like a man of thirty, God bless him, although he's a good ten years older than my Nakhman-Ber. Although my husband doesn't do a stitch of work besides poring over his books, when he comes home, he doesn't grunt like other men and say: "Listen here, bring some food!" The first thing he does when he comes home from the study room in the synagogue, is pick up a book. He reads it and sighs quietly. That means he's hungry. But he'll never say it out loud. What, then? He groans, puts his hand to his heart, and says, "Oh, me." That shows he's really starving! "Want something to eat?" I ask him. "All right," he says. No matter how much I tell him, "I don't understand you. You got a mouth, why

don't you use it? Why do you have to sit there and moan?"—
it does no good. Go speak to the wall. I'd like to see what
would happen if, on purpose, I didn't feed him for three days.
But do you think he's got *that* many bees in his bonnet? How
can a scholar like him be such a ninny? If with what he knows,
he'd just be a little more of a pusher, don't you think he could
be the village rabbi? But, then, what would we do with our
old rabbi? Come to think of it—what are we going to do with
our old cantor? We just got a new one, you know. We
needed him like a hole in the head. We got him so that the old
cantor could starve because—after all—he wasn't much of a
pauper beforehand, anyway. Why'd all this come about? Because the village rich man likes good singing. You want to
hear good voices? Go to the theater and they'll sing you to
death there. If I were only a man I'd show them a thing or
two. Boy, would I take care of them! Do you think I have
any squabbles with them? Nah. I just hate their guts. I can't
stand those rich big-shots. Spiders and rich men! May God not
punish me. I'm not belittling a soul, and I don't like to criticize anyone behind his back. But I'm getting off the track.
Well, that's the way I am, you'll have to excuse me. You
know what they say: a woman has nine measures of talk in
her.

Well, what you get out of the geese. . . . Don't think that
you're in clover once you've sold the goose-fat, all the meat,
and the giblets. If geese didn't have feathers and down, the
whole business wouldn't be worth its weight in salt. When I
start, that is before I even put them into their coops, I feel
them under the armpits, and scrape away the little bit of down
I find there. There's even more after they're killed. Then I
take the feathers and the down separately, and prepare work
for the whole winter. The nights are plenty long and there's
time enough for plucking. So I sit and pluck. I have a little
help, too. My girls. Girls aren't boys, you know. Boys go to
school. But what do girls do? Girls are like a bunch of geese;
they sit at home, eat, and wait to grow up. I sit them down
in front of a sieve and tell them to start plucking feathers. "If
you do," I say, "tomorrow, God willing, I'll smear some

goose-fat on a piece of bread and give it to you. Better yet, I'll make a soup out of gizzards." You should see them rush to work. It's nothing to sneeze at—a soup made out of gizzards. What can I do? We don't even see a piece of meat all week long, not counting the Sabbath. If I didn't sell geese, I don't know what I'd do with my children all week long. Like this, they manage to get hold of a little gullet, a gizzard, a head, a foot, a drop of goose-fat. The smell alone is enough for them. When I lived in Yente's house—and I don't wish this on anyone—my neighbor Genesi told me: "You know, when *Hanuka* rolls around and you start messing around with your Passover geese and kosher-for-Passover goose-fat, a new life comes into my little gang. The smell of the cooking alone makes them dizzy and they think that they're eating goosemeat."

You think it was easy to look at a mob like Genesi's, poor souls, and see them ogling the pot of goose-fat and the frying *grieven*. They didn't even so much as stick their hands out and say "give me." They just stood there and stared, like hungry wolves, licking their lips, their eyes shining. It was pitiful watching them. What can you do? You give them each a little *grieven*—you wet their lips with a bit of goose-fat. I couldn't do any more, though. How can I start feeding so many mouths if I am flooded with a brood of my own, may no harm come to them, and to top it off, have a husband who never earns a wooden kopek and we haven't even paid for the geese yet? I wish I had a third of what I owe. The interest grows like wild mushrooms and you have to pay it. I'm not going to run out on my debts and I'm not going to go bankrupt either, God forbid, like Yente did when she didn't pay her brother-in-law for the other half of the apartment because her son was a student and, as they said, wrote on the Sabbath. Anyway, that's what they say. I don't know. I wasn't there. I hate to talk about things I don't know about and I hate to run other people down. Just let me ask you one question. Why does Yente's son have to study? He's sick too, unfortunately—consumption. The whole family—and I don't wish this on anyone—is consumptive. But let her live to be a hundred and twenty.

I'm her friend. What have I got against her? But on the other hand, she didn't do right by me. You don't go kicking your roommate out of the apartment just before Passover. What was the matter? Menashe the Water-carrier was able to pay the ruble-a-week rent and I wasn't. First let her get a kopek out of him, *then* let her talk. Folks say he's up to his neck in debts. He doesn't even own the hair on his head. He's gotten his money for his winter's work in advance and he's still a pauper. He's married to Peysi, and she's a vixen to boot. May God not punish me. I'm not talking ill of anyone, I hate back-biting you know. But . . . hold up . . . I think I started out to tell you a story! But for the life of me, I can't remember what it was. Women are nothing to sneeze at, you know. They're some brood. Look here. I've mixed up everything under the sun, livers and feathers and last winter's snow. You know what? A woman *was* made with nine measures of talk. I'll just have to put that story off for some other time!

MY FIRST LOVE AFFAIR

1. My First Position and the Power of Pull

He who has sat up late at night burning candles, hungry as all get out, bundled up in a torn, old coat, mulling over the phrase "fresh white bread" in its nominative, genitive, and dative forms while wishing in vain for just a stale piece of black bread; he who has slept on a hard bench with a fist for a pillow while the lamp sputters, the baby cries, the old lady grumbles; he who has had a pair of tattered boots, one with a missing heel, the other with a loose sole which slapped at the pavement and wouldn't fall off; he who has gone to pawn a watch, which the pawnbroker would not take since its case wasn't made of pure silver and its gizzards weren't worth a damn; he who has asked a friend for a loan, seen this friend dig immediately into his pocket and pull out his wallet, then swear that he hadn't a penny; he who has experienced all this first hand, possibly might understand how I felt when I got my first job at twelve rubles a month, plus room, board, and all the trimmings.

I don't want to trouble you with all the details, and what's more, I don't think I have to tell you that I had an uncle, who had an aunt, who had a friend, who had a relative, who had an in-law, who was a rich but simple man who lived in a village. This chap had an only son for whom he sought a tutor in Yiddish, Russian, German, and bookkeeping. Said tutor was to come from a good home and charge next to nothing. Right up my alley!

I took the trouble to run over to my uncle's and asked him to ask his aunt to ask her friend to ask the relative to put in a good word for me with the in-law—that the rich villager should hire no one but me, for there were other young boys

129

in Mazepevke who knew Yiddish, Russian, German, and book-keeping and were quite ready to go out into the big, wide world, so long as there was a job involved.

But this rich man didn't say the good word too quickly. It took him ages to make up his mind. In the first place, did he want a tutor at all? Second of all, if he did hire one—should he take me or the next fellow? Thank goodness, he finally decide to hire a tutor and I was chosen. Knowledge, so he said, played a small role in the choice. Brains were as plentiful as fleas. The important thing was that the tutor came from a good home. Since I fit into that category, I was hired.

That's what my boss said. But—if you'll pardon me—I think he lied through his teeth. My other competitors also came from good homes. No worse than mine. But what swung it? Pull!

Oh, yes. Grand and mighty is the power of pull. And lucky was he who had an uncle, who had an aunt, who had a friend, who had a relative, who had a rich in-law, who lived in a village and had an only son for whom he needed a tutor in Yiddish, Russian, German, and bookkeeping, who would not charge too much.

2. My Boss' Tall Tales Rock Me to Sleep

Who was my boss? What was he? What did he look like? Was he short or tall? Thin or fat? Fair or dark? Actually, this information shouldn't concern you too much. And his name won't make any difference to you, anyway. He may still be alive somewhere, so it wouldn't even be right to mention it. I'd rather report our first conversation, which took place while riding in his elegant horse-drawn carriage. After he had given me a cigar (the first and last cigar I ever smoked), he said, contemplating the gray ash of his black cigar:

"In other words, young man, this is the first time you've come from the city to the country. No doubt you think, young man, that a village is God-knows-what and that we country Jews haven't the faintest notion of the good things

in life. But take a look, if you please, young man, at the life
of a country Jew. He has a house with a courtyard and a
garden. It's a palace. Let me tell you, young man, with no
exaggeration, we have about twenty rooms. What am I saying,
twenty? There are more than thirty! I myself don't know
why we need so many rooms, although we often have company. What am I saying, often? Every week. Every day. In
fact, a day doesn't go by without one, two, or three guests
coming. And what guests, too! A nobleman, a police commissioner, a bailiff, a justice of the peace. Me? I get along with
all of them. I'd like to have a ruble for every time they come
around. I sit at home, and suddenly I see a four-in-hand driving
practically right up to the porch. Who came? I ask. His Excellency, I'm told, the governor himself. Well, you can't be a
pig and not invite him in. You have to receive him properly,
give him the best rooms and the whole garden. And my garden's worth seeing. It's more a forest than a garden! Wait until you see my apples, my pears, my plum trees. And grapes?!
I have everything, thank God, and it's all home grown. Brandies from my own cherries, wine from my own grapes. Even
fish from my own lake—carp, tench, bream—breams, this
big!"

With this, my boss stretched his hands out so far that I had
to lean back to let the bream swim by. He didn't stop spinning
his tall tales. I kept listening and asking for more. Then—I
don't know what did it—the horses' tails swishing, the soft
seat in the rocking carriage, or perhaps it was my boss' yarns,
but I began to doze. It was a warm and pleasant summer night.
A nimble breeze, smooth as satin, blew by every once in a
while and caressed my face. I fell asleep hearing my boss'
snores.

When we arrived, the sun had already sailed over a better
part of the sky. It was a clear, sunny day—all was cheerful
and bright. The sun smiled amiably at me and welcomed me
to my new home.

3. A Pack of Liars—Icy Looks—
A Warm Recommendation

There are all sorts of liars in the world. There are liars who lie just for the fun of it. No one has to twist their arms, so to speak—they have a pair of lips and they blabber. These liars are subdivided into three kinds: a liar for things past, a fibber for things present, and a faker for things future. The first liar will tell you trumped-up cock-and-bull stories and will swear that he saw it with his own eyes, and just you dare dig deep, or look for witnesses, or say it isn't so! A fibber for things present isn't really a liar, but a braggart. He'll tell you that he knows, has, and can do everything—just try and prove otherwise! The faker for things future is a good fellow who'll promise you the moon. He'll hustle and bustle, he'll talk to what's-his-name, he'll arrange things for you—and you have to trust him to a *t*.

All three types of liars know that they're shamming, but think that the next fellow believes them. But there's also the kind of liar who, while spinning his yarn, is convinced that he's telling the truth. He is positive that others believe him and is happy as can be. That chap lives in the world of fantasy. He's a sort of artist who dreams up new tales, and forgets what he's told the night before. His imagination keeps churning out brand-new ideas. One of the latter liars was my boss. You've probably guessed that his palace turned out to be a run-of-the-mill house with far less than thirty rooms. Even the garden was nothing much. Instead of grapes—gooseberries; instead of wine—good old apple cider. Instead of gigantic breams—small pikes, and not from his own lake either. From the fish-market!

A fat woman holding a bunch of keys greeted us. She looked at me with such an icy stare that I felt queasy. By that look, she meant: Who's this blunderhead? My boss saw her look and, in a buttery voice, played up to her:

"Here's the new tutor for the boy. Where is he?"

"The boy's sleeping," she roared in a baritone voice, and

threw me another icy look which could have frozen your insides. It was lucky that my boss asked to be served. He seated me next to him and during the next few minutes, while the samovar was being heated, he told me what his son knew, how well he studied, and how nicely he wrote.

"He's famous for his penmanship! Everyone talks about his letters! German is his mother-tongue. And you ought to hear his French!"

The woman with the keys brought cheese, sour cream, butter, honey, milk, and other delicacies to the table. It wouldn't have been so bad if she hadn't sat down opposite me and thrown glances my way with those sweet eyes of hers. But my boss knew what she was driving at. Immediately, he rattled off my familial lineage. He told her who I was and what I knew. I felt as if my face, my eyes, my very hair were on fire. According to my boss, I was the Baal Shem Tov's grandson, all my ancestors were famous rabbis and noble men of wealth, I was far more clever than a university student, a doctor, and three professors combined. Whether she believed this song and dance, I don't know. But, I think that her icy stare mellowed somewhat.

4. The Boy Eats Like an Army
While his Tutor Starves

The boy turned out to be a strapping lad, handsome, healthy, and happy-go-lucky. He had red cheeks, thick lips, a high, pale forehead, kindly gray eyes, and white hands, as soft as *latkes*. He liked three things: eating, sleeping, and laughing. But above all, he liked to eat. In that house, they ate from morn to midnight. Aside from breakfast, lunch, and supper, tea, coffee, a morning bite, and an afternoon snack—the mother kept sending the boy hot chocolate, bagels, cookies, honey cake, and jam. Quite often, she sent fried chicken livers or just a plain, freshly-baked piece of white bread to keep his soul attached to his body.

His mouth watering, the tutor witnessed all this, swallowing his saliva and calming his appetite with a cigarette. At first, when the tutor hadn't as yet befriended his pupil, he really knew the meaning of hunger. For the lady of the house, the one with the keys, offered him plagues instead of nourishment. There was always something edible around, all sorts of dairy products especially. But, it was all under lock and key. My boss often stood up for me and insisted that I be fed. Then his wife would start jangling her keys, a sign that she was angry, and say: "Of course! What did you think? He eats three times a day! Did you ever . . . ?"

That was a whopper of a lie. Not even once—much less three times a day. Often, I noticed them throwing out hunks of meat and dumping pitchers of milk—at a time when I was passing out in my room for lack of a piece of bread. When my boss wasn't at home, I starved. Luckily, in time, my pupil and I became good friends.

5. My Pupil and I Conspire and Have a Grand Time

One morning, as we sat alone in our special room overlooking the garden, the boy said: "If you want to stay on and be friends, if you don't want to leave—take all these books and chuck them under the table and let's play checkers or 'Sixty-Six.' Better yet, let's lie on our beds and spit at the ceiling."

Without another word, my pupil flung the books under the table, threw himself onto the bed, and spit through his teeth at the ceiling with such remarkable skill that we both burst out laughing.

From that day on, we had a grand time. The pupil taught his tutor the art of checkers and "Sixty-Six." I must admit that until that day, I never knew what a card looked like. But, as soon as I got the knack of the game, I became an addict.

The tutor joined forces with the pupil, scattered all the books to the winds, and played checkers and "Sixty-Six," or lay on the bed and spit at the ceiling, or helped him sample bits of all his snacks. By staying with him, I managed to become well-fed. A couple of months later, yours truly glanced at the mirror and saw a hefty pair of cheeks. He didn't even recognize himself.

No one came into our room except the maid, with food. My boss was rarely at home, and his wife with the keys was busy day and night with her dairy department and never poked her nose into our business. We really had a wonderful time. We were absolutely carefree, without a hint of responsibility to either man or beast. In a nutshell—Paradise!

But once my boss got hold of me:

"Well, how's he doing?"

"Excellently," I said, without flinching.

"See? What did I tell you?" he said, and I wondered how I could look him straight in the eye.

That house, wherein everyone fooled everyone else, wherein everyone bluffed and fibbed, wherein the lie was uppermost and was everywhere—that house was good training for the art of prevarication.

6. The Engaged Couple's First Love Letters— The First Spark is Kindled

Our one duty, though, was picking up the mail and answering the letters. And we had letters every day. I say "we," for we both had to answer them. The letters were written to my pupil from his fiancée, although he himself admitted that he hardly cared for her.

At first, the letters didn't come too often—once a week, or once a fortnight. But, after my arrival, the rate increased and the letters started flying back and forth.

"Here. Read it and answer her. What is she bothering me for?" said my pupil one day, throwing his beloved's letters into my face. I read the letter and liked what she wrote.

My dear, beloved fiancé. I'm sick and tired of your letters, which are as alike as if one mother had borne them. They are as alike as drops of water from a lake. I want to hear something different from you—a fresh word that will warm my heart and brighten my soul. For too cold is the heart, too dark the soul.
From your faithful fiancée

Without delay, I answered thus for my pupil:

My dear and faithful bride-to-be. You write that my words flow
one from the other as if one mother had borne them. How can
it be otherwise if one feeling gave them life? You say they resemble drops of lake water. How can it be otherwise if they stream
from one fount, from one heart? You ask for something different,
something new. Is there anything newer than the word "love"?
Will your soul not be brightened if I think of you, beloved bride-
to-be?
From your faithful fiancé

To this, we received a quick reply.

My dear, beloved fiancé. Your sweet words refreshed and
warmed me and brightened all dark corners. I could swear that I
heard a new melody, a song from Paradise, from a dear, bright
spirit, and I felt as if I'd shed my old skin and taken on a new one.
I feel as if I'm sprouting wings and hovering in the air. A band of
angels comes to greet me and brings regards from my dear beloved fiancé who writes such sweet words. My heart and soul are
totally dedicated to you from now on and forever more.
From your loving and ever faithful fiancée

My dear, sweet, and faithful love. No! You weren't mistaken,
devoted fiancée. No cold and ordinary words were those, but
feelings which streamed from one heart to another—threads
which stretch right out of the heart and join two young souls for
ever and ever. That band of angels, which brought you my regards, returned and brought me an even friendlier greeting from
you. With this band, dear heart of mine, I now send you a fervent
kiss, a sacred kiss from your eternal friend who day and night
carries your bright image in his heart.
From your love-inflamed fiancé

7. Material for an Epistolary Romance

Willy-nilly, a spark comes flying from God-knows-where
and lands on a thatched roof. A little blaze starts. The wind
comes and spreads the flames into a hellish conflagration.

The first letters were the sparks which spread and burned
into demonic flames. The letters became more and more fervent. The fire became more and more intense. An awesome
fire blazed in my heart; flames scorched my whole body and
kindled all my nerves. My blood seethed and boiled. I became
sick. I wasn't myself. Lost my appetite. Couldn't sleep.

Walked in a perpetual daze. My soul was in those letters. They were my only consolation and joy. A letter turned a plain weekday into a holiday. I would open, read, and answer it. All my pupil had to do was copy it and I had to urge him on. Carrying the pain deep down in my heart, affected my health. I had to hide in my room, my head buried in a pillow, and sob quietly, then rise, put up a cheerful front, and sit down to work with my pupil—a game of dominoes or "Sixty-Six."

Luckily, no one noticed that I was fading away, flickering like a dying candle. Luckily, my pupil didn't pay much attention to me. Had he looked closely, he'd have sent me away. I can just imagine what he would have thought of me, had he seen me planting kisses all over his fiancée's letters. How could anyone *not* kiss those letters?

See for yourself. Here's what she wrote:

My angel, my soul, my consolation. I must tell you the truth. I confess to you, my darling, that I didn't know you until now. I never dreamed I'd find in you such a source of lofty feelings, noble thoughts, deep understanding, and such a treasure-house of knowledge. From your wise words, I see how well-read and educated you are. I wonder why I didn't notice this before? It only reveals your innocence and simplicity, which makes you all the more charming. Shouldn't I consider myself lucky that I was fated to meet a person who reflects the best qualities—beauty, intelligence, knowledge, innocence, and goodness? Your goodness shines from your wise words. Your gentle love letters are gifts to me and I thank you a thousand times and beg you not to forget to write.
Your true and ever-loving fiancée

A haze of mystery covered my next letter.

My dear, wise, and kind beloved. You didn't know me for you've never seen me. The person you thought you had seen wasn't really me, but only my reflection. Make believe we've just become friends, that we've never seen each other, that we're both newly born. And oh, how lucky are we that we don't yet know the world, this false and malicious world with its false and malicious people.
Yours, dying with love

This was her answer:

My dear, my love, my angel of God! Your sweet letter, which I've just received, was a closed book to me. A puzzle. You're writing so hazily that I have to rack my brains until I can make out its meaning. And, I think I can proudly say that I understand you perfectly. You say we have to consider ourselves fortunate that we don't yet know the false and malicious world with its false and malicious people. I'm unlucky then, because I happen to know the false and malicious world and its false and malicious people. And how pleasant it is to know that there exists at least one who is humane and fine, true and wise and good, and you are that one, my heaven-sent betrothed. Be well, my dear. Write me what you're reading and what books you recommend. I press your hand with love and remain forever,

Your devoted fiancée

I answered:

My life, my soul, my Paradise. If I'm a source of surprise to you, then imagine what sort of a puzzle and surprise *you* are to *me*! I've never even dreamed of getting such letters from you. From the few Hebrew words which appear in your letters, I see that our holy language isn't foreign to you. For that alone, I think so highly of you that I'm afraid I'm not worthy of mentioning your name. I look at your picture and say to myself—there she is—the ideal Jewish girl. There is my ideal, and I'm ready at a minute's notice to sacrifice myself for you. You ask me what you should read. I'm enclosing a list of the best Russian and foreign classics—Gogol, Turgenev, Tolstoi, Dostoyevsky, Pushkin, Lermontov, Shakespeare, Goethe, Schiller, Heine, Burns. I hope you'll enjoy them. I'm answering your letter immediately, for your letter turns a weekday into a holiday. Be well, my love. Be well, my faithful one. From the depths of my heart,

Your loving and devoted fiancé

She wrote:

My darling, my treasure, my consolation, my heart. I don't know why you're so surprised about the few Hebrew words in my letters. Hebrew—why that's our national tongue. The Five Books of Moses—that's our one and only Jewish national fund. Our entire treasure. What sort of thanks should a Jewish girl get for understanding Hebrew. A girl who hasn't memorized at least a few of Yehuda Halevi's poems should be ashamed of herself, and so should any Jewish girl who has finished high school and doesn't know Mapu, Levinsohn, Smolenskin, Gordon and other Hebrew classics. Many thanks for your list. I'm sorry, but I've already read all those writers and more, like Byron, Swift, Cervantes, Dickens, Thackeray, Shelley, Balzac, Hugo, Sienkewicz, and many more. I wanted to read something new—not a novel, but something serious.

Be well my sweet love and don't think too highly of me, it isn't right. I'm just a plain Jewish girl, devoted to you body and soul.

Your faithful fiancée

Then I wrote . . .

But don't you think it's high time to put an end to this letter business? I'm afraid that it'll turn out to be a collection of
letters rather than a story. I just have one thing to say. These
letters remain hidden to this very day in a corner of my desk.
No man has ever seen them. They're as precious to me as ancient manuscripts, mute witnesses to my first joy and sorrow.
They are dried and faded flowers on the grave of my first romance.

8. I Wallow in Lies and Blush Like a Bride

A man's face will tell you if he's in love. Just look at his
nose. See his eyes roll about. There's a queer smile on his lips.
Ask him about tea, he'll talk about coffee. He always stares at
himself in the mirror. Changes his tie every day. He doesn't
walk, he dances. He's friendly with everyone. And, barring
shyness, he'd have kissed the chimney-sweep.

But no one noticed me. A few times, though, while we were
playing checkers, my pupil asked me: "Are you all here?
You're jumping over your own men!"

Surprised, I asked: "What men?"

Then one night, at the table, my employer pulled me aside
and asked: "Why the long face?"

His wife, jangling her keys, faked a pitying expression, but
deep down she must have felt grand. "He hasn't been eating
for the last few days," she said.

"What's wrong?" my employer asked, then came up with
the answer himself. "It's overwork. Too many books! You
two sit locked up in your room studying for days on end. Take
a walk once in a while."

"When do we have time for walks if we have so much work
to do?" my pupil said. He looked so innocent, that I suddenly
felt like spitting into his face and shouting: "God Almighty.
What liars you people are. One lie after another. One lie
greater than the next!"

But, I kept quiet. Instead of telling the truth, I went one better and told another lie.

"I'm homesick."

"I don't blame him. He has plenty to be homesick for," my employer bolstered the lie with his rich imagination. "His family is not only the finest and foremost family in their town, but you can well say that in the entire region, there's no family like his. The Kovno rabbi—wasn't he related to you?"

"An uncle," I said, unruffled.

"And the Preacher from Porets was your uncle, too, right?"

"A granduncle," I said.

"And the great Epstein? What's the kinship there?"

"Second cousin, three times removed!" I said.

"And Reb Moyshe Halpern is related, too, right?"

"On my mother's side."

"And the Totshiner landowners," he said. "I heard they're quite closely related, isn't that so?"

"Cousins," I said, "on my mother's side."

I was very happy, not with my new-found relatives, but because I remained undisturbed with my sweet dreams and sacred feelings and the precious letters of my pupil's fiancée, which meant more to me than any of my real imaginary friends, and any relatives, close or distant.

This is what she wrote in one of her later letters:

My only consolation. My heavenly angel. Why are you sad? What does it mean? Why have your last letters been so melancholy? Why do you speak of death? What mean those puzzling statements? Why do you think you're the most unfortunate of men? Why do you make me so miserable? Share your secret with me! What kind of secrets can you have from someone who loves you and none other and who counts the days until we meet and are united forever.

To this, the fiancé answered:

Apple of my eye. My divine creature! I beg you, pardon me for those last letters. Forget them. You're right, my love, you're right. I dare not complain. I dare not call myself unfortunate. Unfortunate is he who has never loved and never been loved. I repeat—your letters are all I need. Looking at you once, then dying, would be sufficient for me. But no! I gave you my word that I won't mention death anymore. Do you want to know the great secret? No! You'll never know it until that happy (or unhappy) hour before the wedding when we meet. Then you'll know everything. Meanwhile, be well, my dear divine one, and write, write, write.

Your sadly happy fiancé, who so wants time to stretch on and on

9. The Wedding Preparations—My Foolish Dreams

He who has ever been half as much in love as I will know my bitter-sweet feelings during the start of the wedding preparations. He who has carefully read the preceding chapters will know how I felt when my pupil had fittings for his wedding clothes, which took three weeks of constant sewing to complete. Compared to my pain, Hell was Paradise, and the torments of the grave were nothing at all.

No doubt you're saying—it was caused by jealousy and hatred. God forbid! I knew very well that it was not my pupil she loved, but myself, the real author of the letters. I knew quite well that all I would have to do, upon our meeting, was reveal the secret, that sacred secret. I would just have to say one word and she would understand and everything would be set aright. But how could that be done? How would I even manage to talk to her privately, if but for a minute. I racked my brains over that problem, made thousands of plans, one worse than the other, and dreamed ten thousand dreams, one sillier than the next. I must admit that such awful thoughts came to my head that I'm ashamed to write about them—despite the fact that many years have passed since then.

Don't think that I wanted to do away with my rival or poison him. God save us from such wicked thoughts. I just prayed to God for some sort of miracle, whereby my pupil would get sick, take to bed, and fade away into the next world so that I could step in.

I must confess that I thought of this day and night, expecting my pupil to step into a draft while perspiring, catch cold, start to cough, and develop a fever. Or, perhaps, slip on smooth pavement and break his neck. Or get a rock thrown at his head, accidentally. Or be bitten by a mad dog and go crazy. Or have a storm-uprooted tree fall on him. Anything—so long as he'd make room for me.

But, at the same time, my heart went out to him. Poor innocent soul—he didn't deserve what I wished for him. Why should he die so young? In my heart I mourned him, truly wept over him. I wrote letters of condolence to my love and ended them with a sad poem. In it, I mourned my young pupil who had passed away before his time. I compared the world to a cemetery and him to a young tree.

> The cemetery nightingale bemoans you
> and the stars are dripping tears . . .

I forget the rest of it.

Then my imagination set to work again. A year has passed since his death, and my love and I come to visit his grave, to shed our tears and bring him a gift of sweet-smelling flowers and a poem:

> May flowers bloom on your grave
> and may your soul rest in Paradise.

That flowers bloom on a grave wasn't very likely. But that my pupil bloomed like a rose—of that there was no doubt at all. Day by day, he became healthier. His face shone, his fair skin took on new layers of fat. He was jolly, lively, and happy. Happy not because of love, but because he would be moving to a new, big town among new people, and wouldn't see his own family any more. They made him sick and tired. They bored him to death.

He told me this himself, quite often. But to their face, he said that he'd miss them so much he didn't think he'd live through it.

"But will you miss me?" I asked my pupil.

"Surely," he said, and threw his arms around me. "I'll take you with me. We'll have a great time there. We'll play checkers and go to the theater. I won't ever leave you."

He lied through his teeth, and I knew it. Born and bred in lies, he just had to produce one more.

10. The Guests are Welcomed

I'll never forget the grand reception we got when we came
to the wedding. First of all, they picked us up at the railroad
station with a magnificent coach and brought us to a splendid
house. Each of us was given a separate room, treated first to
pastries and coffee and, a little later, to a dinner of roast duck
and omelets. An endless stream of people swarmed around us,
welcoming us and saying hello. A new face every minute.

They all looked like ants to me. They shimmied before me,
buzzing like flies. I was sunk in my own despondent thoughts:
How can I arrange to see her? Who knows if I'll succeed?
What will happen if she discovers my sacred secret? And if,
God forbid, she . . . ? I was afraid to think of it. It would
be horrible!

Before leaving home, I had put into my pocket—don't be
frightened now, it wasn't a pistol, God forbid—a letter to the
girl. On three pages, I described the course of the romance
and added a short autobiography. But how could I give her
the letter? Through whom? When would she have time to
read it?

The bride's relatives ran back and forth like chickens without heads, hurrying the servants to get the wedding banquet
ready in time; driving the sextons to bring the musicians and
the rabbi. They wanted the ceremony to begin, for the bride
and groom were fasting.

I was witness to the fact that the groom *didn't* fast. In fact,
he helped himself to half a duck, but was telling everyone he
was fasting. He expertly faked the looks of a fasting groom
who pondered deep matters.

Born and bred in lies, he had to lie even on his wedding day.

Meanwhile, the musicians had come and the ceremony of
veiling the bride began. The hullabaloo increased. Everyone
was talking, everyone rushing, everyone made believe he was
doing something. "Hurry, hurry up. Let's go. Come on."

They took us—I don't know who—and brought us—I don't

know where. They told us something, but I don't know what.
My head spun, spots whizzed before my eyes, my ears rang,
and my heart ticked like a clock. Tick-tock.

The musicians were performing. A violin moaned, a trumpet trilled, a flute whistled, and the bass drum boomed. And
my heart ticked like a clock. Tick-tock, tick-tock.

11. The Epilogue to the Romance

Among all the people running back and forth and floating
before my eyes, I noticed another lost soul wandering around
as if he too didn't belong. He was a bespectacled, long-haired
young man who had only one occupation—staring at everything. And he seemed to have fun doing it.

When he looked my way, I had the feeling that he saw right
through me; he saw my heart, my secret, my sacred secret. I
lowered my eyes. But, I still felt his searching stare and knew
that he kept gazing at me. Unwittingly, I looked into those
eyes which pierced my heart, those eyes which magnetized
me.

I don't know how it happened, but we suddenly stood side
by side and talked about the wedding, naturally, the veiling
ceremony, the bride and groom.

Then my pupil's parents led the groom to the bride. She sat
on a chair in the middle of the room, her hair down, her face
in her hands, apparently weeping. The musicians were performing. The violin moaned, the trumpet trilled, the flute
whistled, the bass drum boomed. And my heart—tick-tock,
tick-tock.

A minute more, I thought, in another minute, all is lost.

"What a cow!" the young man with the glasses suddenly
whispered into my ears.

"Where do you see a cow?" I asked him, looking all
around.

"She's sitting right there," he gestured with glasses toward
the bride.

Seeing the bewildered look on my face, he whispered: "She's an ass, a run-of-the-mill domestic animal. Can't even write her name. And she's a hellcat to boot. And look at the fine husband she's getting. You're his tutor, right?"

I don't know if I called him aside, or vice versa. Perhaps we both moved away. But in two minutes flat, we were sitting opposite each other like old friends. The bespectacled young man—he was the bride's tutor—told me hair-raising stories about the bride. I would have been better off not having heard them.

"All right. But her letters," I cried out. "For God's sake, her letters."

Hearing this, the young man held his sides and laughed hysterically.

"Her letters," he laughed. "Oho! Her letters! Oh, I can't take it any more. Her letters!"

"Then, whose were they?"

"Hers!" he continued laughing. *"Her* letters. They were *mine*. My letters. Mine. Mine."

I thought that this young man had surely gone crazy and would soon throw a fit. He grabbed both my hands, walked around the house with me, kept slapping my shoulders, laughing without a stop.

"Hers? Her letters?"

Have you ever had a sweet dream where you see a beautiful palace, excellent food, the finest wines, fruit fresh from the trees, a heavenly scent, it's Paradise! And then, a "she" appears in the form of a golden-haired princess. You don't walk, you float. You rise higher and higher, right up to heaven. Suddenly you hear a whistling coming from the forest, a beating of wings and a grotesque laughter which echoes through the woods and ends with a mournful yawn. You see a deep abyss and you're about to fall. You shiver and wake with a headache. You're not yourself for a long time.

This sweet dream flashed through my mind when the young man stood next to me, laughing at my letters and recounting the girl's good qualities. He laughed, and my blood ran cold.

One drop after another trickled out of my wounded heart and shattered spirit.

In the hall, the musicians were performing. The violin moaned, the trumpet trilled, the flute whistled, the bass drum boomed. And my heart, my heart was drained and empty, and there was gloom and darkness in every corner of my soul.

THREE CALENDARS

You want to know why a Jew like me, a father, handles contraband filth like French postcards? I've got Tolmatshov and Tolmatshov alone to thank for it, may he fry in hell! But since it all happened so long ago, and since Tolmatshov is no more, and since Odessa is back to normal, I think I can come out with the whole truth as to why Tolmatshov was such an anti-Semite. And the truth is, that I'm to blame for most of it, I'm afraid, if not all of it.

Well, now you're probably wondering how a street-hawker like me, who peddles Yiddish newspapers and French postcards on the sly, comes to General Tolmatshov! And what sort of friend am I with generals, anyway? But the answer is, you understand, that every why has its wherefore, and that a Jew is only human. If you can spare a few minutes, I'll tell you an interesting story.

It happened right here in Odessa, many years ago, at this time, during the intermediary days of *Sukkoth*. Generally speaking, Odessa was still the same old Odessa. No one had heard of Tolmatshov, and a Jew could roam around as free as a bird and sell his Yiddish books. Then, there weren't as many Yiddish papers as today. You weren't afraid of anyone, and there was no need to mess around with banned Parisian postcards. In the old days, I used to sell Sabbath and holiday prayer-books and Jewish calendars around Lanjerovski, Katerinenski, and Fankonin streets. You could always run into a Jew there, for that was the area where speculators, agents, and various other Jews hung around waiting for a miracle.

Just like you see me now, I was strolling along on Fankonin Street, the spot where our speculators wear out their shoe-leather looking for business, and I said to myself: where do I get a customer for the few calendars I got left? *Rosh*

Hashana and *Yom Kippur* are gone and forgotten and before
you know it, *Sukkoth* will slip right by and I still haven't gotten rid of my little bit of stock. God knows if I'll ever sell
those bound calendars—for it's the sort of stuff you can't even
give away if it isn't sold before the holidays. Later, they're
completely useless. And I had *three* of them left over from
before the Jewish New Year!

I started off with a hundred and got rid of them on the
street, mostly among the stock speculators. They weren't such
fiery Jews—I mean, they didn't go for Yiddish books and all
that. But when it came to a Jewish calendar for the entire year,
well, even that sold. After all, you had to know when Passover or the memorial day for a loved one came. A Jew is a
Jew after all.

Well, strolling about that way, I stopped near Fankonin and
looked at the group of speculators running back and forth. I
knew every single one of them blind-folded, and I thought:
who can I offer these few calendars to if each one's got his
supply? I don't think I missed a one.

As I stood there thinking, I saw a general with as many
medals as I got hair, sitting at a front table at the outdoor cafe
on Fankonin. He was stirring his coffee with a spoon and talking to a servant, repeating the same thing over and over again.
And each time the servant answered: "I get you, Your Excellency."

What's he trying to tell him? I asked myself. I edged up
closer to the general's table—I'm only human, you know—
and made believe I was looking somewhere else. I heard the
general slowly telling that thick-headed peasant what to do.
He literally put each word into his mouth.

"Remember what I'm saying," the general said. "Go to my
house, at Number 3 Hersonski Street, and tell my wife that
Count Musin-Pushkin is having dinner with us. Don't forget
now. Number 3 Hersonski Street! Count Musin-Pushkin!"

The servant stood at attention. His only words were: "I get
you." When the peasant left, the general called to him again:
"Remember, 3 Hersonski Street. Count Musin-Pushkin!" He
was about to return to his coffee, when he spotted me standing

there almost on top of him, gaping into his glass. Not that I meant any harm by that, God forbid. I just stood there—just like that. Well, he raised his voice and stared right through me.

"What do you want?"

What I want, you won't give me, I thought. But then again, maybe yes! So I got a bright idea. I'm only human, you know. Believe it or not, I told him: "Your Excellency, how would you like to buy a calendar?"

He looked at me. "What sort of a calendar."

"A Jewish calendar," I said.

He looked at me as if I was completely crazy and said, "What do I need a Jewish calendar for?"

"I don't know what you need it for," I said. "But I need money for the holiday. I have three left, you see. How about buying one, Your Excellency?" And I thought: it'll be some neat trick if he'd buy a Jewish calendar.

Well, here's what happened. No sooner did I say the word "Excellency," than he boomed out, "Go away, please."

Believe it or not, my blood froze. I'm only human, you know. I grabbed my bundle and was ready to about face, when suddenly I heard him say "Come back here."

What could I do? I had to go back. He asked me to show him a calendar. I did. Then he wanted to know how much it cost. I told him. He paid me for it right away without bargaining, without saying a word, without anything. How's that for a general? Isn't he worth three speculators?

Well, that's a start, I said to myself, taking my bundle and going. A start was well and good, but what next? Where do you find two other generals like that on whom you can palm off two leftover calendars. Then I got another brilliant idea! I'm only human, you know. Why not offer him a second one? No skin off his back, having two Jewish calendars. But what would he do with two? Come to think of it, what would he do with *one*? Thinking like this, a new idea hit me. I remembered how he tried to pound the address—Number 3 Hersonski Street—into that peasant's thick skull. As I lived and breathed, that was where I could find a home for a second calendar.

Now don't be a bungler, Avram Markovitsh, I said to myself (that's my name, you see), and strike while the iron is
hot. Nab yourself another buyer. Then, without dilly-dallying, I crossed one street after another until I got to Hersonski
Street, and looked for number 3. Sure enough, there it was!
And what a number it was, too! A private, two-story brick
building. Fine and dandy, but what next? Ring the bell and ask
for the general's wife. And that's just what I did, thinking—
I'll be in a pretty fix if a soldier shows up, probably with a
dog to boot. He'll toss me out on my ear and set the dog on
me. That's all I needed!

Two minutes passed, then three. But no one showed up.
What luck I have, I thought. No one's in. But, perhaps the
bell's out of order. Must try again. And believe it or not, I
upped and rang again. Once, twice, three times—finally, the
door swung open and there stood a peasant girl, holding a
broom.

"What do you want?" she said.

I wanted to run real quick, but I took my heart in my hands
—I'm only human, after all—and said: "I have to see the general's wife. It's something personal."

She looked at me as if to say: what a queer bird *he* is. Then,
without so much as a by-your-leave, she slammed the door in
my face. What a welcome! But maybe she'd come back. Then,
again, maybe she'd send the soldier and the dog, I thought, and
wanted to make a quick retreat. But since I was already there
and had rung the bell—it was too late.

Half a minute later, the door opened and there stood a beautiful young woman—all peaches and cream. Was she the general's wife? Couldn't be! Too young. The general's daughter?
Nope. *He* was too young. But time was a-wasting.

"What is it you want?" she said.

What now? I thought. Should I address her as "Your Excellency"? If she really was the general's wife—then it would
be all right. But what if she weren't? Why should I give her
an honor gratis? I'm only human, you know. So I decided to
eliminate the title and start from scratch.

"The general bought a calendar from me and asked me, that

is, told me to deliver it to Number 3 Hersonski Street and
that's where they'd pay me for it. And in case they didn't believe me, the general gave me a sign that Count Pusin-Mushkin
was eating supper here tonight."

She broke into a laugh. "It's not Pusin-Mushkin—but Musin-Pushkin."

So long as you're laughing, lady, I said to myself, you're all
right. "Be that as it may," I said, "Pusin-Mushkin, Mushkin-
Pushkin. What's the difference? So long as the sign is right."
I handed her the calendar. She took it and turned it around
and around, inspecting it from all angles. "How much is it?"
she asked. I told her. Then she took the calendar, paid for it,
and smiled a good-bye. How's that for a lady? Pure gold! She
was worth not only three speculators—she was worth three
dozen! So I got rid of the bigger part of my stock. Only one
was left. I could now go home and eat supper, right?

I had supper and rested, but that one calendar was bothering
me. True, I'd gotten rid of two out of three—was stuck with
only one. But for that very reason, I wanted to get rid of that
last one, too. What good was an old bound calendar? Therefore, I *had* to get rid of it. But how do you go about it, if most
of the speculators already had theirs? No choice but to roam
through town once more. Without dawdling, I took my bundle and went out. Just like that. Since I knew the two main
streets, my feet took me there without being asked. Right to
where the speculators ran around, wearing out their shoe
leather. Where else was there to go? Perhaps God would soon
provide a customer. After all, it was only one little old calendar. And, believe it or not, I wandered back and forth, like a
lion in a cage, looking at the speculators and watching them
scurry about like chickens without heads, looking for business.
Everyone looked to make a ruble. But, in the meantime, while
pacing around and looking toward Fankonin, I spotted another general. He too was full of medals. Here's a neat one, I
thought. It's a God-send. Another general. A customer for my
last calendar.

A thought flew through my head. It's a shame I didn't have
any more calendars. For if generals start to buy Jewish calen-

dars, *all* the speculators can go to hell and take the entire stock-market with them.

While thinking, I looked and realized that it was *my* general. Believe it or not, I recognized him right away. Evidently he recognized me, too. How do I know? I saw him stand up and wave me over to him. Bad situation. What now? All I needed now was to get mixed up with generals. I kicked up my heels and started running, good and proper. I'd figured it out and knew that with such leg-work I'd put three streets between me and him in two minutes flat. That's exactly what happened. Half a minute later, I heard someone tailing after me, hollering for me to stop.

Who was it? Could it be the general himself, in all his glory? What an eager-beaver of a general! Just look what was happening! A Jew had sold an extra calendar—and what a commotion. Generals chasing me. Bad! Bad business! What was the next move? Run faster? But suppose he whistled for the cops? That's all I needed—an arrest! But if I stopped, he'd nab me with that second calendar fraud. Better to make believe that I didn't know what was happening and go my own sweet way—not running, but not crawling, either, just sort of stepping smartly, like a man busy with his own affairs. But what if he caught me and asked why I was running? Then I'd tell him that that was my way of walking.

But here's what happened. He caught up to me. Bad, huh? But listen to the upshot. Well, if you were caught, there was nothing to be done. So, I stopped and looked. But where was the general? General! What general? Baloney! It was just one of the waiters from the Fankonin cafe. He'd run with a napkin tucked under his arm, and was wiping the perspiration from his face.

"Damn you," he said to me, when we both had stopped. "Why'd you take off like a wild billy-goat? The general wants to see you?"

"What general? And how do you know it's me he wants?"

"What do you mean, how do I know? Think I'm deaf? Think I didn't hear the general say: there he goes, the Jew with the books. Catch him and bring him over."

If that's the case, I thought, then all hell hasn't broken loose yet. Doom isn't at hand. I could always think of something at the last minute. I'm only human, you know. Like a flash, a brand new idea hit me. Maybe a miracle would happen and I'd get rid of my last calendar. Without batting an eyelash, I slapped my forehead in mock surprise, spat, and said:

"Well, why didn't you say so in the first place? You should have told me it's the bookish general. He's a queer one. All day long he's been bargaining with me for this book. He's run me to death. It costs a ruble and he keeps offering me a half. I've already told him 75, 70, 60 kopeks. Let's call it quits. But he's as stubborn as a mule and won't budge from that half ruble. I should drop dead right here and now that if this weren't my last book, I wouldn't let him have it for a kopek under the regular price. But since it *is* the last one, as you can see, hand over half a ruble and here—run back and give him this book."

To this day, I don't know who the general was! But my guess is that it was none other than Tolmatshov himself. If not, why did he suddenly let loose such a murderous reign of terror against Jews in general and more so, against Yiddish book-peddlers in particular? We peddlers of Yiddish books and newspapers felt his wrath more than anyone else. To this very day, we don't dare show our faces on the streets selling a Yiddish book or paper. We have to hide it inside our coats like contraband or stolen goods. May my enemies, your enemies, and all enemies of the Jews have as many good years as we have profit out of dealing with hot Yiddish papers. So, I have to have a sideline—French postcards—some loose, some sealed in envelopes. And they're my main item. I handle the newspapers just for fun. But there's a bigger turnover in Parisian picture postcards. The speculators take to them more readily than to the Yiddish papers. Oh me, I know it's a foul business and I'll have to answer for it someday. . . . But what can you do? You're only human. A Jew has to make a living —the kids want to eat. . . . God'll probably forgive me. He'll *have* to forgive me. Has he got a choice? What do you think?

Here it is *Hoshana Rabba* already—and final judgments are being sealed.

May it fall on his head—the judgment, I mean. On Tolmatshov's head! For if it weren't for him, may he rot in hell, I'd still be selling prayer books and Jewish calendars instead of this filth. By the way, can I interest you in something? I just got a new shipment in fresh from Paris.

THERE'S NO DEAD

A month before *Rosh Hashana*, I returned to Kasrilevke to visit my parents' graves.

The ancient Kasrilevke cemetery was much nicer and livelier than the town itself. Here you found little tombstones finer than the nicest of Kasrilevke houses. What good came of the fact that the ground here was as dry as pepper in contrast to the town's muddy, swampy soil? Here, at least, you saw some green growth. In the summer, you saw green grass and two or three pear trees. You heard the twittering birds hopping from branch to branch, talking to one another in their own language. Here you saw the round, blue, skullcap-shaped dome of the sky and the bright warm sun. Not to mention the air! But what difference did it make? One was just as dead here as in town. There was a difference, though. Here, at the cemetery, the dead all lay in one spot. In town, they still walked around. Here, they were at rest and knew of no troubles. In town, they still had troubles and who could tell how many more there were yet in store for them in this world.

I saw a few women stretched out on the graves, crying, screaming, and pleading. One wanted her mother to rise and see what had become of her one and only daughter.

"Oh, if you would only rise, dear, sweet Mama of mine, and look at your one and only daughter, your Sore-Perl, the apple of your eye, and see how badly off she is. Oh, me! Me and my little naked chicks are living with others in a shared apartment. And the children don't have a shirt to their name. You know why? Because your Yisrolik has been sick ever since he went to the fair and caught cold. Now the doctors got hold of him, and I have to give him milk but we can't afford it. The poor kids yell for milk, too, and there is none. Henzil the Tailor, at whose place I'm staying, wants his rent

156

and I can't give it to him. And the long-overdue fees for
Hershel's Hebrew lessons—he's going to be Bar-Mizvah this
year—I don't have money for that either. I don't have money
for anything."

Another woman came to her father, complaining about the
husband the matchmaker sent her. They thought he would be
a bargain. They said he would be a prize. All the girls had
envied her. But he turned out to be a charlatan, a squanderer
who would shell out enormous sums for honors in the synagogue. He also spent a lot for books. He'd sell his own mother
and father for his books, but he didn't give a damn about her
being skin and bones and sick, as well.

The third woman came to bring glad tidings to her dead
husband. She was marrying off her eldest daughter and had
no money for the dowry, not even the first half, which he had
promised to pay. She had neither shirts nor shoes, not to mention money for the wedding expenses—musicians, waiters, this
and that. Where would she get money for that? She'd go out
of her mind if the match were broken, God forbid. What
would she do then?

All the other women cried and bemoaned their troubles,
emptying their bitter hearts by weeping, relieving themselves
by talking to their true loved ones. Perhaps this would make
them feel better. When you cried your heart out, you did feel
better.

As I roamed around among the half-sunken graves and read
the old, rubbed-out inscriptions on the slanting tombstones, I
was seen by Arye, the red-eyed, flaxen-bearded gravedigger.

"Who do you want to see?" he asked.

Reb Arye was so old that no one knew his real age, not
even Arye.

Nevertheless, he kept himself clean and neat and pampered
himself like a spoiled Mama's boy. His shoes were shined; each
hair of his beard was combed. He ate only soft foods and
drank the essence of boiled herbs and rock-candy every morning.

"He has it easy," is what Kasrilevke folk said of Reb Arye,
truly envying him.

"Hello, Reb Arye. How are you?" I said, approaching the old man. It was evening. The sun, about to set, lit up the edges of the tombstones. Reb Arye, shielding his red eyes from the sun, contemplated me and stroked his beard.

"Who are you, my son?" he said. "What do you want here?"

Reb Arye was so old, he could call anyone, my son.

I told him who I was and whom I wanted to see. Then he recognized me and greeted me, smacking his lips and talking with a whistle.

"Oh. Is it really you? I knew your father, even your grandfather, Reb Vevik. What a fine man he was! Your Uncle Pini, too, was a wonderful person. Your Uncle Berke is also buried here. So is your Aunt Khane. I knew them all. They're all dead. All the nicest people have died out. Not a one has remained. Mine have died, too," he sighed, and motioned with his hand. "First I buried my children, all of them. Then my wife died, a saintly woman she was, may I live and be well. Left all alone in my old age. No good."

"What's no good?" I asked him.

"It's no good," he said. "There's no dead."

"No dead?" I asked.

"There's no dead," he said.

"Have they stopped dying in Kasrilevke?" I asked.

"What has dying got to do with it?" he said. "Sure they still die. But who? It's either children, babies, or poor men. You can't make a thing on them, unfortunately. You've got to pass the hat around for shrouds and then after the orphans say the first mourner's prayer, you've got to give them a piece of bread, too. But what can you do? I have no choice." He pointed his dried-out hand toward the crying women. "Those women are stretched out on the graves like princesses. What do I have from them? They swell up like drums, crying! What do they care? Does it cost them anything? And it's me who has to go and show them where their dead are buried, where their mothers and fathers and uncles and aunts are. I've become their father's footman. Sometimes a woman cries so long that she faints. So I have to bring her to, give her some water.

Sometimes even a piece of bread. But where from? How? From the big income I have? There's no dead and you have to keep living and marry off your orphaned granddaughter who's of marrying age. She almost had a groom, the match was about to be made. He wasn't a bad young fellow, a porter, a widower with a few children, but he earned his living, a fine living, in fact. That is—if he had work, he earned money. They even got to meet each other. But before they got engaged, he said: 'Well, what about a dowry?' 'What dowry?' I said. 'I was told you were giving fifty rubles for a dowry,' he said. 'May all my wild nightmare seep into my enemies' skulls! Fifty? Where do I come to having fifty? Do you want me to steal it, or dig up others' shrouds from my graves and sell them?' To make a long story short, nothing came of the match. And if you talk to the Kasrilevke folk they'll insist that they're right. 'Reb Arye, you've got no ground for complaints —God bless you,' they say. 'You have yourself an excellent job.' An excellent job! If by some slight chance there happens to be a fine rich man around, he's been dead a long time. New ones don't come by. There's no dead. None at all!'"

HAPPY NEW YEAR!

Imagine, every single one of them up to Mr. Big himself takes bribes. Don't be shocked now—Mr. Big himself accepts them, too, if he gets an offer. What's that? You don't believe me? You're all laughing, eh? Well, have fun. . . . Ready now? Have you all laughed yourself dry? Now gather round me, brother Jews, and listen to a story that happened a long time ago to none other than my grandfather, may he rest in peace. It happened in the good old days when Czar Nich was boss. What are you nudging me for? Why be scared? You think these peasants sitting here know what we're jabbering about? They won't understand a word, blast them. I won't be obvious and where necessary I'll throw in some Hebrew. Just pay close attention and don't keep interrupting me and everything will be fine.

To make a long story short, it happened in the days of King Ahasuerus—in other words, during the reign of our present Mr. Big's grandfather, after whom he's named. May his grandfather have an easy time of it in the other world, for all the favors and fine and dandy things he let loose against our brethren—Amen. Our fathers and grandfathers just couldn't forget that old Mr. Big. Even when they suddenly awoke from their sleep, they thought well of him. That's how well off they were. In short, their whole life hung on a thread. We were allowed to exist just by the grace of little Mr. Big, or Buttons, as we called him. This Buttons liked to have his palms greased, and loved those Friday night snacks of *gefilte fish* and tumblers of whiskey. So long as this went on, the Jews breathed free and easy, did business, plied their trades, and really had a wonderful time.

But once—and whenever you hear *but once*, you know trouble's coming—something happened. Buttons kicked the

160

bucket. He suddenly just upped and dropped dead and was followed by a new Buttons, a Haman, a villain, a rat, the likes of which you've never seen! He couldn't be greased; he just wouldn't take a thing! They tried slipping him bigger bribes. Still, no. They tried the real thing—big money. Still nothing doing. They invited him for *gefilte fish*. He wouldn't go. They dropped hints about rare liqueurs. He didn't drink. Talk of being ethical! He was as clean as a whistle! If you begged him, he stamped his foot, kicked you out on your ear, and then did things which just weren't done. He kept issuing summonses; he slapped one fine after another on you. He didn't let Jews do business. He didn't let Jewish teachers teach. If he saw a young woman, he'd rip off her marriage wig. If he saw a young man, he'd snip off an earlock. "That's what Mr. Big does, too," he used to say. Then he would beam, get hysterical at his own joke, and shake until the tears came. . . . This made them burn with anger. But nothing could be done. What could Jews do? They did what they always did. They sighed softly, called one meeting after another, trying to think of what to do and how to get rid of such a Haman, the devil take him. They decided to go to my grandfather, Reb Anshel, may he rest in peace. Grandpa Anshel (after whom I'm named) was rich and came from a fine family. He was a follower of a Hasidic *rebbe*, a trustee in the synagogue, a big-shot with the authorities. In brief, a factotum. They came up to him and said: "For goodness sake, Reb Anshel, save the town. Tell us what to do."

My grandfather listened to them and said: "How can I help you, my children? Unless, of course, I can get to see my *rebbe*, may he live and be well. Whatever he'd suggest, we'd do."

No sooner said than done. My grandfather hated long, dragged-out affairs. He wasn't lazy, and money was no object. The town could bear the burden. Where the public's welfare was concerned, how could there be any excuses?

Grandfather Anshel got into his carriage, bade the townspeople goodbye, and left for the *rebbe*'s place one hot summer day. When he arrived, he started telling the *rebbe* the whole story. "It's horrible. It's a catastrophe. We have a man whose hands are clean." The *rebbe* closed one eye and made a motion with his hand, as if to say: hold up. I know everything.

How did he know? Only fools ask such questions. Those *rebbes* knew everything. . . . My grandfather wondered about it, but didn't say a word. He waited for the *rebbe* to speak. A minute later, the *rebbe* called out. "May you be inscribed for a year of health." This astounded my grandfather. How did happy New Year fit in here? Where was the connection? Here it was the height of summer and *Rosh Hashana*, the Jewish New Year, was a long way off. Why the New Year's greeting? But one doesn't question the *rebbe*. Grandfather waited patiently. Before bidding him goodbye, the *rebbe* called him over and said:

"Listen, Anshel" (they were all on a first-name basis with each other, those *Hasidim*), he sighed, "go home in peace and good health. Tell your village that I've wished them a happy New Year. When you arrive home, wait for the big fair. When the fair comes to town, I want you to buy a pair of choice horses, the finest money can buy. I want them to be full-blooded roans. I want both of them to be exactly alike, twins, as if one filly had borne them. They must be completely spotless. Without a freckle. Then, take those horses and hitch them to a carriage, the nicer, the better. Drive them to that city where Mr. Big makes his home. It starts with the letter *P*. When you get there, rest the first day, rest the second day, and rest the third day. The following morning, right after you've said your prayers, and the next afternoon, just before sunset, ride around the palace. But sit in the driver's seat like a lord who's out for a pleasure stroll. And it shall come to pass that, if they stop and ask you: how much do you want for those horses? you will say that you're not a horse-dealer. Now, Anshel," the *rebbe* concluded, "go home, and may God grant you success."

That's exactly what happened. When the big fair came, just like the *rebbe* said it would, my grandfather, Reb Anshel, attended it and bought a pair of full-blooded roans from a gypsy, the likes of which our forefathers never had seen. My grandfather was no connoisseur of horses, but their appearance was made to order—they were exactly alike and spotless, too. Just like the *rebbe* had predicted. After eyeing those horses, my grandfather wouldn't budge. The gypsy, noticing that the horses turned my grandfather's head, naturally put such a price on them that it made Reb Anshel's blood run cold. But there could be no excuses. It was a matter of life or death. The town had to be saved. The Jews had pawned everything they had. He started bargaining with the gypsy—a ruble up, a ruble down. You can be sure that he didn't leave without those horses. He bought them, hitched them to a carriage, and immediately set out for that very place which the *rebbe* had mentioned. He fulfilled everything to the letter. He and the horses arrived in *P* about a month before the start of the Jewish New Year. He rested three days and three nights. Then the next morning after prayers and again before sunset, he drove around the palace gates. He rode slowly. He didn't rush. He had plenty of time and rode back and forth in front of the palace three times. He followed all the *rebbe*'s commands to a *t*.

To make a long story short, he did this one day, two days, three days. Nothing at all happened. He became depressed. What would come of it all? But one mustn't think too deeply about it. If the *rebbe* had said something, surely it wasn't in vain. Listen to what happened! Once, as he was driving in front of the royal palace, he saw a Buttons approaching him, probably one of the adjutants. The adjutant stopped my grandfather, whistling strangely right into his face, inspecting the horses from all angles, like one who understood horse-flesh. Then he asked him:

"Listen here, you, how much do you want for these horses?"

Exactly what the *rebbe* said would happen. Reb Anshel's heart leaped a bit, and he answered as he was told to:

"I'm not a horse-dealer."

The Buttons looked angrily at him. "How do you come to such fine horses?"

This time, grandfather was quiet. He didn't know what to

say, because the *rebbe* didn't mention a question of that sort. The adjutant became infuriated and said:

"Perhaps you've stolen them, huh?"

Now grandfather's heart sank. I hope everything turns out all right, he thought. But he couldn't say a word. Finally, God inspired him with these words:

"Sir. These horses are mine. I bought them from a gypsy at a fair. I have witnesses. A whole townful of Jews."

"So you have witnesses, huh?" the adjutant said. "I know your sort of witnesses."

Then he started whistling again, looking the horses over. Finally, he said: "You know, the Czar liked your horses."

"What's the drawback?" said grandfather. "If he likes the horses, then my horses can be his horses."

Don't ask how Reb Anshel hit upon an idea like that. If it's fated, God gives you bright ideas. Since he was a wise man, as I've already pointed out, he understood that if the *rebbe* told him to parade around the royal palace, there was a reason for it—as you'll soon see.

Well, in a nutshell, they took the horses' reins, and led those full-blooded roans right into the royal courtyard and showed them to Mr. Big himself. As soon as he saw the horses, he couldn't leave them. Some sort of mystic power was in those animals. He looked at those horses for about an hour, staring at them and showing them off to his entire court. In short, he couldn't get enough of them. He fell in love with them at first sight. Meanwhile, grandfather Anshel was standing quietly on the side, watching the goings-on. He recognized Mr. Big immediately; he knew him from his pictures. But, never mind. It didn't faze him at all. He was just a man, like the rest of them. Then Mr. Big approached grandfather, and as soon as he looked at grandfather, a chill ran through his bones. And when he spoke with his lion's voice, grandfather's heart froze.

"How much do you want for those horses?" Mr. Big asked Anshel.

Grandfather could hardly speak. His mouth was dry, and he felt his voice shaking:

"I don't sell horses. But if his majesty has taken a liking to

the horses, and if his majesty will not be angry with me, let the horses be led into his majesty's stables. That's where they belong."

He couldn't say any more, for Mr. Big then looked at grandfather and his soul left him. Then, too, Mr. Big moved closer to Reb Anshel, talking to him. My grandfather practically turned into a heap of bones.

"Listen here. Perhaps you want some special favor. If you do, tell me right now with no bluffs, tricks, flim-flam, or long-winded Jewish commentary. For if you do, it'll cost you dearly."

Well, my dear friends, what do you think went through grandfather Anshel's mind at that time? Surely, the mother's milk in him curdled. But, since Reb Anshel was a brave man, as I told you, it didn't faze him. He plucked up his courage and told Mr. Big:

"Your majesty. King! I swear that I have no underhanded intentions, and I'm not the sort who likes to bluff or trick anyone. I don't ask a thing of his majesty. But I would consider it an honor and the greatest of favors if I could be worthy of having my horses in his majesty's stables and if his majesty would ride them."

Naturally, Mr. Big was moved by these words. He now started talking in a softer tone. His voice, his manner, his words—all changed. He was a new man. Then the Czar left the courtyard and headed for the palace—with grandfather Anshel trailing behind him. It didn't faze him a bit, but his knees shook and his heart ticked like a grandfather clock. Can you imagine—being in the Czar's palace! Wherever you looked, there was only silver and gold and everything was carved out of ivory. Crystal above, marble below, and pure amber on the sides. Amber, the stuff from which pipes and mouthpieces are made. All that wealth made grandfather dizzy, but he controlled himself. Mr. Big walked on with grandfather after him. Then, Mr. Big sat down and asked grandfather to have a seat, too. He offered grandfather a cigar, and grandfather took it and smoked it. It didn't faze him a bit. In the meantime, *she* came in—the Czarina herself,

draped in satin and silk and covered from head to toe with diamonds and other valuable stones which sparkled in front of
your eyes. She was as beautiful as the Queen of Sheba. So
lovely, you couldn't even look at her face. Seeing a Jew in
the king's company, comfortable and smoking a cigar, she
naturally became very angry and looked sternly at him, as if
to say: What's this Jew doing here?

But grandfather Anshel didn't let it bother him. He'd become so high and mighty, nothing bothered him. He continued smoking and didn't so much as glance at her. But she kept
staring at grandfather, looking daggers his way. Mr. Big understood that the guest didn't please her, but he ignored it. He
looked at her and said cheerfully:

"Dushinka, how about some tea?"

She remained silent.

The Czar repeated: "Dushinka. Tea!"

Again, she remained silent.

The Czar didn't delay, but stamped his foot and roared at
the top of his voice: "Dushinka! Tea!"

The window panes shook. It was nothing to sneeze at.
Treason, you know. . . . Immediately, adjutants and generals
started pouring into the place. In a flash, a boiling samovar,
all sorts of home-made jams, egg-bagels, and boiled eggs were
ordered. Boiled eggs—for the Czar's court knew that a pious
Jew wouldn't touch anything but boiled eggs. The Czar asked
him to eat and drink and make himself at home. By and by,
he asked grandfather who he was, what he did, how he earned
his living, and how the Jews of his area were doing. He
wanted to know everything. And he was so friendly, too. Just
imagine, grandfather Anshel answered every single question
one after the other. When it came to the question about the
Jews, he thought: Now's the time to bring up the subject.
Now I'll tell him, and I don't care what happens to me. . . .
Well, he told Mr. Big everything—and Reb Anshel had just
the tongue for it.

"Here's the whole story, your majesty. Your Jews have no
complaints. But if his majesty is in a good mood, and if I have
found favor in his majesty's eyes, and if his majesty will not

be angry at his servant, I shall tell you the whole truth. I'd like you to know, your majesty, that things are all right in your country and that the Jews live by grace of Buttons. If he's just a regular Buttons, it's fine and dandy. But if, God forbid, he isn't, then there's trouble. Not long ago, a new Buttons came into our village—clean as a whistle! And because of that, we're at the end of our rope! There isn't another one like him in the length and breadth of your majesty's entire realm. That a Buttons be incorruptible is something unheard of. It's the eleventh plague!"

Mr. Big looked at him and said: "I'll be honest with you. You're talking in riddles and circles and I haven't got the faintest notion of what you're trying to say. What do you mean by—clean as a whistle? And what do you mean by a—Buttons?"

"By clean as a whistle," grandfather said, "I mean a man whose palms won't be greased. By Buttons, I mean a little Mr. Big whom you appoint to watch over every little town. Well, Buttons watches those towns and in a few years becomes very rich. Who from? The Jews, of course. They've gotten used to it. Because just as Jews know they must pray every morning, they also know that an official must take, and a Jew must give. The same idea is found in our holy books. We always kept giving—for sacrifices, for the Temple, here, there. Having been so kind to your servant until now, you will show your grace and hear him out.

"I want you to know, your majesty, that your whole kingdom, from east to west, from north to south, is filled with takers. The only ones whose palms you can't grease are cripples who have no hands. And even he who has no hands, will tell you to slap it down on the table. There's nothing wrong with that, either. You have to live and let live. The Bible tells us to get along with our neighbor. So our commentator Rashi says—but if his dog barks, muzzle him."

Why are you men looking at me? Seems strange, doesn't it, that a Jew should talk this way to a king? Well, take it or leave it. I wasn't there—that any child will understand. But this is the story that my father—may he rest in peace, heard from *his* father. And I assure you that neither my father nor my grandfather Anshel were liars. The long and the short of it was that my grandfather said goodbye to the Czar and went straight to the *rebbe*, reporting back on his trip.

It was just before *Rosh Hashana*. Once in the re*bbe*'s house, he stood (one always stood before the *rebbe*) and told him the whole story from beginning to end. It turned out that grandfather Anshel needn't have bothered, for the *rebbe* knew all about it anyway. Then why did he let him keep talking? Because it wasn't polite to interrupt a man while he spoke. You see, those *Hasidim* are very strict about etiquette. The next day after the Sabbath service, they all sat around the table, waiting for the *rebbe* to speak. But he decided to talk about a verse which had nothing at all to do with the weekly portion of the Torah. Instead, he expounded on a verse from the chapters of admonition against Israel. The people were beside themselves with surprise.

"In the chapter of admonition in Leviticus," the *rebbe* began with closed eyes, as was the custom, "there is a curse, the simple meaning of which we cannot understand. The Bible says that God will send you a nation whose language you will not be able to understand. The question then arises, what sort of a curse is that? Let me repeat it—God will send you someone whose language you won't understand. How is that possible? That the gentiles (forgive the proximity) don't understand our language—well, that's natural—that's why they're gentiles. But that a Jew won't understand what the gentile is talking about? Where's the connection? Is there anything a Jew doesn't understand? If so, we have to interpret the verse differently. God will send forth a nation whose language you will not understand really means that God will send a gentile whom you won't be able to *talk* to. In other words, he'll be as clean as a whistle. His palms won't be greasable. And a gentile who doesn't take bribes is a catastrophe."

That's how the *rebbe* interpreted the verse from the Bible and the crowd was amazed. They licked their fingers and asked for more. Of course, only my grandfather and those close to the *rebbe* understood him. As soon as the Sabbath ended, Reb Anshel set out for home and just made it in time before the start of the Jewish New Year.

Well, listen to this. On the eve of the New Year, when the Jews were leaving the synagogues after prayers and wishing each other a happy holiday, a year of peace and good health—a rumor flashed through town that our Buttons, that our Haman, may he shrivel up, was fired, and in his place the authorities up-on-high had sent a new little Mr. Big, a man clever and wise, good and kind—in short, a jewel of a gentile, a regular Buttons. He took. He was a taker! But he had one flaw (did you ever see anyone completely perfect?) which was discovered later. He had a mighty dry palm. It had to be greased good and heavy. In fact, he took enough for himself and for the Buttons before him. He took from the quick and the dead.

But the upshot was that the Jews had a gay *Rosh Hashana* and an even gayer *Succoth*. Don't even ask about *Simkhas-Torah!* Then the Jews really had a grand time. It was said that even little Mr. Big, that is, the new Buttons himself, had a few drops and danced with the rest of the Jews. Well, it looks like we've arrived at our station. Be well and have a happy . . .

SOMEONE TO ENVY

In all of Kasrilevke's history, there was no finer funeral than Reb Melekh the Cantor's. Reb Melekh was a pauper, the poorest of the poor, just like the rest of the Kasrilevkite villagers. He received the funeral he did only because he died during the closing service of *Yom Kippur*. Only the saintly die in this manner.

The sun was about to set. It was bidding goodbye to Kasrilevke, shining straight through the old synagogue and lighting up the dead, worn faces, the yellow prayer shawls and the men's white prayer-robes which made them look like living corpses.

These live corpses had long ceased to feel the sensation known as hunger. They just felt their life-strength ebbing. They sat over their prayer book, swaying, refreshing themselves with spirits of ammonia and snuff, singing along with the Cantor.

Reb Melekh the Cantor, a handsome long-bearded, thick-necked man, had been standing on his feet since early that morning. He stood before the Creator with outstretched arms, praying devotedly, crying and pleading for mercy for the people who had chosen him to beg forgiveness for their great sins and ask that they be inscribed for a year of health and peace.

The people in the old synagogue could very well depend on Reb Melekh as intercessor. First of all—his voice. The old townspeople said that in his youth, Reb Melekh had a voice as clear and sharp as the roar of a lion. When he opened his mouth, the walls trembled and the windows shook. As of late, he had become a weeper. He cried as he sang, like a weeping willow, and, looking at him, the whole congregation would burst into tears, too.

As he grew older, his voice became rusty and only the weeping remained—but it was the sort of weeping that could move a wall, or wake the dead.

Reb Melekh lifted his hands, arguing with God in the age-old plaintive melody of the final *Yom Kippur* prayer.

"Oh, Father in Heaven. Oh me! Oh my!"

Hearing this, each person regretted his sins and prayed to God to erase, blot out, forget, and forgive all their transgressions and grant them and their naked, barefoot, and hungry children a good year.

Having reminded themselves of their poor, innocent children, their hearts melted like wax, and they were ready to fast three more days and nights so long as the Eternal One would grant them a year of health.

Meanwhile, Reb Melekh rested and caught his breath. Now he cleared his throat and sang a while in his old tremolo, and then resumed his plaintive cry:

"Oh, Father in Heaven. Oh me! Oh my!"

Suddenly, there was silence and the sound of a thump and a fall was heard. Everyone crowded around whispering.

"Come . . . oh . . . sext . . . oh me . . . sexton!"

Khayim the Sexton ran over, then lifted the Cantor. But Reb Melekh's head hung down, his eyes half open, his face white as chalk, his lips ashen. A bitter smile played on his lips.

The whole congregation pressed forward. They put spirits of ammonia under his nose. They sprinkled water on his face. They pressed his temples. But it was no use. Reb Melekh the Cantor was dead.

When a wolf attacks the flock and devours a lamb, the rest of the lambs panic; they go into a momentary panic. Then they press together and begin to tremble all over.

That's what happened in the old synagogue when Reb Melekh died. First a tumult broke out. An eerie scream was heard from the women's section. Tsviya, the Cantor's wife, had fainted. Looking at her, other women fainted, too.

Reb Yozifl, the village rabbi, signaled the trustees and they banged on the prayer stands for silence. Khayim the Sexton (who had led the morning service) went up to the pulpit and continued praying. The whole congregation prayed until Reb Nisel blew the ram's horn which officially brought *Yom Kippur* to a close. They immediately started the weekday evening service. After that, they went out into the courtyard to recite the benediction for the new moon. Then they went home to break the fast. Some did so by eating a quarter of a chicken, a remnant of the previous day's sacrificial fowl. Some did so by having only bread, herring, and water.

An hour after supper, the entire synagogue courtyard was packed with people. There was no room to breathe. Men and women, boys and girls, even babies, had gathered for the funeral.

The villagers themselves took care of the details, not allowing the sextons the privilege. It was no trifle—the Cantor was an important person.

The night was bright and warm. The moon shone down on Kasrilevke, delighted with the poor people who had come to pay their last respects to Reb Melekh the Cantor before he took his long last journey. When the funeral procession stopped in front of the synagogue, Rabbi Yozifl began his funeral oration. And all the people cried.

Rabbi Yozifl quoted the Bible and the Midrash and showed that Reb Melekh the Cantor's death was not that of an ordinary mortal. Only saintly, very saintly, men died that way. Such saints went straight to Paradise. Everyone ought to envy a man as saintly as he, for not all were worthy of dying at the pulpit during the closing *Yom Kippur* prayer, when God has forgiven man's sins. When a man as saintly as he is laid to rest, the entire village must accompany him. When a man as saintly as he dies, the entire village must cry and mourn.

"Cry then, fellow Jews, mourn this saintly man whom we have lost. Beg him to intercede for us before the Seat of Glory. Perhaps he will pray that we all have a year of peace and health. For it is high time that God had mercy on Kasrilevke and its Jews."

Everyone wept. Tears streamed from their eyes and they felt they had sent a fine emissary to God on their behalf.

At that moment, each person wished he were in Reb Melekh's shoes.

It seemed that Rabbi Yozifl forgot that he was addressing a corpse, and finished his funeral oration with these words:

"Well then, go in peace. Stay healthy and lots of luck to you."

For a long time thereafter, the Kasrilevke folk talked about Reb Melekh the Cantor's death and about the fine funeral he had. Mentioning it, they sighed:

"Ah, yes. There was someone to envy!"

AT THE DOCTOR'S

Just do me one favor, doctor. Listen to me until I finish. I don't mean listen to my heart or anything like that. About my sickness, we'll talk later. In fact, I myself will tell you what's wrong with me. I just want you to listen to what *I* have to say, for not every doctor likes to listen to his patients. Not every doctor lets his patients talk. That's a bad habit of theirs —they don't let their patients open their mouths. All they know is how to write prescriptions, look at their watches and take your pulse, your temperature, and your money. But I've been told you're not that sort of doctor. They say you're still young and you're not yet as passionate for the ruble as the rest of them. That's why I came to consult you about my stomach and get your advice. Look at me now and you're looking at a man with a stomach. Medical science says that *everyone* must have a stomach. But when? On condition that the stomach is a stomach. But when your stomach just isn't a stomach, your life's not worth a damn. I know what you'll say next: man must keep living! But I don't need your help for that. *That* got me the taste of the strap when I was a boy in Hebrew school.

My point is that so long as a man lives, he doesn't want to die. To tell you the truth, I'm not afraid of death at all. First of all, I'm over sixty. And second of all, I'm the sort of fellow to whom life and death are the same. That is, sure, living is better than dying, for who wants to die? Especially a Jew? Especially a father of eleven children, may they live and be well, and a wife—despite the fact that she's my third—but a wife for all that. To make a long story short, I come from Kamenitz, that is, not really from Kamenitz proper, but from a little place not far from Kamenitz. I'm a miller—unfortunately—I own a mill. That is, the mill owns me, for you

175

know what they say. Once you're dragged into it, you're finished. You've got no choice. It's a vicious circle and it just keeps on going. Figure it out for yourself. To buy wheat, I have to put up cash. To sell the flour, I have to give credit. I get a note here, a note there and I have to deal with low-down characters and women. Do you like women, doctor? Go give them an account of things! Why this, why that? Why didn't their Sabbath loaf come out well? Well, what fault is it of mine? Not enough heat in your stove, I say. Rotten yeast, perhaps. Wet wood. So what do they do? They step all over you, make mud of you, and swear that the next time their loaves are going to come flying straight at your head. Do you like having breads aimed at your skull? Those are the retail customers for you. But you think the wholesale buyers are any better? Not on your life!

When a wholesale customer first comes into the mill and wants me to give him credit, he flatters and compliments and sweet-talks me to beat the band. He's so butter-soft you can apply him to a third-degree burn. But when it comes to paying, he rattles off a list of complaints. The shipment came late, the flour-sacks were torn, the flour was bitter, moldy, and stale, and a dozen other phony excuses.

But money?

"Money?" he says. "Send me a bill."

In other words, it's as good as half-paid. Send him a bill and he'll say—tomorrow. Send one the next day and he'll say— the day after tomorrow. There's no end to it. The next thing you do is threaten him with a lawsuit and finally you take him to court. You think that settles it? The court gives you a lien on his house. So what? When you get there, the whole place, lock, stock, and barrel is in his wife's name anyway. What can you do? Call him a crook? Well, let me ask you, how can you not have stomach trouble with a business like this? It's not for nothing that my wife says to me: "Give up the mill, Noah, give it up." She's not my first wife, you know, but my third. And a third wife, they say, is like the December sun. But you can't do away with her, she's still your wife. "Give it up," she says, "let it and the wheat business burn to a crisp and then I'll know you're alive and around."

"Ha," I say, "if it only *would* burn. It's insured for plenty."

"I don't mean it that way," she says. "I mean you're always running here and there. For you there's no Sabbath, no holiday, no wife, no children. Why? Why all the tumult?"

For the life of me, doctor, I myself don't know what I'm dashing around for. But what can I do? That's my nature, the deuce take it. I like to panic and rush. What do I get out of it? Headaches, that's all. But I'll take on any business deal you offer. For me there's no bad deal. Bags, wood, auctions. Anything.

You think the mill is my only business? You're mistaken if you do. For you're looking at a man who's a partner in a timber firm, supplies food for the local jail, and has a share in the meat-tax concession—on which I lose money every year. Doctor, I wish you'd make in a month what I lose in a year. Then you'd say I was a friend of yours. So, why bother with it? To spite them all. Me? I'm a man who likes to win out. I don't care if I ruin the whole town and myself included so long as I win out in the end. I'm not such a bad guy at heart, but I have my little whims. I'm a hot-head. When you step on my honor, I'm dangerous. To top it off, I'm a stubborn mule, as well. In the old days, I took my little synagogue to court just for an "Amen" that didn't please me. I was ready to give my all just to see them lose out. And they did. I can't help it. That's the way I am. The doctors tell me it's nerves and it's got to do, they say, with the stomach. Despite the fact that it makes no sense, logically. What connection is there between nerves and the stomach? Strange bedfellows! After all, where are the nerves and where is the stomach? Doesn't medical science say that the nerves are mostly in the brain? And the stomach . . . the devil knows how far away it is! Wait a minute, doc . . . hear me out. . . . I'll be through in a minute. I want to tell you the whole story so that you'll be able to tell me why this plague had to come upon me, my stomach, I mean.

Maybe it's because I'm always scurrying about and am never at home. Even when I am at home, I'm not at home. It's a joke and I'm ashamed to say it—but I swear I don't even know how many children I have and what their names are. A home's no good without a master and without a father. You ought to take a look at my house—knock wood—and see what a mess it's in. It's like a boat without a rudder. The place is in an uproar and a tumult day and night. It's frightening! Eleven kids from three wives, may no harm come to them, is nothing to sneeze at! While one has tea, the other has a snack. When I'm saying my morning prayers, the other one decides to go to sleep. That one filches a potato, the next one wants some herring. This one wants a dairy meal, that one yells his lungs out for meat! After you're washed and sitting at the table ready to say the blessing over the bread—well, there's no knife in sight to cut the bread with. And in the midst of it the little ones are making a racket, fighting with each other, raising all hell—it's enough to make you run away. Why does all this happen? Because I'm never at home and never have any time for them, and my old lady, God bless her, is too good. Well, that is to say, she's not good. She's more of a softie. She can't handle the children. You have to know how to handle them. So they step all over her. She curses, pinches, rips chunks of flesh out of them, but what good is it? She's a mother, after all. A mother's no father, you know. A father grabs hold of a kid and beats hell out of him. That's what my father did to me. Perhaps your father did the same to you, doctor? What do you say? Well, good for you! I don't know . . . maybe you would have been better off without the beatings. What are you squirming about for? I'm going to finish in a moment.

I'm not just barking at the moon, doctor. I want you to know what sort of life I lead. You think I know how much I'm worth? Possibly I'm rich, quite rich. Then again, chances are that—just between you and me—I don't have much at all. I don't know! All day long it's repairs. Like they say: one window pane goes, another comes in its place. You can't help it. Another thing—whether you can afford it or not, you got to give your child a dowry. Especially if God has been kind and you've got grown daughters. All right, doctor, *you* just try and have three grown daughters—God bless them—and marry them off all in one day and then we'll see if you'll be able to sit home and relax for even a day. Now you know the reason for all my running around from pillar to post. And when you rush about like that you catch cold in the train, or gulp down a quick meal in a flea-bitten inn which gives you heartburn and indigestion. And what about all the odors and stale air in the car—isn't that enough to give you a stomach? My only bit of luck is that nature has protected me and I'm not the sickly sort. I've been immune to sickness since I was a boy. Don't mind me being a scarecrow, all skin and bones. That's what my business did for me. Height like mine runs in the family, by the way. We're all tall and thin. I had a few brothers and they were all like me, may they rest in peace. Nevertheless, I was always healthy, never had any stomach trouble, had nothing to do with doctors or illwinds—may it continue that way! But recently they started stuffing medicines and pills and herbs down my throat. Each one comes with a different remedy. This one says: diet, starve yourself. That one says: don't eat at all. You think that's the end of it? Another quack comes along and tells me to eat, but really pack it in. It looks like doctors prescribe what they themselves enjoy doing. I'm surprised they haven't told me to start swallowing rubles yet. They can drive you crazy. One doctor told me to walk a lot. Just get on my feet and head for God-knows-where. Then the other doctor tells me to lie flat on my back and not budge a muscle. Now try and guess which one of them is the bigger ass! You want more proof? One of them kept me on a fifty-two week silver-chloride diet. Pure silver-chloride. When I went to a second doctor, *that* one told me: "Silver-chloride? God forbid! Silver-chloride will be the death of you." So he prescribed a yellow powder, you probably know which one I mean. Then I went to a third doctor and don't you think he took the yellow powder and ripped up the pre-scription and prescribed an herb? And some herb it was! You can take my word for it that before I got used to that grass I was spitting gall. I used to curse that doctor three times a day, once before each meal when I took the herb. I hope that only half of what I wished him comes true. While taking that herb I used to see the Angel of Death face to face. But what won't a man do for his health's sake? The upshot was that I came back to the first doctor, the one who gave me silver-chloride, and told him the story about the bitter herbs which made my life miserable. He was mad as hell and bawled me out as if I'd stepped on his hat.

"I prescribed silver-chloride," he said. "Silver-chloride! So why are you skipping around like an idiot from one doctor to another?"

"Shh! Tone it down," I said. "You're not alone here. I didn't sign any contracts with you. The next fellow has to make a living too. He's got a wife and family, same as you."

Well, you should have seen him! He blew his stack as if I'd told him God knows what! The long and the short of it was that he asked me to go back to the other doctor.

"I don't need your advice," I told him. "If I want to go, I'll go on my own."

Then I pulled out a ruble and put it on his desk. You think he threw it back at my face? Not at all. They like those little rubles. Boy do they like those rubles! More so than us plain folk. To sit down and examine a patient properly—that they'll never do. They don't let you say an extra word. Recently, I visited a colleague of yours. You know him, so I won't mention his name. I came into his office and before I could say boo he told me to—begging your pardon—strip and lie down on the sofa. Why? He wanted to examine me. Fine and dandy. Examine me! But why can't I say a word? What good does his finger-tapping and pinching do me? But no. He was in a rush. Had no time. He said that there were other people there, on the other side of the door, each waiting for his "next." You doctors have taken up the latest fashions. You have your "nexts" just like the ticket windows at the depot or the stamp lines at the post office. What's that you say? You don't have time either? Oho, now tell me that you *too* have "nexts" waiting out there! You're just a young doctor! Where do you come off having a waiting line? If you continue this way, you hear, you're going to have troubles, not a practice. And you don't have to get hot under the collar about it either. I didn't expect to come here without paying. I'm not the sort of person who'll ask you to do anything for him for nothing. And though you didn't want to hear me out—one thing has nothing to do with the other. I'll pay you for the visit. What's that? You don't want anything for it? Well, I'm not going to force you. You probably have your own source of income. Perhaps you clip bond coupons? Your kitty's swelling, eh? Well, in any case, may God be with you and may the kitty grow and grow. Goodbye! Pardon me if I've taken too much of your time. But that's what a doctor's for.

THREE WIDOWS

1. Widow Number One

You're sadly mistaken, my dear sir. Not all old maids are unhappy and not all bachelors are egoists. You think because sitting here in this room, cigar in mouth and book in hand, you know it all; you've probed deep into the soul and you've got all the answers. Especially since, with the good Lord's help, you've hit upon the right word—psychology. Tsk, tsk. You're really something! It's nothing to be sneezed at—psycho-lo-gy. You know what the word means? Psychology means parsley. It looks pretty, smells nice, and, if you put in into a stew, it's tasty. But go chew parsley raw! Not interested, huh?

Then why tell me about psychology? If you want to know what psychology *really* is, sit yourself down and pay close attention to what I'm going to tell you. Afterward, you can have *your* say about how unhappiness and egoism began. Here am I, an old bachelor—and an old bachelor I'm going to be until my dying day! Why? There you go! You see, you've asked why and you're willing to listen to me. That shows true psychology! But the main thing is not to interrupt me with questions. As you know, I've always been a bit touchy and lately I've become more nervous. Don't worry—I'm not crazy, God forbid. Madness—that's more up your alley. You're married. I don't dare go *meshugge*. I have to remain sane and healthy. Even you'll admit that. In a word—don't interrupt me with questions. And if something still puzzles you after the telling—complain *then*. All right? Well, here we go. But first let's change seats. If you don't mind, *I'll* sit in the rocking chair. I too like a soft comfortable seat, but you'll be better off in my straight-backed chair. You won't doze off.

Now for the story. I hate long-winded introductions. Her
name was Paye, but she was called "the young widow." Why?
Here we go with whys! What's so difficult about that? They
probably called her "the young widow" because she was young
and she was a widow. And think of it! I was younger than
her. How much younger? What difference does it make to
you? If I say younger, I mean younger. And there were people
with wagging tongues who said that since I was a bachelor and
she a young widow . . . you get me? Others even congratulated me and wished me luck. Believe it or not! Even if you
don't believe me, it's no skin off my back. I don't have to brag
to you! She and I were a couple like you and I are a couple.
We just happened to be good friends, no more and no less.
We liked each other. Why do I mention it? You see, I knew
her husband. Not only did I know him, but we were friendly.
That doesn't mean we were friends. I'm just saying we were
friendly. Two different things, you know. You can be
friendly with someone without being friends. And you can be
close friends without being friendly. Anyway, that's my
opinion. I'm not asking you what you think.

Well, I was quite friendly with her husband. I played cards
with him, sometimes even chess. People say I'm a great chess
player. But I'm not bragging. Maybe there are better ones.
I'm just telling you what they say. Her husband was a clever,
well-versed fellow. He knew his stuff. Self-educated too—no
high-school, no college, no diplomas. I'll give you a whole
ruble now for all diplomas. What's that you say? No sale?
As you wish. I hate to talk anyone into anything.

Her husband was rich to boot, very rich. Although I don't
know what you consider rich. In our eyes, a Jew is rich if he
has his fully-furnished home, a thriving business, and a carriage
to take him to and from town. That's what we call rich. We
don't make a big to-do, we don't raise a fuss. We don't aim for
the moon. We take it easy. In short, he had a fine business and
lived well. It was a pleasure to step into his house. Whenever
you dropped in you were welcome. Not like at any other place
where they don't know what to do with you the first time you
come, the hospitality cools off a bit the second time, and the

third time, the reception is so chilly that you catch cold. That's nothing to smile at! I don't mean anyone I know, God forbid. If you come into their house you don't leave without eating and drinking. They treated you like one of their own. You want more? If a button came off your jacket it had to be sewn on on the spot.

You're laughing! You think it's a big joke! A button! What's a button, eh? To a bachelor, my dear friend, a button is an important thing. An entire world. On account of a button a terrible thing once happened. A young man came to look at a girl, a prospective match. The people in the house pointed their fingers at him and laughed. He had a button missing. He went home and hanged himself. But I don't want to get involved in *that* story. I hate to mix one thing with another. . . . Paye and her husband got along so well together. Like a pair of doves. They respected each other much more than some of these highfalutin folk. But—I don't want to knock anyone. Even if you think I do, what do I care? Here's the story.

One day, Pini, Paye's husband, came home sick and was in bed for five days. On the sixth—no more Pini. Just like that! How? Why? Don't ask! He had a little tumor on his neck. They were supposed to operate on it, but didn't. Why? *Y*'s a crooked letter, that's why. After all, we're blessed with doctors. I brought him two doctors. So they argued with each other. One said operate, the other said don't. Meanwhile, the patient died. Imagine that! You can keep all those doctors. If I made a list of how many people they've sent packing to the next world, your hair would stand on end. In fact, they poisoned my own sister. What do I mean by poisoned? Did they feed her arsenic? I'm not crazy enough to tell you that sort of fairy tale. Poisoned means not giving the proper medicine. If they had given her quinine in time, they might have saved her. Don't start fidgeting now. I haven't gone off the track.

Well, that put an end to Pini. I can't tell you what sort of a blow that was to me. A brother, a father couldn't have mourned him any more. Pini! A part of me died with him. Oh the pity of it, the tragedy. The poor widow's grief! Left with a tiny baby, a little flower, pure gold. Our only consolation!

If it weren't for the baby, Rose, I don't see how we could have taken it, she and I. I'm neither a woman, nor a mother who showers praises on babies. But if I tell you that the baby was an exception, take my word for it. Pretty as a picture, she had the best of two beautiful parents. I don't know who was nicer looking, he or she. Pini was handsome, Paye was lovely. The baby had her father's blue eyes. We both loved the baby. I don't know who loved it more, she or I! How is it possible, you ask? She was the mother and I was a stranger. But one thing's got nothing to do with the other. You have to look more deeply into the matter. My connection to the house, my pitying the widow and the innocent little orphans, the baby's charm, and me being as lonely as a stone—take all this, put it together, and you'll have what you call psychology. Not parsley, but pure, unadulterated psychology. Now you'll say I did this because I was in love with the mother. I don't deny that I loved her very much. Do you know how much I loved her? I was always right next to her. I was dying for her. But let her know this?! Not on your life. I spent sleepless nights thinking of how to say it to her. "Listen, Paye, it's like this, you know—I mean, you understand."

But when it came to saying it—I couldn't open my mouth. Go ahead, say that I'm a coward. Say it. What do I care what you say? But think deeply about it—Pini was a true friend of mine. I loved him more than a brother. But here's the problem. Paye! I've just said I was dying for her, haven't I? So the answer is, just *because* I loved her, just because I was crazy for her, just *because* I'd do anything in the world for her—I couldn't say it. But I'm afraid you won't understand me. If I'd have told you *psychology*, you'd have understood. But if I tell you straight from the heart, without any pretensions, then it sounds like a wild tale. But what do I care! You can think what you like. I'm going on my own sweet way and continue the story.

The girl grew up, talked like an adult. A child grows, a tree grows. A radish grows too. But there's a world of difference between one growing thing and another. You have to wait so long to see a baby sit and stand, walk, run and talk! And when

it does all these things, are you through? You want me to be
an old hen and figure out all the things that can happen to a
child: chickenpox, measles, teeth, and so on. But I'm no old
hen and won't take up time with any of these silly things. I
won't tell you any of her clever sayings. She grew and devel-
oped and got smarter each day. I'd say she was like a beautiful
rose, if I wanted to express myself like your novelists, who
understand a rose like a Turk understands Yiddish. Those
novelists are great ones for warming their feet at a fireplace
and writing about nature, green forests, the roaring sea, sandy
hills, and all sorts of flim-flam about things gone by. I can't
stand them and I can't stand their writing. They get on my
nerves. I don't even read them. If I get hold of a book and see
that the sun shone, the moon floated by, the air was fragrant,
the birds tweeted—I fling it across the room. You're laughing,
huh? You say I'm a bit touched. All right, then, so I'm not
all here. At least it can't get any worse.

Well then, Rose grew up and was, of course, raised properly, as befitted an intelligent family. The mother looked after
her education a bit, and I, too, took part. Not a little either,
but a lot. Actually, you can well say that I spent all my time
with the girl, saw to it that she had the best teachers, that she
wasn't late to class, that she took piano lessons and learned to
dance. I was everywere. I, alone. Who else? I handled the
widow's affairs too. If not for me, she would have been ruined.
As is, our Jews duped her. I know you get mad when I say
"our Jews." What else can I say if that's the sort of people
they are. You can call me an anti-Semite. It's your choice. It
doesn't bother me in the least. I go on my own sweet way.
May the anti-Semites have as many plagues as I know what a
Jew is. Don't talk to me about Jews. I've had enough dealings
with them. You know that I own houses and stores which
bring in a large and steady income. I have plenty of contact
with them each time it comes to renewing the leases, fixing up
the houses, collecting the rent. But the gentiles are no better,
though—blast them! However, you would've expected a Jew
to be on a higher level. After all—the Chosen People, as we
say. You think you're doing them a big favor by singing them

this praise. Not at all! What's that you say? You can't stand
this? I don't want to start any arguments with you. Whatever
you say is fine with me. Every man to his own opinion. I don't
care what anyone else thinks. I just know what I think.

Well, where were we? Speaking of the Jews. As soon as
Pini died and Paye was left a widow, all sorts of nice people,
do-gooders, and advice-givers started streaming to her. They
crowded the rooms and wanted to carry away everything she
had. But I stood up in time, said, "hold it!" and took all her
affairs into my hands. She even wanted me as her partner, but
I said: "No! I'm not selling my houses for I don't want any
headaches." So she said: "You don't have to sell your houses.
You can be a partner just like that." Well what do you think
I told her? I told her not to offer me terms like that in the future, for they made me angry. I told her that Pini, may he rest
in peace, didn't deserve that I be paid for my help and my
time. I didn't want any payment. I had so much time I didn't
know what to do with it. When I told the widow this, she remained silent. She lowered her eyes and didn't say boo. If
you're subtle, you'll know what I meant by saying what I
said. Oh, why didn't I tell her right away? Never ask me why!
It just didn't work out. But you can be sure that it would have
been as easy as pie. Just one word and we could have been man
and wife. But as soon as I started thinking of Pini and what
good friends we were . . . I know what you're going to say
—that things weren't so red-hot between Paye and me. You're
sadly mistaken. I told you before that I was dying for her.
And I don't have to start telling you stories about how badly
she wanted me, for you're liable to think that . . . but what
do I care what you think! You better tell your maid to bring
some tea. My throat is as dry as a stick.

Well, then, my dear sir, where did we leave off? The business. Business! That's one thing I'll remember as long as I live.
Exploited left and right! Sucked dry! Get that happy look
off your face. It wasn't me. It was the widow. No one ex-
ploits me. You know why? Because I don't let them. But what
difference does it make—letting them yes, or letting them no,
if you're with crooks, swindlers, and scoundrels who'll con-

found anyone. They tried their damnedest to take our money. But know that money isn't taken from me that quickly. They sweated plenty, they spit blood, damn their hides, until they pumped—you want to know how much? As much as they could. Luckily, I noticed it in time and put my foot down. Enough, I said. I started to cut off all transactions, but just while I was cutting them, they cut her head off. And I mean cut. How could I have let them do it, you ask? I'd love to see how a smartie like you would have given those blackguards the slip. Maybe you would've done better. Could be. I won't argue the point. The only thing that can be said of me is that I'm no businessman. I should care! So long as they don't call me a swindler! No doubt you think it didn't cost me anything. But I don't want to brag. I just want you to know how it all led up to the point where the widow and the bachelor should have joined forces. Only one word was needed. Just one. But I didn't say it. Why? Well, listen, that's where the dog lies buried. Here's where the real psychology begins. The start of a new chapter called Rose. Listen carefully and don't miss a word, for it isn't a concocted tale, understand? It's a living, throbbing story, plucked right out of the heart.

I don't know why, but in each mother there seems to be some sort of hidden force. It gives her the mad desire to see her daughter engaged the minute she outgrows her baby clothes. The mother is the picture of glowing health when she sees young men chasing around her girl. Every boy is a prospective husband to her. His being a nothing, a faker, a gambler, and the devil knows what else doesn't bother her at all. You can be sure that no nobodies and no fakers came within ten feet of us. Because, first of all, Rose wasn't the type to have anything to do with those dancers who could do a neat two-step, curl their hands into a bagel-like flourish, politely scrape their feet, and bow a welcome like an honest-to-goodness officer. That's one. And, second of all, what about me? Do you think I'd stand for any run-of-the-mill fly-by-night getting within look-ing distance of her? I'd sooner break every bone in his body. His name would have been mud.

Once I was at a dance with her, at an aristocratic Jewish

club. You know, those you call the bourgeoisie. Well, one of those dudes came up to her. He bent his elbows like a bagel, tilted his head a bit, and scraped his little foot. A honey-like smile broke over his face and with a squeaky girlish voice, he said . . . The deuce knows what he said! He invited her to dance. You can imagine what sort of a dance he got from me. He'll remember that dance the rest of his life. Well, we certainly had a good laugh over that bungler. That taught the fellows a lesson. If they wanted to meet Rose, they had to meet me first—undergo a little examination—and then proceed. They nicknamed me Cerberus, the watchdog who guards the gates of Paradise. Well, it was no money out of my pocket! But you know who got angry? Rose's mother.

"You're chasing people away from the house," Paye told me.

"What do you mean, people?" I said. "They're not people. They're dogs."

Well, this happened once, twice, three times, until the roof fell in. What do you think happened then? Think we had a fight? You're pretty smart—but you didn't guess this time. Before you start guessing, pay attention.

One day, I came into my widow's place and found a guest there, a young man about twenty or thirty. There are some sort of young folk—you can never tell how old they are. This chap, there's no denying it, was a charming fellow, the sort you take a liking to right away. He had a kind face and gentle eyes. Couldn't complain about him. Do you know why? Because I hate those overly sweet characters with their sugary faces and honeyed smiles. I can't stand looking at those nasty, smiling, yes-men. They'll say yes to an August snowstorm and agree to fish growing on a cherry tree. If I run into someone like that, I just want to smear honey all over him and let the bees have a picnic. You want to know what this young man's name was? What's the difference? Let's say he was called Shapiro. Satisfied? He was a bookkeeper in a distillery, not just bookkeeper, but virtual boss. And, what's more, he had more to say in that place than the real boss. But what's the good of being boss if you don't trust your workers? You may think differently. But I'm not asking you.

In short, they introduced me to this young Shapiro the Bookkeeper, the boss, a sincere boy who played an excellent game of chess. That is, no worse than mine. If you want to think he's a better player than I, go ahead. But I told you I don't make a big chess player of myself. All right, so be a prophet and foresee that there's a whole romance involved. And what a romance! What a passion! What an ass I was not to see it right away. Imagine, I myself added fuel to the fire, praised Shapiro to high heaven, made a fuss over him. May all the chess sets and all the chess-players burn to a crisp! While I kept playing chess with him, his mind was elsewhere. I took his queen and he took my Rose. I checkmated him in ten moves and he checkmated me in three. For his fourth move, that is, the fourth time he came, the widow called me aside. There was a strange light in her eyes as she told me the good news. Things clicked. The match was on. Rose was engaged to Shapiro. My widow was in seventh heaven and gushed with congratulations for me and her and both of us.

I don't want to tell you what happened to me when I heard the glad tidings. You'll say that I'm a gangster, a madman, a lunatic. That's what the widow said, too. First she laughed, then she bawled me out and started crying. This was followed by an attack of hysteria with all the trimmings. What a conflict. Well, the blister finally burst and we had hard words. We didn't spare each other, and in one half-hour we said more truths to each other than we did in our entire twenty-year friendship. I told her quite openly that she was my Angel of Death, that she slaughtered me without a knife, that she'd taken away from me my only consolation, had broken my heart and had taken my soul—Rose—away from me and had given her to another.

She replied that if anyone was an Angel of Death, it was I and no one else, and if anyone had broken another's heart, it was I who broke hers and not all at once either, but slowly, bit by bit, over a period of eighteen years. What she meant by

that—well, I don't have to tell you. Any fool would know.
I'm not obliged to tell you what I answered. I can only say
that I didn't act like a gentleman. That is—I was rude, quite
rude. I grabbed my hat, slammed the door, and ran out like
a madman. I gave my word that I'd never set foot in that house
again. Well, what do you think? You're a scholar of sorts. What
does your psychology have to say for that? What was I to do
next? Drown myself? Buy a pistol? Or hang myself on a
tree? It's obvious that I neither drowned, shot, nor hanged
myself, thank God. As to what happened later, we can save
that for another time. You won't burst if you wait a while.
I have to be off to my widows. They're expecting me for
supper.

2. Widow Number Two

Why'd I let you wait so long? Because I wanted to. When
I tell a story, I tell it when *I* want to *tell* it, not when *you* want
to *hear* it. It's obvious that you want to hear it pretty badly.
Everyone wants to listen to a story, especially a good one.
After all, what do you care if you sit at home smoking an
after-dinner cigar in a comfortable chair while I tear my lungs
out talking. The fact that the teller eats his heart out—what's
that to you? So long as you hear a fine tale. No, no, I don't
mean you, don't get scared. You just pay close attention to
what I'm telling you. Despite the fact that what I shall tell you
now has nothing to do with what I told you last time, I'd
still like you to remember what I said, because there is a little
bit of a connection between them. Not only a little, but a lot.
If you've forgotten anything, I'll remind you. In fact, I'll tell
you the whole story in a nutshell.

I had a friend Pini, who had a wife Paye, who had a daughter Rose. Pini died, leaving Paye a widow. I was a friend of
the family, a secretary, a brother. I was mad about her. But
I didn't have the courage to tell her. So passed the best years
of our lives. Her daughter grew up, the rose bloomed, and I

was a lost soul. Completely lost. Then out of the blue there came Shapiro the Bookkeeper who didn't play a bad game of chess and Rose fell for him. So, I poured all the stored-up bitterness within me onto the mother, had a fight, slammed the door, and swore never to set foot in their house again. Happy now?

Now I know that you want to know one thing. Did I keep my word? But after all, you're a . . . what do you call it . . . a psychologist. In that case, *you* tell *me*—was I supposed to keep my word or not? Aha! You're not saying a thing. Do you know why? Because you don't know. Here's what happened.

I roamed all over town that night, like a maniac. I measured the length and breadth of each street at least three times, came home at dawn, looked over all my papers, tore many of them up—I hate old papers, you see—packed my things and wrote letters to a few acquaintances. I have neither friends nor relatives, thank goodness. I'm as lonely as a stone. I left instructions about the disposal of my houses and stores, and when I finished doing all this, I sat down on my bed, held my head, and thought and thought and thought until sunrise. I washed, dressed, and went to see my widow. I rang the bell, was admitted, told the maid I'd have some coffee until Paye got up. My widow got up and when she saw me, she stood without moving, her face pale, her eyes puffy. It seems that she too didn't get too much sleep that night. The first thing I said were these three words. "What's Rose doing?"

As I said this, Rose herself came in, lovely as the day, bright as sunshine, good as God. Seeing me, she blushed, then came up to me and patted me on the head, just like a baby. Then she looked into my eyes and burst out laughing. What do I mean by that? It was not an insulting laugh, but one which so charmed you that soon you, the world, the very walls were laughing. Yes, my dear friend, that's the sort of power she has to this day. For her laughter I'd give away everything I have. Even now! The only trouble is, she doesn't laugh any more. She has her troubles, poor thing, and ah me, there's no room for laughter. But I hate to put one thing before another. I like things to be in their proper order. In that case, let's proceed in order.

Do you know what it's like to marry off a daughter? You don't? Then you're better off! I know very well what it's like, even though it was someone else's daughter. I'll never forget it. What was I supposed to do, I ask you, if my widow Paye was the sort of woman who was used to having everything prepared for her? Whose fault is it if not mine? I taught them, mother and daughter both, that if they ever needed anything, all they had to do was tell me and, although the world turned upside down, they'd have it within the hour. Money—they came to me. Need a doctor—they came to me. Hire a cook—me. A dancing instructor—yours truly. Clothes, shoes, a tailor, butcher, baker, candlestick maker—me. A pen, a pin, a screw, me, me, me. Don't you think I told them, "what's going to become of you? A dish rag!" That's what I told them, but they laughed. Everything was one big joke. There are people like that, you know. Not many, but they're around. It's my luck that their path had to cross mine. Who had to play nursemaid to others' children? Me! Who had to go *meshugge* with other peoples' troubles? Me! Who had to dance at others' weddings? Me! Who had to mourn at others' graves? Me! Who asked you to, you say. But my answer is, who asks you to run into a burning house and save someone else's child? Who asks you to jump into the water when another is drowning? Who asks you to make faces when someone else is in pain? You'll probably say that you don't run, jump, or make faces. Well then, you're an animal. I'm no animal. I'm human. I don't make myself out to be an idealist. I'm an ordinary, run-of-the-mill person and a confirmed old bachelor to boot. Despite the fact that your psychology says that an old bachelor is an egoist. Maybe that in itself is egoism. What's that? You hate that sort of philosophizing? Me, too. All right, then, we had to marry off my widow's daughter, Rose, and I had to make believe I was one of the family. Did I have a choice? And knowing me and my quirks you know how much I liked that. I hate that expression, "one of the family." Call me lackey, servant, footman, call me whatever you like, but don't call me "one of the family." But my widow was all aglow with the new name she had—"in-law." Call her "in-law" and she melted with joy. "Well, you'll soon be a mother-in-law," I told her. She lit up like a bulb. "I hope I live to see it," she said. What a mother-in-law! You should have seen her at the wedding. Pretty as a picture. And young, too. You'd never guess they were mother and daughter. You'd swear they were sisters. I just kept staring at her under the bridal canopy and thought: What an idiot you are! You lonely old character. Here's your chance. With just one word you can stop being lonely. With just one glance . . . you'll build your own home, plant your own garden . . . and you'll step into Paradise. You'll live a peaceful life among your own true loved ones. Get Rose out of your mind. Rose isn't for you. Rose is a baby compared to you. Don't be foolish. Look at the mother! Just say the word, you dumb ass. Tell *her* and no one else. What are you dilly-dallying for? Can't you see how she's looking at you? Just look at her eyes!

That's what I said to myself as I met Paye's eyes and I felt part of my heart breaking. I felt such pity for her. You listening? Pity was what I felt. Nothing more than pity. There was a time I had another feeling. Now, only pity remained. But talking of pity, maybe I'm to be pitied too. And maybe I more than her? Did I owe her something? Why did she keep still until now. Why was she silent now? Where is it written that I had to tell her and that she couldn't tell me. Shyness, you're going to say. The way of the world. That's the way convention has it. Well, I laugh at your convention. It makes no difference to me if *he* or *she* says it first. People are people. If she says nothing, I say nothing. You want to call it stubbornness, ambition, lunacy? Call it what you will. I told you once before that it makes no difference to me. I'm pouring my heart out to you because I want us both to analyze it and find out where the loose screw is. Maybe the answer is that Paye and I had never been alone for two minutes. There was always someone else around who took up our time, our thoughts, our feelings, our troubles, and our joys. All these belonged to others, not to us. But that we be alone together—not on your life! It's as if we were both made to cater to others. First it was Pini. Then the good Lord sent us little Rose. Now he'd sent us another bundle of joy: a freeloading son-in-law. But he was the right man. Any Jew would want a son-in-law like him. You know, I'm not easily impressed and don't flatter the next fellow. I don't overdo songs of praise or exaggerate compliments. I'll just say that the word "angel" was an insult to the young man. Satisfied? If there is a heaven and if angels do flutter around up there, and if those angels are no worse than Shapiro, then I tell you it pays to drop dead and be with them rather than with the two-legged beasts who spend their time down here under God's skies and pollute the earth. I'll bet you'll say that I'm a misanthrope, a hater of mankind. If people would treat *you* the way they've treated *us*, you wouldn't be a misanthrope but an out-and-out cut-throat. You'd take a knife, stand smack in the middle of the street, and kill people like sheep. And, anyway, what sort of queer tradition do you have here, letting a man talk for hours on end and not even offering him a glass of water. Tell the maid to make tea.

Well then, where was I? Our bundle of joy, Shapiro. I've already told you he was the manager of a distillery. Not only manager, but over-all boss. Everything was under his supervision, everything was in his name. You can't imagine how much they trusted him. They loved him like a son. It's not hard to imagine that the two owners, partners and crooks (they'll forgive me since they're long time residents of the other world—America) were big shots at the wedding. They gave him a chestful of silver, made themselves out to be open-hearted and kind, like honest-to-goodness philanthropists. And you know how much I adore philanthropists, especially if they're bosses who come to my party and display their philanthropy for all to see and show everyone that they appreciate another man's work. Perhaps because of him they had become rich? If it weren't for Shapiro, those two probably wouldn't be philanthropists today. Wipe that smile off your face. It's uncalled for. My dear sir, I don't make myself out to be a socialist, but I hate a philanthropic boss. Why do I

say this? Do I have any proof? You'll soon hear what a philanthropic boss can do. You'd think if with God's help you
had a good business, which brought in several thousand rubles
each year, and if you had a man you could trust as your first-
hand assistant, you wouldn't lose any sleep at night. You could
even go abroad and have a wonderful time. But you know
"our Jews." Yes, I know, you hate that term, but I'll say it
again. "Our Jews." They never have enough. A Jew likes to
do business, run around, finagle, brag, put on a big show. Let
everyone see! Let everyone hear! In short, my Shapiro's bosses
weren't satisfied with having such a top-notch business in such
sure hands. They started investing in forests and lots; they
went into auctions and mortgages, into wheat and corn. They
got a mad desire to creep into real estate. There was a rush for
real estate. They burned with excitement until they themselves were burned up and dragged our Shapiro into the mess
with promissory notes. They grabbed whatever cash there
was and ran off to America. Folks say they're doing all right
for themselves over there. But they left Shapiro with debts up
to the neck, notes which he himself had signed. Every single
one. There was a big scandal, and it reached the point where
they didn't care whether he was just an employee or boss—he
had to cover the notes. But since he didn't have a kopek, he
was bankrupt. And since he couldn't show that he was bankrupt due to some extraordinary misfortune, it was called fraud-
ulent bankruptcy. In other words, he was a rogue and rogues
were clapped into jail because the world hates a rogue. You
can go bankrupt a dozen and one times so long as you do it
correctly and with finesse. Why, then you can thumb your
nose at the public. You buy yourself a house with all the
trimmings, become one of the town's elite. You arrange the
finest marriages, you air opinions left and right, you step on
other people's toes, you elbow your way into high society, all
the way into the four hundred who lead the town by its nose.
You think you're great, you huff and puff with pride, you
swell like a turkey, you don't recognize old friends, and you
become so impressed with yourself that the deuce himself almost takes you. You'll pardon me, but you understand that it's

not you I mean. I'm just talking to the wall. The long and short of it was that my boy Shapiro couldn't take this humiliation—and another thing—he was all upset about the poor widows and orphans. (His bosses, you see, didn't spare anyone. They grabbed whatever they could.) He took poison.

I don't think what he took and where he took it from should make any difference to you. And why poison in the first place? And what sort of letter did he write me? What did he say? And how did he bid goodbye to Rose and me and the mother? All these things are just sentimental eyewash which the novelists use to squeeze tears out of silly readers. In a word: he not only poisoned himself, he poisoned all of us. We three were so broken up, so deep in grief, so numb with pain that we didn't even shed a tear. Not a one of us. We were stunned, dumbfounded. We were as good as dead. We would have been the happiest people alive if someone had come and chopped all our heads off with one blow. You listening? You can say what you want—I can't stand those who come to console you after a tragedy. Their make-believe sad expressions which say: Thank God it isn't me. Their wooden talk which makes no sense, their false praises, their long faces when they leave. You want more? You know, it's customary for every young lout on such occasions to look into the Book of Job, although they can't make head or tail out of it. Even that custom sickens me. What's that? I'm a heretic? Is that heresy in your eyes? And what about tripping up an innocent fellow, getting him to sign promissory notes and then sneaking off to America and leaving the other fellow to poison himself and three other innocent folk—what would you call that? Isn't that heresy? And wouldn't you label that an unjust act of God? But how can you complain against God? Well look and see what this very same Job has to say, that book which everyone reads, but no one understands. You're not saying a word, eh? Me, too, for you can talk until you burst and no one'll give you the answer. You can rehash the words: The Lord gave and the Lord has taken away—until you're blue in the face, and you won't be any the wiser. What's that you say? Philosophizing is like chewing straw? My very words!

Now, back to the widow. What am I saying, widow? I mean my two widows. Rose, a widow too! That's a laugh. It was fate's cruel joke. It was so tragic that one could only laugh. Rose a widow! You should have seen her. A fifteen-year-old couldn't have looked younger. A widow! But that's not all. Rose was a mother, too. Three months after Shapiro's death the baby came and the house was full of its sounds. They called her Feygele and she became queen of the household. Everything was done for Feygele. Wherever you walked or sat or went it was only Feygele, Feygele, Feygele. If I were religious and believed in Providence, as you call it, I'd say that God rewarded us for our suffering and sent the baby as consolation. But you know I'm not much of a believer, and I have my doubts about you, too. What's that? You want to convince me that you *are* a believer? Fine and dandy. I don't care. So long as you yourself are sure that you're no hypocrite. Listen! I hate Jewish hypocrites as much as a good Jew hates pork. Be as religious as ten thousand demons, but be sincere about it. If you're a faker, a saint in masquerade, then you're not one of my boys and you can fry in hell for all I care and I have no further use for you. That's the sort of guy I am!

Where were we? Oh yes, Feygele. As soon as Feygele appeared, everything blossomed, everyone smiled and was happy. All our faces shone. Our eyes brightened. One with the baby, we were all born anew. And what's more, Rose, who hadn't smiled for ages, suddenly began to laugh her strange old laugh which charmed you into laughter too—although you really wanted to cry. That's what Feygele did when she opened her eyes and looked at us with the first gleam of understanding. Not to mention the first time we saw a smile on her lips. Both widows practically went out of their minds with astonishment. When I came, they ran to me with such vigor that I was scared half to death.

"Oh, where were you a minute ago?" they pounced on me.

"What is it? What happened?" I asked, frightened.

"Why just half a minute ago Feygele laughed. Her first laugh."

"Is that all?" I said coldly. But deep down I was very happy,

not so much for the smile but because my two widows were
so overjoyed. Well now you can imagine what happened when
she started teething. The young widow, Rose, was the first to
feel it. So she called the older widow, Paye, and they both
tested it with a glass to see if it was really a tooth. When they
were sure it was, they made such a tumult that I ran in from
the next room with my heart in my mouth.

"What happened?"

"A tooth."

"It's your imagination," I said purposely, to tease them.
Then both widows took my finger and made me feel the little
point in Feygele's warm mouth which could be—which *was*
—a tooth.

"Well?" they both asked and waited for me to bring regards from the tooth. I played innocent. I loved teasing them.
I asked:

"Well what?"

"Is it or isn't it a tooth?"

"Of course. What did you expect?"

Since it *was* a tooth, why then Feygele was a genius the
likes of which hadn't been seen on earth. And being a genius,
she deserved to be kissed until she started to cry. Then I tore
the baby out of their arms and quieted her down, for I soothed
her best of all. In fact, you can well say that she liked my hair
better than anyone else's. Her tiny fingers liked to mangle
my nose better than any other nose in the world. Feeling those
little fingers was seventh heaven. You longed to kiss each part
of those white and tiny, smooth and soft little fingers a thousand times. I know you're looking at me and thinking: he's a
woman at heart. For if he weren't he wouldn't love children
so much. A good guess, right? Here's the story. What I am at
heart, I don't know. But I do know that I love children. That's
a fact. Who, then, are you supposed to love if not babies. You
want me to love those adults with the double chins and packed
pot-bellies whose whole life is one long lunch, Havana cigar,
and game of cards? Or do you want me to love those noble-
hearted public servants who live off the community's kitty
while they raise a racket and holler to beat the band that all

their labors are for the public good? Or perhaps you want me to love those sweet young things who want to change the world, who call me a "bourgeois" and want to make me sell my houses and divide it with them in the name of expropriation? Or perhaps you'll tell me to love those bloated women, those fattened cows whose only ideals besides clothes, diamonds, and the theater are eating and flirting with other men? Perhaps you want me to adore those short-haired old maids who were called "nihilists" in my day and today operate under other dandy nicknames? Go ahead, say it: I'm such a grouch and such a misanthrope because I'm an old bachelor. And that's why I don't like anyone. Say what you want. It doesn't bother me in the least. I'll just keep on talking.

Where was I? Oh yes, Feygele and how we loved her. All three of us devoted ourselves body and soul to that baby, for it sweetened the bitterness in our lives. It gave us fresh energy to carry the yoke of this foolish and botched-up world. For me, especially, the child was a source of secret hopes. You'll understand what I mean if you remember what Rose meant to me. The more the baby grew, the more the hope grew in my heart that my loneliness would once and for all be ended and I too would know what a normal life was. I wasn't alone with that thought. This same hope budded in Paye's heart, although we never mentioned it. But it was as clear as day to all three of us that someday it would have to be. You'll ask: how can people understand one another without talking? Well that shows that you really know psychology. But not people! I'll paint you a picture and you'll see how people can talk without words and read each other's eyes.

It's a summer night. The milky-way streaks the sky. I wanted to say that the stars glittered, sparkled, shone. But, then I remembered that that's the way it's written in a book. I don't want to rehash anyone else's words. I've told you already that I hate their descriptions of nature. They resemble nature as much as I do the Turkish Sultan. Anyway, it was a summer night, one of those rare and warm, clear and beautiful nights which makes a poet out of the least sensitive soul and makes him long for something he cannot put his finger on. Some sort of holy spirit fills him and he sinks into a sacred calm. He stares into the deep blue skullcap which we call the sky and feels that it is whispering secrets to the earth, continuing that eternal dialogue which people call godliness.

Well, what do you say to my descriptions of nature? You don't like them? Well, now I'm exposed! But wait, you're not through yet! I forgot to tell you about the beetles—queer, fat, brown beetles which come in the dark, beating their wings, humming and buzzing and bumping into the walls and windows, then falling to the floor, their skirts damaged. There, they finally quiet down. But don't worry . . . they'll rest for a while on the ground then start the whole business all over again. Now, all four of us were sitting on the porch, facing the garden. Feygele was big, she would soon be four, and she was talking like a grown-up. She talked and asked questions. Loads of them. Why is the sky the sky, the earth the earth? When is night and when is day? Why is it dark at night and light during the day? Why does Mama call Grandma "Mama" and why does Grandma call Mama "Rose"? Why am I her uncle and not her father? Why does Uncle look at Grandma and Grandma at Mama and why is Mama red in the face? You can imagine what laughs this caused. When Feygele asked what we were laughing about, we laughed even more. The result is, we looked at each other and knew quite well the meaning of that look. We needed no words. Words were unnecessary. Words were made only for babblers, women, and lawyers. Like Bismarck once said: "Words were given to us to hide our thoughts." Animals, birds, and other creatures, don't they get along without speech? The tree grows, the flower blossoms, a blade of grass sprouts, stays close to the earth, kisses the sunbeam—where's their speech? Eyes, my dear sir, human eyes are great things. What eyes can tell you in a minute, a mouth will never say in a day. Our looking at one another that night was a page, a chapter in our mutual history. Better yet, it was a poem, a song, the pathetic song of three lost lives, three crippled souls, who because of various entanglements couldn't drink from the fountain called happiness and from the spring called love. . . . Unwittingly, I've just come out with the word love. Believe me, it disgusts me. You know why? Because your writers use this sacred word so often it becomes a workaday expression. When your writers use the word "love," it's sacrilege. The word "love" has to pour out of you like a prayer to God. It has to flow forth in a song without words, in a song of pure poetry. And it doesn't have to rhyme either. When I read rhymes like moon-June, love-dove, and other such stuff your poets dream up, it seems that I'm gulping raw beans followed by a dessert of blotters. You may not like my image, but you don't have to make a face. In a minute I'm going to finish the story of widow number two and I'm going to make it quick, for I hate people yawning in my face.

Tell me, did you ever have a toothache so bad that the tooth had to come out? But instead of pulling it right away, you put it off from day to day until, with heavy heart, you finally go to the dentist. You come to his office and see the sign on his door: Doctor So-and-so—office hours from 8 to 1 and 1 to 8. You look at your watch and say to yourself: then what's my rush?

You turn around and head for home, but, meanwhile, your tooth is killing you. Well, that's exactly how it was with me and Rose. I left my house every morning with the thought that it had to happen today and no excuses. First I'd talk it over with my widow number one. She'd blush, lower her eyes, and say, "It's all right with me. Now talk it over with Rose." Then I'd leave widow number one and go to widow number two and say: "Listen, Rose, here's the story." Well, with that in mind, I grabbed my hat and came to my widow's house. Feygele came running into my arms, threw her hands round my neck, kissed my glasses, and begged me to ask Grandma and Mama—they'd listen to me—that she not go to school or play or dance that day, but be allowed to go to the zoo with Uncle. They had brought new monkeys, monkeys so funny your sides hurt from laughing. Well, how could you refuse and not take her to the zoo to see the funny monkeys?

"What's going to become of the child?" widow number one grumbled.

"He's spoiling the child," widow number two echoed.

And Uncle paid no more attention to the two widows than to the man in the moon. He took Feygele and went to the zoo and introduced her to the new monkeys whose antics made you roll with laughter. That's the way it was. There was a different alibi every time. Days passed. Weeks. Years. The child got older, began to understand things you don't speak of. It was a sort of silent agreement among us three that we'd wait until the girl grew up. When Feygele would grow up and pick her mate, our hands would no longer be tied. Then we'd set our lives aright and build a new home for ourselves. Everyone made plans—each in his own heart—about how we would live together. The young couple—Feygele and her husband. The old couple—Rose and I. And the widow—Grandma Paye—would rule over us all. What a life that would be! The only problem was—when would we see it come true? We couldn't wait for Feygele to grow up, pick a young man, and marry. Like the saying has it: keep living and you'll live to see it. I hate clichés like that. Do you like them? Wonderful! Enjoy yourself!

Well then, keep living and you'll live to see it. Feygele grew up, matured, chose a husband. And *there's* where the dog lies buried. Here's where your real psychology begins. You know, looking at your watch is entirely uncalled for. I won't tell you any more today in any case. I have to go now. My widows won't know what to think. If you want to hear the story of widow number three, I don't mind if you pick yourself up and come to visit me. If not—it's up to you. I won't drag you over by the coat-tails. You'll come of your own free will. So long!

3. Widow Number Three

It's good you came at a time when I'm at home. What I mean is, I'm always at home. For myself, not the next fellow. Every man has his own habits. For instance, I'm used to having the cat sit opposite me when I eat. I won't eat without my cat. Here she is. Kootchie-kootchie-koo! What do you say to her?

Smart as a whip. She'll never help herself to anything. Even gold. Do you like her fur? What's that? You hate cats? Silly old prejudice, a remnant of Hebrew-school days. Don't tell me! Don't make excuses. How do you like your tea? With milk or plain? I take it with milk, too. Scat . . . beat it, puss. The deuce take it!! There's nothing she likes better than milk. She won't go near butter, but once she spots milk, she must take a lick.

You know I hate long-winded introductions, but here I have to say something. I hate when people smile. Laugh as much as you please. But don't smile. Do you remember everything I've told you? If you don't, don't be bashful. People smarter than us also forget sometimes. It looks like I'll have to give you a quick résumé of what happened. I had a friend, Pini, who had a wife, Paye, who had a baby girl named Rose. Then Pini died, and Paye was left a widow. I became one of the family. We both loved each other. But we never spoke of it. Kept it to ourselves. So passed our best years. Meanwhile, her daughter, Rose, grew up and I was mad about her. Then in slipped a Shapiro, a good bookkeeper and a fine chess player. Rose fell for him. I had a fight with Paye and left thinking I'd never again set foot in that house. I didn't keep my word and came back on the next day and once again made myself at home. I masqueraded as "one of the family" and we celebrated the wedding of Rose to Shapiro, the boy who managed his bosses' business, even signed their notes. They pulled a fast one and ran off to America, leaving him with their debts. He committed suicide and Rose remained a widow.

Now there's two widows. Just as Paye, my widow number one, was left with a baby after Pini's death, so Rose was left with a baby after Shapiro's death. We loved the baby and were so devoted to her that we didn't have time to think of my romance with widow number two, Rose. We put it off until Feygele grew up. Well, when she finally got older . . . Look, do me a favor! When I'm telling a story, don't read! It's a disgusting habit! You better listen to what I'm saying, for there's a new story beginning.

You can say what you like about me, but I've never been

fanatic or stubborn. I've always kept up with the times. I never went backward nor stood still like others, who always complain about the modern generation and their newfangled ideas.

I can't stand these old wiseguys with their eternal pretensions who say: look at the egg starting to teach the hen. Who came first, the chicken or the egg? What a bunch of asses they are! On the contrary. Just *because* it's younger, is the egg better, smarter, more skillful. The older generation must listen carefully to the younger, because they're fresh out of the shell. They study, they desire, they seek, they find, they accomplish. What else? Want them to be like you, moldy old scholars who sit themselves down on books from the year one and refuse to budge? The only thing I'm angry at the young ones about is that they belittle us, they push us completely out of the picture. They don't even call us asses and donkeys. We're nobodies. We don't exist. We're not even here. And that's the end of that. Just imagine, three young popinjays come into our place. I mean the widows' place. And they didn't come to see the widows either, but the granddaughter, Feygele. Whether they're students or not, the devil himself knows. But they wear black shirts, they don't have haircuts, they don't introduce themselves, they have sharp tongues and Karl Marx is their god. He's not their Moses mind you, but their god. Well, what do I care? Let him be their god. I'm not going to do myself in on account of that. Especially since I myself am close to the socialist ideal. I'm also familiar with capital, the proletariat, economic struggle, and all that. And if you want to know—I myself—get that smile off your face. No, I don't belong to any organization, God forbid. But I'm certainly not a down-at-the-heels tailor, either.

Well then, these three characters came to visit us every day. One's name was Finkel, the second was called Bomstein, and the third, Gruzevitsh. They came and felt perfectly at home. That's the way my two widows are. When a visitor came they didn't know what to do first. They went all out for them, especially bargains like those three, one of whom was surely a candidate for Feygele. What I mean is, they were all candi-

dates, but she couldn't marry three of them, so one of them it
had to be . . . But go guess which one it was if the thing was
never even mentioned. Nothing was sure. They asked no one.
Who were they to ask? The mother? What did they give a hang
about the mother? She was a young woman with a pretty face
and that was the end of that. The grandmother? Who was
she? She was only a hostess who had to see to it that there was
enough to eat and drink when they came visiting. Not only
eat and drink, but glut and guzzle. Me? I don't come into the
picture at all. What am I to them? An extra seat at the table.
No more than that? You'd think they'd throw a word my
way? Unless of course it was: pass the salt, pass the sugar, or,
got a match? And all that without a please or a thank you. If
they wanted a match they'd make a striking motion with their
hands, or they'd stick out their lips while I was smoking a
cigar—just like speaking to a deaf-mute. Aside from that—
not a word. Sometimes they came and found only me in the
house. So they sat down in a corner and talked to each other,
or sprawled on the sofa and yawned. You'd think they'd say
something just to be polite. But no. Just as if I wasn't there.
Certainly, I wouldn't start talking to them first. I'm not like
the others who slipped them ten thousand little flatteries, a
load of sweet talk and sugar-coated smiles. The guy I'm going
to kowtow to hasn't been born yet. And it's not because I'm
such a proud one either. All right, let's say I am proud. Call it
what you want. You can keep your opinions to yourself. But
bragging is one thing I hate. I just want to tell you the sort of
breed those three big-shots were. Once, when I came out and
asked if any of them played chess, you should have seen the
looks on their faces. You should have heard them cackling. I
thought, what sort of crime is it to be a socialist *and* a chess
player, too. Karl Marx won't turn over in his grave. But there's
no talking to them. I don't give a damn about them. They can
go straight to hell for all I care. But I was burned up at Feygele
—why did she laugh along with them? Why should every
single thing they said be sacred to her, as if they were God's
own words at Sinai? What sort of pagan worship was it these
young folks practiced? What sort of new fanaticism? A brand

new *Hasidic* movement! Karl Marx was the *rebbe* and they were his devotees. And after Marx was there no one? Where were Kant, Spinoza, Schopenhauer? Where were Shakespeare, Heine, Goethe, Schiller, Spenser, and hundreds of other great men who also had something clever to say? Of course they weren't as wise as Karl Marx, but at least they didn't prattle nonsense. I must tell you that I'm not one to let a fellow spit into my face. I hate stuck up folk and I love making them angry. If they say black, I'll say white. On purpose. And go fight me if you want. Once I heard them say that Tolstoi was a nobody. I'm not a Tolstoi fan. Not one to make a god of him and his new philosophy which makes of Jesus something he never was. But as an artist, I think Tolstoi is on the same plane as Shakespeare. If you don't agree with me, I'm not going to eat my heart out. You know me. So, I purposely brought Feygele one of Tolstoi's books to read. You ought to see the face she made as she pushed Tolstoi aside. What's the matter? Finkel, Bomstein, and Gruzevitsh—none of them liked Tolstoi.

Then I really blew my top. When I have to, you see, I can be a meanie. I made mud of all three of them. I told them that Karl Marx was a theory and that theories change. Today it was this theory, tomorrow that one. But Tolstoi was a great artist and art remains forever.

Well, you should have seen them flare up. If you had provoked the Baal Shem Tov himself, his disciples couldn't have been angrier. The long and short of it was, if my two widows hadn't interfered there would have been a royal scandal. But, I saw later that I was an ass. After all, I should have apologized to them! You know why? Because Feygele wanted it that way. And if that's what she wants, that's what it'll have to be. If she tells me today to pick up the house and move it, don't you think I'd do it?

That girl not only charmed me, but made me a devoted slave. She destroyed my will and made a robot of me. Mine wasn't the only head she turned. She put us all into a dither with the match she made. She picked Gruzevitsh, a chemical student in his third year. He wasn't a bad chap, but nothing extraordinary. There were plenty worse. But first of all, he came from a fine family. That's very important. Say what you will, but it counts in the end. Don't get excited—I didn't mention noble lineage! I can only say that who you stem from counts. If you come from a bunch of louts, I don't care how educated you are, you'll still remain a lout. I'm not going to talk about his other qualities. Their sort—to give the devil his due—are good and honest and noble so long as they keep true to themselves. But as soon as they step out into the big wide world and become somebodies, watch out! They're worse than anyone else. If a nobody puts one over on you, he'll hide. If a somebody swindles you, he'll show you logically that you're the swindler, not he. But why lose time with silly philosophizing! At the age of seventeen, our Feygele became Mrs. Gruzevitsh. I won't chew your ears off with long stories about the wedding, who arranged it, who paid for it, and the tumult in the widows' place. The mother lived to bring her consolation to the wedding canopy. The grandmother had the joy of seeing her grandchild married. And me? The fool! What sort of joyous occasion was it for me? That the youngest one had been married off? But listen to this. Our entire joy lasted no longer than *Purim*. The third day after the wedding, Gruzevitsh was taken to jail over a small matter. They just happened to run across a whole storehouse of bombs and dynamite. And since he was a chemist, and a famous one at that, suspicion fell on him. In addition, a few of his own letters had been found. In short, they took him in.

I had my work cut out for me. I ran from pillar to post, greasing palms, and got headaches and plagues. It didn't do a bit of good. Once caught in a mess like that, you might as well kiss everyone goodbye. Picture the suffering of the little seventeen-year-old girl. The anguish of her mother, Rose, and of the grandmother. The wrath of God fell on that house.

And let me tell you, business was none too good, either. I started feeling the pinch in my pocket. I became frisky, schemed and swindled, mortgaged some of my houses, and the money just melted away. When the cash went, I sold a few of my stores outright. I'm not telling you how clever I was and

I'm not bragging. I just want to show you what my widows were like. They gave no thought to what they were living on, where the money was coming from, and what they'd do for future support. It didn't concern them in the least. I had to worry about everything. Everything had to be on my shoulders. I had to knock myself out. Who asked me to? God knows! It came by itself. I'd like to see you in my shoes under the same conditions, among people each of whom is finer than the next. You can never get peeved at them, can never hate them, can never hold a grudge against them. And if some wild spirit got into you and you flared up at them and went home angry—all that was needed was for you to return and look them in the eye, listen to their first hello and all your anger went with the wind. In a flash, you forgot your rage and you were ready once again to go to hell and back for them. That's the sort of creatures they are. Well, what can you do? Not to mention Feygele. She was a gift of God. One look from her deep, beautiful, and nearsighted eyes was enough to drive you wild. Take it easy now, I don't mean you, I mean myself. For she drove me crazy marrying that Misha Gruzevitsh. The whole house was full of Misha. No one could eat, no one could sleep, no one could live. What was up? Misha! Misha was taken away. Misha was clapped into jail. They were going to try him. He had to be saved. But those cold-blooded characters didn't let me near him. Neither me nor her. No one. I saw that it looked bad, that the least he would get off with, if he were lucky, would be life imprisonment, if not hanging. I see you're not comfortable in this chair. Why don't you sit over here by the window? Perhaps I've bored you a bit? But it's no great tragedy. My burden is heavier than yours. It's nothing to you. You'll hear me out (I'll soon finish) and then you'll go home. But I live with this TNT forever.

Where were we? Oh yes, hanging. You've probably read in the papers that they hanged two men yesterday. Today they're hanging a few more. There's no difference nowadays between hanging people and killing chickens. And what do you do while all this is going on? You sit in your rocking chair smoking a Havana cigar, or you have yourself a snack—

a fresh cup of coffee and hot buttered rolls. Do you care if
they're hanging a man, who twitches and trembles during the
last moments of his agony, someone you knew, one near and
dear to you, someone who only yesterday was as full of life as
you are now? Do you care if his warm body lies there—a body
from whom the hangman has taken the life? Or if out there
a man is suffering; he wants to die quickly, but he can't, for
the hangman didn't tighten the noose properly or it broke and
he's left dangling there, half-dead, half-alive, and with dying
eyes begging the judges to render justice quickly? What's
that? You can't stand that sort of talk? Are you a softie? I'm
just as soft as you are. Just imagine, since I'd been everywhere,
I knew the exact moment he was to be hanged. Then, I read
in the papers how one of the three—they hanged all three you
see—put up a struggle with death. That was Bomstein. He was
heavy and so they had to hang him twice. That's how they
wrote about it in the papers. And we all read it. That is, not
all of us, only Rose and I. We hid the papers from the grandmother and from Feygele. That's how we added another
widow to the household. Widow number three.

Grief descended upon us all—a silent, death-like grief which
neither words nor colors can describe. A grief you don't dare
write about, for writing about it would profane it. If one of
your writers had described that grief, I would have broken
his arm. It was a grief about which you could not, must not,
dare not speak. We lived in memories, in the past. Three
widows—three lives. Not complete lives, but half lives. Not
half lives, either—but fragments. Just the start of lives. Each
had started so well, so poetically. It flashed for a moment, then
was snuffed out. I'm not talking about myself. I don't count.
But I see them every day, spend my evenings with them, talking of the good old days, remembering stories and events of
my dear friend Pini, the kind and honest Shapiro, the hero
Misha Gruzevitsh, who was written up in all the papers and
described as a near-genius in the field of chemistry. Every
time I leave them, I leave with heavy heart, peeved at myself.
Why have I thrown away my life so foolishly, I ask myself.
Where was my first mistake and what will be my last? I love

all three of them. Each one of them is precious to me. Each of them might have been mine and still might be. Each one of them thinks me a dear and a bore, a necessity and a nuisance. If I don't show up one day, they're as gloomy as anything. And if I overstay a half hour, they simply show me the door. They don't take a step without consulting me. If I scold them about something, they say I'm a busybody. So I get angry and run away and lock myself up with my cat and tell the maid to tell any callers that I've gone away. Then I work at my diary, which I've been keeping for thirty-six years. It's quite an interesting book, you may be sure! I keep it for myself, only. For no one else. This literature of yours—it doesn't even deserve having a book like mine. Maybe I'll show it to you some-day. But no one else. For no money in the world!

But half an hour later, there's a knocking at my door. Who is it, I want to know. "It's the maid from the widows' place. They want you to come for lunch. What should I tell her?" "Tell her I'll be right over."

Well? What have you got to say now? Where's your psy-chology? You're in a rush, eh? I'll join you. I have to visit my three widows. Just a minute, though. I want to leave word to feed the cat, because I'm liable to spend the whole day there. We play cards. For money! You ought to see how everyone likes to win. And if a mistake's made, we lay into each other—I into them, they into me. None of us spares the other. When someone else makes a mistake in cards, I'm liable to rip him to shreds. What's that smile on your face for? Believe me, I know what's in the back of your mind. I see right through you, but I laugh at you and your grandmother, too. You're thinking: What an old bachelor. What an old grouch!

THE PASSOVER EVE VAGABONDS

1. Kicked out of Paradise

"Thank God Purim's over and done with. Now we can start planning for Passover."

That's what Mama said the morning after Purim as she carefully inspected the four corners of the parlor like a chicken about to lay an egg. There, a few days later, we saw some hay and two boxes, upon which stood a little barrel covered by a coarse, white piece of cloth. Father and I were called into the parlor and warned about three dozen times that I not dare enter that room again, look at it from a distance, or even breathe in the general area. Immediately thereafter, the parlor door was shut, and, with all due respect, we were told to bid a hearty goodbye to the room and not set foot into it until Passover.

From that moment on, the parlor had a magnetic charm for me and I was strongly tempted to peep into that forbidden corner, if even from afar. While munching on my afternoon snack—a piece of bread smeared with chicken fat—I joyfully looked into the bright parlor. There stood the red sofa, made of the same tawny wood used for violins, the three-legged, semi-circular table, the oval, well cut mirror, and the magnificent, hand-decorated picture hanging on the east wall which faced Jerusalem. It was a work of art which Father had made when still a young man. Oh my, what *didn't* appear on it? Bears and lions, wildcats and eagles, birds and ram's horns, citrons and candelabras, the Passover plate with stars of David on it, leaves and buttons, circles, loops, and an infinite number of curlicues and dots. It was hard to believe that a human hand could have drawn all that. How talented he is, I thought. Father is perfect.

214

"May the devil not take you! Standing with bread at the Passover door. May you not burn in hell," Mama shouted, and with two sharp pinching fingers led me by my left ear to Father.

"Go ahead. Take a good look at your son and heir. With bread in his hands, he looked into the parlor where the Passover borscht is."

Father faked a solemn expression, shook his head, pursed his lips and clucked:

"Tsk, tsk. Off with you, you little brat."

When Mama turned to go, I noticed a sly little smile on Father's lips. As Mama faced him again, the serious look returned. He took me by the hand, put me in the adjoining chair, and told me not to look into the parlor again. It was forbidden.

"Not even from far away?" I asked.

But Father didn't hear me. He had returned to his book, deep in thought and silent study. Again I sneaked up to the parlor and peeked through a crack in the door. Before me was a Paradise of fine things: a set of brand-new crockery, shiny pots, a meat cleaver, a salting board. In addition, two ropes of onions were strung on the wall, adding charm to the room. The parlor was all set for Passover! Passover! Passover!

2. From Bad to Worse

"Perhaps I can trouble your honors to move yourselves and your books out of here and go to the big alcove?" Mama ordered.

She was dressed in white, had a white kerchief on her head, and held a long stick in one hand and a feather duster in the other. She bent her head back and looked up to the ceiling.

"Sosil. Come here with the brush! Come on, get a move on, girl. Show your face."

Sosil, the maid, a white cloth on her head too, appeared with a wet rag and a pail of whitewash. She set to work, slapping the wet brush across the ceiling, splash, splash. The two women looked like live white-shrouded corpses and both were as angry as could be.

But they didn't let me watch this rare comedy for long. First, they told me that a young boy wasn't supposed to stand and watch the ceiling being whitewashed for Passover. Then, in an angrier tone:

"Listen here! How about heading for the alcove?"

Saying this, Mama took me by the hand and showed me where to go. Since I wasn't too eager to leave, I returned and met Sosil. She pushed me away from her and said: "What a child! Always getting under your feet!"

"Go. Run off, for goodness sake. Go to your father," Mama said, and pushed me toward Sosil, who caught me and threw me back at Mama, saying: "I've never seen such a stubborn child in my life."

"He hasn't learned his lesson," Mama said and slapped my rump. Sosil grabbed me and dabbed some whitewash on my nose and I stumbled into Father's room, like a wet kitten, and burst into tears.

Father looked up from his books, tried his best to console me, put me on his lap, and started studying again.

3. From the Alcove to the Pantry

"Excuse me, boss," said Sosil to Father, "but the boss-lady told me to tell you to move to the pantry."

The maid came into the alcove armed with all her tools, painted white as a ghost. We had to pack ourselves and our books to the pantry, a place no bigger than a yawn. One bed stood there, and in it slept the maid and, to my great shame, I. Sosil, you understand, was a relative, and had been with us for many years. "When I came," she once said to me, "you weren't even born yet. You grew up under my care," she said. "If it weren't for me you'd be God knows where," she announced, "for wherever there was a tumult, a hodge-podge, a mess—you were in the midst of it and I saved you from the muddle. And that's the thanks you give me, huh?" she said, "biting the hand that fed you? Well, don't you deserve a thrashing?" she said.

That's how Sosil used to talk to me, smacking me and tugging my hair, as well. And—wonder of wonders—no one
protested. Neither Father nor Mama took my part. Sosil did
whatever she pleased with me. Just as if I was hers, not theirs.

I took to a corner of the pantry, sat down on the floor, looking at Father as he rubbed his forehead, chewed his beard,
swayed, and sighed, "Well, that's how it is. . . ." Just then
Sosil came in with her equipment and asked us to move a bit
further.

"Where, now?" asked Father, completely bewildered.

"How do I know?" Sosil said, and started whitewashing
the place.

"Into the little storeroom," said Mama, coming into the
pantry. With her long stick and new feather-duster, she
looked like a fully-armed enemy in a surprise attack.

"The storeroom is as cold as a stone." Father tried to beg
his way out.

"A stone-cold plague on him," said Mama.

"Sure! They're freezing on the streets now, come spring,"
Sosil mocked, and started splashing her wet brush on the dry
walls. We had to pick ourselves up and move to the storeroom, where we both shivered with cold. You couldn't say
the place was conducive to studying. The little storeroom was
narrow and dark. Two people could hardly stand there without stepping on each other's toes. But because of that, it was
a miniature Paradise for me. Just imagine, there were little
shelves for me to climb. But Father wouldn't let me. He said
I'd fall and break my neck. But who paid any attention to
him? No sooner was he into his books, than I was—yippee!—
on the first, the second, the third shelf.

"Cock-a-doodle-doo!" I crowed at the top of my voice,
wanting to show Father my great talent. I raised my head and
before I knew it, had banged into the ceiling with such force
that it practically knocked all my teeth out. Father became
frightened and raised a fuss. Then Sosil, followed by Mama,
came a-running, and both of them plowed into me for all they
were worth.

"Did you ever see such a wild boy?" Mama asked.

"That's no boy. That's a little demon," Sosil said, adding that in a little while we'd be asked—begging our pardon a thousand times—to move ourselves to the kitchen, for most of the house was already painted-for-Passover.

4. From the Storeroom to the Kitchen

In the kitchen I saw the big-browed Moyshe-Ber sitting with Father on the dairy-bench. They weren't studying now, but pouring out their bitter hearts to each other. Father complained about his pre-Passover travels, saying, that for the past few days he'd been sent packing from one place to another. "I've become a vagabond. Gone into exile, tramping from one place to the next."

But Moyshe-Ber said, "That's nothing. I have it much worse. I've been kicked out of the house altogether."

I looked at the big-browed Moyshe-Ber and for the life of me couldn't understand how such a big Jew with such huge eyebrows could have been kicked out of his own house. Bit by bit they slipped back into their old strange talk. Maimonides, Yehuda Halevi's Kuzari, Philosophy, Spinoza, and other such nonsense which went in one ear and out the other.

The gray cat, sitting on the stove and licking its paws, was more interesting. Sosil said a cat licking herself meant a guest was coming. But I just couldn't understand how the cat knew we were going to have company. I went up to the cat and started teasing her. First, I wanted to touch her paw. But nothing doing. Then, I taught her to beg and stood her up on her hind legs. She didn't like this either. "Attention!" I told her, and slapped her nose. She closed her eyes and turned away, stuck out her tongue, and yawned as if to say: Why does this boy bother me so? What does he want of my life? But her behavior annoyed me. Why does the cat have to be such a stubborn mule, I thought, and kept teasing her until she suddenly bared her sharp claws and scratched my hand. "Mama, help," I yelled. Mama and Sosil rushed in in an uproar and I got my share of it from both of them. Next time

I'd know not to fool around with cats, they said. Cats! All told there was only one little cat and they called it *cats*.

"Go wash up," Mama told Father. "We'll have our last pre-Passover meal in the cellar."

Sosil took the poker and started moving the pots around on the stove, paying no attention to either me, my father or Moyshe-Ber. Moreover, she let Moyshe-Ber know that she couldn't understand what he was doing here on the eve of Passover. That's the proper time to be home, she said, instead of lolling around in neighbors' houses. Moyshe-Ber took the hint, said goodbye, and we all went down to the cellar for our last pre-Passover meal.

5. From the Kitchen Down to the Cellar

I couldn't understand why Father made faces, shrugged his shoulders, and grumbled: "What a vagabond life!" What sort of catastrophe was it having one meal in the cellar? How could the smell of sour pickles, stinking cabbage, and crocks full of dairy products harm anyone? What was so terrible about making a table out of two upside-down barrels and a noodle-board, and using other barrels for chairs? Just the opposite. I thought it was much better that way, and more fun, too. While doing so, you could ride around the cellar on the barrel. But what if you fell? If you fell you got up and rolled around again. The only trouble was that Sosil was on a sharp lookout to foil my attempts.

"He's got himself a new game," she said. "He's dying to break a leg."

That was a lot of hooey. I no more wanted to break a leg than she did. I don't know what she wanted of me. She always picked on me and looked at the black side of things. If I ran, she said I'd break my skull. If I went near anything, she said I'd smash it. If I chewed on a button, she had a fit: "The blunderhead is going to choke himself." But I used to get even with her when I was sick. The minute I felt out of sorts, she turned the world upside-down fussing over me, and didn't know whether she was coming or going.

"Now, take the child upstairs," Mama said, after we had finished grace. "We have to clean up the last bit of leaven from the cellar too." Before Father asked her where to go, she added: "Up to the attic for a couple of hours."

"Because the floors are still wet," Sosil added quickly. "But see to it that the little bungler doesn't tumble out of the attic and break all his bones!"

"Bite your tongue!" Mama yelled, as Sosil hurried me on with a push from behind.

"Well, get a move on, bungler. Move!"

Father followed me and I heard him grumbling: "The attic! What next? There's a vagabond gypsy's life for you."

What a strange one Father was. Going up to the attic displeased him. If it were up to me, I'd like every week to be the week before Passover where I would have to climb up to the attic. First of all, the climbing itself was fun. On a regular weekday I could stretch out and die—and they wouldn't let me go up to the attic. And now I scrambled up the stairs like a little devil. Father came after me, saying; "Take it easy. Take it slowly," but who took it easy? Who took it slowly? I felt as if I'd sprouted wings and was flying, flying.

6. From the Cellar to the Attic—and that's all

You ought to see the looks of our attic. It was smack full of treasures—smashed lamps, broken pots, clothes so old you couldn't tell if they were men's or women's underwear. I found an old piece of fur there, too. As soon as I touched it, it crumbled like snow. Pages from old sacred books, the burned exhaust pipe of an old samovar, a sackful of feathers, a rusty strainer, and an old palm-branch lay on the floor, stretched out like a lord. Not to mention the planks and boards and the roof! The roof was made of pure shingle and I could touch it with my bare hands. Being able to touch the ceiling was nothing to sneeze at.

Father sat down on a cross-beam, picked up the loose pages, attached one to another, and started reading them. I stood next to the little attic window and had a picture-postcard view of all of Kasrilevke. I saw all the houses and all their roofs, black and gray, red and green. The people walking in the streets seemed tiny and I thought that ours was the finest village in the world. I peeked into our own courtyard and saw all the neighbors washing and scrubbing, scraping and rubbing, making the tables and benches kosher-for-Passover. They carried huge pots of boiling water, heated irons and red-hot bricks, all of which gave off a white vapor. It tumbled and turned until it disappeared like smoke. The smell of spring was in the air. Little streamlets flowed in the streets, goats bleated, and a man wearing cord-wrapped boots was hauling himself and a white horse through the mud. That happened to be Azriel the Wagoner. The poor devil beat his horse, who just about managed to drag his feet through the mud. He was delivering a load of matzohs to someone. Then I remembered that we had bought our matzohs a long time ago and had them locked in the cupboard over which a white sheet had been hung. In addition, we had a basketful of eggs, a jar of Passover chicken-fat, two ropes of onions on the wall, and many other delicacies for the holiday. I thought of the new clothes I'd have for Passover and my heart melted with joy.

"Boss," we heard a voice from downstairs. "Sorry to trouble you, but you'll have to come down and air out the books."

Father stood up and spat out angrily: "Damn this vagabond existence."

It was beyond me why Father wasn't happy. What could be more fun than standing outside, airing the books. I dashed from the window to the attic door, then—clompety-clomp—head-over-heels down the stairs, I went into the kitchen.

I don't know what happened next! I just know that after the fall I was ill for a long time. They tell me I almost didn't recover. But as you can see, I'm as hale and hearty as ever, may it continue that way. Except for that one scar on my face, my shortness of breath, and the constant twitch in my eyes, I'm in perfect shape.

HOMESICK

There isn't a thing in the world about which Kasrilevke does not know. There isn't a bit of news that the little people of Kasrilevke don't get to hear.

Truth of the matter is, when the news does come, it comes late, and not first-hand, either. But so what? It's no great catastrophe. Just the opposite—I think it's an advantage, a great advantage.

Just between you and me, what great loss is it to the Kasrilevke Jews if they hear of the good news, wonderful events, and great happenings the world over a month or two later, God forbid, or even a year later? Some catastrophe!

In a nutshell, one day the little people of Kasrilevke discovered—late, albeit—the existence of the word "Zionism."

At first, not everyone knew what "Zionism" meant. Later, when they found out that it is simply derived from the word "Zion," which appears in their prayer books, and that the Zionists were a group of people who wanted to send all the Jews to Palestine—the Kasrilevkites mocked, and jeered. They split their sides laughing. Their laughter could be heard a mile away. As I live and breathe, the jokes they cracked about Doctor Herzl, Doctor Nordau, and all the other doctors were worth putting into a book. I guarantee that those quips had more punch to them than those licorice-sweet *bon mots* which were printed in the Jewish calendars.

The Kasrilevkites have one good quality—once they laugh, they keep laughing. But, having had their fill, they start thinking about the topic, mulling over it until they begin to understand. That's exactly what happened with Zionism. First they laughed, poked fun, cracked jokes. Then they took notice of what was being said in the papers, reading and re-reading and properly digesting it. Later, when they heard talk of a

bank, a Jewish bank with Jewish shares, they understood that
it was the real thing. For shares meant business and business
meant money. And what couldn't money accomplish in today's world?

Money talked, especially to the red-fezzed Turk, who was
a pauper along with the rest of the Kasrilevkites. From that
day on they took to Zionism with a vengeance. The Kasrilevkites, thank heaven, were a pliable sort. That which yesterday was as crooked as a serpent and as difficult as dividing the
Red Sea, was today as easy as pie. There could be nothing
easier. It was like gobbling up a bagel or smoking a cigarette.
What could be easier than buying Palestine from the Turks?
Let's face it—what *could* block it? Money was no problem.
No question of money was involved. One Rothschild (if
only he wanted to) could buy up not only Palestine and
Istanbul, but all the Turks to boot. The price was nothing to
worry about, either. Since it was business, they would bargain! In any case, what was one ruble more or less. But there
was only one hitch. Suppose the Turks didn't want to sell.
Eh, nonsense! Why shouldn't they want to sell? And, second of all, if we really get down to it, we were none-too-
distant kin. In fact, we were close relatives. Second cousins,
three times removed. Jews and Turks. Isaac and Ishmael.

The long and short of it was that they called one meeting,
then two and three, and with the help of God a group was
organized. The members elected a president, a vice president,
a secretary, and corresponding secretary, as in all civilized
towns. Everyone promised his share of Zionist dues. Some, a
kopek a week, some, two. The young people held fiery
speeches. The words Zion, Zionism, and Zionists were loudly
accented. The names of Doctor Herzl, Doctor Nordau, and
all the rest of the doctors were heard more frequently. Membership kept increasing and a big batch of money was collected. They called a big meeting and sat down to decide
what to do with the money. Should they leave the capital in
Kasrilevke and establish a separate fund for the Kasrilevke
Zionists, should they send it to the Zionist headquarters, or
should they wait a little longer until more money was col-

lected and the town could be a shareholder of the Jewish bank?

This meeting was one of the stormiest ever held in Kasrilevke. Opinions were split. Many supported the Zionist headquarters, saying that they were duty-bound to help the central office. If not, where would it get money from? Others argued that the headquarters could get along without Kasrilevke. We're not obliged to worry about the rest of the world, they said. Does anyone worry about Kasrilevke? It'll be enough if each one takes care of himself, they thought.

Then the president, Noah, stood up and made a passionate speech. A rich man's son-in-law, he was a young, beardless intellectual.

"For four thousand years these pyramids have stared down at you," he began in too high a voice. "This is what the great Napoleon said to his guards before capturing Egypt. I want to start my speech to you with practically the same words. It's been nearly two thousand years, brothers, since we found ourselves, not high up on the pyramids, but buried in the earth, six feet under. For almost two thousand years we've been waiting, not for our guards, but for the Messiah to come and redeem us from the Exile and bring us to the land of our forefathers, the land of Israel. For almost two thousand years we've been fasting on the Seventeenth Day of Tammuz, we abstain from meat for nine days, and comes the Ninth Day of Ab, we sit on the earth in our stocking feet and mourn the destruction of our Temple. For almost two thousand years we've been mentioning Jerusalem seventy-seven times a day. Now let us ask—what have we done for Zion's sake and for Jerusalem's sake?"

It's a crime, that, unlike other civilized towns, there was no stenographer in Kasrilevke to cover that meeting and transcribe every single word of Noah's excellent speech. Therefore, the end of his talent-packed talk must suffice.

"Now that we've been worthy of living to see this day," Noah said, perspiring, "when the poor sick Israelite has awakened from his slumber and is now stretching his weary bones, looking at the world around him, and saying: 'House of Jacob!

Come, let us go!'—we must not depend on anyone else. We must neither look for miracles nor wait for great men. For if you wait for great men, you'll just keep waiting. It's easier to be struck by lightning than to squeeze a ruble out of a rich man for Zionist purposes. We alone must start building our glorious home. As our sage Hillel said: 'If I am not for myself, who will be?' Surely we can be proud of having lived to see the day when Jews can talk about their own bank. But we must see to it that Kasrilevke should not be outdone by other towns and that Kasrilevkites too should have a share in our own Jewish bank. However, gentlemen, I have to tell you that according to the figures, as our treasurer will soon show, we haven't even collected enough money to buy one share. The greater half of the sum is still missing—that is, about five-six rubles. Therefore, it is only right, brothers, that you put yourselves out right here and now and chip in as much as you can and see to it that the sum of ten rubles is reached and no excuses. Let our brethren the world over know that Kasrilevke too has its Zionists in whose hearts the holy flame of Zion is burning. Let Doctor Herzl know that his hard work on our behalf is not in vain."

Thank God Kasrilevke still knew nothing about applause and shouts of "bravo." It's a good thing, too. The tumult and racket are ear-splitting enough as is. If they'd clap and yell "bravo," you would be deafened to boot, damn it. In Kasrilevke, when you liked what someone said, you went up to him and slapped him on the shoulders.

"Well, what do you say to our president, huh?"

"What a mouthpiece, the devil take it."

"He knows his stuff. He brought in the Talmud and other sacred books, mixed this and that . . ."

"You have to be a professor to remember all that stuff by heart."

"You ass! He sits day and night poring over his books."

In a word, the result was, a share was to be bought. But, that was easier said than done. How do you cross the bridge if some Jews were hidden away in a hole called Kasrilevke and the Jewish bank was God-knows-where out in London?

Well, then the hullabaloo began. Letters! Letters here, letters there. Shmaye, the corresponding secretary of the Kasrilevke Zionists, wrote his fingers to the bone, so to speak, until he finally found out where and how to send the money. When he did find out where and how to send it, a new catastrophe came in the person of the Kasrilevke postmaster. The well-known postal official was a fat, spoiled character, who couldn't stand the smell of garlic (although he himself loved it). As soon as two Jews walked into the post-office, he held his nose, made fun of them, and mimicked their Yiddish.

When Shmaye handed the postmaster the package, he flung it back at the secretary's face. It wasn't addressed properly, he said. The next time the postmaster threw it back at him again. Bring sealing wax, he was told. The third time the postmaster could find no fault. He inspected the package from all angles, melted the wax, and stamped it. Avoiding Shmaye's eye, he said:

"What sort of business do you have sending money to London?"

Our Shmaye, evidently, blurted out the reply. Or perhaps he was just showing off for the postmaster. (All correspondents are show-offs.)

"The money is going right into our Jewish bank!"

The postmaster looked at Shmaye, astonished. "A Yid bank? Where do Jews come to banks?"

Shmaye thought it over. Since you're such an anti-Semite, he thought, I'll show you what a Yid bank is. He started giving him a song and dance about the Jewish bank being the leading bank in the world. (All correspondents like to exaggerate.) The bank had assets of more than two hundred thousand million English pounds sterling. Pure gold. It was hard to convert it to Russian money, for a pound sterling was equal to about a hundred rubles. . . .

The postmaster licked the seal, pressed the molten wax, and said: "Now you're lying like a dog! A pound sterling isn't more than ten rubles."

"That's a plain pound sterling," Shmaye alibied, "but a golden pound is worth much more."

"Get on with you, you nitwit," the postmaster laughed, "Who are you telling stories to? A Jew just has to be a rascal. He must fool someone! Anyone else in my shoes wouldn't even accept your package. Do you know that I can put you, your package, and your whole congregation under arrest for sending our money to London. We work, we sweat, we plow the earth with our noses, and when the Jews come everything's prepared for them. They'll swill and glut and then take and ship our gold the devil knows where to some Yid bank."

When Shmaye saw that he had kicked off a pack of troubles, he held his breath and kept still as a mouse. He would have given anything to have taken his words back. But it was too late. (Plenty of correspondents would be quite glad to take back their lie- and fib-packed reports. But nothing doing. There was no taking it back!) Satisfied that he had the receipt, Shmaye left the office like a cowed puppy.

Having sent the money, the Kasrilevkites looked forward daily to the arrival of the share. One, two, three, four months passed—but neither money nor goods arrived. They came running to the secretary, the correspondent that is, and asked if by any chance he'd sent the money to the wrong place. Perhaps he hadn't addressed the package properly. Poor Shmaye had his work cut out for him. It wasn't enough that he had to write letters to committees, to Zionist headquarters, and to London, but he also had to listen to all the Kasrilevkites complaints and jests, which pierced him to the seventh rib. The whole business played right into the hands of those anti-Zionists, that is—the devout and pious Jews and the *Hasidim* who didn't think much of Zionism.

"Oho! Didn't we know that it would end up this way? Didn't we tell you right away that they'd cheat you out of the few rubles? What are you going to do now, take them to court?"

But God pitied our corresponding secretary. One fine morning, a letter from London arrived saying that the purchased share was there—not in Kasrilevke, but at the border. It just had to be officially stamped. Again, one, two, three, four months went by. Still, no share. The local wiseguys started harping on the secretary. Where was the share? Are they still stamping it? As was their custom, they spared no barbs. That business of official stamping galled Shmaye more than the share itself. That stamping made him spit blood. He rolled up his sleeves and started writing letters to Jewish communities all over the world.

"Is it fair?" he wrote. "Are such things done? Is it possible to hold a share and stamp it so long? Even if it had to be stamped with ten thousand stamps, you'd think it would have been stamped by now."

To the local Zionists he said: "What's the difference? If you've waited so long—wait a bit longer. Surely you won't have to wait any longer than you've waited until now."

That's exactly what happened. Nine months later, a package came for Rabbi Yozifl. Our corresponding secretary didn't have it come in his own name, because he wanted no further dealings with the postmaster. When the package arrived, a general membership meeting was called in the rabbi's house. Since all Jews (and Kasrilevke Jews certainly) were always in a rush and each one wanted to be first, it's no surprise that they pushed and crowded, climbed over one another, and tore the share in the Jewish bank out of their neighbor's hands.

The Kasrilevke Jews looked at the share for a long time. First they sighed and then each one had something else to say. The mood in the house seemed brighter, more cheerful. Their spirits were heightened, as are a man's who, while among strangers, yearns for his homeland, looks forward to some news, and suddenly gets wonderful regards from home. The people in Rabbi Yozifl's house felt happy, yet something tugged at their hearts. They felt like dancing, yet wanted to have a good cry at the same time.

Later, when everyone had his fill of looking at the share, Rabbi Yozifl (who, though a rabbi, didn't like to be the center of things) said: "Now, let me have a look."

He put a pair of spectacles on his nose, gazed and gazed some more, slowly inspecting the share from all sides. Seeing Hebrew letters and words in the holy tongue, he donned his Sabbath hat, recited the proper benediction proper to a new occasion, and again stared at the share. A sadness came over his face and you could have sworn that there were tears in his eyes.

"Rabbi! What are you so sad about?" they asked him. "We have to be happy. We'll have to finish off by dancing! Why are you feeling this way?"

Rabbi Yozifl didn't answer right away. From an inner pocket in his cloak, he took out some sort of a handkerchief. He pretended to blow his nose, but in reality wiped his eyes and said with a sigh, his voice breaking: "Just a touch of homesickness."

ON AMERICA

"America is all bluff. All Americans are bluffers. . . ."

That's what strangers say. Being greenhorns, they don't know what they're talking about. The fact is that America can't even shine Kasrilevke's shoes when it comes to bluffing. And our own Berel-Ayzik could put *all* the American bluffers into his side pocket.

You'll realize who Berel-Ayzik is when I tell you that if a Kasrilevkite starts jabbering a mile a minute, or as they say in America, talks himself blue in the face, he's shut up with these words: "Regards from Berel-Ayzik." He gets the hint and buttons his lip.

There's a story they tell in Kasrilevke about a fresh lout which tells a lot about Berel-Ayzik. On Easter, the Christians have a custom of greeting one another with the news that Christ is risen. The other answers by saying: True, he is risen. Well, once a Christian met up with this fresh lout of a Jew and said: "Christ is risen." The Jew felt his stomach churning. What should he do now? Saying "he is risen," would be against his belief. Saying no, he's not alive, might get him into a pickle. So he thought about it and said to the Christian: "Yes, that's what our Berel-Ayzik told us today." Just imagine, it was this very Berel-Ayzik who spent a few years in America before he returned to Kasrilevke. Picture the wonderful stories he told about that country.

"First of all—the land itself. A land flowing with milk and honey. People make money left and right. Beggars use two hands. They rake it in. And there's so much business there, it makes you dizzy. You do whatever you please. Want a factory —it's a factory. Want to open a store—fine. Want to push a pushcart, that's permitted, too. Or you can become a pedlar, even work in a shop! It's a free country. You can swell from hunger, die in the street, and no one'll bother you, no one'll say a word.

"As for its size. The width of its streets! The height of its buildings! They have a structure called the Woolworth building. Its tip scratches the clouds and then some. They say it has several hundred floors. How do you get to the top? With a ladder called an elevator. To get to the top floor, you board the elevator early in the morning and you reach your floor by sunset.

"Once I wanted to find out, just for the fun of it, what it looked like up there, and I'm not sorry I went. What I saw, I'll never see again. What I felt up there cannot even be described. Just imagine, I stood at the top and looked down. Suddenly I felt a queer kind of smooth and icy cold on my left cheek. Not so much like ice as jello, slippery and nappy-like. Slowly I turned to my left and looked—it was the moon.

"And their way of life. It's all rush and panic, hustle and bustle. Hurry-up is what they call it. They do everything quickly. They even rush when they eat. They dash into a restaurant and order a glass of whiskey. I myself saw a man being served a plate which had something fresh and quivering on it. As the man lifted his knife, half of it flew off to one side, half to the other, and that put an end to that man's lunch.

"But you ought to see how healthy they are. Men as strong as steel. They have a habit of fighting in the middle of the street. Not that they want to kill you, knock your eye out, or push a few teeth down your throat like they do here. God forbid! They fight just for fun. They roll up their sleeves and slug away to see who beats who. Boxing is what they call it. One day, while carrying some merchandise, I took a walk in the Bronx. Suddenly two young boys started up with me. They wanted to box. "No, sir," I said. "I don't box." Well, we argued back and forth, but they wouldn't let me leave. I thought it over: if that's the way you feel about it, I'll show you a thing or two. I put my package down, took off my coat, and they beat the daylights out of me. I made it away, my life hanging by a hair. Since then, all the money in the world won't get me to box.

"Not to mention the respect we Jews have there. No people are as honored and exalted there as the Jew. A Jew's a big shot there. It's a mark of distinction to be a Jew. On *Sukkoth* you can meet Jews carrying citrons and palm-branches even on Fifth Avenue. And they're not even afraid of being arrested. If I tell you that they love Jews it has nothing to do with the fact that they hate a Jewish beard and earlocks. Whiskers are what they call them. If they see a Jew with whiskers, they leave the Jew alone, but tug away at his whiskers until he has to snip them off. That's why most of the Jews don't wear beards or earlocks. Their faces are as smooth as glass. It's hard to tell who's a Jew and who isn't. You can't tell by the beard and by the language, but at least you can recognize him by his hurried walk and by his hands when he talks. But aside from that, they're Jews down to the last drop. They observe all the Jewish customs, love all Jewish foods, celebrate all the Jewish holidays. Passover is Passover! Matzohs are baked all year round. And there's even a separate factory for the bitter herbs we use during that holiday. Thousands upon thousands of workers sit in that factory and make bitter herbs. And they even make a living from it. America's nothing to sneeze at!"

"Yes, Berel-Ayzik, what you say is all very well and good. But just tell us one more thing. Do they die in America like they do here? Or do they live forever?"

"Of course they die! Why shouldn't they die? When they drop dead in America, they drop dead by the thousands each day. Ten and twenty thousands. Even thirty thousand. They drop dead by the streetful. Entire cities get swallowed up like Korah in the Bible. They just sink right into the ground and disappear. America's nothing to sneeze at."

"Then what's the big deal with Americans? In other words, they die like us."

"As for dying, sure they die. But it's *how* you die—that's the thing. Dying is the same all over. It's death that kills them. The main thing is the burial. That's it! First of all, in America it's customary to know where you're going to be buried. The man himself, while he's still alive, goes to the cemetery and picks out his own plot. He bargains for it until the price suits him. Then he takes his wife, goes out to the cemetery, and says: "See, dear? That's where you'll be. That's where I'll be. That's where our children'll be." The next thing he does is go to the funeral office and order whichever class funeral he wants. They come in three classes—first, second, and third. The first-class affair is for the real rich men, millionaires. It costs a thousand dollars. That's what I call a funeral! The sun shines, the weather is lovely. The coffin lies on a black, silver-plated catafalque. The horses wear black harnesses and white plumes. The rabbis and cantors and sextons are dressed in white-buttoned, black outfits. Carriages follow the coffin—carriages without end. All the children of all the Hebrew schools assemble at one point and they slowly sing the verse from the Psalms: "Righteousness shall go before him and shall set his steps on the way." This chant makes the town's rafters ring. It's no trifle! A thousand dollars!

"The second-class funeral is quite nice, too. It only costs five hundred dollars, but can't compete with the first-class affair. The weather isn't too peachy. The coffin lies on a black catafalque, but it isn't silver-plated. The horses and the rabbis are dressed in black—no plumes, no buttons. Carriages follow, but not as many as in the first-class affair. Children come, but only from a few Hebrew schools and they don't stretch the verse out as much. "Righteousness shall go before him and shall set his steps on the way." They use the mournful Psalms melody as befits the five hundred dollar rate.

"The third-class funeral is a shabby one and costs only a hundred dollars. The weather is cold and foggy. The coffin has no catafalque. There are two horses and two reverends. Not a carriage in sight. The children from one Hebrew school dash off their line without a tune. They mumble it so sleepily you can hardly hear them. After all, it only costs a hundred dollars. What can you expect for a hundred dollars?"

"Yes, but what happens, Berel-Ayzik, to a man who doesn't even have the hundred?"

"He's in hot water. Without money, it's bad all over. The pauper is half dead and buried anyway. But don't get any wrong ideas. Even in America they don't let the poor man lie

around unburied. They give him a free funeral. It doesn't even
cost him a penny. It's a pathetic funeral, to be sure. There's
no ceremony whatever. There's no hint of a horse or a rev-
erend. It rains cats and dogs. Only two sextons come, the first
sexton on one side, the second on the other, and in the middle,
the corpse himself. Then all three drag their feet over to the
cemetery. It's hell being born without money. It's a lousy
world . . . ! By the way, can anybody here spare an extra
cigarette?'

75,000

Troubles, you say? You call *everything* troubles. But *I* think that since the beginning of time and the creation of the Jewish people, a trouble like mine hasn't been heard, felt, or seen even in the wildest dream. If you have the time, move up a bit, pay close attention, and I'll tell you the story of 75,000 from *a* to *z*, down to the very last detail.

The whole affair makes my chest tighten; it gags me; it sends a stream of fire through me. I feel that I *must* get it out of my system. You get the picture? Just do me one favor. If I interrupt my story or get sidetracked and start jabbering about Boyberik, just lead me back to it. Ever since this business of the 75,000, you see, my ears have been ringing—and I usually forget where I'm at. I don't wish the likes of it on you! You get the picture? By the way, can you spare 75,000 —damn it—I mean, a cigarette?

Well then, where was I? Oh, yes, the 75,000. . . . You're looking at a man whose lottery ticket won the 75,000 rubles this past May 1. At first you might think: well what's there to listen to? Don't plenty of people win money? Don't folks say that a man from Nikolay won two hundred thousand and a young bookkeeper from Odessa forty thousand rubles? But not a peep is heard from them. Everything is fine and dandy. True, right, everyone expects the big prizes. One hundred thirty-six million people envy us. You get the picture? But the point is, there's no comparing one prize and another. The story of *this* prize is an amazing one which weaves into, around, and out of itself. You really have to prop yourself up and hear me out to the end to understand what's going on.

First of all, let me introduce myself. I'm not going to give you a song and dance that I'm a great scholar, philosopher, or man of wealth. You're looking at a plain, down-to-earth Jew who has his own house and a respected name in town, as well. You get the picture? True, I once had money, lots of it. Then again, how can I say lots? Certainly Brodsky had much more. But, in any case, I did have a few thousand rubles. Then, God took pity on me, as they say, and I was bitten by the bug-to-get-rich-quick. I started selling wheat in the famine-stricken districts and was left flat broke. But at least I could still meet my debts. No doubt you think that as soon as I lost the money I became depressed. Well then, you don't know me. Money means no more to me than—I don't know—a cigarette butt! It means absolutely nothing to me. How do I mean nothing? Sure, money is important, but to go fight over it, or kill yourself for it—not on your life! When you don't have what you need, if you can't live properly, if you can't give the donation you'd like to give—*then* things are bad. Take my word for it —when they ask one villager for a three-ruble contribution for the communal funds and skip *me*, it annoys the daylights out of me. You get the picture? I'd rather get hell from my wife as to why there's no money for Sabbath provisions than say no to a poor man while I still have forty kopeks jangling in my pocket. You get the picture? That's the sort of madman I am. By the way, do you have forty . . . damn it . . . I mean a match?

Well then, where was I? Oh, yes, the rubles. I lost the few rubles and was left without a kopek to my name. Having lost my few rubles and being left without a kopek to my name, I told my wife one fine morning:

"Tsipora, listen to what I've got to say. We're clean broke."

"What do you mean by clean broke?" she said.

"We don't even have a kopek to our name."

Well, being a female, she immediately started bawling. "Oh, my God. We're sunk. We're lost. We're six feet under. What are you talking about Yakov-Yosil—where's all your money?"

"Shush up! Pipe down! What are you raising such a racket for? Who says it was my money? God gave and God took. Or like they say: Ivan never had and never will have money. Who says that Yakov-Yosil is supposed to have two maids, a four-room apartment and wear a silken Sabbath cloak? There's plenty of Jews who are starving. But do they die? If you keep asking why this, why that, the world wouldn't exist for long."

I cited other examples and proverbs and my wife finally admitted that I was right. You get the picture? You ought to know that I'm married to a woman I'm proud of. She has a good head on her shoulders. You don't have to plead too long to make your point. She stopped her sniffling and fussing immediately and even took to consoling me, saying that the whole thing was probably fated, that God is a merciful Father and would watch over us. . . .

Without dilly-dallying, I sub-leased my apartment, moved into one tiny room and kitchen, and, begging your pardon, dismissed the maids. My wife, may she live and be well, rolled up her sleeves and became the cook. And I let it be known that I, Reb Yakov-Yosil, was to be called Pauper. What do I mean by Pauper? As you can well imagine, there are plenty poorer than me. After all, I still had an apartment, a piece of property from which I could make my livelihood. The only trouble was that there were four weeks in the month. Had there been only two weeks in a month, maybe our expenses and income would have balanced. Each month always had two extra weeks and, naturally, that's no good. But, never mind. Like they say—you get used to troubles. Let me tell you, being a poor man is the most peaceful thing in the world. Your mind is free of headaches, payments, loans, rat-races, and a topsy-turvy world. But wait—there's a God up above who says: What good is it, Yakov-Yosil, having peace of mind and living without troubles? Do you have a ticket to the lottery? Well, here's 75,000 for you, go break your neck with it! You get the picture? By the way, do you happen to have a ticket—damn it—I mean, a cigarette?

Well then, where was I? Oh, yes, the lottery ticket. Ticket? You think it's so simple for a Jew to have a ticket and collect the 75,000? Wait just a minute. First of all, why does a Jew have a ticket? So that he can pawn it and get some money for it. Well then, why don't you go into a bank, Yakov-Yosil, you ass, and get some cash for it? But the excuses are that in the first place there are no banks in our village and, secondly, what do I need the bank for? Can't a bank go bankrupt if it has a mind to? Then again, things do operate in an orderly manner in this orderly world and no one was grabbing the ticket out of my hand. Who wanted my ticket anyway? You get the picture? Well, that's what I thought at the time. On second thought, perhaps I didn't really think at all. But I decided: my tenant, a fine young man, a gentleman and a scholar, was a money-lender. Why not pawn the ticket with him? If he'd give me 200 for it, I'd take it. Why shouldn't I? So I went over to him—Birnbaum, he was called—and said:

"Mr. Birnbaum, would you give me 200 rubles for my ticket?"

"I'll give you 200 rubles for your ticket," he said.

"How much interest would I have to pay?" I said.

"How much interest do you want me to charge you?" he said.

"How do I know?" I said. "Charge me bank rates."

"I'll charge you bank rates," he said.

In a nutshell, we settled on the interest, I pawned my ticket for five months, and took the 200 rubles. You get the picture? Then why don't you take a receipt from him, Yakov-Yosil, you ass, stating that you left such-and-such a ticket of series and number so-and-so. But, no! Just the opposite. Birnbaum took a receipt from *me* that I borrowed 200 rubles for five months and left him such-and-such a ticket of series and number so-and-so. And if I didn't pay the 200 rubles in time, said ticket would be his and I would have nothing on him. You get the picture? You know what I thought then? I thought: what's there to be afraid of? In any case, if I'd redeem the ticket at the proper time and pay my debt, everything would be fine and dandy. If not, I'd pay him the interest due and he'd just have to wait. Why wouldn't he wait? Why should he care, so long as he got the interest? You get the picture? Well, here's what happened. When the time came, naturally, I didn't redeem the ticket. Five months passed, then another five. Slowly it stretched on into two years and five months. I kept paying the interest, of course. That is, sometimes I paid, sometimes not. What was I afraid of? Would he sell the ticket? He wouldn't sell my ticket. Why should he sell my ticket? Anyway, that's what I thought at the time. On second thought, perhaps I really didn't think at all. Meanwhile, times were bad, business was rotten; the extra weeks in the months kept piling up and I worked my fingers to the bone. What was one to do? Just live and be well—there were always plenty of troubles! And this situation lasted until Passover.

But this year, before Passover, God sent a little business my way. I bought a few carloads of millet. The price of millet skyrocketed. I sold the millet and, thank heaven, made a neat profit on the millet. I had myself a Passover that Brodsky himself would have envied. Not owing a kopek to a soul and having a few hundred rubles to your name to boot was nothing to sneeze at. I was riding high—you get the picture? So why don't you take two hundred rubles, Yakov-Yosil, you ass, and pay Birnbaum and buy back your lottery ticket? But, no. I decided—what's the rush? He won't run away with the ticket. After Passover will be time enough. If not, I'll pay the interest and take a receipt for the ticket. Anyway, that's what I thought then. On second thought, perhaps I didn't really think at all. You get the picture? I upped and turned the money into sacks which I stored in a warehouse. Well, thank goodness for a miracle—the lock was jimmied that night. It happened right after Passover, on April 30, the night before the May 1 lottery drawing. All my sacks were stolen! I was flat broke again.

"Tsipora," I said to my wife. "You know what? We're flat broke again."

"What do you mean flat broke?"

"We don't even have a *sack* to our name," I said.

"What do you mean? Where did the sacks disappear to?"

"They've been carried off! Right out of the warehouse!"

Being a woman, naturally, she started bawling and wailing.

"Shush up, Tsipora," I said. "Don't yell. You're not alone here. Make believe the house burned down and we got out of it naked as the day we were born. Does that make you feel any better?"

"What a comparison?" she said. "Is that why they have to steal your sacks?"

"What's one thing got to do with the other?" I said. "Mark my words, the sacks will be found."

"How are they going to get to you?" she said. "Are the crooks going to present you with the sacks just because you're called Yakov-Yosil? They don't have anything better to do, eh?"

"Go on!" I said. "You're a ninny. Man can't even imagine the wonders of God!"

Well, here's what happened! The sacks, of course, were goners. What sacks? Where sacks? But I ran around like a madman, contacted the police, searched high and low, poked into every rat-hole. But it was a lost cause. Like trying to find yesterday. You get the picture? My head was in another world, my heart was in my throat, my mouth was dry—I was completely depressed. But around noon, while standing near the local stock exchange, that is, near the pharmacy on the marketplace, a thought flew through my mind: after all, today's some sort of judgment day. The lottery drawing— the first of May. God can do anything! We have an Almighty God. If only He wills it, He can make me and my whole family happy.

Then, remembering the stolen sacks, I forgot all about the first of May lottery drawing and started looking for the sacks again. I had a little clue and kept searching the whole day into the rest of that night and on until the dawn of May 2. I was in a complete daze, I hadn't eaten for twenty-four hours and here it was 1 P.M. and I was passing out. You get the picture?

When I came home, my wife pounced on me: "How about washing up and having a bite? Haven't you had enough of that sack affair. Your sacks are sticking like a bone in my throat. The devil take those sacks. Do you have to kill your- self on account of those sacks? We'll be no better off with or without the sacks. What a business with sacks! Here sacks, there sacks. All I hear is sacks, sacks, sacks."

"You know, wife, dear?" I said. "Let's forget about the sacks, huh? I've been sacked enough as is. Now *you* come

along and rub salt into my wounds. Sacks, sacks, sacks." You
get the picture? Can I trouble you for a sack—damn it—I
mean, another cigarette?

Well then, where was I? Oh yes, the sacks. Well, it was a
lost cause. What to do? I wasn't going to kill myself for them.
I washed and sat down to eat, but—nothing doing! My appetite was gone.

"What's wrong with you, Yakov-Yosil?" asked my wife,
God bless her. "Who crossed you today?"

"I myself don't know what the matter is," I said, left the
table in the middle of the meal, and lay down on the sofa. No
sooner did I stretch out than the paper was delivered. Why
then don't you take it, Yakov-Yosil, you ass, and see if perhaps your ticket won a prize? After all, it *is* May 2d. But no
go. I didn't know if it was the second of May, the twenty-first
of June, or the Ides of March Slave. You get the picture?
Well then, I picked up the paper and started reading it like
the prayer book—from the very beginning. The long and the
short of it was that I lay there reading all sorts of news. Shoot-
ings and hanging, stabbings and murders. The English and the
Boers. Naturally, it all went in one ear and out the other. Who
gave a damn about the English and the Boers when my sacks
were gone! The whole pack of them weren't worth one of my
stolen sacks. Anyway, that's what I thought at the time. But
on second thought, perhaps I really didn't think at all. I flipped
from one page to the next, scanning, and then I saw—LOTTERY
DRAWING. Suddenly a thought hit me. Perhaps my ticket has
won 500 rubles at least. That would be a handy heaven-sent
substitute for my sacks. I went through the list of winners of
500 rubles. Nothing. The 1,000 ruble section. Nothing. Certainly not 5, 8, or 10,000. I kept this up until I got to the
75,000 listing. As I looked at that number, I saw stars and felt
a violent pounding in my head. Series 2289, number 12. I
could have sworn it was my number. But then again, how does
a bungler like me come to such a big prize? I took a long look
at the numbers and—great God!—it was my number. I wanted
to rise from the sofa—but couldn't. I was glued to it. I wanted
to call "Tsipora"—but couldn't. My tongue was stuck to my

palate. Mustering all my strength, I got up, went to my desk, and looked at my note book. As I lived and breathed—series 2289, number 12.

"Tsipora," I said, my hands shaking, my teeth chattering. "Know what? The stolen sacks have been found."

She looked at me as if I were crazy.

"What are you talking about. Do you know what you're saying?"

"I'm just trying to tell you," I said, "that God has paid us back for our sacks a thousand-fold and then some. Our ticket has been picked and we've won a barrelful of cash."

"Are you serious, Yakov-Yosil, or are you teasing?"

"Teasing?" I said. "I'm quite serious. We ought to be congratulated. We've won money."

"How much have we won?" she said, looking me straight in the eye, as if to say: if you're lying, better watch out!

"Well, for example, how much do you think we've won?"

"How do I know?" she said. "Probably a few hundred rubles."

"Why not a few thousand?" I said.

"How much is a few thousand?" she said. "Five? Six? Or perhaps all of seven?"

"You can't think of anything higher, can you?"

"Ten thousand?"

"Use your head," I said. "More."

"Fifteen thousand?"

"More."

"Twenty, twenty-five?"

"More!"

"Tell me, Yakov-Yosil, don't tease me!"

"Tsipora," I said, taking her hand and squeezing it. "We've won a gold mine. We're in the chips. You've never even dreamed of the amount we've won!"

"Well, tell me how much we've won, Yakov-Yosil, don't keep me in suspense!"

"We've won a load of money," I said, "a treasure-chest, a grand total of 75,000 rubles. You hear, Tsipora? 75,000!"

"God be praised," she said, and started running around the

room, wringing her hands. "May your name be blessed for looking down upon us, too, and making us happy. Thank you, dear God, thank you. Are you sure, Yakov-Yosil? Is there no error, heaven forbid? Praised is your name, dear God, true and merciful Father! The whole family will be over-joyed, our good friends will be happy, our enemies will eat their hearts out. Such a load of money, knock wood, is nothing to sneeze at. How much did you say, Yakov-Yosil, 75,000?"

"75,000," I said. "Give me my coat, Tsipora, and I'll be on my way."

"Where are you off to?"

"What do you mean, where? I have to step into Birnbaum's place. That's where I've pawned my lottery ticket. And I don't even have a receipt for it."

As soon as she heard these words, she turned all colors, grabbed both my hands and said, "Yakov-Yosil, in God's name, don't go now. Think it over first. Think of what you're doing, where you're going and what you're going to say. Don't forget, it's 75,000!"

"You're talking like a fishwife," I said. "So what if it's 75,000. Am I a child?"

"Listen to me, Yakov-Yosil," she said. "Think it over first. Consult a good friend. Don't go there right now. I won't let you."

To make a long story short, you know quite well that when a woman puts her foot down, she wins. We called in a good friend and told him the whole story. Having heard us out, he said that my wife was right, for 75,000 was no trifle; in the meantime, someone else had my ticket and I had no receipt for it; money was tempting and who knows what evil thoughts might come to him. After all, it was 75,000.

You get the picture? Well, how shall I put it? The both of them put me into such a blue funk that I myself became frightened and started suspecting God knows what. How should I handle the situation? We decided that I take 200 rubles (cash was to be had at a moment's notice—a prize winner was good security), plus another man who would stand outside the door while I spoke to Birnbaum, paid him my debt and the interest,

and bought back my ticket. In any case, if he gave back the
ticket—fine. If not, I would at least have a witness. You get
the picture? But all this would be grand, I thought, if he still
didn't know that the ticket had won the 75,000. But what to
do if he too had a paper and noticed the winning number?
What would I do if he'd say: "First of all, I returned the ticket
a long time ago. Second of all, that's not the number you gave
me, and third of all, you never gave me a ticket at all." You
get the picture? Unless, of course, miraculously, he hadn't as
yet heard about the prize.

"Remember now, Yakov-Yosil, it's no trifle. You're going
for 75,000. Don't let them see a hint or a trace of that 75,000
on your face. But no matter what happens, remember that
your life is worth 75 times 75,000."

Those were my wife's words, God bless her. She took me
by the hands and asked me to give her my word, my word of
honor, that I'd remain calm. Calm? How could I be calm when
my heart was pounding away and my thoughts buzzed a mile a
minute. I couldn't forgive myself. Yakov-Yosil, you ass, how
could you give Birnbaum, a complete stranger, a ticket worth
75,000, and not even take a receipt or say a word. By the way,
do you have a word—damn it,—I mean, a cigarette?

Well then, where was I? Oh yes, Birnbaum. I would be in
a pretty pickle, I thought, if Birnbaum had read the paper
and already learned of the 75,000, perhaps even before I did.
Then I would come up to him and say: "God be with you,
Mr. Birnbaum."

"Greetings," he would say. "What's the good word?"

"Where's my ticket?" I would say.

"What ticket?" he would say.

"The ticket of series 2289, number 12, which I've pawned
with you."

He would look at me, wide-eyed and innocent.

Thoughts like these flashed through my mind. I felt my
chest tightening; I had a choking sensation in my throat; I
couldn't catch my breath. But what was the upshot? I came
to Birnbaum's house and asked where he was. Sleeping, they
told me. Sleeping? An excellent sign that he doesn't suspect

a thing. Blessed are you, dear God! I entered the house and met his wife, Feygele, in the kitchen. It was hot, smoky, and knee-deep in filth.

"Reb Yakov-Yosil! Welcome! What a surprise!" said Feygele. She invited me in, seated me at the head of the table, and asked why haven't I come around.

"How do I know why? I don't know myself," I said, looking her straight in the eye, thinking: *"Does* she know or *doesn't* she know."

"Well, what are you doing, Reb Yakov-Yosil?"

"What should I be doing?" I said. "You've probably heard about my bundle of troubles."

"What troubles?"

"What?" I said. "Haven't you heard about the affair of the stolen sacks?"

"Is *that* all?" she said. "That's an old story by now. I thought it was something new."

Something new? Was it the 75,000 she meant? I thought, and looked into her eyes. But they told me absolutely nothing.

"How about having a glass of tea, Reb Yakov-Yosil, until my husband gets up. I'll have the samovar heated."

"A glass of tea? Sure. Why not?" I said. But my heart thumped, I couldn't catch my breath, my mouth was dry, the room was hot, I was sweating, Feygele was chattering away and for the life of me I didn't know what the devil she was talking about. My head, you see, was in that little room where Birnbaum slept, snoring away so lustily. You get the picture?

"Why aren't you drinking?" said Feygele.

"What then am I doing?" I said, and kept stirring the spoon in the glass.

"You've been playing with the spoon for an hour," she said, "and you haven't even taken a sip."

"Thanks," I said. "I don't drink cold—I mean, hot tea. I like the tea to stand a while and get good and hot . . . I mean, good and cold. What I mean to say is, I like the tea to heat up, I mean cool off."

"You seem to be in a complete dither, Reb Yakov-Yosil," she said. "You're in such a daze, you don't know what you're saying. Is that what the stolen sacks have done to you? With God's help, the sacks will be found. I heard they found a clue. Wait, there's my husband, stirring. He's getting up now. Here he comes."

Birnbaum appeared, wearing a silk skullcap. He was still sleepy and rubbed his eyes, looking at me out of the corner of his eye.

"How are you, Reb Yakov-Yosil?"

My first thought was—does he know or doesn't he? At first, it seemed that he did not know. Then again, perhaps he did.

"How do you expect me to be?" I said. "You heard about my bad luck with the sacks."

"That incident has whiskers already. Tell us something new. Feygele, how about some jam? Sleep has left a funny taste in my mouth," Birnbaum said, making a face.

Well, so long as he was asking for jam, it was a good sign that he knew nothing, I thought. We started a conversation about . . . the devil knows what! It made no sense at all. My stomach was churning; I was gagging; I felt as if I were passing out. In another minute I'd topple over and start yelling: "Help, fellow Jews, it's 75,000!" You get the picture? Finally, with the good Lord's help, I brought up the subject of interest.

"I can give you some of the interest, Mr. Birnbaum," I said, "that is, I can pay up the entire interest for the ticket."

"With pleasure," he said, tasting a spoonful of jam, "with all due respect, why not?"

"How much do I owe you?"

"Do you want to know what's coming to me, or do you really want to pay cash?"

"No, no," I said. "I mean cash."

"Feygele," he called, "bring the account book over."

Hearing these words, I felt as if I'd come back from the dead. Poor chap, he didn't know the first thing about the prize.

After paying the interest, I told him: "Excuse me, Mr. Birnbaum, but note in your book that you got the interest for the ticket of series 2289, number 12."

"Feygele," he said, "note that it was paid for ticket series 2289, number 12."

He doesn't know a thing, I thought, and started talking about the ticket: it didn't pay to own one and have to pay interest on it. Then I asked: "What will become of the ticket?"

"Why bring it up now?" he asked, staring at me out of the corner of his eye.

That look made my heart leap. I didn't like the looks of that look. You get the picture? But I covered up immediately and said:

"I mentioned it because the ticket's costing me an arm and a leg. I swear, you ought to extend the loan and take 1 per cent less. Like they say—for friendship's sake."

"No," he said. "Anything else, yes, but this—no. If you want it under the old terms, fine. If not, pay me my money and pawn your ticket elsewhere."

"Even now?" I asked and my heart hammered away within me; rappety-rap, rappety-rap.

"This very minute," he said.

"Here's your money," I said, taking out the 200 rubles, my heart in my mouth.

"Take the money," he said to Feygele, bending over his tea and tasting a spoonful of jam. This was followed by another spoonful, and then a third, a fourth, a fifth. I was dying to get hold of my lottery ticket, and here he was eating jam. Every wasted moment was costing me my health. But you can't be a glutton about it. If he liked jam, let him enjoy it. It wasn't proper to drive someone by the scuff of his neck. So I had to sit and nurse my bleeding heart until he'd put an end to that jam-gobbling. You get the picture? Do you happen to have some jam . . . damn it . . . I mean a cigarette?

Well then, where was I? Oh, yes, Birnbaum eating jam. Having finished, he wiped his lips and said: "Reb Yakov Yosil, I've taken the money. I've been paid the interest, and now I have to give you the ticket, right?"

"Seems fair," I said, faking a nonchalant expression. But I nearly dropped dead out of sheer joy.

"There's only one hitch," he said. "I can't give you the ticket today."

As soon as he said this I felt something tearing in my heart.

I came down from seventh heaven back to earth. I don't know what kept me on my feet.

"What's wrong, Mr. Birnbaum?" I asked, "why can't you give me the ticket?"

"Because I don't have it here."

"What do you mean, you don't have it here?"

"It's at the bank."

Hearing this, I felt better and fell into a deep thought.

"What are you thinking about?"

"Nothing special. I was just wondering how I and the ticket'll get together."

"Simple," he said. "Tomorow I'll go into town and bring it to you."

"Fine," I stood, said goodbye, made a motion for the door, but immediately turned back.

"How do you like that? What a businessman I am! I've returned your money, paid the interest, but you still have the ticket. At least give me a receipt for it."

"What good will a receipt do you?" he asked. "Don't you trust me for 200 rubles without a receipt?"

"Perhaps you're right," I said, heading back to the door. Then I turned around again and added: "No. It's isn't right. It isn't business-like. If someone else has your ticket, you should have a receipt for it. Listen to me, Mr. Birnbaum— give me a receipt. Why not give me a receipt?"

Suddenly Birnbaum picked himself up and went back to his little curtained-off room and called his wife.

"Mr. Birnbaum," I shouted, "I know why you've called Feygele. You're going to tell her to send the maid out for the paper. Since today's the second of May you want to look and see if your ticket's won any money. But why bother? *I'll* tell you the news. My ticket, thank God, has won prize money."

Birnbaum turned all colors.

"Is that so?" he said. "May God be with you. How much did the ticket win?"

"The ticket has struck gold," I said, "may all Jews have like luck. And that's why I want a receipt from you, you get the picture?"

"As I said before, may God grant you the entire 200,000," he said. "From the bottom of my heart, believe me, I don't begrudge it to you. Come on now, how much did the ticket bring in? Don't be afraid to say it."

"Mr. Birnbaum," I said, "why drag it out and why beat around the bush? The ticket has won 75,000—you have the ticket, the interest is paid, the capital I've returned, and now give me my ticket. But you say you don't have it, that it's in the bank. Then hand over a receipt and let's get this affair over with."

It was no use. A wild look came into Birnbaum's eyes; his face became inflamed. Seeing that he was in a bad way, I took him aside and held his hands.

"Dear friend. Have pity on me and on yourself. Tell me what you want. We'll come to an understanding. But don't torment me. I can hardly stand on my feet as it is. Tell me how much you want and give me a receipt for the ticket. It's no use —I won't leave without a receipt, for its a question of 75,000 rubles."

"What do you want me to say?" he said, his eyes blazing. "We'll let people mediate. Whatever they say, we'll do."

"What do you want other people for?" I said. "Let's be people ourselves. In the name of God, Birnbaum, listen to me. How much do you want? Let's not have it come to ridicule and scandal."

"Only mediation!" he said. "Whatever they say, I'll do."

Seeing that it would do no good, I opened the door and told my witness: "Zeydl. You can go now!" Zeydl took off like a bat out of hell and spread the news all over town: Yakov-Yosil's lottery ticket had won 75,000 rubles and Birnbaum had it and wouldn't give it back. You get the picture? That's all they needed. A half hour later, Birnbaum's place was packed, and the street was filled with a tumultuous crowd, yelling on top of their voices.

"Ticket!"

"Yakov-Yosil!"

"Birnbaum!"

"75,000."

The crowd sided with me. Some banged on the table, others promised to beat the daylights out of Birnbaum and smash his house to bits. And they weren't kidding either. But the upshot was, we'd let the town's rich man decide. Whatever he'd say would be done. The entire kit and kaboodle went over to his place.

You ought to know that our town's rich man is a soft-spoken, decent, and honest gentleman. He hates all this mediation business. But, since the whole pack of us swooped down on his home, shouting, "Save us"—for, if not, they'd tear the place apart—he had no choice but to take on the burden. We promised that his decision would be final, and poor Birnbaum had to sign the ticket over to the rich man. We all agreed to go into town, either the next day or the day after that, God willing, and take the ticket out of the bank. I would pay Birnbaum whatever sum the rich man ordered. You get the picture? Now you probably think that that finished it. Tsk, tsk, tsk. The fun's just beginning. You see, I had a partner to the ticket. Did you ever know a Jew who owned a ticket outright? Who was my partner? My partner happened to be my own brother, Henikh, who lived in a small village not far from here. It was because of *him*, really, that I pawned the ticket with Birnbaum. I mean, just the reverse, that is, it was because of *me* that my brother had the ticket pawned by Birnbaum. You get the picture? But there's a long story that goes with it, which I must tell you from *a* to *z* to make it clear.

Well then, where was I? Oh, yes, my brother Henikh. Well, I have a brother Henikh—may he live to be a hundred and twenty—what can I say? It isn't right to talk about your own brother, is it? It's like cutting your nose to spite your face. But, never mind. Don't ask! My brother and I don't think much of each other, you get the picture? May God repay me for all the things I've done for him. I can well boast that I set him on his feet. Save God alone, I'm the one who made a man out of him. But I don't have to impress you! You get the picture? So, when he sends me a lottery ticket and asks me to either sell it or pawn it for 200 rubles and send him the

money—you'd think I've got the right and privilege to do so,
eh? But once that was done, do you think he gave a damn
about the ticket? Do you think he ever gave it a second
thought? *I* took care of it, *I* insured it, *I* paid the interest on it.
What did he care? And when with God's help the ticket won
a prize, who beat his head against the wall with Birnbaum? Who
almost got apoplexy before a way out of the dilemma was
found? Finally, when we got down to brass tacks, my brother
argued:

"Who asked you to drop dead for my ticket?"

Well, did you ever? How's that for gall? I tell you, this
boorish attitude peeved me no end.

"Since you're such a low-down ass, who says the ticket is
yours?" I said.

"Then whose is it?"

"Whose ever it is, it is," I said. "But in the meantime, we
have to get it out of strange hands. Seventy-five thousand
rubles is no trifle, you know."

You get the picture?

Well, how was I repaid? With scandal! With him banging
on tables and smashing my chairs. Listen, if the whole world
and his brother says you can't make a skullcap out of a sow's
ear, they're probably right. Why fight with my brother for
nothing, I decided. One hundred thirty-six million envy our
prize and we brothers, sons of one mother and father, end up
squabbling over it. My ticket, your ticket—phoo! It was a
damn shame. Our first move was to redeem the ticket. That
was preferable to all else, right? But go argue with an ignora-
mus. I'm referring to my own brother, Henikh, may God not
punish me for these words. Had he only told me beforehand
what was eating him—that the ticket wasn't like all others,
that there was a snag in the proceedings—I would have known
what to do! But when do you think he mentioned the snag?
Way, way later, when the ticket had long been signed over
to the rich man and the judge had, begging your pardon, impounded the ticket in the bank, called for an investigation,
that is, summoned each of us to give him all the facts about the
ticket.

"How did you get this ticket?" he asked me. "What connection has Birnbaum with it? And how does the rich man
fit in?"

Believe me, it was some to-do, you get the picture? What
has the judge got to do with us? Why does he have to know
all these stories? But listen, here's where the real snag begins—
the sort of snag one cannot get out of. Like a bone stuck in
your throat which won't go up or down. It just chokes you.
Do you want to know the source of that snag? It originated
with some sort of a priest, a monk. You get the picture? There
was this monk in my brother's village with whom Henikh had
dealings for many years. On his word alone, he used to borrow
money from the monk and sell him merchandise. They got
along like friends. You get the picture?

But then something happened. According to the monk—
and go believe him and his word of honor—my brother came
to him one day and said: "Father, I need a small loan, 200
rubles. I have to go to the fair."

"How can I give you something I don't have?" the monk
said.

"That's no excuse," said my brother. "I need the 200 badly."

"What a queer Jew you are," the monk said. "I tell you, I
have no money. But, if you wish, I can lend you a lottery
ticket for which you might get some money."

"You get the picture? That's the very same ticket which
won the 75,000. Anyway, that's what the monk said, and go
believe him and his word of honor. Now that the ticket won
the prize, the monk naturally came running to my brother and
said: "The ticket has won a neat prize, thank God."

"That's what they say," my brother said.

"Well, what'll happen?" said the monk.

"Well, what do you expect to happen?" my brother said.

To make a long story short, they argued back and forth.
One said this, the other that. One said cheese, the other, beans.
But neither of them had anything signed in black and white.
You get the picture? Then again, my brother, at any rate, had
the ticket. But what did the monk have? Aggravation! The
upshot was, the monk begged Henikh to give him at least a

few thousand rubles. Then why don't you button his lip
with a couple of thousand rubles, you mangy lout, and let him
stop pestering you?

"He doesn't have it coming to him," my brother argued.
"It's my ticket. May I drop dead if I didn't buy that ticket
from him three years ago."

Well, that might have been the end of it. But you know our
Jews, God bless them. The village itself is oh such a fine one.
Perhaps you've heard of it. Naginsk, it's called, and like its
name it's full of nags and tattle-tales, may it burn to a crisp at
high noon! In short, they informed the monk that he could
make a federal case out of the incident. They advised him
not to fritter his time away but go right to the district attor-
ney's office in the big city and tell him that some Jews cheated
him out of a ticket which had won 75,000 and wouldn't give
it back to him. You get the picture? Well, the monk didn't
waste time and did everything he had to do—even more than
he had to. It was then that they impounded the ticket and,
gradually, the hodge-podge grew. And it was no laughing
matter, either. As if things weren't bad enough, another problem entered the picture, another snag—a monk! Wanting to
settle, my brother offered him ten, then fifteen thousand, but
the monk turned a deaf ear to him. That monk was so
dazed, he himself didn't know what he wanted. And that's the
story of the snag. You get the picture?

Well then, where was I? Oh, yes, the snag. We couldn't do
a thing with this heaven-sent snag. Couldn't turn left, couldn't
turn right. But there's a great God up above who, like they
say, punishes with one stroke and heals with the other. So, we
found some people, buddies and pals, brothers-in-arms, do-
gooders, and just plain hangers-on who stepped into the midst
of the affair and tried to make peace. They finagled here and
there, they ran from party to party—from my brother Henikh
to the monk, from the monk to my brother, from me to Birnbaum, from Birnbaum to me, from both of us to my brother,
and from all three of us to the monk. We hustled and bustled,
traveled and argued. In brief, after much difficulty, they
finally smoothed things over. Don't ask *what* or *how* they

smoothed over. So long as things were smooth. Like they say: you stew up your troubles and eat a hearty meal.

Or as my brother put it when he met the monk.

"Your grace, this isn't the greatest decision in the world, but let's split it down the line."

"All right, we'll split it. But you're still a swindler, Henikh."

"I drink to your health, father," said my brother offering him a glass of whisky. We all drank bottoms-up, kissed each other. Everything was fine and dandy. Everyone was satisfied. Satisfied? How could *anyone* be satisfied if each of us practically had 75,000 in our grip and had let it slip away. Blast it! You want to know how it happened? Here are the plain facts. I'm not even going to talk about myself. So what if I don't have the 75,000! I don't give a damn. But I ask you, what would my brother Henikh have done if I hadn't wired him about our 75,000 ruble prize? Do you know what someone else in my shoes would have done, seeing such big money? He would have buttoned his lip and mum's the word. What brother? Who's Henikh? Let him think I sold the ticket outright. Or that I pawned it with Birnbaum and didn't buy it back in time. For doesn't Birnbaum have a receipt from me saying that I pawned ticket number such-and-such and if I don't buy it back in time then said ticket would be his? You get the picture? But the point is, I swear I never so much as thought of any fast deal like that! You're looking at a man who doesn't give a damn for money. When you get down to it, what *is* money? Dirt! Like my wife says, so long as you got your health and everything else you need. . . . But, then again, it was aggravating. After all, it was 75,000. You get the picture?

Now take Birnbaum, for instance. He's completely innocent. Poor chap, he let the 75,000 slip right through his fingers. Simply an honest and high-minded young man was he, who wanted absolutely no gain from a ticket not his own. He only wanted people to judge. To hear what others would say. You get the picture? For otherwise the situation would have been peaches and cream for him. After all, he had my note saying that if I didn't buy back the lottery ticket within a cer-

tain time, then that ticket numbered such-and-such would
be . . . you get the picture? Well, as luck had it, that very
ticket won the 75,000. Now, I ask you, isn't that enough to
give you a fit? So much for two poor devils into whose
pockets the 75,000 had almost come. Right?

The third poor devil was my brother, Henikh. He moped
around like a dead chicken. It was *indeed* a pity that he was
getting such a small share of the prize. After all, he was used
to winning no less than 75,000 *every* year, *twice* a year, in
fact! He went around yelling: "What do they want of me?
Give to the monk, give to my brother, give to Birnbaum. They
want to make a pauper out of me." You get the picture?

The fourth man, the monk that is, was certainly a poor
devil. He swore, and you had to believe his word of honor,
that he couldn't understand why the Jews were splitting up his
money. "Henikh, at least, despite the fact that he's a swindler
and deserves to be locked up, is, after all, a home-town friend.
But the rest of the bunch? What sort of partners are they to
my ticket?" You get the picture? Well, try and speak to a
monk and explain the meaning of honesty—that one was a
brother who could have taken the entire sum without anyone
saying boo, and the other was such an honorable young man,
who had my note which stated that lottery ticket number
such-and-such . . . you get the picture? Did Birnbaum have
any ill-intent? Did he demand anything? Did he have any
complaints? God forbid! He only wanted to call in outsiders
to judge. Whatever other people would say! He'd suddenly
fallen in love with people. You get the picture?

Well then, four people each won a part of the 75,000 and
each of them lost the full 75,000. Four ruined, unhappy souls.
But having settled, there was no use crying over spilled milk.
Perhaps it was fated. Well then, what was the next move?
To go and share the prize—that is, all four of us would have
to go to the bank, take the ticket, collect our money, divide it,
and shout congratulations over a glass of wine. Right? Well,
take it easy, hold your horses! First of all, the ticket had been
impounded by the judge. So the first thing to be done was to
liberate it. But the monk didn't want that done until his share

of the prize was guaranteed. You get the picture? But how
could his share be guaranteed? Only by taking it from the
rich man's account and writing it over to Henikh and the
monk. But the rich man didn't want to hear of it, and rightly
so. Here's what he said:

"What do I care about someone else's ticket. How can I
order the release of a 75,000 ruble ticket which isn't mine and
which has been impounded, if I don't even know whose it is.
First it belonged to Birnbaum and Yakov-Yosil. Now, the
latest is that it belongs to a Henikh and a monk. Later, other
owners will show up, other Henikhs and other monks. What
will I do if each of them demands the 75,000 from me?
Friends, where would I get all that cash? I'm not Brodsky, you
know."

You get the picture? Then a run-around with lawyers
started. And laywers are just like doctors. Whatever one says,
the other says just the opposite. But they all take money and
give advice. Each of them, different advice. One lawyer said
that the rich man could very well hand the ticket over to anyone he wished. Another said that he could not hand it over
under *any* circumstances. A third comes to say that he *had*
to release it, for, if not, he could get himself into hot water
for *not* handing it over. Then came another lawyer who said
that the best thing would be for the rich man to wash his hands
of the ticket altogether. Another lawyer said: mention it not!
If he washed his hands of the ticket, the ticket would be left
dangling in mid-air, and then he'd *really* be in hot water. Another lawyer said: just the opposite. If he *didn't* give up the
ticket he'd be in hot water. Then a new lawyer showed up
with a new idea: The rich man could either give it up or not
—he'd have a pack of troubles in any case. You get the picture? But I think the rich man had himself a pack of troubles
anyway. Aside from the fact that they kept annoying him
every minute, he had to hustle into the big city every week,
run from one lawyer to the next, pay their fees, and beg them
to have pity and tell him how to get rid of that load of TNT
he'd latched on to. It *was* a pity, I tell you, a downright shame!
They took an honest, easy-going chap who wouldn't hurt a

fly, hung a pack of troubles on his back, and told him to keep it. But what ever for? Why does he have to carry such a load of TNT? Because others wanted to make peace and do a man a good turn . . . you get the picture? Do you happen to have another load of TNT—damn it—I mean another cigarette?

Well then, where was I? Oh yes, the TNT they hung on to our rich man's back. No doubt you want to know what happened to it. Nothing. The TNT was still TNT. It was still up in the air. Our rich man hopped back and forth to the big city, seeing the money-grabbing, advice-giving lawyers. This one said this, that one said that, and the third one said neither this nor that, but, as you'd expect, something entirely different. How it would end up, only God knew, for no human mind could conceive of the outcome. If, heaven forbid, it ended up in court, who knew what the result could be. You get the picture?

But, in the meantime, who was buried six feet under? Yakov-Yosil! I had dealings with the whole city—what am I saying, *city?* The whole world! Everyone pointed at me and said: "There goes the 75,000." I was cut off from business; I didn't have a kopek in my pocket; it was worse than before. My wife was ashamed to show her face at the marketplace— they kept calling her, "the new Mrs. Well-to-do." At the synagogue, they honored me in an entirely new fashion. They figured out how much I'd have to contribute to the communal funds, how much to give my poor relatives, and what I'd do with what's left over. One said, I'd probably become a money-lender. Another suggested that I become a wheat-dealer again. A third proved that it would be best for me to open up a business office. That way I'd have the finest business in town, for which office in our town had a capital of 75,000? And they're speaking of cold, ready cash. You get the picture? For our village is made up of a mob of doubting Thomases. No one believes that there's a merchant in town who has twenty-five rubles he can call his own. I want you to know that our village is a right and proper one—it hasn't gone to the dogs yet. Not much! People look twice before they leap into things. There are plenty of loafers who, for lack of anything better to do, go from Shmerel to Berel and slander the whole world. They have no business of their own, so they mind everyone else's. They assemble in front of the marketplace drugstore known as the stock-exchange and they estimate everyone's worth. They quiver and quake if someone else is making money. They're pleased as punch if someone goes into the red. Now you can imagine what sort of blue funk the town fell into when they heard about the 75,000. They've been jabbering about it from dawn to dusk ever since. They exchange quips and thorny digs. They eat each other's hearts out and cut each other to the quick.

"Why didn't *you* win the 75,000 rubles? You could have well used them."

"Why didn't *you?* You need it more than *I* do!"

So as to vex them, one calculator figured out that I was the richest man in the village. Quite simple, he said. I'd won 75,000, he said, and my apartment was worth 6 or 7,000. That made a grand total of 85,000, nearly 100,000 rubles, he said. Then, after all, he thought, if a Jew says that he had 100,000 rubles, you could well depend on his having 200,000, for if he's valued at 200,000, the calculator said, he doesn't even have 100,000. In other words, I had 200,000, and was therefore the richest man in town. But if you ask: aren't there any men richer than me? I'll answer—how can we tell? Who has crept into their pockets or counted their cash? Who knows if they haven't come down in the world? You get the picture? This really rankled many people to the core. They just couldn't take it, poor souls. Why should a down-and-out Jew suddenly and out of the blue fall into 75,000, without lifting a finger?

There's a rich old miserly bachelor in our village. One day, our gang purposely sent Mendel the Beard over to his house to deliver the good news that Yakov-Yosil had won 75,000. He got so sick—may you be spared—that they thought his end had come. Tsk, tsk, what a pity! He stumbled around in a dither for days. But, after he heard about the snag and the incident with my brother Henikh, he fully recovered. "Better let the monk get the money," he said. "Why should a Jew get

such a big sum?" You get the picture? I bet you think that
at least those close to me don't begrudge me the money! But
they're so riled they're liable to drown me in a teacup. Take
my word for it, if the 75,000 would have been mine and mine
alone, the picture would have been entirely different. Everyone would have gotten his share—relatives and friends alike.
However, since things are the way they are—what can I do?
But never mind, the family can well start preparing big purses
and see what they can tap out of my brother. After all,
Henikh is a big sport. When he starts shelling out, the world
will stand up and take notice. There's a rumor that he's already earmarked a dowry of 72 to 75 rubles for his poor unmarried sister. He's also given all of a hundred rubles to his
aged father. Let his old man know and realize that his son has
won 75,000. You get the picture? So much for local relatives.
As for far-off kin . . . they just kept dropping in out of nowhere, each with his own hard-luck story. Many of them had
already started arranging matches and weddings on account
of the prize money. Some of them got divorced so that they'd
be able to remarry into richer circles. Well, at least they're
relatives. Like they say: suffer with your own. You get the
picture? But complete strangers? Must I bear the brunt of
their troubles? Have I deserved a fate like that? What wrong
have I done? I wish a 75,000 ruble prize on all my enemies.
I swear that I can no longer stand all those congratulations,
those sweet fawning smiles and little flatteries. People I've
never before seen in my life come up to me and ask my advice.

"We've heard about you, Reb Yakov-Yosil. We've known
all along what a wise man you are. Don't you think that this
has anything to do with the big prize with which God has
blessed you. Heaven forbid. We dropped in just like that to
pour our hearts out to you."

You get the picture? One man even came from some queer
town in a distant land whose name I've forgotten and where
my grandfather's grandma had never been. One day, the door
suddenly opens up and in walks a Jew who puts his bundles
on the floor.

"Hello."

"Hello yourself. Where you from?"

"From hunger! Are you Reb Yakov-Yosil?"

"That's me. What's the good word?"

"Are you really *the* Yakov-Yosil who won the 75,000? I purposely came to see you. What I mean is, I was passing by anyway and I heard that you'd won the 75,000, so I decided to drop in for a day. I wanted to set my eyes on that lucky man who'd won 75,000. It's no trifle. After all, it is 75,000!"

You get the picture? Go explain to each and everyone the details about Birnbaum who wanted mediation, a brother named Henikh, the snag in the proceedings, the rich man, the load of TNT, the lawyers, the devils, the plagues! I swear, I was better off before the 75,000 than now, after the 75,000. Certainly things were quieter. To tell you the truth, I'm afraid for my life now! Just the other day, I was in the big city, seeing the lawyers. That night, I met up with some scoundrel who lured me to his home in the downtown slums, supposedly for a cup of tea. When I got there, I met another one of the gang, a decent-enough looking fellow with a long beard, sitting and studying. He greeted me, rose to light a cigarette, but suddenly put out the light instead. All of us were left in the dark. You get the picture? I swear, here's another story worth telling, but it's quite late and you're in a rush to get home. Anyway, this story is linked up with another one. Like they say: a pimple on a blister, a blister on a boil. You get the picture?

Well then, where was I? Oh, yes, at the end of the story. You think that's the end of it? Hold your horses, take it easy! This is just the start. What am I saying, *start?* The start hasn't even begun yet! And whose fault is it? My very own! Then again, why mine? How do I know? After all, I'm just a human being made out of flesh and blood, like they say. And, if misfortune is fated, is there any getting around it? Why is it my fault that I . . . but wait a minute. You're not supposed to put the horse before the cart, I mean, the cart before the horse. Let me tell you the whole story, not from the very beginning, but from the beginning of the end. In any case, if you remember, after much worry and trouble, we finally decided with the good Lord's help to share the winnings. Naturally, this was easier said than done. There was plenty of yelling and bickering among us. The monk argued—why are Birnbaum and I getting a share? My brother Henikh was hell-bent upon me relying on *his* honesty, good will, and sense of understanding. And my Birnbaum shouted that he didn't want a thing— he only wanted people to mediate, to hear what others would say. You get the picture? Well then, some brokers poked their noses in—three of them at once. They sweated over it, straightened things out, and put an end to the affair. And, if you remember, the upshot was . . . well what *was* it? We decided to get together, all four of us that is, and take a trip to the big city, secure release of the ticket, pick up our bit of money, split it, and wish each other a fond farewell. But all this was fine and dandy if you had a ticket. But what if there was no ticket? Could one say there was no ticket? Actually, there *was* a ticket, but do you remember *where* it was? Locked up in a bank under another person's name, and, begging your pardon, it had been impounded by the court to boot. Try and release a ticket like that! Well what could we do? The first thing we'd have to do was put an end to the affair. Once that happened, we'd see what was to be done next. You get the picture? But who *could* put an end to it. The monk, naturally. But he said, if you remember, that he wanted a guarantee— that the ticket should be written over to him—and then he'd see to it that the affair was closed. You think he was right, right? Who, then, was supposed to hand over the ticket so that the affair could be ended? The rich man, naturally. So we came to our rich man and asked him to sign the ticket over to the monk and then the whole affair would be closed. But, once again, our rich man rightly argued: "What do you want of me? Why latch another affair onto this one?"

"You're right," we said, "but what can we do if you're the only one who can put an end to this business."

"But is it my fault?" he said. "Put an end to the affair or not put an end to the affair. What affair is it of mine?"

You get the picture? Do you have an extra affair?—damn it—I mean, a cigarette?

Well then, where was I? Oh, yes, putting an end to the affair. We got advice here and there and finally decided to sue.
Since it came to suing, we had to go to a lawyer. Since it came
to a lawyer, we had to go to the big city. Then the question
arose—which lawyer? One said to go to *this* lawyer, another
said, *that* one. The outcome was, we had no choice and went
to them both. What one lawyer said, the other, naturally, op-
posed. A third one pulled something entirely new out of his
hat. We were in a bad fix, so we went to a fourth lawyer. In
a word, do I have to tell you what sort of breed lawyers are?
Lawyers and doctors are one and the same plague. Lawyers
and doctors were created for the specific purpose of contra-
dicting each other. Whatever one says, the other must say
just the opposite. They're just like the Aramaic translation of
the Bible. I have a friend who says that the Aramaic translator
was a spiteful wretch. For instance, if the biblical Hebrew
says: "And he said," the Aramaic says: "And he saith." And
when the Bible says: "And he spoke," what harm is there,
Mr. Translator, in saying: "And he spoke"? But no! The
Aramaic says: "And he spake." Well, can you go fight him?
You get the picture? One lawyer said that all four of us ought
to serve notice against the bank and the rich man because they
weren't giving us the ticket. Good idea—huh? Comes the other
lawyer and says, only two of us, Birnbaum and myself, should
serve notice on the rich man because he isn't asking the bank
to hand the ticket over. That too seemed to be a good idea,
right? But, then, the third lawyer said: what has Yakov-Yosil
to do with the bank? Does the bank know him? Did it have
any dealings with him? Let Birnbaum alone serve notice, not
on the bank, but on the rich man. For is the bank at fault if
Birnbaum himself had recently ordered transfer of the ticket
from his to the rich man's account? Sounds logical, right?
Then another lawyer came and said that neither I nor Birnbaum should serve notice. The monk and Henikh should serve
notice. That made sense too, eh? Then another lawyer came
and hit upon this plan. We should not sue at all. Let's take a
look and see how the ticket came to be in the rich man's name.
Birnbaum put it there. Where did he get it from? Me. Where

did I get hold of it? From my brother, Henikh. Who did he get it from? He borrowed, I mean, bought it from the monk. Henikh said *bought*, the monk said *borrowed*. What difference did it make? It was a lost cause. In that case, let the monk demand it from my brother, my brother from me, me from Birnbaum, and Birnbaum from . . . from whom? Birnbaum from the bank. But the bank says that they don't know Birnbaum any longer—only the rich man. Then let Birnbaum demand it from the rich man and he from the bank. But the rich man was afraid of—of what?—of being sued. But there was another way out, said the lawyer. Birnbaum would sign a note and release the rich man, I'd release Birnbaum, my brother would release me, and the monk would release my brother. How's that for a brainstorm? Could there be anything better? Then another lawyer popped up and asked a silly question: Hold everything! How do we know that the trail of the ticket ends with the monk? Suppose there's another character hiding in a closet who's going to jump out tomorrow with a batch of witnesses and documents and claim: "The ticket's mine. Help! Where's my ticket?" What would happen then? He wouldn't demand the ticket, he'd demand the 75,000. Who from? None other than the rich man. But the rich man had a release note from Birnbaum, Birnbaum had one from me, I had one from my brother Henikh, and Henikh had one from the monk. The next step, the lawyer said, would be for the rich man to sue Birnbaum, Birnbaum me, I my brother, my brother the monk. Like the Passover song: *One Only Kid*—"the cat ate the kid, the dog ate the cat, the stick beat the dog, the fire burned the stick, the water put out the fire, the ox drank the water, the slaughterer killed the ox," and so on. You get the picture? Things were in a bad way again! What were we to do? We had to go to one of Russia's biggest lawyers, Kopernikov himself, and from him to the greatest lawyer of them all. In short, we didn't leave out a single one. We literally lawyered our heads off. Morning, noon, and night all we heard was lawyer, lawyer, lawyer. Do you happen to have a lawyer on you— damn it—I mean, a cigarette?

Well then, where was I? Oh yes, the lawyers. Finally, with

the help of God, they hit upon a solution. After all—they are lawyers! What did they advise? Here's what they advised: Before we did anything else, I and Birnbaum, both of us that is, should sign a notarized statement saying that we two had absolutely nothing to do with the ticket; that we weren't parties to the affair at all; that the ticket was sent to me by brother Henikh who took, that is, bought it from the monk; and that Henikh asked me to pawn it which I did through Birnbaum for 200 rubles. In other words, the story as it really happened, the honest to goodness 100 per cent truth. When you get down to it, isn't the truth better than alibis, flim-flam, or makeshift excuses? But nobody thought of it before, you get the picture? But hold up, I'm not through yet. What did he mean by me and Birnbaum giving ouselves a slap in the face like that? What would become of our share in the prize money? What would happen later if the other two would say: kiss my —. Ought I depend on my brother's honesty and the monk's word of honor? But you'll say that we'd signed a paper and had drunk toasts. Nonsense! A piece of paper costs a kopek and toasts can be drunk every day, like they say, so long as there's a drop of whisky around. Then what did I and Birnbaum want? We just wanted a guarantee. We wanted our shares of the prize guaranteed. You get the picture? Here's where the picnic began.

"Guarantees!" they said. "Where do they come off deserving guarantees? It's enough they're getting money which doesn't belong to them. But guarantees?"

This touched us to the quick. "What do you mean? We deserve it for our honesty, you so and sos. It's enough that we're doing you a favor," we said. "We could have taken the whole 75,000 and no cock would have crowed. And you still complain?"

"In other words," they said, "we have to thank you and pinch your cheek, besides."

Those were Henikh's words. This got my goat! We exchanged tit for tat and had a row, as is customary among brothers. But—in a nutshell— things worked out. They would give us a guarantee. What sort? Receipts? A receipt is as strong as a thatched roof. Notes? They aren't worth the paper they're written on. What then? Cash? Like my grandma, may she rest in peace, used to say: "The best check is ready cash." But where would they get cash if in those days not a soul had any. What am I saying—not a soul? There *was* cash around, and lots of it, but the Brodskys had it.

"In short," I said, "it's all a lot of hot air. Until there's a guarantee, I'm not signing."

"What sort of guarantee?"

"Any kind at all, so long as it's a guarantee. I just don't want everyone to call me an ass later on."

You get the picture? That's number one. And my buddy, Birnbaum, took up his old battle-cry—mediation! Since he was about to sign over his part of the ticket permanently, he wanted to let other people judge. He would go by whatever they would say.

"Again people," I said. "I thought we dropped that. What good will they do you?"

"I want to hear what others will say, you understand," Birnbaum said. "Perhaps they'll find that I have nothing coming to me, then why should I take money for nothing?"

You get the picture? I'm screaming for a guarantee, and he's calling for mediation.

"We'll get the guarantee later," he said, "first let's see what other people will say!"

"You're on that people binge again, huh? You've got my head spinning with your people. Let's get a guarantee first. That's more important."

Well then, where was I? Oh, yes, the guarantee. Well, they gave us a guarantee, legally and properly connected each one of us to the other, and we all signed it at the notary's. The papers were presented at the right place and we again started going to lawyers, drawing up documents, documents of this and that sort, dashing into the big city every Monday and Thursday, paying good money to sleep in bedbug-ridden hotels (a plain inn wasn't good enough for them), dining on fried roaches, which the menu listed as roast beef (plain stew wasn't good enough for them), perspiring like in a Turkish bath, broiling in the sun, scuffing over the hot cobblestones, deafened by the city noises and dead-tired from the rush and the tumult. And for what? Big deal! 75,000! I wished the whole business would come to an end. Like my wife said, may she live and be well: "A bird in the hand is worth two in the bush. Your 75,000 has put 75 holes into my heart. And with due respect for all the glory—what do I need all this for?"

"Go on," I said, "you're a fishwife and you'll always be one."

But yet, I felt she was right. What good did that sum do me if I couldn't use it for shopping. All I did was breed unnecessary enemies. This one envied me, that one begrudged me the prize, afraid that I might get the money, for why should Yakov-Yosil come into such big money? You get the picture? It cost us plenty of health until we finally got the good word that the whole affair was over and done with. The whole affair was an affair no more. And you can imagine what a sight for sore eyes that ticket was. Think we got to see it so quickly? Hold your horses! Take it slowly! First, we had to wait a month in case anyone wanted to protest the settlement. I don't think I slept one night that month. I had such queer dreams. More than once—you get the picture?—I would wake up in the middle of the night yelling in a voice not my own: "Tsipora, I'm flying!"

"Where you flying to?" she said. "Flying all of a sudden! Spit three times and tell me your dream."

"I had a fine dream. I dreamed I had wings and was flying and was being followed by wild creatures—by flying serpents and dragons who wanted to kill me."

That happened once. The second time, I dreamed I was sitting on a sack, a huge inflated sack of red rubber which had "75,000" marked on it in large numbers. It was a summer Saturday and the whole town, men, women, and children, had gone out for an afternoon stroll. They all stopped and stared at me. Then—suddenly—BANG! There was a roar and my rubber sack burst. I felt myself falling, falling and screaming, "Tsipora, it burst."

"God be with you. Who? Who burst? May my enemies

burst!" my wife said. Naturally, she thought the dream was all for the good, as a wife usually does.

Well then, where was I? Oh, yes, getting the ticket. When it came to taking the ticket out of the bank, something new came up. Who would participate? Everyone trusted himself to the core, but I wasn't obliged to rely on anyone *else's* honesty. It was too great a temptation. After all, it was 75,000 rubles. You get the picture? The upshot was—you didn't trust me—I don't trust you! Then let's all go together. What did that mean? It meant all ten of us. How come *ten?* Figure it out for yourself and you'll see. I'm one, Birnbaum is two, the monk is three, my brother Henikh is four, and three lawyers (the monk's, my brother's and the one representing Birnbaum and me). That makes a grand total of seven people—may no evil eye harm them. Then what about the three brokers who stuck their noses into the affair and brought us to terms? That makes an even ten. At first, it was a bit strange. My brother Henikh kicked up a storm about such a big mob coming. He thought that two would have been enough—he and the monk. He didn't at all like the idea that no one had faith in his honesty or the monk's word of honor. But it did him as much good as barking at the moon! Each one had a different and legitimate argument. For instance, I said that I *had* to go, for I was a brother. Not for dignity's sake, but because one brother would very well thumb his nose at the other. And what could I do to him then? Sue him? My own brother? My Birnbaum argued, if Henikh's own brother didn't trust him, why should he, a complete stranger, depend on miracles? He said that he'd done his duty. You couldn't say he was completely wrong either. There was no question about the three lawyers going. They *had* to be there, they said, for there would be plenty to legalize, notarize, and authorize. That left the brokers. The brokers claimed that they too had to come along and all three of them to boot. They were old hands at the game, they said; they were trained at the school of hard knocks; they'd gotten their experience at the Yehupetz stock exchange and knew what brokers' fees meant. Like the match-

maker's commission, it was the sort of fee that had to be paid
on the spot. You get the picture?

We arranged to come, not all at once, but one by one. Since
each of us anticipated being first, however, we all met at sunrise in front of the bank. We paced around for a long time
until they opened the doors and let us in to take our ticket. I
don't have to tell you what a bank is. A bank hates to rush—
it takes its time. What did it care about a ticket, Yakov-Yosil,
75,000, monks, Henikhs, Birnbaums, the poor brokers who
wanted a little commission, and the rest of the lookers-on?
The bank didn't give a damn about it all. One smoked, another prattled nonsense, this one drank a glass of tea, that one
sharpened a pencil, another read the paper. He had his nose
buried in it and wouldn't have lifted it for all the tea in China.
We walked around, yawned, coughed. We were on pins and
needles, waiting for the big moment. But the bookkeeper still
had not arrived. When he came, the cashier was still missing.
When the cashier showed up, the director had yet to come.
Where was he? Sleeping! In other words, the owner of the
bank was still snoozing. After all, what did he care about
tickets, Yakov-Yosil, 75,000, monks, Henikhs, Birnbaums,
the poor brokers who wanted a little commission, and the rest
of the lookers-on? How much did a director like him earn? I
wondered. Six thousand for sure, maybe 8, and possibly all of
10,000 rubles. Why not? Poor chap overworked himself,
didn't he? I swear, I would have taken his job for half the sum,
a third of it, and I would have been more devoted and harder-
working. That's what I thought at the time. On second
thought, perhaps I didn't really think at all. You get the picture? Finally, the director came. As soon as he showed up,
naturally, we all pounced on him at once. This evidently
frightened him and he waved us away. The three lawyers and
the monk went up to him and gave him the documents. You
get the picture? The director locked himself up in his office
with the papers and we had to wait and wait and wait. We
waited until the moment we all waited for arrived. The director came out of his office accompanied by a fat aristocratic-

looking gentleman. The director—begging your pardon—turned his backside to us and started an endless conversation with the blue-blood. What did he care about the ticket, Yakov-Yosil, 75,000, monks, Henikhs, Birnbaums, the poor brokers who wanted a little commission, and the rest of the lookers-on? Suddenly, the director turned around and said:

"Your papers are ready. Go to the cashier."

Now couldn't he have told us that at the beginning? With papers in hand, we dashed to the cashier, gave them to him, and thought that would be the end of it. But the upshot was, we hadn't even begun yet. The cashier was busy counting 100- and 500-ruble notes and had a table covered with piles of gold before him. How much money was there? Oh me, if I had a tenth of that—I'd laugh at the ticket. That's what I thought at the time. On second thought, perhaps I didn't really think at all. The cashier kept counting and didn't throw so much as a glance our way. What did he care about a ticket, Yakov-Yosil, 75,000, monks, Henikhs, Birnbaums, the poor brokers who wanted a little commission, and the rest of the lookers-on? The gold flew through his hands with a sweet tinkle. The music of gold! You get the picture?

Well then, where was I? Oh, yes, the gold. Having counted the gold, he pushed his glasses to his forehead and snatched the papers out of our hands. His fingers flipped expertly through them as if counting 100-ruble notes. He opened a drawer and removed a huge packet. From it he withdrew a large envelope. He ripped it open and took out *the* lottery ticket. "Who'll take it?" he asked. Ten pairs of hands shot out at him.

"Nothing doing," the cashier said. "I can't give the ticket to so many hands. Choose one of your group."

We then picked the oldest of the three lawyers. He slowly took the ticket with both hands, as if he were holding a baby about to be circumcised, and brought it first to the monk, then to my brother Henikh, then to me and Birnbaum, to both of us that is, to see if the ticket was the authentic one. The monk said he recognized it even while the cashier held it. He could tell by a certain sign. What the sign was—he wasn't saying. My

brother Henikh swore that if, for instance, he were awakened
at two in the morning and shown the ticket, he would immediately have recognized it. You get the picture? It so happened that I and Birnbaum *didn't* recognize the ticket. Why
should I say something when I hadn't a leg to stand on? We
carefully went over the series number and the number 12.
Like they say: that's the main thing. Right? Then we immediately hurried over to the State Bank to cash our ticket and
take that sweet bundle of 75,000. We all walked, although it
was up-hill all the way. The oldest lawyer held the ticket over
his head with two hands so as not to lose it and so that no one
would suspect him, God forbid, of pulling a switch. You could
never tell—it was such a jinxed ticket! You get the picture?
We weren't ten now, we were more than twenty. Where did
we pick up so many people—God bless them? I'll tell you.
First of all, some good friends from my village just happened
to be in the big city that day. Seeing that we were already on
our way to the State Bank to pick up our 75,000, they decided
to join us and watch the pay-off. For it wasn't every day that
an event like that could be seen. In short—what a procession
it was! At the State Bank, we were royally welcomed. Even
the corporal who guarded the door was thrown for a loop
when he saw so many Jews, and in their midst, a monk, swoop-
ing down at him. Nevertheless, he received us politely and
admitted us into the bank, one by one. We saw those we had
to see, said what we had to say, and were brought over to an
official with a head as bald as a soup-bowl. They gave him the
ticket and whispered something we couldn't hear. The baldy
who sat at the other side of the latticed cage looked up, stared
severely at us through his glasses, and continued working. He
held a sharp little knife—you get the picture?—and scratched
something into a notebook. He kept scratching and scratching. While he scratched, we stood there with our hearts in our
mouths, watching him. The rest of the people watched us,
inspecting us from head to toe. The bald official still kept
scratching, and the rest of the clerks sat and counted money.
Money wasn't the word for it! There was so much of it, it
was like rubbish. Stacks of gold! It glittered before your eyes.

The sight of it made your head whirl. Its tinkle made your
ears buzz. Money, I wondered, who invented this thing which
caused so much suffering and useless struggle. For money, one
man was ready to swallow the next. Neither brother, sister,
father, child, neighbor, friend, loved one existed—only money,
money, money. Anyway, that's what I thought at the time.
On second thought, perhaps I didn't really think at all. You
get the picture? The official didn't stop scratching away. For
what concern of his was the ticket, Yakov-Yosil, 75,000,
monks, Henikhs, Birnbaums, the poor brokers who wanted a
little commission, and the rest of the lookers-on? But there
was a limit to everything. Finally, God took pity on us. The
official stopped scratching, put his sharp little knife into his
jacket pocket, took out a clean handkerchief, and royally
blew his nose. Then he took the ticket, just as if it were a
piece of scrap paper, opened a book, and started looking. First
at the ticket, then at the book, then again at the ticket, and
again at the book. This smartie probably thinks the ticket is
a fake, I thought. Scratch and sniff away for all you're worth.
The ticket is no fake, it's the real thing. Suddenly, I saw him
take the ticket and practically throw it at our faces, saying
(and I remember it word for word): "Who told you that this
ticket won the 75,000?"

You get the picture? Who told us? Did you ever . . . ?

"What do you mean who told us?" we said. "The ticket
itself told us we won the 75,000. Series 2289, number 12."

"Yes," he said, quite seriously, "that's true. Series 2289, number 12 *has* won the 75,000 rubles. But your ticket is series
2298, number 12. A slight error."

Well how do you like that? What can I say? When he first
told us this we were all in a dither. We thought: either he's
nuts, we're crazy, or perhaps it was all a dream. We looked
at one another. Then, we finally remembered to have a look
at the ticket. Yes, as we lived and breathed! Series 2298, number 12. You get the picture?

Well, my dear friend, what more can I say? I couldn't even
describe a tenth of what happened, and you'd never be able
to write it up. No one could possibly picture the scene which

took place in the bank when we stood rooted, dumbstruck, looking at one another. Their faces were filled with—how shall I put it?—their faces weren't human any more—you get the picture? They were the faces of animals and beasts, beasts in human form. If looks could kill—there would have been wholesale murder that day. But so what? What was wrong? You've dreamed a dream of 75,000? Well, was it worth losing your life over it? Aside from money, wasn't life worth living? They were men completely crazy, you get the picture? But no one riled me so much as my buddy, Birnbaum. At least, the rest of the gang tried to make excuses and shift the blame on to the next fellow. The monk put the entire blame on my brother Henikh. Henikh said he didn't know a thing about the 75,000 and wouldn't have known a thing if it weren't for my congratulatory telegram. You get the picture?

"You certainly know how to read the paper, brother mine," Henikh said.

"Why didn't *you* look?" I asked.

"You were the big-shot," he said. "You had the ticket. You *owned* it."

Did you hear that? Before, when 75,000 rubles were involved, they wanted to cut me out altogether. Now that the dam had broken, I had become the real owner of the ticket. You get the picture? But never mind. I, Yakov-Yosil, who had always been the scapegoat, would take the entire blame. Fine, it's all my fault. But then, you asses, where were *your* eyes? You yourselves had seen all the papers and receipts and documents at least two dozen times, and there the series number 2298, number 12, was plainly written, while series number 2289, number 12, actually won the prize. Why didn't you think of looking and seeing that the 9 came before the 8? And when the ticket was in your hands, couldn't you have checked with the official list of winning numbers to see which series won the 75,000—series 2298 or 2289? You spared no effort in gathering up a mob and invading the bank. Why? Because you thought you'd be collecting. You get the picture? But Birnbaum burned me up most of all. You should have seen him standing there on the side like a complete stranger, as if the whole affair were no concern of his. A minute before, he'd been whipping up a storm. Mediation! Other people's judgment! And now he stood there, like a poor lamb, innocent as all get out. This cut me to the core and I decided to get even with him for the way he had tortured me that second of May, if you remember, when I stood and begged for the ticket like one before a thief.

"Mr. Birnbaum," I said, "now's the time to hear what people have to say. There are plenty of people here in the bank now—God bless them. Why so quiet? Don't you want to hear what others will say? You've given up on people, huh?"

The entire crowd stood there and had the time of their life. I can't tell you what they enjoyed more—me calling Birnbaum to the court of public opinion, or the kick they got out of the whole affair of 75,000 coming to naught. I can swear by anything under the sun that I don't give a damn for the money. Let it fry in hell for all I care. The only thing that bothers me is this: When they just *thought* I had 75,000, then Yakov-Yosil was known as Reb Yakov-Yosil. Now that it was known that Yakov-Yosil had beans and not 75,000, he was through. He was no longer Reb Yakov-Yosil. You leper-headed bastards! What sins did I commit? Yes 75,000, no 75,000. What difference did it make? Listen to me, Mr. Sholem Aleichem, you can sure be proud of your Jews and of the whole world! I tell you it's a lousy world. Phooey! It's a false and foolish world, a world led astray. But admit it—aren't your ears ringing and isn't your head spinning from my story of 75,000? Sorry that I've chewed your ears off. Live and be well—you get the picture?—and God grant us better business in days to come.

AGENTS

A One-act Play

Characters:

MENAKHEM-MENDEL CANDLETWISTER—a young villager wearing a brand-new suit, a new, ill-fitting hat, and a collar so tight it makes his eyes pop. He holds a shiny, huge brief-case on his lap.

MARK MOYSEYEVITSH LAMPLIGHTER—a young dandy, also with a huge briefcase.

AKIM ISAKOVITSH FISHMONGER—a huge man who has a propensity for overeating, also with a huge briefcase.

LAZAR KONSTANTINOVITSH TURTLEDOVE—a man with a large beard and a larger family—a wife with a brood of children, one smaller than the next.

OTHER PASSENGERS.

The scene:
The entire act takes place in the third-class section of a train. Some sit, some lie stretched out, some sleep. Suitcases and various packages on the shelves. Stage front, sitting alone in a seat is MENAKHEM-MENDEL, *contemplating his new suit and talking to himself.*

MENAKHEM-MENDEL: Well, at least I'm well dressed. Look just like a groom. Dandied up like a bride. Only thing is—the pants are too tight and the collar—oh that collar—it's enough to make one choke. Main thing is—I'm traveling! Think I know whereto? "You'll make a terrific agent," they said. "Your name's your passport," they said. "Just listen to the sound of it. Menakhem-Mendel Candletwister. It's known far and wide," they said, "like a bad coin. In Yehupetz, in Boyberik, in Mazepevke! Where isn't it known?" they said.

"Travel among your Jews," they said, "and lots of luck to you. Assure them to death," they said. Only thing is, how do you go about assuring them to death? The devil only knows how you do it—despite the fact that they trained me for two days to be an agent and even gave me an advance. And that's the most important thing, isn't it? For all agents get advances! If it weren't for the advances, they say, there would be no agents. Aside from that, they packed my briefcase full of constructions—I mean, instructions as to how an agent is supposed to act while assuring someone to death. I better start reading the con . . . the instructions, I mean. (*He opens his briefcase and takes out a letter.*)

Well, speaking of the devil—here's a letter from my wife, Sheyne-Sheyndl. Like my mother-in-law says: "If you look for the scissors, you'll find the broom." In any case, I better re-read what the old lady has to say, God bless her. It's dull here, anyway. Nothing to do. (*He reads.*)

"To my dear and respected, noble and wise husband, Reb Menakhem-Mendel, may his light never dim. The first thing I want to tell you is that we're all in good health, thank God, and hope to hear the same from you." (*Looks up.*) Thank God they're healthy, at least. (*Reads.*) "The second thing I want to tell you is this, you mangy heretic . . ." (*Looks up.*) There she goes with her compliments, again. (*Reads.*)

"May you have the same strength, you heretic, to rot away in that dead and dingy town of Yehupetz—may you and it both burn to a crisp—the way I have strength to drag my feet around. For the doctor has told me to get off them and lie down, may he himself soon lie down in the cemetery and have you for a neighbor. Like Mama says . . ." (*Looks up.*) Aha! Here comes her mother's saying. (*Reads.*)

"Like Mama says: 'To make the long winter nights more pleasant for you both'—There's an ill-wind for you—God has sent my fine and dandy breadwinner a new occupation. He's going to assure people's deaths. What in the world does that mean, Mendel? How can you do such a thing?" (*Looks up.*) Poor thing. She doesn't have the faintest idea of what it's all about. (*Reads.*) "You're downright crazy—may you go

crazy for all Jews and gentiles, too. Like Mama says . . ."
(*Looks up.*) There she goes with her mother again. (*Reads.*)
"Like Mama says: 'Drop a horse's reins and watch him take
off.' It's not enough that you've been a jack of all trades:
broker, stoker, butcher, baker, candlestick-maker, swindler,
jester, and matchmaker. Everyone has had some contact with
you in one way or another. And now you have to start up
with dead-and-alive corpses. Like Mama says: 'Just you wait,
he'll end up as a wet-nurse somewhere in Poland.' Wouldn't
you have been a thousand times better off in the war against
Japan . . ." (*Looks up.*) Of course! I'm running. (*Reads.*)
"And come home like Moyshe-Velvele did, God spare us
all, with no hands, no feet, no life in him at all. Like Mama
says: 'Does the bullet know whom its shooting?' Just remember what I've got to say, Mendel. And I'm saying it now in all
good intent. May riots and plagues, cankers and agues come
upon you and . . ."

Enter: LAMPLIGHTER *carrying a huge suitcase. He looks for
a seat. Approaches* MENAKHEM-MENDEL.

LAMPLIGHTER: Do you mind?

MENAKHEM-MENDEL: (*Puts the letter away.*) Of course
not. (*Aside.*) He looks like a likely customer. Has a fine suitcase. Maybe I can assure him to death.

LAMPLIGHTER: (*Puts his suitcase away and sits down next
to Mendel. He takes out a cigarette.*) Do you have a match
by any chance? (*Aside.*) I have to feel him out.

MENAKHEM-MENDEL: Why not. (*He gives him a match.
Aside.*) I'm glad he started first.

LAMPLIGHTER: (*Offers* MENAKHEM-MENDEL *a cigarette.*)
Smoke? (*Aside.*) This country yokel with the new outfit is
a likely customer. Maybe I can do some business with him.
Perhaps I can eke just a small premium out of him to cover my
expenses.

MENAKHEM-MENDEL: (*Accepts the cigarette.*) Oh. Sure
I'll smoke, why not? (*Smokes and talks to himself.*) Seems
like quite a fine chap. God willing, he'll surely let himself be
assured to death.

L-L: (*Aside.*) With a hick like him, I'd better shift into high gear. It's nice riding in the train, isn't it? Not like it used to be. When we had to go by horse and wagon, time just dragged on and on and on.

MM: On and on and on.

L-L: We were at the mercy of the wagoner—just like his horses.

MM: Like his horses.

L-L: He used to pack the wagon full with all sorts of people.

MM: All sorts of people.

L-L: Men and women, sacks of flour, a cantor, a goat, a priest. . . .

MM: A goat, a priest.

L-L: And when it came to a hill he used to ask our pardon and tell us to get off.

MM: Tell us to get off.

L-L: And now we ride like gentlemen. We sit in the train and have a smoke! And that's that!

MM: That's that!

L-L: The only advantage the horse and buggy had was safety. You never worried about an accident, God forbid, a catastrophe of any sort, like the wagon turning over and you diving out head-first like the seagulls.

MM: Head-first like the seagulls.

L-L: It's good if you're insured for at least a few thousand rubles after your death, so that your wife and kids, God forbid, won't have to go begging from door to door.

MM: Begging from door to door. (*Aside.*) He's beating a straight path, like a clever horse.

L-L: (*Aside.*) He keeps wagging after me like a little pony. (*Aloud.*) For you know, that so long as the wheel turns, it turns.

MM: It turns.

L-L: And once it stops turning—the machine stops.

MM: The machine stops.

L-L: (*Aside.*) He's letting himself be led on. Just got to head straight for the stable. (*Aloud.*) The only trouble is that not everyone can guarantee his family's upkeep with money. Today's expenses, you know, with today's, um . . .

MM: With today's um . . . um . . .

L-L: Then the least you can do is buy a little policy.

MM: A little policy, at least. (*Aside.*) As I live and breathe, this is a God-send.

L-L: I just remembered something that happened in our town. A down-and-out villager who never even had a thousand rubles to his name, you understand, and never saw a hundred-ruble note in his life, had enough sense to insure himself in time for a few thousand rubles. Recently he was killed in a train wreck—may this never happen to you—and his wife got five thousand rubles cash in one lump sum.

MM: Cash in a lump sum! That's just what happened in our town. The exact same thing happened in our town, but not with five thousand, but ten thousand. That's the God's honest truth, as I live and breathe.

L-L: (*Surprised.*) Ten thousand rubles?

MM: Ten thousand rubles.

L-L: What did they do with all that money?

MM: What do you think they did. They opened up a smart little shop!

L-L: Really? Are they making money?

MM: What a question! They're raking it in!

L-L: (*Aside.*) Now's the time. I've got him right where I want him. (*Aloud.*) It's not right to say we envy a dead man, but the living, you get me, all have wives and children. (*He sighs.*) Everyone should insure himself.

MM: (*Sighs, too.*) That's just what I say. (*Aside.*) I'll strike now, while the iron's hot.

L-L: (*Sighs.*) He who sees the writing on the wall and acts —well, that man's pretty lucky.

MM: (*Sighs.*) A wise man looks to the future—and the whole thing doesn't come to too much either. After all, what does it amount to?

L-L: (*Excitedly.*) Depends how old you are. I think we can arrange the whole thing right here and now.

MM: (*Excitedly.*) Why not?

L-L: We can have the physical afterward, have it notarized, you get me?

MM: That should be our last worry. The most important is the amount.

L-L: (*Grabs his briefcase.*) It's not the amount that's important, but the age.

MM: (*Grabs his briefcase.*) Of course, it's the age. How old are you?

L-L: Me? What difference does it make how old *I* am?

MM: What do you mean what difference does it make? You just said the important thing is the age.

L-L: What's going on here? Do you want to insure *me*?

MM: What do you think? Did you want to assure *me*?

L-L: What the—are you an agent too?

MM: (*Proudly.*) Not only an agent, but a sub-agent.

L-L: (*Stands, introduces himself politely, but with a touch of superiority.*) Mark Moyseyevitsh Lamplighter, district agent and adjuster of Equitable.

MM: (*Stands and introduces himself.*) Menakhem-Mendel Candletwister, sub-agent of Metropolitan.

Enter: FISHMONGER, *carrying two suitcases. He looks for a seat.*

FISHMONGER: May I?

L-L: If you please.

MM: Do. Do.

FISH: (*Sits opposite them. He opens one suitcase and takes out all sorts of bottles and packages of food. He stands the suitcase on its end and uses it as a table.*) You see it pays to take along everything you need, for you can't get what you want at every station. And I don't eat just anything that's available. I watch out for my stomach. That doesn't mean that I have a bad stomach, God forbid. It's in tip-top shape and I hope it always remains that way. Only thing is—I'm afraid to upset it. Your belly's like a boiler, you hear? If, heaven forbid, the kettle stops seething, then the whole machine goes to pot. (*He opens a bottle and pours himself a drink.*) Well, brother Jews, here's to your health! (*He pours a glass for* MENAKHEM-MENDEL.) Here, try a drop. It's my own brew, made from orange peels.

MM: (*Aside.*) Seems to be an outgoing sort of fellow. Perhaps I can assure him to death. (*Aloud.*) Thanks. How about him? (*Points to* LAMPLIGHTER.)

L-L: (*To* MM.) Drink it down. (*Aside.*) Here's a friendly chap. I'll insure him and make my expenses.

FISH: (*Has a second shot and offers one to* L-L.) Here, taste this and have some of these anchovies as a chaser. Top-notch anchovies. Well, what do you say? Am I right or wrong? Fresh as daisies, right? I never travel without anchovies. You can never tell what can happen on a trip! You have to watch what you eat on the way, for your health is the most important thing you have. (*Opens up a salami. He eats and shares it with the others.*) If you've tasted my anchovies, you certainly can taste my salami. Don't worry—it's fresh and kosher. When I buy salami, I don't buy just any salami. For health is the most important thing you have. You know, when you start thinking about death, you start worrying about your life. Especially if you've got a wife and two young kids at home who are the apples of your eye.

L-L: Just two?

MM: Is that all?

FISH: (*Chewing.*) Isn't that enough? What happens if you kick the bucket, God forbid?

L-L: (*Eating.*) With a shape like yours?

MM: (*Eating.*) With a body like yours, knock wood.

FISH: (*Chewing.*) Forget that I'm such a. . . . If I didn't eat I'd be long gone. (*Opens up another package.*) Go ahead. Have some of this smoked meat. It's cold, but fresh. When I buy meat, I don't buy just any meat. Why don't you help yourself to some sour pickles? They're manna from heaven, not pickles. Before I leave the house, my wife, God bless her, starts packing lunches and just keeps packing and packing. Go ahead, have some brandy. My wife made it herself.

L-L: (*Drinks.*) You got yourself a devoted Mrs.

MM: A devoted Mrs. is what you got.

FISH: One in a million. Words can't describe her.

L-L: That's no wife you got, that's a treasure.

MM: She's a treasure, she's no wife.

FISH: I can't begin to tell you! It's just impossible.

L-L: (*Aside.*) Now's the time. I think things will click. (*Aloud.*) A wife like that must be protected.

MM: (*Aside.*) The way is paved. (*Aloud.*) There's a woman that deserves respect. That's a woman for you.

FISH: (*Peeling an orange.*) How can I describe her? Here, have an orange. They're excellent. When I buy oranges I don't just buy any old oranges. She put these in to the lunchbox, too, my wife did.

L-L: (*Peeling an orange.*) A wife like yours just shouldn't be left alone suddenly, God forbid. You know, in case of an accident, heaven forbid. You get me? In any case, I think that you ought to provide for your wife, especially one with children. Especially traveling folk like us.

MM: (*Aside.*) As I live and breathe, he's not doing a bad job. (*Aloud.*) After all, we're travelers, that's what we are.

FISH: It's my opinion too, that a wife has to be left with something. She should know she'll have a capital of at least ten thousand rubles. And there's only one way of going about it.

L-L: (*Excitedly.*) Taking out insurance?

MM: (*Excitedly.*) Assuring yourself to death?

FISH: How did you ever guess? You took the words right out of my mouth.

L-L: It's only logical. How else can people like us provide for our wives.

MM: It's as easy as pie.

FISH: You're absolutely right. You can pay it off in installments. And it doesn't cost too much. Which of you two is interested?

L-L: (*Makes a dash for his briefcase.*) Me, of course. (*Looks* MENAKHEM-MENDEL *up and down.*)

MM: (*Grabs his briefcase.*) I will, naturally.

FISH: In other words, you both want to. Well, that's even better. (*Bends down to his briefcase.*) Don't worry, there won't be any difficulties with the doctor.

L-L: It can be notarized later. The main thing is the age.

MM: We can always get a doctor's note. The important thing is—how old are you?

FISH: Me?

L-L: Who, then?

MM: Who'd you think, me?

FISH: What are you talking about, didn't you want *me* to ins . . . ?

L-L: You—us? We wanted to write *you* a pol. . . .

FISH: You—me? What the . . . are you agen . . . ?

L-L: Of course we're agents! How about you?

MM: Of course we're agents! Who are you?

FISH: (*Stands, brushes the crumbs off his lap and jacket, shakes hands.*) I have the honor of introducing myself. Akim Iskovitsh Fishmonger, inspector and organizing director of New York Life . . .

L-L: Well then, you're one of us. I'm Mark Moyseyevitsh Lamplighter, district agent and adjuster of the Equitable Company. (*He throws a haughty glance at Menakhem-Mendel.*)

MM: So you're really one of us after all? (*with elegance*) My name is Menakhem-Mendel Candletwister, sub-agent of Metropolitan Life . . .

Enter TURTLEDOVE *and his mob, carrying a bunch of suitcases, packages, bags, and bundles. He looks for empty seats.*

TURTLEDOVE: Is this spot taken?

FISH: Not at all.

L-L: Sit right down.

MM: With pleasure.

The newcomer starts seating his family, putting his luggage away. They raise a racket. One yells: "Lunch, mama, lunch." Another wants a drink. The mother is busy cracking nuts and popping them into each child's mouth. She holds a baby on her lap. The older kids rush for the window and elbow one another out of the way. The father treats one to a slap, pinches another, and cuffs a third on the neck.

FISH: (*Aside.*) A man like that should certainly be insured. (*Aloud.*) A trip's no fun with so many children, eh?

L-L: (*Aside.*) A likely subject for a policy—he and his kids. (*Aloud.*) Not easy with so many children, right?

MM: (*Aside.*) Maybe this man will let himself be assured to death. (*Aloud.*) It's pretty hard with so many children, isn't it?

TURT: As hard as death.

FISH: They're pretty spoiled, aren't they?

L-L: You let them have their way, huh?

MM: Spoiled brats, right?

TURT: (*He smacks the oldest boy away from the window.*) Not so spoiled as loved.

FISH: You've got a bunch of fine children.

L-L: They're smart as whips, knock wood.

MM: Knock wood, they sure are clever.

TURT: They're not bad. They're good at school. Well brought up. Upbringing—that's the important thing. (*Calls over his oldest boy.*) Abrasha, come over here. (*Abrasha refuses and gets slapped.*) See this little runt. (*He points to a second boy.*) He's got some head on his shoulders. A genius he is. But, what a devil! He's got an answer for everything. Talk to him and he'll make mud out of you. You see that one —with the dirty face? He's a wise one. Pays no more attention to his mother than the man in the moon. But me, they respect. That is, they wouldn't listen to me either, if it weren't for my strap. And boy do I use it? Left and right! Children, you understand, have to be taught, brought up, that is. Upbringing is the most important thing. See that little monkey, the one my wife's feeding nuts to? What a mouth he has! He's not even four yet, but he pronounces each word like a grown-up. Davidke. Come over here. (*The little monkey called Davidke refuses to slide off his mother's lap, but turns around and faces his father.*) Tell me, Davidke, what's your name?

DAVIDKE: (*Mumbles.*) Mum, mum, mum?

TURT: Davidke, tell mama to give you some prune-whip.

DAVIDKE: (*Turns to his mama.*) Mum, mum, mum.

TURT: Well, what do you say to that? Says each word like an adult.

FISH: (*Beaming.*) Children like that deserve a lot.

L-L: You have to provide well for children like that.

MM: They deserve to be provided for.

TURT: And how! You see these gray hairs. (*Points to his beard.*) I'm married only fifteen years!

FISH: (*Shaking his head.*) Tsk, tsk, tsk.

L-L: What a gang, God bless them!

MM: God bless them, what a gang!

TURT: You have to support them, dress them, give them shoes, teach them, bring them up. Upbringing—that's the most important thing. What I mean to say is—I'm not complaining, God forbid. Thank heaven I've got a good job and with these hands make my few thousand rubles each year. (*He displays his ten fingers.*) But when I look at my mob, God bless them, and start thinking, what if something should happen, heaven forbid . . . you get me? So long as you're healthy everything is fine, but one . . . you understand?

FISH: We understand perfectly. We're family men ourselves. We know the troubles involved in raising kids.

L-L: Providing for kids is one of the greatest deeds.

MM: It's a great deed, it is, providing for kids.

TURT: That's what I keep telling my wife and everyone I meet. What would middle-class folk like us do if there weren't any means for . . . ?

FISH: . . . insuring them!

L-L: Insuring them in case of death.

MM: Assuring them to death.

TURT: (*Excitedly.*) I see that you're quite familiar with all this, and that you're all ready to go through with it. Well, all I can do is congratulate you. You're doing a fine thing!

FISH: (*Very excited.*) We're just doing our duty.

L-L: What our conscience tells us.

MM: We're only doing what's right.

TURT: Well then, may all your wishes come true. Live happy and long lives and may God bless you like you've blessed me and my wife and kids. They look up to me, poor things, for I'm their only provider. (*Opens up a briefcase.*) What amount do you want?

FISH: (*Takes his briefcase.*) How do *we* know what amount?

L-L: (*Takes his briefcase.*) How can we tell you what to do?

MM: You want us to tell you what to do?

TURT: (*Astounded.*) What do you mean, you—me? It's *I* who want . . .

FISH: (*Beside himself.*) You mean *you* wanted to put this thing over?

L-L: You wanted to insure *us* in case of death?

MM: You wanted to assure us to death? Us?

TURT: What did you think? You—me? What the . . . are you agents too?

FISH: Ho-ho! Of course. How about you?

L-L: Certainly we're agents. What about you?

MM: Of course we're agents. And you?

TURT: (*Elegantly.*) Lazar Konstantinovitsh Turtledove, inspector-general and organizing director of Mutual Life.

FISH: Akim Iskovitsh Fishmonger, inspector and organizing director of New York Life.

L-L: (*With dignity.*) Mark Moyseyevitsh Lamplighter, district agent and adjuster of the Equitable Company. (*Looks down his nose at Menakhem-Mendel.*)

MM: (*With pride.*) And I'm Menakhem-Mendel Candletwister, sub-agent of Metropolitan Life. (*They all shake hands and exchange cards.* MENAKHEM-MENDEL *searches his pockets for a card.*) How do you like that? I don't have my card on me.

TURT: (*Sighs.*) It's a tough racket, huh?

FISH: (*Sighing.*) As hard as dividing the Red Sea. You meet somebody and hope, maybe . . .

L-L: (*Looks haughtily at Menakhem-Mendel.*) You understand? It wouldn't be so bad if there weren't so *many* agents. Plenty of competition, you know.

MM: I don't give a damn for big words like competition. Let's be honest. Business is lousy and we're all in one hell of a fix.

THE RUINED PASSOVER

"Pardon me, Reb Yisroel, but can you have the boy's new suit ready for Passover?"

That's what Mama shouted to the stone-deaf tailor at the top of her lungs. Yisroel, tall and long-faced, constantly kept cotton in his ears. He half-smiled and waved his hands, as if to say: Sure it'll be ready. Why not?

"In that case, please measure him. But only on condition the suit'll be finished in time for the holiday."

Yisroel looked at Mama, as if to say: What a queer woman. Isn't one promise enough? From his chest pocket, he withdrew a long, paper measuring-tape and a pair of English shears. He then began measuring me up and down and from side to side. Mama stood next to me, giving orders:

"Longer. Make it longer. Wider. Make it wider. For God's sake, don't make the pants too small. And I want the jacket to be pleated. Make it a few inches longer. That's it! I don't want the waist to be tight, God forbid. I want it to look nice and proper. More, more! Don't be stingy with the cloth . . . the boy is growing."

Yisroel the Tailor knew quite well that a boy grew, but he continued working without saying a word. After taking all my measurements, he nudged me, as if to say: You can go now. You're all finished. I very much wanted the jacket to have the fashionable pocket and slit in the back. But I didn't know who to turn to. Yisroel rolled up the tape with two fingers and stammered broken sentences to my mother:

"It's a hard season . . . just before the holiday . . . lots of mud in the streets . . . fish expensive . . . potatoes like gold . . . not an egg in sight . . . lots of work . . . new clothes ordered? . . . no . . . just patches. If the rich Reb Yehoshua Hersh orders his old coat turned inside out, times are pretty bad . . . Reb Yehoshua himself! These are some times, huh? You can't beat it."

But this didn't impress Mama too much. She interrupted him with:

"How much will the whole thing come to, Reb Yisroel?"

The deaf Yisroel took a bone snuff-box out of his jacket pocket, poured some snuff into the hollow of his palm, slowly brought his hand up to his nose, and expertly sniffed it into his nostrils. Not a drop landed on his mustache. Then he waved his hand and said:

"Tsk, what's the difference? We won't quarrel about it. You know what I mean? Reb Yehoshua-Hersh. Turn an old coat inside out! Things are bad."

"Now don't forget what I asked you, Reb Yisroel. I don't want it tight or small. I want a pleat. And the waist—wide and roomy."

"How about a sl . . . ?" I started to say.

"Shh, let me finish," Mama said, and banged her elbow into my ribs. "Remember, now. Neither small nor tight. A roomy waist and a pleat. For God's sake, a pleat."

"How about a pocket?" I tried again.

"Will you shut up?" Mama said. "Did you ever see a boy like that, mixing in whenever grown-ups are talking?"

The deaf Yisroel took the package of cloth under his arm, rubbed two fingers over the *mezuza* on the doorpost and said:

"In other words, you really want it finished by Passover! Well, have a happy holiday."

2.

"Well, speaking of the devil, here's Reb Gedalye. I was about to send for you again."

Gedalye the Shoemaker was an ex-soldier. His front teeth were missing and his huge round beard was scraggly in the center. Gedalye was a jolly sort of man who moved with a little dancing gait as he spoke.

"Reb Gedalye," Mama said to him, "can you have a pair of shoes made for me by Passover?"

"So you want it without fail for Passover, eh?" He asked

Mama. "It's downright amazing! Everyone wants the stuff for Passover. I've promised Khayele, Reb Motel's wife, two pairs of women's boots. One for her and one for her daughter. I have to make *them* up. Reb Shimele's Yosele ordered four pairs of shoes for Passover. I have to make those. Then there's a long-standing promise to Reb Avrohom's Feygele for a pair of women's boots. Neither storm nor earthquake will stop me —they'll have to be ready for Passover. Moyshe the tailor asked for a pair of tips—I can't refuse him. Zyama the Joiner's shoes need a pair of heels. There's no getting around it. Asne the widow's daughter latched herself on to me and begged in the name of God that . . ."

"Let's make it short and sweet," Mama interrupted. "In other words, you *won't* have it done by Passover? In that case I'll send for the other shoemaker."

"Why shouldn't I have them done?" he said, wriggling. "For you, I'll put off the rest of the work. Your shoes, with God's help, will *have* to be finished for Passover. And no excuses!"

Gedalye the Shoemaker pulled out a piece of blue paper, bent down on one knee and measured my foot.

"Make it a wee bit larger," said Mama, "a little more . . . more . . . don't be stingy with a slice of leather! That's it. It shouldn't squeeze his toes, God forbid."

"Squeeze his toes," Gedalye repeated.

"I want the best leather, Reb Gedalye. You understand. No rotten stuff."

"Rotten," said Reb Gedalye.

"And I want good soles on them. I don't want them to wear out quickly."

"Wear out."

"And I don't want the heels to fall off, God forbid."

"Fall off," Gedalye said.

"Now you can go to Hebrew school," Mama told me. "I hope you at least appreciate what we're doing for you. If only you'd want to study, you could make something of yourself. If not, what will become of you? Absolutely nothing. You'll be a dog-catcher."

I myself didn't know what would become of me. I didn't know if I'd become a somebody, a nobody, or a dog-catcher. All I knew was that at that moment I wanted the shoes to squeak. Boy, did I want squeaky shoes!

"Why are you standing there like a scarecrow?" said Mama. "Why don't you go to school? Go on! You're not going to get anything else."

Gedalye started to go, then turned around. "In other words, you definitely want it for Passover," he said. "Happy holiday!"

3.

Coming home from school, I stopped off at the tailor's to see about the slit and the pocket.

The deaf Yisroel stood, jacketless, in front of a huge table, wearing a broad pair of ritual fringes, immersed in his work. Draped around his neck were several long threads. Pins were stuck in his vest. He made chalk marks, snipped cloth and scratched his back with a bent middle finger, talking to him- self as usual.

"Go make them pleats . . . they want it roomy . . . and nice . . . what from? . . . the air? You can cut your fingers to the bone . . . you just about make . . ."

A few tailor's apprentices sat around the table sewing, sing- ing a song, their skillful needles flying. One jaundiced-looking, freckle-faced boy with a bit of a sunken nose sang in a bell- like voice, sewing to the rhythm:

> Oh you're going,
> Oh you're going,
> and you're leaving me alo-o-one . . .

The others answered with a little scream.

> I'll stab myself!
> I'll hang myself!
> I'll drown myself!
> I'll do myself some ha-a-a-rm!

"What do you want, little boy?" Yisroel asked.

"A slit," I said.

"What?" He bent his head down to me.

"A slit," I yelled into his ear.

"A slit?"

"A slit!"

"Where do you want the slit?"

"In the back."

"What do you want in the back?"

"A slit. And a pocket, too."

"What sort of a slit? What kind of pocket?" Basye, the tailor's wife, butted in. She was a tiny woman, who performed three jobs at once. She rocked the baby with her foot, darned a sock with her hands, and fussed and fumed with her mouth. "What the devil! Slits and pockets! Where do we have material for a pocket? Pockets he wants! Let his mother send cloth for pockets and he'll get them. There's a fine how-do-you-do! Pockets!"

I began to regret the whole business. I just hoped Mama wouldn't hear about it.

"In other words, you really want to have a slit?" Yisroel asked me and took out his little snuff box. "Go home, little boy, you'll have yourself a slit."

"And a pocket, too?" I asked, pulling a long, sad face.

"Go home, little boy," he said. "I'll see that you have everything."

Happy as can be, I whizzed over to the shoemaker's place to ask about the squeak in my shoes.

But Gedalye the Shoemaker wasn't in. His assistant, Karpe, sat at the bench working on a sole. Karpe was a healthy, broad-boned peasant lad with a pock-marked face, wearing a leather head-band to hold down his stiff, black hair.

"What do you want, boy?" he asked in Yiddish, then showed off his knowledge of a few Yiddish phrases.

"I have to see your boss, Reb Gedalye," I said in Russian.

"Boss gone to circumcision party. To get drink," he said in his halting Yiddish, and tapped his Adam's apple to make his point.

I sat down in a leather-covered bench opposite him and started a long discussion about leather, leather-goods, shoes, soles, nails, until I got to the subject of squeaks. He spoke

Yiddish, I, Russian. When he didn't understand me, I talked
with my hands.

"I'm talking your language, you ninny," I said. "I want you
to tell me why a shoe squeaks."

"Better keep talking Yiddish," Karpe said. He licked the
sole and scratched a mark into it with his black thumb-nail.

"Why does it squeak?" I asked in Yiddish now. "What do
you put into the shoes to make them squeak?"

"Oh, squeaks?" said Karpe. "Sugar makes them squeak."

"Is that all? Sugar? How come?"

"With sugar," Karpe explained, "it clomps-clomps, squeak-
squeaks."

"Oh," I said. "The ground-up sugar probably crackles
there. Don't you put anything else in?"

"A little whisky," Karpe said, "a little bit of whisky."

"Whisky? You mean vodka. Why vodka? I can see sugar
making it squeak. But how come vodka? What's that good
for?"

Karpe strained himself in Yiddish and finally made me understand the reason for it. Before you put the sugar into the
shoes, he told me, you have to soak the soles in vodka, otherwise the sugar won't take.

"Now I get it," I said. "If there's no vodka, the sugar goes
to waste. And if there's no sugar, there's no squeak. Like the
Mishna says: 'If there's no food, there's no Torah.' "

I opened my purse and gave Karpe my entire fortune. All
the money I'd collected for *Hanuka* and *Purim*. I bade him a
friendly goodbye. Karpe slipped his big, black, tar-smeared
hand into mine and rattled off a Yiddish ditty.

I ran home to grab a bite, then went back to school to brag
about the new clothes and shoes that were being made for me.
A jacket with a pocket and a slit in the back. And shoes which
squeaked. Really squeaked!

4.

"Mama, school's out," I said, as I came running home from
school a few days before Passover.

"Big deal! May you live to bring home better news," Mama

said, completely in a dither prior to the holiday. She tied kerchiefs around both maids' heads, gave them brushes, brooms,
and feather dusters. She herself had a kerchief on her head, and
all three women cleaned and rubbed, washed and scrubbed,
making everything kosher-for-Passover. I didn't know what
to do with myself. No matter where I sat or stood or went—
it was the wrong place.

"Get away from the Passover cupboard with your bready
clothes," Mama screamed, as if I were lighting matches near
gunpowder.

"Easy there! You're stepping on a Passover sack."

"Don't even look in that direction. That's where the Passover borscht is!"

I kept moving from one spot to another and got under
everyone's feet. They slapped and pinched and smacked me.

"May your rabbi shrivel up! Couldn't he keep you in school
one more day, so you wouldn't spin around here like a top?
As if there isn't enough work to be done! In civilized homes
the children sit in one place, they do. Can't you pick yourself
up and do something—how about reviewing the Four Questions?"

"Mama," I said, "I know the Four Questions by heart."

"Big deal!" she said, "as if it didn't cost me plenty to get
you to learn them."

I just about managed to survive until evening when Father
went around the house, holding a candle, a wooden spoon,
and a feather duster, looking for last signs of breadcrumbs
which he himself had previously placed on the window
sills.

Only twenty-four hours left, I thought. One day and one
night. Then I'll have my new holiday clothes and be dressed
like a prince. I'll have a new jacket with a pocket and a slit in
the back. And my shoes will squeak!

"What's that squeaking I hear?" Mama would surely ask.

And I'd pretend not to know what's going on. Then there'd
be the Passover ceremony, the Hagada, the Four Questions,
the four cups of wine and the holiday goodies; *latkes,* dump-

lings, *kugels*. Thinking of these treats, my mouth started to water. I had hardly eaten a thing that day.

"Recite your bedtime prayer and go to sleep. There's no supper tonight. It's the eve of Passover."

I went to sleep and dreamed it was Passover. I arrived at the synagogue with my father . . . my new clothes crackle . . . my shoes squeak . . . Squeak, squeak. . . . "Who's *that?*" strangers ask. "That's Motel, Moyshe-Khayim's little boy." Suddenly, from out of nowhere, there appears a black, kinky-haired dog. With a growl, he attacks me, grabs hold of my jacket, and wants to run away. Frightened, Father stands rooted and shouts: "Beat it, scat!" The dog pays no attention and tugs at me from behind, just where the split and the pocket are. He rips half the jacket and begins to run. I run after him with all my might and lose a shoe. I stop in a mud puddle— one shoe on, one shoe off. I start yelling and crying: "Help, help!" Then I awoke and saw our maid, Beyle, standing next to me, pulling the quilt and tugging at my leg.

"Look at him. You can't wake him. Wake up, lazybones. Your mother told me to get you up. We have to get rid of the last of the leaven."

5.

Father threw the wooden spoon, the feather duster, and the remaining bread crumbs into the oven. The house was ready for Passover. The whole place was spotless and kosher. The table was set. The four cups smiled at me from afar. Before long, Passover would come. Soon I'd be dressed in my holiday clothes. But until the tailor and the shoemaker delivered my things, my mother made *me* kosher-for-Passover. She washed my hair and scrubbed my head with an egg and hot-water solution, and tore my hair out as she combed me. I writhed. She pinched and slapped me and hit me with her elbow.

"Will you stop squirming like a worm? Did you ever see a child who won't stand still? You do him a favor and he doesn't appreciate it."

I lived through the scrubbing ordeal, thank God, then sat
waiting for my new clothes, watching my father who had
just come from the bath-house with wet earlocks. He sat
studying the *Code of Law*, swaying back and forth, chanting
with a Talmud melody:

"For bitter herbs we use horseradish. Since it is hard, the
radish may be grated."

I looked at my father and thought: he's the most devout
Jew in the world; ours is the most kosher Passover; no one
would have finer clothes than I. But why weren't they here
yet? What was wrong? Perhaps they weren't finished in time
for Passover, God forbid. Of that, I didn't even want to think.
How would I be able to set foot in the synagogue? What
would my friends say? How would I be able to sit down at
the table? May it never happen, I hoped. I wouldn't be able
to stand it.

As I sat thinking these sad thoughts, the door opened and
Yisroel the tailor came in with his handiwork. Joyfully, I
jumped up, knocked the bench over, tripped, and nearly
broke my neck. Mama ran in from the kitchen, holding a
Passover ladle.

"Where'd that noise come from? Who fell? Oh, it's you,
eh? may you not go straight to blazes! You're a devil, a
demon, not a boy. Didn't you get banged up, God forbid?
Good for you! Don't jump! Don't run! Walk like a human
being!"

Then to Yisroel she said: "Well, you kept your word, Reb
Yisroel. I was about to send for you."

Yisroel half-smiled and waved his hand, as if to say: That'd
be something, as I live and breathe! Me not keep my word?

Mama put her ladle away and helped me into my new
trousers. Then she put on my new set of ritual fringes which
she herself had made for me in honor of Passover. Over that
she put my jacket, happy that it was wide and roomy.

I put my hand behind my back. Thunderations! There was
no hint of either a slit or a pocket. Everything was sewn
smooth and proper.

"What sort of an animal is this?" Mama asked suddenly, and started turning me around.

Yisroel took out his snuff box, poured a bit of the tobacco onto his palm, and sniffed into his nose.

"What sort of an animal is this?" Mama repeated, and spun me around again.

"Where do you see an animal?" Yisroel asked, and turned me the other way. "That's the pleat you wanted. You asked for a pleat. Did you forget about it?"

"Some pleat!" Mama said, and whirled me around once more. "What a botched-up job, blast it! Phoo! It's a shame. As I live and breathe, it's a shame!"

But this didn't faze Yisroel. God forbid! He looked me up and down like a professor and said that the suit fitted me perfectly. It couldn't be any better.

"Even Paris can't beat this work. It sings, as I live and breathe, the jacket literally sings."

"What do you say to the way it sings?" said Mama, bringing me over to Father. "What do you say to this song?"

Father spun me around, looked at the jacket, and concluded that the *trousers* were a bit too long.

Yisroel took out his snuff box and offered my father some snuff.

"The trousers *are* a bit longish, Reb Yisroel."

"What's that? Longish? Don't you know what to do? Roll up the cuffs!"

"Perhaps you're right," my father said. "But what do you do if they're too wide. If they look like two sacks?"

"Some fault! It's like saying—the bride's too beautiful," said Reb Yisroel, taking a pinch of snuff. "Wide, you say? Too tight is a thousand times worse."

I didn't stop feeling the back of the jacket. I kept looking for the slit and the pocket.

"What are you looking for back there?" said Mama. "Yesterday's snow?"

That old liar, I thought, and looked at Yisroel as if he were a thief. "You deaf ass! To the blazes with you and your daddy!"

"Wear it well," the deaf Yisroel told me, reckoning the cost of the work. Then, Father again took up the *Code of Law* and continued chanting: "He who has forgotten to eat the last piece of matzoh . . ."

"Wear it well," said Mama, after Yisroel had gone. She couldn't stop looking at the jacket. "Just don't start any of your shenanigans. Don't get into fights with the peasant boys and then with the help of God you'll wear it and wear it in good health."

6.

"Well, speaking of the devil, here comes Reb Gedalye," said Mama. "Are the boy's shoes finished?"

"And how!" he said with his little dance-like gait, carrying the shoes with two fingers, as if carrying a metal hoop of live fish, fresh out of the lake. "It's downright amazing! Everyone and his brother wants them for Passover. I worked myself to the bone, slaved away at shoes instead of sleeping. Once I give my word, I don't care if the world comes to an end."

Mama then put the shoes on me, squeezing and feeling the leather, asking if it pinched me anywhere at all?

"Pinch?" Gedalye said, "I think that another pair of feet could fit into those shoes."

"Stand up and we'll see," said Mama.

I stood and bent the sole, listening for the squeak. But where? what? when? Not a peep came out of them.

"What are you bending the soles for?" said Mama. "Take your time, the year's plenty long. I'll bet that you'll have them ripped, God willing, by next Passover. Now take a walk over to Yekhiel the Hatter and they'll get you a hat for the holiday. But be careful with the shoes. Step lightly on the soles. They're not made of iron."

We walked through the courtyard to Yekhiel's shop, which was right next door. Yekhiel was born white, hair and all, but since he always worked with hats dyed black, he was always smeared with soot. Both sides of his nose were always blue and his fingers black as ink.

"Well, hello, look what the cat dragged in," Yekhiel said, good-humoredly. "Do you want the hat for yourself, or for your boy?"

"For my son," said Father with pride. "But show me something proper . . . something . . . you know what I mean?"

"For instance?" Yekhiel said, looking over the hat-filled shelves.

"For instance," Father said, sticking out his fingers. "I want it to be nice and fine and good and cheap and . . . you know what I mean?"

"I have just the thing you're looking for," said Yekhiel, taking some hats down from the shelf. As he fetched each hat, it twisted and spun on its way down, as if by magic. He put one hat after another on my head, moved away, looked at my face, and said, smiling: "May God bless us! What a perfect fit! Well, how do you like that hat? That's some hat, eh?"

"No, Reb Yekhiel, that's not what I had in mind," said Father, sticking out his fingers again. "I want the hat to be Jewish, you know what I mean, yet stylish, without any fancy doodads. It should be proper and . . . and . . . you know what I mean?"

"Well, why didn't you say so?" said Yekhiel, using a long pole to bring down a hat from the topmost shelf. It was sort of oval, soft-brimmed, and full of checked colors. He held it on one finger and spun it quickly, like a windmill. Carefully, as if my head were made of glass and he were afraid of breaking it, he put it on the tip of my head. The hat barely touched my head. He congratulated himself and wished himself a year of bliss. On his word of honor, it was the only one of its kind in the store. Father bargained a long time for it. Yekhiel vowed that he was selling it so cheaply only for us. Practically below cost, he swore, wishing himself a kosher Passover and lots of health.

I saw that the hat was to Father's liking, for he stepped back and kept looking at it and smoothing down my earlocks.

"I hope it lasts through the summer, at least," said Father.

"Two summers," Yekhiel said, sidling up to him. "Three

summers! As I live and breathe, that's some hat. Wear it well!"

By the time I got home, the hat had flopped over my ears. It was a bit too big, I felt.

"It's no tragedy. So long as it isn't too tight," said Mama, pulling the hat over my nose. "Just don't keep taking it off and putting it on. Don't touch it. Wear it well."

7.

When Father and I came into the synagogue, all my friends were already there: Itsik and Berel, Leybl and Ayzik, Tsodik and Velvel, Shmaye and Kopel, Meyerl and Khayim-Sholem, Shakhne and Shepsl. All were dressed in their holiday best. All wore new jackets, new shoes, new hats. But no one wore such an old-fashioned, long jacket with a pleat as I did. No one wore the kind of shoes I wore. And no one's hat was as queer as mine. I'm not even talking about slits and squeaks. They sure fooled me. They sure made a clown out of me!

The gang greeted me with laughter.

"Oh! So these are the clothes you bragged about? Where's the slit in the back, huh? Where's the pocket you mentioned? Why don't we hear the squeak in your shoes?"

As if I wasn't feeling blue enough, they rubbed salt into my wounds. Everyone threw another dig my way:

ITSIK: What sort of jerket is that you got?

BEREL: That's no jerket, that's a junket.

LEYBL: It's a smock.

AYZIK: It's a dress.

TSODIK: A petticoat!

VELVEL: And look at those pants. They're looney.

SHMAYE: Pantalooney!

KOPEL: A pair of long-johns with leather clompers.

MEYERL: And that hut of a hat.

KHAYIM-SHOLEM: A stove-pipe.

SHAKHNE: A noodle-pot.

SHEPSL: A slop-pail.

I was so boiling mad, I couldn't even hear the fine praying of Hersh-Ber the Cantor. Only when the congregation was wishing one another "Happy Holiday," did I finally recover.

I returned with Father, heavy-hearted and depressed. I just about managed to drag my legs home. A fire burned within me. I couldn't enjoy a thing. Neither the four cups of wine, the Four Questions, the Hagada we'd read, the delicious peppered fish we'd eat with sauce-soaked matzoh, the hot dumplings and *latkes*, nor the rest of the tasty dishes. None of it meant a thing to me. Nothing attracted me. It all disgusted me. Everything was spoiled, ruined. . . .

At the table, Father, the king, sat dressed in a white linen robe, wearing his satin hat, reclining in his pillowed easy-chair. Mama, the queen, sat next to him, wearing her splendid wedding-dress, a silk kerchief, and a necklace of beautiful pearls which made her so charming. I, the prince, sat opposite them, outfitted from head to toe in brand-new clothes. To my left sat Beyle the maid, wearing a new calico dress and a white, starched apron, which crackled and rustled like a matzoh. To my right sat Breyne, the mustached cook, her hair covered with a new yellow kerchief. She held her head with one hand and swayed back and forth, all set to listen to the Hagada.

"This bread of affliction," sang the king in a fine voice, as the queen, her face shining like a star, helped him lift the plate with the matzohs. Beyle lowered her red hands to her apron, which rattled like a newspaper. No sooner did Breyne hear something in Hebrew, than she pulled a religious face and contorted her features, ready to have a good cry. Everyone was in high spirits; everyone was in a holiday mood. But the prince wasn't in step with the rest of them. His heart had turned to stone. A mist came over his eyes. Were it not for the Passover feast, he would have begun to weep. A spell of crying, perhaps, would have done him good.

"This year we are slaves, but next year we shall be free men," the king sang proudly and sat, making himself comfortable in the pillowed easy-chair.

Then, everyone sat, waiting for the prince to rise and ask the Four Questions: "Wherefore is this night different from all other nights?"—to which the king would answer: "We were slaves for Pharaoh in Egypt. . . ." But the prince sat as if he were tacked to the chair. He couldn't budge.

"Well?" the king motioned to him.

"Get up," said the queen. "Ask your father the Four Questions."

The prince didn't move. He felt as if someone had taken him by the throat with a pair of tongs and was throttling the life out of him. He bent his head to a side. He felt his eyes popping from their sockets. Two round pearl-like tears trickled from his eyes, rolled down his cheeks, and fell on the Hagada.

"What is it? Why the tears all of a sudden in the middle of Passover service?" the queen yelled in a rage. "Is that your thanks for the new clothes we made you for the holiday?"

The prince wanted to stop crying, but couldn't. The tears pinched and choked him. Suddenly an entire fountain, a wellspring of tears opened up.

"Tell us, what is it? What hurts you? Speak up. Answer! Or do you want Father to lay you down and give you a sound thrashing in honor of Passover?"

The prince stood up and stuttered:

"Question! I want to ask you four fathers . . . I mean, father . . . I want to ask you four que . . . que . . . que . . ."

The prince's legs buckled under him and he fell, his head on the white tablecloth, crying and sniffling like a baby.

A ruined . . . a completely ruined . . . Passover!

FROM THE RIVIERA

Don't ask me what the Riviera is. I *used* to be in the dark about it and I hope you *remain* that way. I wish *I* never got to know it. So you want to know all about the Riviera in a nutshell, huh? In three short words it's: Jew-boy give cash! Riviera—that's a spot in Italy dreamed up by the doctors in order to wring the public dry. The sky there is always clear. We have the same sky here. Same sun, too. But the sea bothers the daylights out of you. It rears and roars; it makes your head spin. But you keep paying. For what? For nothing at all. Absolutely nothing. Because you're an ass and have let yourself be hoodwinked into the Riviera—shell out! And you certainly do!

Just try and outsmart them, try not to pay! Do you think they argue with you? Insult you? Embarrass you? God forbid! They're as good as gold to you. They kill you with kindness. But the Riviera has one good point—and there's no denying it—it surely is warm there. Wherever it's warm, folks say, you don't cough as much. And there it is warm all year round, winter and summer.

Does it make sense? Surely it makes sense. If the sun shines —it's warm. But what of it! If it gets hot enough, our village is no icebox either. So, they come back at you with—fresh air! True, the air isn't bad there. Smells quite good, in fact. Like perfume. But it's not the *air*, really. It's the oranges they grow. Then again, is it worth going all the way out there just for that? I don't know! There's plenty of air all over, I think. And oranges can be bought here, too. But the doctors say there's no comparing one type air with another. Perfumed air can cure. That's what the doctors say. But who cares what doctors say. Go listen to doctors! Why do they they tell you that the Mediterranean soaks every sickness out of you? I don't deny it. Perhaps it is a sickness-soaker. All *I* know is that it soaked every last kopek out of me—that sea. And not so much the sea as those doctors. God sent a doctor my way, there at the Riviera . . . how should I put it? He was some doctor! That is, he was quite a likable fellow, otherwise. A Jew, to boot. And what a Jew! He spoke Yiddish just like you and me. And what a juicy, spicy, free-and-easy Yiddish, too. It was a pleasure listening to him. But the way he took you for a ride! Boy, could he take you for a ride! And you know, I'm just the sort to be taken. He certainly found the right customer. I made up my mind—you hear?—and let myself be led by the nose right up to the last minute. I saw right off who I was dealing with. But I played dumb. You want to soak me. Go ahead and soak me.

First off he sounded me out, examined me, tapped me with little hammers and bangers, tubes and pipes, and told me to come the next day. I said to him: "Pardon me, doctor, but I'm not familiar with the local procedure. How much do I owe you?" He looked at me through his glasses, his hands in his pockets, and said: "We'll get to that later." Fine, I thought. Later is fine with me. When I came the next day, we went through the same rigamarole. He examined me, sounded me out, pinched and hammered me. Then he told me to come the next day and get an injection.

"Pardon me, doctor," I asked him. "How much do I owe you?"

"Later," he said.

Wonderful! Later was fine. The next day, he gave me a shot and told me to come the following day for a massage. I came for the massage and he massaged me, that is, he rubbed the spot where I'd been injected and told me to come the next day for another shot.

"How much do I owe you?" I asked.

"Later," he said.

Fine. I didn't care. And that's the way it went, from day to day. One day he gave me a shot, the next day he massaged the sore spot. That swindle didn't appeal to me from the start. You want to get me coming and going, eh? Well, go right

ahead. But why make it a slap-down, dragged-out affair? Who
said you need one day for a shot and another one for the massage? It seems to me that both operations done in one day
would be better. It's logical. Inject and rub it in at the same
time. But what's the point? Procedure? Of course not! Then
I had to assume that he wanted to milk me dry. Well, try it!
Perhaps I'm not milkable. Perhaps there's nothing to milk
from? Do you know me? Did you ever look into my pockets?
Have you counted my cash?

Well, here's what happened. A month later, he mailed me a
bill. As soon as I looked at it I saw stars. Each injection cost
10 francs (there they soak you in francs), and each massage
cost five. Not a bad little bill, eh? Cures like that can make a
rich man out of you. What should I do? I thought. Bargain
with him? That I could always do later. If that wise-guy didn't
demand his money, why should I rush? So I kept getting his
injections every other day. I come—he injects. The winter
came and went. Before I knew it, Purim had arrived. Time to
start thinking of the trip back home. Especially since my
health, thank God, was good—quite good. In fact, I can well
say—and why deny it?—I hope it never gets any worse. Of
course, better has no limits. In that case, I had to say goodbye
to that smartie of a doctor and go home. When I saw him,
I said: "I'm going home."

"Have a nice trip," he said.

"Well, what about the bill?" I said. "I have to pay you off,
don't I?"

He looked at me through his glasses, his hands in his
pockets, as if to say: What's keeping you from paying?

"I hope you'll pardon me, doctor," I said, "but before we
settle the account, I'd like to tell you a story, if you can spare
the time."

"I really don't have the time to spare, but if it's short, tell it."

I sat down and told him the following tale:

"Looking at me, you can see I'm an average Jew. Thank
heaven, I also have five boys, God bless them. Four of them
happen to be fine and talented. But one of them—may you
be spared a like fate—is the devil-knows-what! Didn't want

to study—not a bit. A bad boy. We slapped him, beat him, but we couldn't knock the mule out of him. Neither kindness nor threats helped. A bad boy. Well, what was I to do?

"Put him into apprenticeship," my wife suggested.

"What? You want him to be a *worker?* Over my dead body!"

"What then? What'll you gain if you beat him to death?" she said.

I considered it and decided she was right. I made a deal and turned him over to the best tailor in town.

"Take this prize-package," I said, "and make a workman out of him."

I signed a contract with the tailor. By the end of three years, he would have to make a tailor of my son and I would pay the master-tailor three hundred rubles. After the first year, he came around, took the first hundred, and signed for it. Wonderful! Another year passed by. The tailor returned, took the second hundred, signed for it. Fine and dandy. The third year passed by—but my tailor didn't show up. I waited a week, then two. Nothing! What had happened? I took a walk over to the tailor's place.

"Mr. Tailor," I said, "why haven't you come for the third hundred?"

"You don't owe it to me," he said.

"It doesn't make sense," I said.

"It makes plenty of sense! Three things make a tailor. First of all, he must know the work itself. Second of all, he must know how to make off with a piece of left-over material. If you want to call it robbery—go right ahead. Call it what you will. Third of all, a tailor must know how to drink, that is, celebrate a festival with a few drops. Your son, then, is two-thirds of a tailor. When it comes to thievery, he's quite handy. When it comes to liquor, he can hold his own with the best of souses. But a tailor he is not, and never will be. Therefore, why take the third hundred?"

After listening to this story, the doctor asked: "Well, what's your point?"

"My point is," I said, "that your work, like any other work,

consists of three things. First of all, you have to be a good doctor. Second of all, you have to be honest. Third of all, a doctor
has to know how to make money. Which of the first two
points is outstanding on your part, I don't know. But as I live
and breathe, you surely know how to present a bill. Now,
let's dicker over the price. . . ."

May a plague wrack my enemies for every ruble I bargained
off the bill. I ended up paying less than a *third* of it. But the
cure wasn't even worth *that* much. For had I stayed at home
and done nothing, and were I destined to get better—I would
have gotten better *anyway*. So what good's the Riviera?

A HOME AWAY FROM HOME

1. A Windfall—We Shoo the Wolf Away— Doctors Order a Change of Air

Don't ask me how it happened or why! Don't ask me to describe the headaches and heartaches that finally brought it about! Don't even ask me why it had to happen to me and no one else. But thanks to the good Lord in heaven, I finally had a windfall before Passover and put across a neat deal which netted me a fat few thousands, all in one heap.

When a fat bundle like that falls your way, the first order of the day is to shoo the wolf from the door. You do this by clouting him in the head with a newly-bought bench, coat, pillow, a pair of quilts, a new set of dishes, a fine piece of cloth, a piano—whatever's handy, you fling at him! To make a long story short, I sent that wolf straight to blazes and paid off the butcher, the grocer, the Hebrew teacher, and all the other creditors who were knocking at the door. I wish all our friends could have had the sort of Passover we celebrated that year! We enjoyed the best matzohs, the finest fish, the most expensive wines, the juiciest *knaidloch* (and in the synagogue, the juiciest honors) and were all stylishly dressed.

But all this high living caught up with us pretty quickly. It went straight to our stomachs (may it never happen to you!). So we began calling doctors. The doctors, in turn, began writing prescriptions, taking money, and forking out advice that I, my wife, and children had to have a change of air, that one could not live more than an hour without air. (That's exactly what they said.) The upshot was, in June, right after *Shevuoth*, we would rent a summer cottage in the country, move out of the big city to Boyberik, and start breathing.

To tell you the truth, it wasn't the air so much as Boyberik

itself that attracted us. Taking a summer cottage in Boyberik
was rated very highly by the Yehupetz folk. They thought
it quite the fashion—like hard-springed easy chairs which are
never sat in, the parlor piano which no one ever plays, and
similar stylish furnishings. When two Yehupetz residents met,
the first thing they said was:

"Where are you going this summer?"

"Boyberik. Where else? How about you?"

"Boyberik, naturally. Got your cottage yet?"

"And how? Well, how about you?"

"And *what* a cottage! Where's yours?"

"Right on the main street, of course. And yours?"

"Same place."

And so on.

2. Into Paradise, Which the Agents Ruin

Right after *Shevuoth,* my wife and I took the train to
Boyberik to look for a cottage. We were charmed by the
green forests, the fresh air, the tweeting birds, and the neat
summer houses, each of which looked like a well-dressed bride
on her wedding day. We had a good mind not to go back to
noisy Yehupetz with its hot streets and awful night smells.

"Well, what do you say to this, Khaye-Etel?" I said to my
wife.

"What should I say? May all money be burned to a crisp!"

"It looks like the Yehupetz blue-bloods know what's good
for them. It's Paradise."

"May they burst wide open!" she said good-naturedly.

We walked around in that Garden of Eden just like Adam
and Eve before the fall. But the Boyberik real-estate agents
ruined our little Paradise for us. Each one dragged us to see *his*
cottage. Each one said that his was better, bigger, and cheaper.
Among the agents were a swarthy, one-eyed fellow who carried a whip, and a red-head with a twisted face. The red-head
grabbed us by the lapel and began dragging us around town.
Then up spoke the swarthy Cyclops and latched on to our
sleeves.

"Why go with that crook? He'll lead you straight to the lower depths of hell!"

"Shut your face, you black devil," the red-head said. "In another minute, I'll fix your other eye."

Without dilly-dallying, he punched the black devil in the nose. Then, Blackie lashed out with his whip and made a bloody mess of the red-head, roaring that he'd bring him to the police and use us as witnesses. Hearing the word "police," we took off like two madmen.

3. The Big Move—Little Troubles—Much Shame

The trip to Boyberik from Yehupetz is a snap—it only takes half an hour. But to move out to a summer cottage with wife and children, bed and bedding, meat and dairy dishes, and all the rest of the junk—that, I wish on my enemies! The minute you're on your way, the wife gets into a dither and turns into a deadly bundle of nerves. At a time like that, you'd be better off leaving her alone. While holding the keys, she runs around yelling: "The keys, the keys! What a house! Anything you put down disappears. God save us from a house like this and from children like ours! Children? They're devils one and all. They're fiends and demons, not children."

These children had a habit of getting under your feet just when they saw you were busiest. So they got pushed, slapped, smacked. They started bawling and screaming. They raised a racket and then all hell would break loose. And talk of packing! Knock wood—you had to gather up the entire household —sort it, pack it, wrap it, tie it, and not forget a thing. And then, as if in spite, when everything was at the depot, you looked around and discovered that you'd forgotten to include your wife's hat with the little flowers, the canary and its cage, the inkwell, canes and parasols, and other such silly things which popped up the last minute—like the exhaust pipe for the samovar.

"What'll we do without that chimney?" my wife yelled.

"What am I going to do without a hat? And what about the poor canary? It'll drop dead."

The long and the short of it was, we had to take all those things with us. But who was to carry them if everyone was loaded down from top to toe with all sorts of baskets, boxes, packages, and bundles? Guess who? Me! I had no choice. So I took the exhaust pipe in one hand, and the canary cage in the other. Then what about the hat and the rest of the junk? I got an idea. I put the exhaust pipe under one arm and the hat under another, so that it wouldn't get crushed. Then, what about the inkwell? That I slipped into my pocket and, with heart in mouth, headed for the station.

When I got there, the fun began. Tickets! For the life of me I couldn't figure out how many tickets I needed. So I counted my gang. The wife was one, then there were eight children—God bless them—six of them big ones. That made it seven tickets so far. The two little ones went for half-fare. That made it eight. Grandma made it nine. Three maids brought it up to twelve. An even dozen. Lucky it wasn't thirteen. Thirteen was an unlucky number. Naturally, I forgot to include myself. Then—*clang, clang. All aboard!* As the crowd started pushing, my wife called me.

"What's taking you so long? We're going to be late because of you."

The children helped her out by yelling. "Hurry up, pop, hurry up. You'll be late."

I ran into the car and got tangled up with the edge of the exhaust pipe. At first, it wouldn't fit through the door. I dropped the hat. When I bent down to pick it up, the inkwell overturned and leaked all over the hat. My wife flew off the handle and rightly so.

"Butter-fingers! What a clay pigeon! Who asked you to carry my hat? Who needs your favors? What am I going to do now, without a hat?"

I told her I was going to buy her a dozen hats, so long as she would pipe down. She said she didn't need my favors and needed the hats like a hole in the head. Fifty sets of eyes were

on me. I blushed and started to perspire. The children started
to fight for space near the window. Lucky it's happening on
the train, I thought. I'd really have taken care of them if I
weren't so ashamed of a scene. Then my little one came up and
asked, "papa, where's the canary?"

I looked into the cage. No bird. I looked all around—
searched my cuffs, my pockets. "Where could it have disappeared to? When could it have gotten out?" I said.

One wise-guy asked what sort of bird it was. Another asked
how much it cost. Some whispered among themselves and
others were hysterical with laughter. One white-toothed
young man suggested that as soon as I got to Boyberik I
ought to wire back to Yehupetz and ask them to look for the
bird. They all cracked up. I was tempted to take him by the
throat and chuck him out the window. Luckily, the conductor
and inspector walked in just then and everyone took out his
ticket.

When he came to me, he asked who were the twelve tickets
for. I figured it out: the wife, six big kids, two little ones,
grandma, and the three maids.

"And where's your ticket?" the conductor said, staring at
me as if I were a thief trying to sneak a free ride.

I became rattled and looked all over for the ticket.

"Where is your ticket?"

I peeked into the exhaust pipe of the samovar. I searched
each pocket. But no ticket. My wife, seeing that I was looking
for something, asked:

"What is it now? What'd you lose *this* time? Have you got
your gold watch? See if you still have it? Or have you got
beans instead of the watch?"

"I didn't lose a thing," I said angrily, picked up the exhaust
pipe, and flung it out the window. "To hell with you and
head first, too."

That's the story in a nutshell of our first trip to Boyberik
from Yehupetz.

4. Door to Door Service—Jews by the Dozen—
The Slaughterer's Son

We had just started unpacking, hardly had time to get our bearings, when from all sides salesmen swamped our cottage offering all sorts of dainties. Chickens, eggs, vegetables, and dairy-products, edibles, salted and smoked, and other merchandise like groceries, fancy-goods, even furs. They sold practically everything.

"What do you say to this?" I asked my wife.

"What should I say?" she said. "May all money be burned to a crisp!"

After the salesmen had gone, Jews carrying no samples at all started streaming in and out of the house and we began to make friends.

"Hello, there. Lot's of luck!" a new man said.

"Hello yourself," I said, "what's the good word?"

"Nothing. Wood's my business. I thought you might need some wood, so I stopped by."

Then the women came and started introducing themselves. The milk woman, the cheese and butter woman, the poultry woman, the bread woman. Each of them came with a recommendation. Then, a wave of paupers descended upon us. They appeared singly and in pairs—alms collectors by the dozen, just like in a big city.

"You seem to have plenty of Jews in Boyberik, don't you?" I said.

"Knock wood," said a tall, sleepy-voiced, pale-faced young man. He wore a long sack which he called his wrap, as if to say: You can call me either a *Hasid* or an aristocrat. It's up to you.

"How many Jews in this town?" I asked.

"Better ask how many non-Jews there are."

"What do you mean—is this Palestine? Can Jews live here without any trouble?"

"Just the opposite. Jews aren't allowed to live here at all."

"Then how come they live here if it's forbidden?"

"Just like you see," he said.

"What are you?" I asked the young man.

"What am I?" he said. "I'm a Jew."

"It's as plain as the nose on your face that you're not a peasant, God forbid," I said. "What I mean is—who are you?"

"Who am I? Well, I'm the local slaughterer's son."

"What do you do?"

"What do I do? Well, perhaps I'll soon do something once more. But in the meantime, I'm not doing anything at all."

"Then what do you want here?"

"What do I want? Well, I came to ask if you'd give us something for our Hebrew school."

"You mean to tell me that you have a Hebrew school, too, in Boyberik?"

"Nah," he said. "It'd be fine and dandy if we did have one."

"Then you mean to say that you *don't* have a Hebrew school here. Then what're you collecting money for?" I asked.

"What for? For the local Hebrew school!"

"But if you have no funds, how'd you get a Hebrew school?"

"A fact's a fact."

Then I heard my wife yelling: "Why waste your time with that nincompoop. Be good enough to drag yourself over here and help unpack, set up the furniture, and put some nails into the walls."

I said goodbye to the slaughterer's son and went to work.

5. I Hammer Nails—
My Wife Introduces Me to Our Neighbors

Banging nails into the walls—that was my life. If I saw an empty wall, I filled it top to bottom with nails. What could I do? That was my weakness. I couldn't stand seeing a wall without nails.

"Who's banging there?" came a voice from the other side of the wall.

"What's all the banging for?" came another voice from behind another wall.

"From dawn to dusk, all this guy does is hammer nails into walls," said a third voice, from behind another wall.

"Why don't you bang your *head* against the wall?" a woman's voice said.

"Khaye-Etel," I called. "Do you know who's screeching out there?"

"Why shouldn't I know?" she said. "That's the woman from Greydik—the one whose husband left her and ran away to America. She has bad eyes and gets silver chloride treatment in town from Dr. Mandelbaum, twice a week."

"Where do you get all your information from?" I asked.

"What do you mean?" she said. "I've made friends with almost all the neighbors already. The kitchens are together here. We're a varied bunch, you know. Aristocrats from Yehupetz, rich men and poor villagers. There's a dry goods man from the big city's slums, a money-lender from Main Street, a fire insurance agent, a choir member, a teacher, a cashier in a mill, a stock-broker, two students, three women, and a fourth one from Lithuania."

"It's a regular zoo," I said.

"The women are quite nice. They're from out of town and came here to take care of themselves. One is from Zvenirodke. She's as thin as a stringbean and the poor thing coughs all night long. The other one is from Restopol. She's got a wooden leg. The third one is from Greydik, the one with the bad eyes. The Lithuanian is a fine one, too. She has teeth trouble, God spare me. She's going crazy."

"Let her suffer with it!"

"Let her suffer with it? What have you got against her? Do you know her? She happens to be a fine person, gentle and honest."

"It's quite possible."

"What do you mean it's possible? What sort of talk is that?"

"Shush," I said. "Don't holler. Look. There's a woman hobbling this way."

"That's the peg-leg from Restopol," she said, and went toward her with a smile of welcome.

6. The Peg-leg and Her Many Ills—
Her Tirade—My Escape

"Have a seat! Sit right down. Why don't you sit down?" my wife said, bringing her a chair.

"Thanks. It's quite all right," she said, sitting and stretching out her bad leg. "I don't know who dreamed up this Boyberik," she sighed.

"Air-shmair. It's a load of hooey. I've been here for a week already and haven't even improved this much. (She touched the nail of her pinkie.) I wish the doctors were as slow in finding out what's wrong with themselves as they are with me."

"Why'd they send you to Boyberik? What's wrong with you? Any special sickness?"

"My sickness!" she said, bending her wooden leg. "If only I had one sickness it would be fine and dandy. The trouble is that there isn't an illness under the sun that I *don't* have. But if you ask me what hurts, I don't know. I'm rooming with a woman from Zverinodke. She's got lung trouble. But that's nothing. At least she knows what's wrong with her. Or take the woman from Greydik with the bad eyes. She knows she has to visit Dr. Mandelbaum twice a week and that's that. Or take the Lithuanian with the teeth. It's bad enough if one tooth hurts. But all thirty-two of them? May it never happen to me! They say that she may have some sort of rheumatism. She caught cold in a bath. Now, she's clawing at the walls with pain. I tell you, you've got to be made of iron to stand her screaming. And whose fault is it? The men! (She threw a nasty look my way.) If I had a toothache like that I'd pull all my husband's teeth out."

"Why's the husband guilty if his wife has a toothache?" I said.

"Oh. Is that so?" the woman stretched her wooden leg and snorted. "What about having a baby, that's nothing, huh? Carrying it and nursing it and weaning it and chicken pox and measles and teething and cooking cereals and washing diapers and sewing shirts and darning socks and spanking them and scrubbing and combing them? Aha! You don't want to hear that! No time, eh? You just want to take the kids for a walk in the woods. You don't hear what you don't want to hear. I know your type. Pull your hat down over your ears some more, go ahead! It won't hurt you none. The truth should be told, even to a father!"

7. My Gang's Version of Paradise— A Matchmaker's Advice

My gang consisted of eight, God bless them. Three grown girls, two younger ones, and three little boys. Poor things. They all starved a bit in the bad days. They had their share of hard times. Now they all wanted to have a good time. Like us, they wanted Paradise on earth. But each had his own private picture of Paradise. My oldest daughter wanted a doctor from Yehupetz, and Yehupetz only. The other girl wanted a lawyer from Odessa. No other place would do. The third wanted a graduate engineer. He could come from anywhere. My boys' Paradise was something quite different. One was under the impression that the greatest thing in the world was riding a horse of his own. The other one wanted a bicycle. "I'd be the happiest boy alive if you'd buy me a bike," he said. The third just wanted a red shirt, a pair of trousers tucked right into shiny boots, and a puppy chasing after him. And I had to buy everything, for my wife, may she live and be well, loves each child so much that they got whatever they want. Especially since, with God's help, we could now afford it— why should we deny them the pleasure? Until now, we've mentioned things which money could buy. But proper matches for the girls? A doctor from Yehupetz? A lawyer from Odessa? A graduate engineer?

On the other hand, money *could* get you as many doctors and lawyers and engineers as you wanted. As soon as they found out that I was in the chips, I'd gotten letters from matchmakers the world over. For instance, the matchmaker from Smargon had already come beating at my door. He offered me twenty-seven matches and insulted me to boot.

"Is it my fault," I told him, "that my daughters don't want any pre-arranged marriages?"

"What then do they want?"

"They want something to come out of . . . meeting someone . . . out of love."

"Is that so? That's the way they've been brought up, eh? Love is what they want, huh? Well then, I'll give you a bit of advice. Let them sleep on the window sills. Then someone will take pity on you, kidnap them, and run away with them."

Any other time, the matchmaker from Smargon would have cracked the door open with his head. But if you had three eligible daughters at one and the same time, you had to swallow your pride and keep quiet.

To tell you a secret—we really went out to Boyberik for our daughters' sake. Perhaps God would be merciful, I thought, and something good would come of it. For here in Boyberik, the finest matches from Yehupetz were arranged. It's logical, for the world's an open place during the summer season. The forest is huge. The depot is always full of people. There are gardens, theaters. Boys and girls meet a dozen times a day, look at each other, smile, exchange a few words. They get acquainted, they stroll in the woods. They take out rowboats and sing songs. At night, they sit in the moonlight, counting the stars and sighing. The next thing you know, the wedding bells are ringing in Yehupetz!

8. Creatures of the Forest—Couples at Large— The Secret of the Trees

If you think that the Boyberik forest is like any other forest in the world, you're sadly mistaken. Here, you could roam alone to your heart's content without giving it a moment's thought. No bandits would take you by surprise, God forbid. You wouldn't meet up with wolves, wild goats or harmful beasts. Here, you could meet other sorts of creatures. A Jew from the town of Yadeshliv, who wandered around, free as a bird, hawking and spitting; a sick woman, who either held on to a tree coughing lustily, or lay on the ground trying to catch her breath; the rich patients stretched out in hammocks which looked like suspended coffins. Plus other sorts of creatures who suffered and did not want to die, for they believed in witchcraft, doctors, prescriptions, woods, fresh air, and other such fantasies.

Jews like to stick together. They can be as sick as the devil, but they hate to sit alone. Their motto is: Come what may— so long as we're together. There were spots in the Boyberik wood which served as a sort of club, or (forgive the proximity) a little synagogue, where all the sick could meet. Well, meeting led to talking and talking led to backbiting and slander.

Walking through the woods with my family, I spotted a group of men and women sitting in a circle in various positions, looking like a bunch of cadavers.

"Moyshe, do you know who he is?" said one of them, pointing at us.

"How should I know?" Moyshe said, coughing, "the devil knows who they are!"

"Shush," said a third, "they must be the newcomers who moved into that huge summer cottage this morning."

"If so," said still another, sitting up, leaning on his scrawny, stick-like hands, "if that's the ones you mean, I've got something juicy to tell you about them."

Hearing that something juicy was about to be told, the cadavers suddenly came to life. The man with the scrawny hands coughed himself content and then whispered his story to the whole gang. They listened with pleasure, staring at me and my daughters.

"Breyne," one woman yelled to another, "which of the three girls do you like best?"

"The middle one," Breyne shouted.

"Do you agree, Sore-Zisel? Is it the middle one?"

"No," Sore-Zisel said, "all the middle's one's got is nice hair —and that's it. I like the little one. If it weren't for that nose, she'd be a beauty."

"Pipe down," one of the men yelled at them. "Just look at those geese honking away."

We kept walking and met other characters. They sat around green tables, playing noisy games of cards.

"I've got threes."

"So what?"

"Threes take the pot, right?"

"Well?"

"Well, I've got three of them."

"Good by me. What have you got?"

"Three jacks."

"Eyewash! What have *you* got?"

"Three queens."

"Dump them! Kings take it. Show money."

"No you don't. Aces talk. Kings walk!"

Apparently, these people didn't even think of death. Among them were the sort who came from Yehupetz to Boyberik not for its beautiful woods and fresh air, but for the sole purpose of card-plyaing.

A bit further on, we started meeting couples, boys and girls taking walks in the woods. One couple strolled along, holding hands. They gazed at each other, then broke into a queer little song and danced to its rhythm:

> I like apples, I like stew,
> But most of all, dear, I like you.

Another couple was practicing running. Either that, or they were playing tag. She ran, and he chased her. When he tried to catch her, she dodged. A third couple played switch; she put on his cap; he put on her coat. Go do them something! Others hopped around crazily, yelling at the top of their lungs: "Hi-ho, hi-ho," listening for the echo.

But the forest stood silent and still. It wasn't in the least concerned with all the goings-on. Proudly, the tall pine trees with their sweet-smelling needles stretched to the clear blue sky. Rest assured—they wouldn't breathe a word.

You know what? I think the Boyberik forest outdoes the most famous matchmakers in the world.

9. Eating Under Open Skies—Paupers' Investments— The Peg-leg's Husband—The Ladies' Palaver

Coming home from the forest, we found a table set for us on our porch. Surrounded by shrubbery on all sides, we sat down to our first meal under the open sky. A chorus of birds, musicians without pay, accompanied our meal with song, trilling and chirping in every way. Every once in a while, they would flit down to the table, nab a crumb, and fly away.

"Khaye-Etel," I said. "What do you say? It's nice having a meal in the fresh air after a walk in the woods, isn't it?"

"What do you want me to say?" she said, in her usual manner, "I told you already: May all money be burned to a crisp! The only trouble is that things are too open here. Everyone knows what's cooking in everyone else's pot. The woman from Greydik, the one who's getting eye treatments in the big city, pokes her nose into everything, and the woman from Restopol asked our maids to tell her our life story, starting from the day we got married."

Suddenly, a bunch of beggars appeared. "Brother Jews! How about some alms?" Behind them were a host of others.

"Where are you from?" I asked one of them.

"Yehupetz," he said.

"And you're living here?"

"God forbid!" he said. "We commute."

"Then you have traveling expenses," I said. "Do you at least make the price of the fare?"

"Sometimes yes, sometimes no," he said. "Sometimes we make expenses, sometimes we end up in the red. That's how every business is. You got to speckalate. And that's just what we do: speckalate."

When they left, someone else came.

"How do you do? Hearty appetite," said a young man,

wearing a silk fedora and a wide set of ritual fringes. He puffed at a cigarette as he watched us eating.

"Hello," I said, "join us."

"No thanks! Eat hearty!" he said, and kept smoking.

"Where are you from?"

"Restopol. I came to visit my sick wife. She lives here too, you know."

"Oh, so you're her husband. What's your name?"

"Khayim-Wolf."

"Did you come to tell me something special, Reb Khayim-Wolf?"

"No," he said solemnly, "I saw you eating, so I purposely came closer to see a Jew eating without a hat."

"You know," I said, "that reminds me of something that happened in Konotop, a town your local *rebbe* recently visited. A certain anti-*Hasid* dropped in to see him. He was the sort that didn't give a damn for Hasidic *rebbes*. He put a ruble on the table in front of your Restopol *rebbe* and didn't say a word. 'What do you want?' the *rebbe* asked him. The man then took out another ruble and put it on the table, still not saying a word. Again the *rebbe* asked him: 'What is it you want?' The man answered, 'Nothing. I just wanted to see a Jew taking money for nothing.' "

Khayim-Wolf turned around, spit, and left.

"What do you say to your girl-friend's husband, Khaye-Etel?"

"What do you want me to say?" she said. "Your Yehupetz blue-bloods with their diamond earrings are no better. All they do is giggle. In fact, one of them, a woman with plenty of diamonds, who reads all day long—well, you should have seen the storm she raised about a chicken. She suspected her neighbor, another woman loaded down with diamonds, of stealing . . ."

"Hee-hee-hee-hee," came a woman's giggling squeals. But in their tone was heard a bit of anguish. Then another woman started cursing away, using words like: Big mouth, killer, hunchback, snot-nose, slut, and bitch.

"Wow," I said. "She certainly knows her Yiddish."

"And would you believe it!" Khaye-Etel said, "to me she won't say a word of Yiddish. For the life of her, when she talks, she'll use only Russian and German."

10. The Hot Wall—A Nightingale's Song and a Merchant's Thoughts

Knocked out from the day's work, we all fell into our beds like dead ones and went to sleep. After a three hour snooze, I dreamed I was in the upper shelf of a Turkish bath and that someone was giving me a drubbing with a birch switch. What a pleasure!

"Turn up the steam," I shouted. "Turn it up high."

"God be with you! What are you screaming about? What is it?" my wife woke me.

"It's awfully hot here," I said. "I'm soaked through and through. Just touch the wall, Khaye-Etel. it's steaming like an oven."

"Thunderations!" Khaye-Etel screamed, and drew her arm back. "The wall's as hot as fire."

"It looks like the cottages have central heating."

"Wise-guy! Did you ever hear of summer cottages with heat. You're as crazy as a fox. It's the wall where the oven is, that's all. Is that so hard to understand?"

"What difference does it make if I *do* understand. The fact remains that it's so hot, you can melt."

I got up and opened the window. Immediately, a cool breeze swept into the room, bringing with it the perfumed scent of flowers and other rare aromas. I stuck my head out the window, entranced by the beautiful and sweet-smelling summer night.

The dark blue sky was starred with twinkling diamonds. Sunk in the grayish mist, the silvery moon peeped through the leaves. Little by little, the mist dispersed like puffs of smoke and soon the moon was perfectly clear and bright. From the woods came the strange call of birds. I listened carefully, hardly daring to breathe. I was in heaven. I hadn't heard singing like that in ages. It was the sweet singer of the night, the nightingale. It didn't sleep and didn't let others sleep, but brought to the fore long-buried feelings and thoughts which had nothing at all to do with rubles, profits, and business pursuits.

My thoughts carried me to another world, long gone. They took me back to my silly, but so very happy childhood, a world which would never return. For a moment, I was another person. I didn't want to leave the window. I felt like staying there all night. But, suddenly, the chronic workaday thoughts returned: wife and children, girls of marriageable age, headaches, business affairs, rubles. . . .

There's no denying it, I thought. That little fellow can certainly sing. But, ought a busy man whose thoughts are of making a living spend a whole night gazing at the moon, counting the stars, and listening to the nightingale? One just doesn't do things like that.

I closed the window and went back to sleep.

11. Fancy-goods—a Cold Shower— The Peg-leg's Husband's Compromise

"Fancy-goods for sale," someone yelled right into my ear. "Scented soaps. Fine soap. Say, do you need some good soap?"

"Soap? What sort of soap?" I awoke, scared out of my wits. I sat up in bed, rubbed my eyes, and saw a man with a dark, dog-like face and wide open nostrils staring at me.

"Any kind you want," the dog-face said. "Essence of Violets, Breath of Spring, Summer-Mist, or Jasmine. They're all sweet-smelling. Take anyone you want. They're cheap."

"What's going on here? Help! Help! Help!" my wife awoke with a yell. Seeing that black face gaping at her through the window, she passed out.

"It's all right," I said, trying to bring her to. "It's nothing, nothing at all. It's only a salesman."

"Madam," the man addressed my wife, "why'd you get so scared? Have I got horns?"

"Where do you come off crawling through other people's windows when they're sleeping?" she said.

"In the country, you ought to get up early," he told her.
"Suppose we didn't sleep all night?" I said.

"Then what'd you do?"

"None of your business," I said. "Beat it."

"When it's time to go," he said, "I won't ask your permission. Well, aren't you the big-shots. You come to the country and you stretch yourselves out like a bunch of lords. It's not enough that you get door-to-door service, but you got to be sore about it, too, huh?"

"You're an impudent lout!"

"An impudent lout, eh?" he smiled. "What's that? What does it mean? Well, I see you're a hot-head. Madam, let me make a sale. Buy yourself a fine little brooch. It's the latest thing."

I couldn't take it any more. I picked up the water pitcher and dumped its contents on his head. He raised the roof! Then, all the neighbors and all the help came around and turned the place into a fish-market. That was no way to treat a poor Jew, they all said.

"In any case," they complained, "if you don't want to buy, don't. But to insult a poor salesman for no reason whatsoever and throw the slop-pail at him! Phoo! That's no way for a decent man to act!"

Hearing them talk that way, the salesman said: "I'm going straight to the police and put an end to it. Let them settle this."

Then the man from Restopol interfered and suggested a compromise—I should beg the salesman's pardon and buy something from him.

"That would only be fair," he said. "That's the fairest thing. Letting a poor Jew make a kopek is a far-better deed than eating without a hat."

"It's only fair," the whole crowd shouted. "It's only fair."

"If you dare buy a kopek's worth of stuff from this man all hell's going to break loose!"

Now you tell me who to listen to!

12. Dawn in the Forest—
Patients—Their Desires and Complaints

Early in the morning, when all are still asleep, the Boyberik wood was a pleasure. It looked like a handsome groom, combed and washed and all dandied up for the wedding. You didn't see any of the people who wandered around all day long. You only heard the peeping and twittering of thousands of little creatures. They sang and hummed and chirped, jumped from branch to branch, flew from one tree to another, and touched the diamond-like, sparkling drops of dew which still hung on the leaves. Then, suddenly, a whole flock of birds broke into an uproar, fighting and screeching. What's the matter? They were bickering over a worm. One bird had found a worm, took to a branch ready for a snack, and kept looking about, this way and that. Another bird spotted this and flew over.

"Chirp-chirp. Where'd you find a worm so early?"

"Tweet, tweet. What's the difference, so long as I found it?"

"Chirp-chirp. Give me a little piece."

"Look around, find one, grab it, and then it'll be yours."

"Chirp-chirp. Hey, fellows. Come over here and you'll see something," the bird called his friends, stretching his little neck.

"Twit-twit. What's going on here?" the other birds asked, flying over.

"Chirp-chirp. A little worm," he yelled.

"Twit-twit. A worm. A worm. A worm," they all yelled.

Some attacked the bird with the worm, others defended it. The bird dropped the worm and a new one, a total stranger, nabbed it. The poor bird was downcast. It lowered its wings, puffing up, shivering, and fluttering. Then, it sharpened its beak on a little branch, spread its wings, and flew off, looking for another morsel—anything to fill its empty stomach.

Down below, the earth, too, was not silent. Thousands of little creatures jumped and hopped, crept and crawled. Flies and bugs, beetles and worms, snakes and lizards of all colors, spiders and ants by the thousands. One carried a dead fly into his lair, a snack for his little ones. This one a piece of grass, that one a bit of weed for the thatched hut. Another carried a piece of straw ten times its size. But all went out to work to guarantee survival for another day. The air was full of gnats, mannerless as the devil, who jumped right at your face, and all sorts of insects who seemed to thrive on wind alone. They fluttered and spun, doing nothing but humming and whizzing, having a wonderful time. They buzzingly whispered into your ear, nipped you when you weren't looking, sucked out a bit of blood and flew away. Everything in nature was alive and busy, fussing with itself for the sake of its belly.

Later, the people started streaming into the wood. The same Jews with their bottles and their hammocks which looked like swinging coffins.

"Are you folks living in Boyberik?" I asked a group of poor, sick Jews from Yadeshliv out of curiosity. Their dried-out wives leaned on the trees, coughing.

"What a question?" a few women answered at once. "Where do we come off living in a summer cottage? We're poor workers from Yehupetz."

"Then what are you doing in Boyberik?"

"It's no fun being here, believe me," said one man. "We're staying at the local sanatorium."

"Free?"

"What then? For pay?"

"Then who pays for your stay?"

"Who do you think pays?" they said. "What's the matter? Can't the Yehupetz money-bags afford it? Don't you think they have enough? God grant that they get as sick as us— then we'd treat them better than they treat us."

"What's wrong? Aren't you happy here?"

"What a queer character you are!" they said. "Expect us to be dancing for joy?"

"Then what's missing?"

"We wish we had all that's missing. First of all, they've torn us away from our homes, our wives, and our children. Then, they've put us out here in the country. They stuff us like geese and pack us with medicines and milk and the kefir* which the Tartar brews. They tell us to loll around in the woods and get fresh air all day long. To top it off they tell us not to worry. And that's easier said than done."

"Is that all?" I said.

"What about spitting?" A man with dark glasses began coughing. "Spitting's nothing, eh?"

"What sort of spitting?" I asked.

"The fact that we're not allowed to spit," he said. "If a man wants to cough and spit, they don't let him. The doctor set up a system where every patient has to carry his own spitoon. Now, I ask you, is that the doings of a sane man?"

"How about the sheets, the bedding, and the laundry?" said a woman with ashen lips. "The doctors tell us to change them every minute. Did you ever hear of such a crazy thing? My question is: what has a white sheet got to do with my coughing? If I change my blouse *ten* times a day, will I stop coughing?"

"And the way they feed us," said a fiery-eyed man.

"What's the matter, don't they feed you?" I asked.

"You want them not to feed us at *all*?" he said, his eyes flashing. "Feed us, they do, but not everything can be called food. We've been here three summers, thank heaven, and we're dying for a plate of borscht. For three summers in a row, they've been stuffing us with soups and roast chicken, with milk and soft-boiled eggs. Every day—soup and roast chicken, and, again, milk and soft-boiled eggs. Like they say—you can even get sick of champagne. But we just want a chunk of garlic-flavored roast meat and some chopped onions with chicken-fat. Or a piece of radish for a change. Or perk us up with a bowl of borscht. But they tell us that the doctors say no. They tell us that we're well enough to eat cutlets or fresh steak, roast chicken, bouillon and crackers, and follow it up with milk or the kefir which the Tartar brews. What good are those dishes to us, we argue. Give us what we like. In any case, if you've undertaken to give us room and board and

* Kefir: a Caucasian drink, a fermented liquor made from milk.

service and medical treatment, you have to ask *us* what *we* like
and not what that wise-guy of a doctor dreams up. If this is a
hospital, then let us poor get the benefit and not the doctors.
Try having a hospital without us poor folk! Try to people it
with doctors and see how far you get. Am I right or wrong?"

Hearing them speaking Yiddish, my little children shouted:
"Papa, they're Jews!" and called me out of the wood.

Ever since I had made my fat few thousands and university
students had started flocking to the house, we no longer spoke
Yiddish. Although the students were of Jewish parentage, and
themselves seemed Jewish too, our children followed their example and stopped talking Yiddish to us. They said that Yiddish wasn't spoken any more. Well, what can you do with
them?

13. Boyberik Villagers—The Hebrew School

After returning home from the forest, I met two Jews in
front of the house, one short and fat, the other tall and thin.

"Who are you?" I asked them.

"We're from here," they said, "that is, local house-holders."

"Well, what's the good word?"

"Nothing. We just wanted to ask you if our slaughterer's
son was here?"

"Sort of a young man with a long jacket, a green vest, and
a white tie?"

"Yes, that's the one," they said. "Did he ask you for a donation for the Hebrew school?"

"Right!"

"Well, did you pledge something?"

"Why not?"

"Well—if you've pledged, you've pledged," they said, ex-
changing glances. "It's a farce with you summer boarders,
pure farce. No matter who comes to you for money, you
shell out. None of you ever laugh in their faces."

"What's up? Don't you think much of the local Hebrew
school?"

"What Hebrew school? Like you see this noodle-pudding,
you see a Hebrew school. Do we have any poor children here

for whom we need a Hebrew school? Just out of curiosity, ask the Yehupetz Hebrew teacher, the journalist, about it. He'll give you all the dope."

"In other words, you think that one should not give *any-thing* to the Hebrew school?"

"It's got nothing to do with what *we* think. Can we air opinions about what's going on in your pocket? Can we stop you if you want to burn your money? God forbid, we're not the sort of people who'll slander others. But if you only knew *who* our slaughterer's son is and *what* he is, you'd have a fit. Excuse us for bothering you. Good day!"

They walked away, then returned.

"Listen, do us a favor. Don't tell a soul that we've talked to you about the slaughterer's son, the Hebrew school or anything else. We said it just in passing, simply for your own information, you understand? All right then. Bye."

"Bye."

As soon as they left, another two came up. One wore a derby, the other a cap.

"Who are *you?*" I asked them.

"We're local. That is, we live here."

"Well, what's the good word?"

"Nothing. We just wanted to ask you if you just had two visitors?"

"One short and fat, the other tall and thin?"

"Right, right," they said. "Didn't they talk to you about the slaughterer's son and the local Hebrew school?"

"What Hebrew school?" I said. "Do you *have* a Hebrew school here in Boyberik?"

"Ha. A Hebrew school!" they said. "May we have a hunk of gold for every pupil! Those other Jews no doubt told you we don't, huh?"

"Do you have any poor children here?" I asked them.

"And how! We should have a thousand rubles for every child that walks around barefoot and naked. Those other two probably told you we don't, eh? Those Jews are downright amazing! Listen! This isn't the place for it, after all, you're a stranger. But if we told you just a fraction of the

332   STORIES AND SATIRES

goings-on in our town, you'd jump out of your pants. Take
our word for it when we tell you that we don't give a rap
for the slaughterer's son. We need him like a hole in the
head. Then what's the point? The young man happens to be
a fine fellow. Just by the very fact that he devotes himself
to such a noble and sacred purpose as the Hebrew school.
It's nothing to sneeze at—a Hebrew school! Of course, you
know what our sages have said about Hebrew schools. Obvious, isn't it? There's nothing grander! So two Jews decide
to come along and spoil everything. You can just burst!
Why? Because in this town there's two of everything—
two slaughterer's, two synagogues, two political parties.
Whatever one does, the other does just the opposite. And
to top it off, the Hebrew teacher from Yehupetz, the journalist, stuck his two cents' worth in and wanted to know why
we opened a Hebrew school without him."

"In other words," I said, "you say that I shouldn't pay any
attention to them and that I *should* contribute to the Hebrew
school."

"What's that got to do with it?" they said. "Can we tell
you what to do. Of course, it's a good deed to support poor
children who go around barefoot and naked and have nothing to do. You're not forced to listen to all the lying talk
which others tell you. As you can see, our town is pretty
poor, but full of intrigues, gossip-mongers, envy, and hatred.
Just name it, we have it, God forbid, we don't want to talk
behind anybody's back. But since we happened to mention it,
we brought it up. Excuse us if we've annoyed you. Good
day."

They walked away, then came back.

"We just want to ask you—don't tell anyone we've talked
about two slaughterers, two synagogues, intrigues, this and
that, the man in the moon. We told you just so you'd know.
You understand? So long!"

"So long," I said.

As soon as they left, two others came. One carried a parasol, the other a cane. They went through the same rigamarole
from scratch.

"Well, who are you and what's the good word?" I said.

"We're local villagers. We stopped by for no special reason. We only want to ask you if two fellows were just here. One wore a derby, the other a cap. They probably told you a lot of phony stories about the local Hebrew school and seventy-seven pupils, defended the slaughterer's son, said that there were two slaughterers, two synagogues, two parties, and probably slandered the Hebrew teacher from Yehupetz, the journalist, and said he was a glory-seeker who loved to whip up intrigues. Right? Just as if we'd been here all along, listening! Oh, me! If you only knew half of what's going on here! If we started telling you about the matzoh-fund, or the free-loan society we wanted to set up, or the local bathhouse we tried to build, you'd go crazy."

I stopped them, and said I didn't need their matzoh-funds, their free-loan society, their bath, even their journalistic Hebrew teacher. I didn't want to go crazy, I told them. They said goodbye and left. But no sooner did they go when two shrimps appeared, both wearing derbies and carrying canes.

Seeing another team of two, I went up to them and, without waiting for formal introductions, said:

"Pardon me, dear friends, you're probably local landlords who are here for no special reason, but you simply came by to find out if I've just seen two Jews, one with a parasol, the other with a cane. Now, I tell you that there was no one here at all. I know nothing about slaughterers, teachers from Yehupetz who double as journalists, intrigues, Hebrew schools, matzoh-funds, or bathhouses. Nothing. Nothing at all. A hearty good-day to you both. Khaye-Etel, warm up the samovar!"

14. Gone Is the Maid—Gone Is the Water— Gone Is Friendship—Gone Am I

"You want the samovar, huh?" my wife said. "You'll just have to wait for it. There isn't a soul in the house. We don't have a drop of water. We're completely ruined. Your fine

and dandy Yehupetz aristocrats—may they burn in hell—
talked our maid into leaving."

"What do you mean by that? Talked her into leaving!"

"Just look at that ninny. He doesn't know how you go
about talking a maid into leaving. Tsk, tsk! Poor fellow!"
Khaye-Etel said. "Just let me get a hold of them and wish
them a fiery, stormy, black, and dingy . . ."

"Pipe down," I told her. "Listen to me, Khaye-Etel, and
keep quiet. We're not at home now. We're still boarders at
a summer cottage."

"Summer cottage, my eye!" she said. "This place takes the
cake. It should have burned with the rest of Boyberik before
we even rented it. How many times did I tell you we don't
need a summer cottage. So you got it into your head to do
what everyone and his neighbor does. They all run to Boyberik, so we run here, too. What would you do if all the Jews
decided to chop off their noses?"

My wife, God bless her, is just like a machine. Once she's
wound up, there's no stopping her. She'll just talk until she
talks herself dry. While my wife was arguing with the blue-
bloods about our maid, I went into the kitchen to see if the
cook would prepare the samovar. But she gave me some royal
welcome!

"You'll just wait until I heat up the samovar for you," she
said. "That's none of my business, the samovar. It's enough
that I have to live in this dandy dog-house of a summer cottage. You got yourself cottages in the head! You got so much
luxury you don't know what to do next. That's number one.
Now for number two. Why don't you ask me where I'll get
water from?"

"What sort of question is that? Don't we have a well here?"

"Oho! In other words," she said, "you want *me* to go draw
water for *you*? Oh, may my enemies not live to see the day
when I, Basye-Beyle the Sexton's wife become a water-carrier. It's enough I have to work for others in my old age. Woe
is me! Look what's become of me. If my Raphael, may he
rest in peace, would get up and look at his Basye-Beyle, he'd
drop dead again!"

Basye-Beyle started sniffling like a little baby. I felt a lump in my throat and told her:

"You know what? Give me the bucket and the rope and I'll try to draw some water myself."

I took the bucket and walked to the well. I turned the rope this way and that, but nothing happened. It's easier to break into ten Yehupetz stores, I thought, then get a bucketful of water here. Then while lowering the bucket, the rope slipped out of my hand and—plop!—down the well it went. No bucket, no rope, no water.

"I could have sworn it would have happened," said Basye-Beyle. "Neither the rope nor the pail belonged to us. Who asked you to go get water? In all my days I've never. What a character! You have to stick your nose into every pot! Where am I going to get another pail now? What am I going to cook with?"

As I retreated from the kitchen, my wife ran smack into me, crying.

"God be with you, Khaye-Etel, what's up?"

"He wanted a summer cottage," she wailed. "He wanted the fresh air of Boyberik. You should have seen the fresh air I just got from your high and mighty ladies. They insulted me like a maid. The little scene I just had was worth our whole trip! I thought that those female fishmongers would side with me. But the upshot was that the woman from Rostopol threw it up to me that our kitchen wasn't kosher, that we mixed dairy and meat dishes. But you know who disappointed me most of all? The blind bat. You know, the one who gets chloride treatments. May her eyes fall out—dear God!"

"If you don't shut your yap," came a woman's voice from the other side of the wall, "we'll slap all your teeth down your throat. We'll pay no mind to your grown daughters for whose sake you've come here to nab husbands. We'll pay no mind to your husband who pulled a fast deal and made himself a few thousand rubles—which will last you no longer than a quick amen. May the Jewish Exile be as brief! We've seen your type Yehupetz big-shots. Today they ride on rubber tires, and tomorrow they don't have a shoe to their name."

Well, I thought. The day started off on the wrong foot. It's a bad sign. I alibied that I had some business in town and ran for the railroad station.

15. Suffering—Variations to a Card Game— How to Sell an Estate—The Yehupetz Trolley

The Boyberik summer residents who commuted to Yehupetz were evidently great sinners. For they were sentenced to suffer in this world, to fry in hell while the spark of life was still in them. Their fate was to stew all day long in town, scamper here and there like chickens with their heads cut off while loaded down with packages, barely having enough time to gulp down a quick-plague sandwich, watching the clock all the time, living in perpetual fear of missing the train back to Boyberik.

But when talking to your friends, you bragged that a summer cottage was something out of this world. The main thing, of course, was the fresh air. The air was Paradise itself. So used were the summer commuters to this "Paradise," they thought it their permanent lot in life. They even stopped complaining. They were like prisoners who knew they would have to serve their time (the summer), and then be free. There was nothing to be done about it. If, with the help of the good Lord, they nabbed a seat on the train, they were in clover. But not everyone was that fortunate. You had to elbow your way into a seat and you had to have luck besides. For sometimes even after the smoke had cleared and you were already seated, a beardless someone (you couldn't tell if he was Jewish or not) came up to you and said, "Ahem . . . if you don't mind."

The car I got into was packed tight with Boyberik residents. Many sat and many more stood on their own two feet. They started chatting about business. One mentioned that the banks were going bankrupt. Another said he had a good note due soon.

"What do you call a good note?" Someone wanted to know.

"One signed by a man who's sure to pay up," the man answered. "But he's *such* a sure one that he too is going bankrupt soon, you get me? You can make a neat profit with a note like that. I made myself two notes that way, in fact, while swinging in a hammock."

"It isn't worth the paper it's written on," the other answered. "How much can you make on notes? But sugar—in that there's sure profit. Why just yesterday, Yankele made four hundred tons of sugar."

"Four hundred tons of sugar?" the crowd asked, excitedly. "How much did it go for? Who bought it? Who sold it?"

A long palaver started about sugar, and everyone figured out how much Yankele and his gang made on the deal.

"I'm afraid it was six times four hundred tons," someone said, "the devil take them."

"And I'm afraid it was more than that," said another, sighing. "May troubles plague them, dear God!"

Further along in the car sat the profiteers themselves, talking sugar. Was the price going up or down? Each one aired an opinion and contradicted his neighbor's. They all ripped to shreds the minister who hardly let any sugar flow into the market. Each one gave his plan and said that if he were minister, he'd do a much better job.

But not everyone in the car talked about banks, notes, or sugar. There were some who spoke of other things.

"Just listen to this one," a man said. "We were playing "21." We started early in the morning and we didn't stop until 2 A.M. I just couldn't get a good hand, so help me God. If I bought a card, it was the death of me. If I didn't, the card would have been my gold mine. If I *did* get a good card, I held on to it for so long it didn't do me any good. In short, they took me to the cleaners to the tune of 145 rubles! In my first hand, I had a king and then bought another one, so the banker gets an ace and king. Another time I had a king and ace and really raised the chips. So the banker gets the ace and king of spades. I thought I'd blow my stack. The 145 went like water."

"Wait a minute," someone said. "Listen to what happened
to me. This is even better. We were once sitting and playing
poker. It was the fifth night of *Hanuka*. I got a bug in me to
take the next card blind, a-la-Leyb. This time I got myself a
three. The long and short of it was that I flew off the handle
and fizzled away a ruble sixty and wished that Reb Leyb
would shrivel up."

"Pardon me for asking," someone from the other side of the
car said, "but I'm from Zvenirod. We play poker there too.
That is, we play all sorts of card games, but mostly poker. Do
me a favor, will you, and tell me what a-la-Leyb is?"

"Don't you know what a-la-Leyb is?" said another from
the group, "I'll clear it up for you right away. There's a chap
by the name of Leyb in Yehupetz. A hail-fellow-well-met.
Sticks his nose into every pot. Once he introduced something
new. If in one round the first person bought a card blind, the
last would also have to do it. So we called this move a-la-
Leyb. Now you get the point?"

"So what of it?" the man from Zvenirod asked, stretching
his neck. "Is it a sure-fire charm?"

"May he live to regret it," the other man said, and everyone laughed.

In another corner of the car, two Jews were quietly talking. One was a red-head, the other a blackie. The red-head
wore his hat way back on his head, had his sleeves rolled up,
held a magnifying glass in his hand, and perspired as he spoke.
The blackie was penciling something into a little notebook.

THE RED-HEAD: Put down one estate in the Kherson re-
gion.
BLACKIE: But I need one in the Podol region.
RED: Then jot down 1,300 acres in Podol.
BLACKIE: That's not enough.
RED: Make it 1,800.
BLACKIE: Listen, 1,800 isn't enough, either. I need at least
3,000.
RED: Then put down 3,400 acres of rich, black earth.

BLACKIE: I have no use for just bare land. I need some forest on it too.

RED: There's 600 acres of woodland on it.

BLACKIE: That's not enough. I need at least 1,000 acres of wood. My boss, you understand, likes the forest.

RED: That's what I meant—1,200 acres of woodland.

BLACKIE: What sort of woods are they?

RED: What sort? Pine forests. The real stuff which everyone goes for. Each and every pine tree is a tall beauty. You've never set eyes on the likes of them.

BLACKIE: Pines are no good to me. I need oak.

RED: Damn it! That's what I meant to say. Oak! The best oaks in the world. They're cedars of Lebanon. Each oak is so huge you can't even chop it down.

BLACKIE: Is there a courtyard on the estate? My boss needs a great big courtyard.

RED: And what a courtyard! There's none like this one. Jot down that it's a palace of about twenty rooms. What am I saying twenty? There's thirty for sure. Tell you what. Put down forty. On my responsibility.

BLACKIE: What about a lake? My boss wants a lake on the estate.

RED: And what a lake it is! First of all it's huge, and to top it off, it's full of fish. (He shows Blackie the palm of his hand.) Here's the estate, and right here's the lake.

BLACKIE: How do you get out there? My boss likes it close to the railroad.

RED: It's a stone's throw away. Less than a half mile. What am I saying? It's less than a quarter of a mile away. Just a few steps. Here's the station and here's the estate. (Again, he shows him the palm of his hand.)

"Shh. Get set. We're approaching Yehupetz," said one of the crowd, jumping out of his seat. He dashed to the door, ready to grab a seat in the trolley. The rest of the crew trailed right after him. More skill was needed to grab a seat in the trolley than in the train. In the trolley, there was a wild rush and they literally crawled all over you. It was frightful! Here,

manners went to the dogs. It made no difference if you were
gentile, Jew, with a beard or without. Even if you were a
woman. You pushed her and pressed her until you heard the
breath rattling in her throat. If she happened to be sitting, you
plopped yourself down on her lap. And just let her dare and
say: Get off me. Here, you had to be on the lookout for
pick-pockets, too. You'd be better off leaving your watch at
home. If you ever plan on riding in a Yehupetz trolley with
a gold watch (even a silver one will do), by the end of the
trip you'll be one watch lighter.

16. Guests—A Jolly Uncle, A Morose Aunt— Tears in Vain

Coming home from the city half-dead, hot as hell, and hungry, too, my little children ran toward me with a shout:

"Papa, papa. We have guests."

"Well, look who's back! God save you and your guests
both," said my wife. "It's your family. As soon as they found
out you made some money, they decided to drop in from
God knows where. I'd like to know where they kept themselves when the wolf was knocking at the door."

It's been quiet for too long, I thought, and walked to
the house. Coming toward me, I saw a bearded old man with
a corpse-like face and sunken cheeks. With him was a short,
red-nosed woman, wearing a yellow silk scarf tucked behind
her ears and, despite the heat, a shawl on her shoulders. She
bowed awkwardly, wiped her nose with the back of her
hand, and said sweetly:

"Don't you recognize me? Go on, go on! I'm Yentel, Aunt
Zlate's daughter. And this is my father, your Uncle Zalman.
Hasn't he aged terribly? I've made friends with all your chil-
dren already. One's prettier than the next—God bless them."

"Hello, Uncle," I said. "Where are you coming from?"

"It's wonderful here," he said loudly, smacking his lips with
pleasure. "It can't be any better, you hear? Well, what's new

with you? I haven't seen you for ages, you hear? Isn't that so? Must be twenty-two years, right? Maybe even more. Wait, wait. I'll tell you exactly, in a minute. How long has it been since Yentel's wedding. We haven't seen each other since then. How's your health, eh? And how's business?"

"Pretty good, thank God," I said. "And how are you doing?"

"Straight from our village, Avritsh," he shouted. "First I went to your house in Yehupetz, knocked at the door. No answer. In short, they told me that you're here in Boyberik. What are you doing here, huh? Spending your summer here, right? Well, say something!"

"He doesn't hear well," Yentel said. "Since my mother died —may I be spared—he's become deaf—may you be spared. He's not just hard of hearing either. Deaf as a stone!"

"It's top-notch here, you hear? Excellent, eh?" Uncle Zalman yelled as if I were the deaf one, not he. "I tell you, this place is great. You hear? Paradise! Right? God willing, I plan to spend one or two weeks here, maybe even three, eh?"

"We wanted to take a room," Yentel alibied, "but father insisted—only here. He said that you'd be insulted if we stayed with strangers. He said that he's your beloved uncle and it wouldn't be proper to go anywhere else."

"Wonderful! But who are those two?" I pointed to a couple sitting on the porch, blowing at their hot tea, having the time of their lives.

"The devil only knows," whispered Yentel. She wiped her lips and looked at the two. "They look like man and wife. They came into our car at Khvastev and have been riding with us ever since. So naturally we got to talking along the way. Where are you going? Where are *you* going? This and that and the other thing—to make a long story short, they found out we were heading this way and that you're in the chips now, knock wood . . . you get me? They say they're relatives and close ones, too. How? I asked them. They said it's as tight as a knot. But you can't get any details out of them. As soon as he starts talking, she interrupts him. As soon as she starts, he butts in. There's no end to it. But, never mind that—I'd rather you hear *me* out! After all, we're first cousins."

Yentel then started to pour out her bitter heart to me. A sad story it was. The poor thing was having a hard time of it now. That is, they'd never had an *easy* time of it. In fact, she said, since her wedding, she hadn't seen one good day. But, never mind. Like they say, things always get worse. But, of late, her situation had really been bad. Not a kopek to be earned and they needed so much.

"In addition, there are other headaches. Here it's a son being drafted, there it's marrying off a daughter. Here a work-animal drops dead, there the store burns down. We didn't even save a broom. Well you'd think that things were hunky-dory all around, right? Then what happens? Your daughter, not quite thirteen, pretty, full of life, good as gold, ups and dies all of a sudden. She was called Sosil, after Aunt Sosye. Like her, she was always strong and healthy, nothing ever hurt her. One day she comes home from the market and, as she's putting her basket away, I notice she's white as a sheet. 'Oh my God, what's the matter with you?' I said. 'Nothing,' she said. 'I have a little headache.' I felt her forehead—as hot as fire. 'Lie down for a while, I'll call the doctor,' I said. 'What do I need a doctor for?' she said. 'It's a waste of two rubles. It'll soon pass. It'd be better if I salted the meat and peeled some potatoes,' she said. But I saw she was fading, so I put her into bed against her will—oh, me!—and went for the doctor. But where was he? Where could he be? Doctor! Doctor! The doctor, the deuce take it, was somewhere on the other side of town. But that's no excuse. I need a doctor. Well, I brought that fine doctor back to the house, but when I came in I found her—oh, I wish it on my enemies—with her tongue hanging out, her eyes rolled back, the whites showing. 'Sosil,' I said, 'don't you know me?' But go talk to the wall! She didn't last through the night. She was such a beauty, so healthy, so good. How could you bury a child like that?"

Yentel burst into tears and wailed like a little baby. Looking at her, I felt the tears starting to choke me.

"What's the matter? Why all the crying?" Khaye-Etel came over to me.

I wanted to tell her, but the words stuck in my throat. I swallowed the tears, plucked up some strength, and said:

"The poor thing lost a child . . . thir . . . thir . . . thirteen . . . y . . . y . . . yea . . ."

"When did this happen?" Khaye-Etel asked in a fright.

"About nine or ten years ago," Yentel said, and nudged her father. "Papa, how long is it since Sosil died? You ought to know exactly."

"From Avritsh here?" said Uncle Zalman. "As the crow flies it's about sixty, maybe even seventy miles, eh?"

To prevent an outburst of laughter, I made believe I lost my glasses, bent to look for them, and dashed up the porch stairs to meet the new guests. They were still blowing at the hot tea, having a wonderful time.

17. The Couple—Tight-as-a-Knot—An Endless Tale

I approached the couple and found them bathed in sweat from the tea. The man wore a broad-brimmed satin hat and the woman a wig with a white part. They were both pretty hefty—together, they would have tipped the scales at over six hundred pounds. I sat down and started talking to them about this and that, asking them where they were from and who they were.

"You'll soon find out who we are," the man said, wiping his brow with his shirt sleeves. "But first, I want you to answer one question. Your maternal grandfather was called Reb Mordekhay, right?"

"That's right," I said.

"Dead, eh?" he asked.

"Sure," I said, "dead a long time."

"Blessed be the righteous judge," he said. He shook his head mournfully and spat three times. "What an honest man he was. When it came to studying Torah, he was a genius. Of him it can be said; blessed is the memory of the righteous. And how's your grandmother Khanele doing?"

"She's dead, too."

"May she have a bright and splendid Paradise! A fine woman!" he said, and turned to his wife. "You never met them, so you can never know what a couple Reb Mordekhay and Khanele were. You hear?" he said, turning to me, "you don't know what a pair of grandparents you had. Oh, what a couple they were!"

"I *know* I had a grandmother and grandfather," I said. "But who are *you?*"

"I'll tell you in a minute," he said, rolling his sleeves up to the elbows. He took hold of his beard and started swaying, smiling, and talking in a sing-song voice.

"Your own grandfather was a Korsishever from Korishev. There, he had two sisters, Nekhamele and Zisele. Nekhamele had two husbands. That is, she married twice. Her first husband was Leybele Korsishever from Korsishev. Her second husband was called Reb Simkhele, also from the same town. This Reb Simkhele was a widower when he married Nekhamele. Now pay close attention. His first wife was from Korsishev too. Dveyrele was her name and she was a close relative of your grandfather's. Understand? Now your grandfather married her to—you listening?—his brother-in-law, Reb Simkhele, at a time when Simkhele wasn't as yet his brother-in-law. Then, when Dveyrele died, Simkhele took your grandfather's sister, Aunt Nekhamele, and they had a daughter called Reyzele, after his mother Reyze, who happened to be your grandfather's aunt. Then Reb Simkhele's Reyzele married Meyerl from Manestrishtsh who comes from your grandmother's side—get the connection? It's as tight as a knot!"

"Tight as a knot," his wife interrupted, "but he forgot to say how Reyzele was related to her husband. So I'll tell you. Your grandmother Khanele from Korsishev had an uncle in Mezshbizsh who was called Neyakh . . ."

"You're all wet," her husband broke in. "She got herself all tangled up with uncles in Mezshbizsh. Just let me set things straight and you'll see the kinship. To make a long story short, your grandfather's other sister, Zisele, married a man from Holeypoli. Reb Leyvenyu was his name. She had no children from him, so she divorced him. Then she married again, this time a man from Manestrishtsh—Reb Naftoli Manestrishtsher. From him she had five sons and seven daughters . . ."

"Just the opposite," his wife interrupted, "seven sons and five daughters."

"I mean seven sons and five daughters." He counted them off on his fingers. "Borukhel, Khayimkel, Yankele, Hertsele, Berishel, Fishele, Yosele. Then there's the five girls. Etele, Rivkele, Hodele, Feygele, and Kreyndele. At least that's the way I remember them. Then Borukhel died and Yankele got married in Korsishev, took Aunt Nekhamele's girl, Reyzele, who was your grandfather's niece. In other words your grandmother was matched up with your grandfather. Get the link-up now? It's as tight as a knot. Go ahead, let me hear you say it isn't!"

"That's right," I said, "it *is* as tight as a knot. But what's it got to do with you? Who are *you*?"

"Well did you ever!" he said. "This very same Naftoli Manestrishtsher whom I told you about was the father of the two girls Etele and Rivkele. So Etele married Reb Moyshe-Leyb Radomishler's son, who happened to be in the family anyway, because Naftoli's sister married Moyshe-Leyb's brother! You see what's going on here?"

"Where'd you leave Rivkele?" his wife said, all set to start telling the story. But her husband didn't let her. He covered her mouth with his hand and shouted:

"Hold your horses with Rivkele! What's your rush? She'll stay in one piece. I won't hide her in my pocket. Well, where was I? Oh, yes. Etele from Manestrishtsh married a kinsman from Radomishel, like I told you, but Rivkele took a fanatic idler named Henikh from Manestrishtsh, married him, and they had a daughter called Genedel."

"There's a fine how-do-you-do!" his wife said. "Where

does Genedel fit in here? Genedel was Etele Radomishel's daughter."

"Isn't that what I said?"

"You said she was Aunt Rivkele's daughter!"

"You're daydreaming! I didn't even start talking about Rivkele."

"Oh, my God," his wife said, getting fidgety, "you can get apoplexy from him. You just finished figuring out Aunt Rivkele's family ties . . . that she married in Manestrishtsh and took that fanatic loafer, Henikh . . ."

"She gets me all confused," the husband said. "Where was I? Well then, Rivkele from Manestrishtsh had a daughter, I mean a son, who was called Mendel, and Etele from Radomishel had a son—daughter, I mean, whose name was Genedel. So they matched up. That is, Rivkele's daughter Mendel married Etele's son Genedel. No, it's the other way around. Rivkele's son Genedel married Etele's daughter Mendel . . ."

"Blast you!" his wife spat out, jumping up and clapping her hands. "Did you ever hear of a son named Genedel and a daughter, Mendel. Did you ever see a Genedel have a wife named Mendel?"

"You're getting me all confused," the husband said, and continued talking. But this time Khaye-Etel came in.

"The table's all set. Let's eat," she said, turning to me. "Invite the guests in, dear. They're probably starved."

At the table, my relative continued with my grandmother Nekhamele's uncle Neyakh from Mezshbizsh. Like the biblical Noah, he too had three sons. They weren't called Shem, Ham, and Japeth, but Shimele, Khemele, and Yokel. A new and endless thread of relatives and matches was unfurled here. It twisted and turned, it was knotted and tied. It was a story without an end. Luckily Uncle Zalman—God bless him —interrupted:

"How much do you pay here for a pound of meat? In Avritsh, the price is pretty steep. You know why? Because of the tax. We have our government meat-tax representative. But he's a downright pig! Is your tax-man a pig too? They're all a bunch of bastards, may they all drop dead. Isn't that so?"

My silken-hatted kinsman stopped, held his fork half-way to his mouth, and gaped at Uncle Zalman as if he were a highway robber. Why did the old man interrupt him in the middle, he seemed to say. But Uncle Zalman paid him no more mind than the man in the moon. He went on his own merry way, telling stories about the tax representative and other folk from Avritsh, eating quite lustily all the while.

18. Where to Bed the Family—The Trip Abroad

After the meal, my wife asked worriedly: "Where are they going to sleep? They're very welcome and all that, but we can't very well put them up outside."

"Ask me another!" I said. "I plan to put Uncle Zalman right here on the porch. Yentel will sleep with the kids. The tight-as-a-knot couple can sleep next to the hot wall. Let them enjoy the cottage. Just feel that breeze, Khaye-Etel. It's getting cloudy. Look like we're going to have rain."

"I certainly hope so," she said. "The sun's been roasting us all day long. It's high time for a change here. What a summer cottage! What air! I sure hope that God sends down such a deluge that it drowns all the summer cottages, its residents, and all of Boyberik in one—dear God!"

In a little while, the sky was covered by thick clouds. Suddenly, it became dark, as if someone had put the sun out. The birds hid in their nests. The air became thicker and heavier. A flash of lightning cut through and blinded the eyes. Immediately afterward, a peal of thunder tumbled and roared, echoing from one horizon to another.

"I think it's going to rain," Uncle Zalman said, looking up to the sky. The minute he said it, it started pouring cats and dogs. It kept coming down harder and harder. Lightning flashed and lit up the thick blue darkness. Thunder roared through the forest.

"I think the rain's going to stay," Uncle Zalman said. "With God's help, it'll just keep on raining."

"May you live to tell better news." Khaye-Etel jumped

up in a fright. Every once in a while, she dashed into the house.

"What are you looking for?" I asked her.

"To see if there's any leaks from the ceiling," she said, jumping up again. "It's dripping right onto the bed. We've got to put a pot underneath it."

"We had a downpour like this in Avritsh, too," Uncle Zalman said, "about twenty or maybe even thirty years ago, eh? It flooded the whole town. They rowed around in little rowboats, they did. Boy, was it dark."

"Where's everybody?" a voice came from inside the house. "Come over here. Give me a hand. Help!"

I sprang into the house. Oh my God! What a catastrophe! The rain was coming in through the windows, the ceiling was leaking. Khaye-Etel had rolled up her skirt. She held a little pillow in one hand, a frying pan in the other, and was yelling: "Help, give me a hand. Help! Help!"

"What are you doing?" I asked. "What sort of stuff are you dragging from the house? Let's run away and save *ourselves*. Where are the little ones?"

"Papa, come here," they called from the other room, happily standing ankle-deep in water, dancing and splashing, making waves and singing:

> Rain, rain go away
> come again another day.

"Help! Help! Save us someone! We're lost!" Khaye-Etel yelled, standing like a statue in the puddle.

"Save the children, the children," Yentel screeched, and didn't budge.

"Why doesn't someone get the children?" the couple hollered, standing where they were.

"You know what?" said Uncle Zalman. "I think it'd be a good idea if you took the little ones to a safer place. It seems to me as if there's going to be a flood. . . ."

I'm rushing to bring this story of a "Home Away From Home" to a close. For Khaye-Etel and I are about to take a trip abroad to the hot springs. The doctors decided that we ought to drink special mineral waters and bathe in the mineral springs. And, besides, we just want to take a look at the world. After all, if God's been good and you can afford it—why not? We're not leaving the kids alone in Boyberik, heaven forbid. We made Yentel the boss of the household and because of her Uncle Zalman is staying on, too. The tight-as-a-knot couple wanted to spend the whole summer with us, but my wife let them know that God-willing things would be gay enough in Boyberik without them. So they packed up and left. Where *we're* going to I haven't the faintest idea. Most likely the doctors'll steer us to the right place. Since we're going to a German-speaking land, we have to start getting used to their language. So to keep in practice, we'll bid you goodbye by saying: "Adieu!"

TO THE HOT SPRINGS

1. A Nervous Wife—The Lady from Bobroysk—Home-Made Jam

"It's better to break a leg than to marry" is what one philosopher said. But I'm afraid it wasn't Socrates. *I* say: you're better off remaining unborn than having a wife with a nervous condition.

I'm neither a philosopher nor a writer who sits at home and dreams up stories. I'm just an average fellow with some property, who, with the help of God, raked in a neat little pile, shooed the wolf from the door, moved bag and baggage to the summer house in Boyberik, and then befriended doctors, prescriptions, pharmacies, the water cure, massages, troubles, and plagues. Hallelujah!

Of all the calamities in the world, the biggest is the doctor. Not so much the doctor either, as his waiting room where you have to sweat it out by leafing through the magazines scattered on the end-tables, and look at a bunch of strange faces. You gape at them and they stare at you, and, not having anything better to do, you start talking.

"You been coming here for a long time?"

"What's wrong with you?"

"Which hot springs are you going to?" And so on.

My wife, Khaye-Etel, may she live and be well, is the sort of person who hates to keep still. So she started jabbering with a woman from Bobroysk. Attached herself to her like a leech. What she saw in that woman I don't know. But they became friends immediately. A minute later, my wife informed me that they both had the same sickness. What do you think was wrong with them? Not a darn thing. They just imagined they *had* everything anybody else *complained* about. If someone had pains in the side—they got the pains, too. If someone had a toothache—their teeth hurt. Ears—their ears, too. Feet—the same story. Whatever was to be had—they had. And the woman from Bobroysk—she'd traveled all over the world, tried every medicine under the sun. But nothing helped her.

"Well, what does the doctor say?" my Khaye-Etel asked her kindly.

"What should he say? He doesn't know himself. He says its a nervous condition and tells me to go abroad to the hot springs."

On that very same day, Khaye-Etel came down with a nervous condition. It wasn't a plain case either. There are all sorts of nervous conditions. I just hope that God doesn't count the nights I sat up with her. Things got so bad that I couldn't take a step, cough, move. The slightest thing I said led to: "What have you got against my nerves?"

To make a long story short, the result was that we had to go abroad for the water cure. Where to? They'd let us know at the professor's in Vienna or Berlin. While I applied for my passport, my wife started preparing clothes and hats for the trip, bought suitcases, straw satchels and baskets, and boiled up some home-made jam. You might well ask—what do clothes and hats and baskets and home-made jam have to do with a man like me?

"Plenty," my wife said, "you're going just like me. So you can put yourself out a bit too!"

The words "put yourself out" were delivered in a manner beyond description. Only men with nervous wives will recognize that sly tone of voice.

Then started a tornado of clothes, stores, shops, tailors, fashions, magazines. Having lived through those three weeks, I was sure I'd live to be a hundred. My wife set out, once and for all, to play the sport in Vienna and Berlin and to put Marienbad, Francesenbad, Baden-Baden, and all the other hot springs to eternal shame. As we stood and packed our things, I paid the bills and settled with the dressmaker, paying her for cloth, buttons, and hooks; brushes, ribbons, and lace; satin,

silk, and cheesecloth; pins, foulard, and feathers; and once
again, cloth, buttons, and bows.

Luckily, I had a phone in the house and just then someone
called me—bless him.

"Who is it?"

"Is this the government commissary?" the voice said.

Boy, have you got the wrong number, I thought. But I
didn't hang up. I just held the receiver in one hand and with
the other paid off the dressmaker and was in seventh heaven.
Finally got rid of her and her bill.

Then my wife came in. "What sort of jam should I prepare
for the trip?"

"Any kind you want."

"What do you mean, any kind *I* want? How about you?"

"I can get along without jam."

"Well, can you beat that! He can get along without jam.
In other words, everything I do is for *myself*. Because I'm
the glutton, I'm the hog."

"For God's sake, Khaye-Etel, pipe down. Boil up some rose-
leaf jam and let's be done with it."

"So it should get moldy and we should have to throw it
out, huh?"

"Then make it cherries. Cook up some cherries."

"Sure! I have nothing better to do than sit down and start
pitting them."

"You know what? Boil blackberries."

"So they should shrink away, eh smartie?"

"Boil up raspberries."

"So I should sweat over them until they're done. You expect
me to drop dead in that kitchen, don't you?"

"Then cook peaches. Stew plums. Heat up apples. Boil shoe-
leather. Parasols! Lamps! Meat-cleavers! Cradles!"

Draw your own conclusion as to the aftermath of that little
jam-session. I'm not obliged to tell you everything!

2. Torments of the Graves Explained

Our sages paint all sorts of gloomy pictures of the torments of the grave. As for hell—that's even worse. It seems that then they didn't have wives with nervous conditions, never went abroad to the hot springs baths, didn't carry half a ton of luggage, not counting suitcases, baskets, and all sorts of little bundles. They also didn't take any home-made jam with them. If I was fated for torments of the grave, I had my share of it in the railway depot in Boyberik before departing. As for hell—that opened up for me while riding with Khaye-Etel on our way abroad.

It's easy to just stand and watch the hullabaloo when the express arrives, stops for only five minutes, and you have to rush and buy tickets, check the luggage with the porter, kiss all the children—God bless them—goodbye, dash into the car with your wife, and with all your packages, bundles, and suitcases, look for seats which aren't there.

I was glad I nabbed a seat for Khaye-Etel, at least. But she wasn't satisfied. She didn't like sitting opposite a huge priest who frightened her half to death. She didn't like my not having a seat and my having to stand holding the bundles. She didn't like my forgetting (due to the mad rush) to tell the maid and the children many important things.

But thanks to the priest, who felt sorry for me and moved over a bit, I was able to squeeze into a part of a seat and could look around and see where I was. With all the scurrying back and forth, with all the tumult, my head was spinning like a top, and I had the feeling that I'd forgotten something. But I didn't know what it was. That's why I was deep in thought and didn't quite hear Khaye-Etel saying to me:

"Look here, did you at least put away the baggage receipts?"

"Which receipts?"

"From the luggage!"

"That's it!"

"What is it with you? You're so rattled you don't hear people talking to you!"

Then I remembered that I had forgotten to take the receipts from the porter. Not knowing what to do, I started running—but I didn't know where! My wife's nerves couldn't take this and she threw her head back, all set to faint. Things began to hum in the car. The passengers gathered and found out all about the baggage stubs. They gave all sorts of advice as to what to do, who I should wire, and how to act at the border.

It looked as if our trip had a blight on it from the start. I began to regret the whole business. The health it was costing me here wouldn't come back in the three months at the hot springs. And it certainly wasn't doing my blood pressure any good, either. I heaped a barrelful of curses on the hot springs, the doctors, the whole trip abroad. Just let half of what I wished them come true!

But you get used to all sorts of troubles. The train wouldn't go back for the sake of my stubs, and no one was obliged to bear the brunt of my ill-luck. Nevertheless, I was happy that my wife found and made friends with two women. As soon as she found out that they too were traveling to the hot springs, they went into such a dither, you'd think they'd won first prize in a lottery and were about to divvy up the cash.

One of them was a heavily-powdered woman from the town of Uman, wearing a little hat. Since it was her second trip abroad, she spoke more German than Yiddish and knew every place on the map. The other one—a young woman from Yehupetz on her first trip out of the country—held on to the Uman woman like a little baby and followed her wherever she went.

"Who are you?" I asked the young woman. "And who is your husband?"

"I don't think you'll know him," she said. "His name is Brodsky."

The name Brodsky from Yehupetz hit me like a load of dynamite. The young woman's value shot up 99 per cent in my eyes.

"What do you mean? Expect me not to know Brodsky?

Who doesn't know the sugar millionaire? From which side of the family are you? Lyov or Lazar?"

"Neither," she said, "We're Brodskys, it's true. But not *the* Brodskys. My husband is a real estate agent."

Suddenly, her value crashed and I didn't want to listen to her any more.

But Khaye-Etel wasn't that way at all. She was pleased as punch with the two. First of all, she wrung all the foreign news out of the Uman woman. That was like found money for both of us. Secondly, she found out about diseases of whose existence she'd never known. Listen to the queer sickness that the Brodsky woman had. One night she dreamed she had swallowed a full set of false teeth. From that day on she felt them clicking away in her stomach and no one could convince her it was all in her mind. After all, she knew better than the doctors that the teeth were there inside of her. Therefore, she was on her way to Vienna; the professor would tell her where to go from there.

It was catching. No sooner said than done. My Khaye-Etel immediately reminded herself that she had once lost a tooth at night and never did find it. The upshot was—she must have swallowed it that night. In fact, she often felt a queer, stinging pain inside of her and didn't know what it was from.

"Luckily, there's no one here with a bitten-off nose," I said. But no one even cracked a smile at my little joke. Just the opposite. I noticed that the three women were looking daggers my way. They teamed up and agreed to give me the cold shoulder. But I had the pleasure of getting even with them all.

Suddenly, the lady from Uman shot out of her seat with a yelp—as if her dress were on fire. All the passengers in the car dashed over, shouting:

"What is it? What happened?"

It was nothing much. Up there on the shelf, in one of the straw satchels, one of Khaye-Etel's jars of jam had broken and was slowly leaking through the straw and dripping right onto the lady's hat and silk blouse, which became glued to the seat. I'm not even going to talk about the damage we had in the satchel itself. I'm just saying how embarrassed we were in front of all those people in the train. Everyone cracked jokes, one flatter than the next. There was one man with blue-tinted specs and thick lips who had a head as bald as an egg. He must have thought a lot of himself, for he kept looking into a little mirror, twisting his mustache. He said that the woman would now be as sweet as honey, and went into an uproar at his own joke. Then there was a fat old man with a huge golden chain on his belly and a thick cigar between his teeth. He said something off-color and made the whole crowd laugh. But the women didn't laugh. Their friendship shattered like glass; it fizzled into thin air like a puff of smoke; it disappeared like a dream. The heavily powdered woman from Uman was as mad as hell. The poor thing couldn't understand how anyone could take home-made jam on a trip. So my wife, who had also flown off the handle, answered by saying that it was a matter of taste. "Some take home-made jam, others, war-paint."

I think that the woman knew what Khaye-Etel was driving at. At the very next station, she and her friend from Yehupetz picked up all their luggage and moved to another car without so much as a by-your-leave. Well—at least they left two empty seats!

"It's all your fault."

I'll let the reader guess who said this.

3. An Introduction of Sorts— What Marienbad is and Does—The Ekatrineslav Lady— Volotshisk Station—I Buy and Get Rid of a Bargain

My wife, praised be the Lord, is the sort of person who hates to sit alone, staring at the four walls, as she puts it. She likes to hear others talking and loves to chew the fat herself. When it's quiet in the house, her ears start buzzing and her nerves can't take it. If we're alone at home and have run out of talk (what do husband and wife have to talk about anyway?), she asks me why am I so quiet, why don't I say something?

"What should I talk to you about?" I asked. "We've been talking now for more than twenty years. There's no more stuff left . . ."

"Why do you always find stuff when we're among strangers? Make believe *I'm* a stranger."

Well, try and find an alibi for that one!

I've mentioned all this as a sort of introduction, so that you shouldn't be surprised at my joy when Khaye-Etel, thank God, had finally found someone to talk to during the trip. I myself went looking for a partner for her. In the next car, I found a huge woman from Ekatrineslav traveling with her engaged daughter. That is, a daughter who should have been engaged, who *wanted* to be engaged, for it was high time for her to be hitched. For that very reason, she was taking the girl to Marienbad.

Hearing the word Marienbad, my wife got all excited, because that place tempted her so much. Why Marienbad? You'll never know the logic behind it, just like you'll never know why one likes white, the other black. It depends on your taste. If everybody picked one place to go to, then all the other places would be left empty.

"So you're going to Marienbad, too?" Khaye-Etel asked the woman happily, throwing her a look, as if to say: why is this mountain of a woman going to the hot springs anyway? What could possibly be wrong with *her?* But the Ekatrineslav woman, evidently reading my wife's thoughts, explained:

"I go to Marienbad every summer. Not for any cure, God forbid. I'm the picture of health, thank God. (As anyone could see.) I just hope it continues that way. (Amen!) Then why am I going? To reduce! After six weeks in Marienbad, I leave them about thirty pounds. (Oho!) In that way, Marienbad acts like a medicine for me. The only hitch is that when I come back home to Ekatrineslav, I gain back the thirty pounds I left in Marienbad, plus twenty more (may no evil eye harm you! I thought), for the appetite I develop just kills me."

"Then wouldn't it be better for you to stop going to Marienbad?" I said.

"What are you talking about?" she said. "I have to go there to reduce and get rid of the thirty pounds."

"But you gain them right back," I said, "plus twenty more. That's 1 per cent of a ton each year."

"I didn't know you were such an accountant," the woman threw a dig my way, and my wife looked at me as if to say: mind you own business, scoundrel! So I bit my tongue. I sat and looked at the Ekatrineslav woman and thought of what would happen to her if she lived another twenty years and kept going to Marienbad losing thirty pounds, then gaining them back, with interest. Twenty times twenty is four hundred pounds—exactly one fifth of a ton.

"Volotshisk Station next," the conductor shouted, taking our tickets. All the passengers grabbed their bundles, happy at the approaching frontier.

But for me, there was nothing to be happy about. God himself knew if they were going to give me my luggage without the stubs. For those pieces of paper which I had forgotten to take from the porter, I had to telegraph back to Boyberik.

"What are we going to do if, God forbid, they're not going to give us our luggage?" my wife asked.

"Why look at the black side of things? What if they *do* give it to us?"

Well, here's what happened. When we came to the station, they started passing the buck. A young employee sent us to an older one. The older one to one still older. One said there was a telegram. Another said there wasn't. One said there was a telegram to release the luggage. Another said there was a telegram not to release it. To make a long story short, we had to wire again and wait for an answer.

What about my wife? Would you really like to know what I got from her? If with God's help you too have to whiz away to the hot springs with your wife like I did, and if you too forget the luggage stubs like I did, and if you too have to hang around a station for an extra twenty-four hours like I did— then you too will know the stuff your wife's made of.

The one stroke of good luck we had was that the Ekatrineslav woman and her daughter also had to wait another day.

But for a different reason. Her sister, also on her way to Marienbad, was due on the next train from Odessa, having missed the first one.

"Is your sister, also such a . . . um . . . ?" I asked, and stopped in the middle.

"Such a what?"

"Such a . . . what I mean is . . . is she also going to reduce?"

"Just the opposite," she said. "She's too thin as is. So she goes to fix herself and gains fifteen pounds every year. But when she comes home, she loses those fifteen pounds and fifteen more. She hardly eats a thing. She's so delicate!"

"That means that in ten years," I said, "she loses a hundred fifty pounds. Soon there'll be nothing left of her."

"Who's asking you for your statistics?" my wife swooped down on me, and rightly so. "You've got figures on the brain. My great accountant here. You'll be better off figuring out how much extra the luggage is costing you on account of you're such an absent-minded professor. Go find out if an answer came to our telegram."

Naturally, no answer had come. Things didn't move that quickly. Having nothing to do, I decided to take a walk along the streets. Though Volotshisk was right on the border, it was a small village, like all the Jewish villages in creation. It had a marketplace, stores, and Jews who wandered around with canes in hand and had nothing to do. Since no one knew me, I bought a pound of gooseberries and strolled around town eating them from the paper bag. All of a sudden, I saw a queer animal, the likes of which I'd never seen before. It was some sort of a tall horse covered with yellow, shaggy hair. It was bald in spots, had a split lip, and two humps on its back. I could have sworn it was a camel. A swarthy gypsy was sitting on the ground, warmly wrapped in a coarse white cloth, looking as if he was disgusted with the whole world.

I approached, looking at him and at the two-humped beast with the split lip.

"What's that?" I asked. "A camel?"

"A camel," he said, not looking me in the eye.

"How much is it?" I said, coming closer.

Suddenly, the gypsy stood up, stretched himself into Goliath-length, and shone his eyes straight into mine.

"You buying?"

"Why not?" I said, pulling his leg. "What do you want for it?"

"A hundred and ten rubles," he said. "How much you offering?"

"Twenty-five," I said, still pulling his leg.

"Put up," he said, and took my arm in such a friendly manner that I was afraid to slip away from him. I looked around me and thought: what do I do now? Should I buy it? But then what would I do with a camel? On the other hand, I was afraid not to buy it. He might start swinging. I really don't know what happened to me—but I took out the twenty-five rubles and had myself a camel.

Strangely enough, just as I was a nonentity on the streets before, I now became the center of attraction. People gathered round, staring at me and at the bargain I'd bought.

"Say, old man," someone called out, "how much you want for that walking corpse?"

At first, I just wanted to get my money back. Then I thought I'd take a five ruble loss, then ten, then fifteen. But no go. In fact, when I wanted to give the camel away for nothing, they told me to keep it myself.

What to do? Leave him in the middle of the marketplace and beat it?

First of all, I was ashamed to do it, and, secondly, I was afraid they'd follow me to the station and let my wife in on the deal.

To make a long story short, I paid a few rubles over and above the cost and got rid of the pest. Coming back to the station, I found Khaye-Etel in tears. What was up? The telegram from Boyberik had been here all along, even before we had come. We had telegraphed in vain. We would get our luggage in the evening.

"Where did you disappear to?" my wife asked. "How can

a man just go away for a whole day and wander around God knows where, doing God knows what?"

What you don't know, won't hurt you, I thought. And thank heaven for that!

As soon as we left that town, I began to feel much better. While there, I kept looking around, afraid that at any moment someone would be bringing my bargain back on a leash. The headaches I had with the passport control, the troubles I had on account of my wife's home-made jam, which had a heavy duty slapped on it, the papers which got lost, the fact that the money-changers slipped a fast one over on me and did me out of nine rubles—all this was nothing compared to that silly deal with the camel. I couldn't get it out of my head until the good Lord sent another misfortune my way in Cracow. And that's the next thing I'm going to write about.

4. What a Wife Can Do—
Behatted Men, Bewigged Women—
A Discourse on Jewelry—The Wife Passes Out

What became of that fat woman from Ekatrineslav, her string-bean sister, and her daughter who was dying to get engaged, I don't know. They either evaporated or moved to another car. I wanted to look for them but my wife put her foot down and rightly so.

"Here's a fine how-do-you-do!" she said. "No sooner do we cross the border than you want to leave me all alone in a foreign country and chase after strange women."

"But it's for your own good," I tried to excuse myself, but only succeeded in making it worse.

"First of all, I don't need your favors," she said. "I can do without them. Second of all, if things get too boring, I'll find my own friends."

That's exactly what happened. Just outside of Lemberg the train filled up with passengers. And what passengers they were! Jews wearing queer hats, long, belted black coats and odd-looking shoes and socks. And their wives. So pious! They wore short jackets and were as heavily veiled as rabbi's wives. And their sing-song way of speaking! They all gabbed at once. From deep down in their throats. Talked with their hands, too.

"Are these Germans?" Khaye-Etel asked.

"Well, what do you think of them?" I said.

"It's like Palestine, here," my wife said.

"As I live and breathe, you're so right. You hit the nail right on the head."

We both felt so at home with these people. As if we'd come not into a foreign land, but into Berditshev or one of our village fairs. The only difference was that in trains in our part of the country a group like that would be insulted left and right. The crowd would complain that the Jews were everywhere and were taking over the country. Then the familiar name-calling would begin: "Yid, Jew-boys, exploiters," and other sweet labels which, thank heaven, we'd gotten used to already.

Of course, we got acquainted quickly and started lively conversations. Hearing that we were from Russia, these westerners gave us queer looks, as if we were apes or something. To them, we were human, somehow—then again. . . . They asked pointed, detailed questions, and wanted to know what was cooking in each pot: what did we eat, who was our *rebbe*, were we ever in St. Petersburg or Moscow?

At first, one might think that they had nothing to do but talk politics. But later on, after chatting with them for a while, I found out that they spoke of nothing else but baked fish, stuffed geese, roast veal, and other things which pertained to the realm of the stomach.

All this took place on the men's side of the fence. My wife and those pious women talked about entirely different things. The latest fashions were discussed. What *we* were wearing and what *they* were wearing. And although we were only Russians and they were from the West, the upshot was that we followed the latest styles more readily.

"For example," my Khaye-Etel told the women, "take your jewelry and take ours. If one of our *fraus* (here, Khaye-Etel used the German word instead of the Yiddish—she was learning fast!), for instance, were caught with two bombs like that in her ears, she'd be chased down the street."

These words were aimed at a bewigged woman from Lemberg, who had two huge golden earrings dangling and waggling from her ears.

"And what sort of earrings do they wear in Russia?" asked a red-faced, sniffly-eyed woman, who until now had been sitting in a corner, quiet as a mouse.

"Back home, earrings are earrings," said Khaye-Etel, and without any further ado, started to unpack the big trunk. She then displayed the box with all the jewelry I'd ever bought her since I started making money.

It made a big hit with the group. All the women, and some men, too, crowded around, looking into the box and at the pretty earrings, valuable rings, pearl necklaces, and the rest of the gems with which she wouldn't part for even a day.

"What good will jewelry do you at the hot springs?" I had asked her back home, before the trip. "Who knows? Maybe it'll get stolen, God forbid."

"And what about me? Bite your tongue!" she said. "You always have to imagine the worst."

I should care, I thought. It's your jewelry and your decision.

In the meantime, I must confess, I got so involved in political and other talk with these westerners, that I forgot all about Khaye-Etel. When did I first remember she was alive? When the fat German conductor with his queer hat and huge clumsy-looking key came through, cawing, "Cra-cow, Cra-cow," in his high-pitched crow-like voice. As to what he said after that —the devil only knows.

"Here's where we're going to have a bite," my wife said.

She took me by the arm, quite aristocratic-like, and we strolled through the magnificent terminal, as chipper as a honeymoon couple. Moments of bliss and beautiful blue-skied days like these were rare in the lifetime of a married pair. For the most part, there were either clouds or rain, freezing cold waves, or merciless hot spells which took their toll. Even after a sudden cloudburst, the sun would shine for a while and then disappear again.

If it's been any different with you—well then, you were born lucky, as they say. Such beautifully sunny and happy days, I must admit, came none too often in our lives. Who was more at fault? I really don't know. By nature, I'm pretty spiteful. My wife had a nervous condition. Put spite and nerves together—it's like cat and dog—soon the fur begins to fly. But, since we ran into a fine, bright day, we took advantage of it and enjoyed ourselves to the utmost.

"Khaye-Etel, dear, what do you say to this carefree land? Isn't it nice here?"

"Paradise," she said, in her usual manner, looking at me with such warmth that I realized there was no one prettier than she.

"What do you say, darling," I said, "would you like to live here always?"

"With you? Of course."

"With the one you love, even in an tent," I said, just the way the books do.

Then, she smiled one of those smiles which gladden heaven and earth. Everyone took on a new appearance. Even the conductor passing by. The cop with his huge horse. The poor German beggar waiting for a handout. It all took on a new color, a new form. Everything smiled and sang, danced and welcomed us.

"Khaye-Etel?"

"What is it, dear?"

"Let's give each other our word of honor that from now on we'll get along peacefully. We won't fight any more, we won't . . ."

Suddenly, she tore her hand out of mine, stepped back and yelled in an odd voice. "The box. The box!"

"God help you! What box?"

"The jewelry box," she screamed, and dropped into a dead faint.

Everyone in the terminal gathered around. Within a minute, a doctor and a druggist had appeared and they brought Khaye-

Etel around. When she came to, the real tears began to flow.

"Oh me, oh me! My jewels! My jewels!"

Nothing helped. Neither kind words, nor promises to buy her other gems. She didn't want to hear a word. She bawled, she wrung her hands, she fainted, she was going crazy.

"Woe is me! All is lost! My jewelry! All the jewels are gone!"

The jewels *were* gone, but the colossal woman from Ekatrineslav and her not-quite engaged daughter were found.

"Oh my God! What happened to you?" the huge woman asked. As soon as she found out about the loss, she wrung her hands and asked how could anyone flash jewelry so openly? Everyone who heard the news pulled a sad face and asked the same question.

"It's all his fault. Him and his big, fat mouth," Khaye-Etel said.

There's no need telling you who she meant, is there?

5. Nerves on the Rampage Again— The Odessa Citron—The Wife Gets Sore— Remedy to the Malady—Aunt Nekhame from Otseles

Before we got to Vienna, Khaye-Etel really got sick. Too many troubles, evidently, and this ruined my trip at the very outset. It was hard to say what was wrong with her. But you could tell her nerves were played out just by looking at *me*. Don't laugh. You can tell by a man's face if his wife's got a nervous condition. Show me any man, and within a minute I'll tell you if his wife is nervous or not. You just have to have a crackerjack eye.

An awful lot of cures for nervous conditions are on the market, but there isn't a one that's worth its salt. The most effective remedy is to leave the patient alone. That's exactly what I did. No matter what she said to me, I never talked back. I just swallowed a mouthful of air and kept still. Sometimes this combination of her talking and my keeping quiet, ended up in a brawl. But I wasn't afraid of a scene in the train. For right opposite me sat the mountainous woman from Ekatrineslav, who didn't stop nibbling; her not-quite engaged daughter, who kept staring into a mirror, inspecting the pimples on her face; and her thin-as-a-broomstick sister from Odessa, who was so delicate and yellowish, she looked like the citron used for *Sukkoth*.

Although the women were so chummy before, they exchanged neither glances nor words now. Khaye-Etel didn't even want *me* to talk to them. But, as if in spite, the three kept asking me to do things for them. Bring down a suitcase, unpack a bundle, close the window, buy something at the terminal, and like chores one must perform while exiled among a pack of women. But the yellowish citron from Odessa annoyed me most of all. Although ugly as sin, she put on such airs one would think there was none like her on earth. I was tempted to tell her the truth. Madam, whether you know it or not, your face would stop a clock!

Haven't you ever had something silly at the tip of your tongue that was just dying to be said? I once got smacked for something like that. More than once, too. But since we're talking about the hot springs, let's not get sidetracked.

To make a long story short, the women bossed me around and my wife fumed and fussed at them, at me, and at the rest of the world something awful. I had the funny feeling that a full-fledged storm was brewing and that pretty soon I'd have a minor catastrophe on my hands. But, since the good Lord is kind and gracious, he decided to send the remedy before the malady. He pitied me and sent a new lady to save me. Back home, she'd be called a fishwife, but since she was on her way to the hot springs, I'll call her a lady. Walking through our car, she spotted Khaye-Etel, ran over, fell on her neck, and the two started raining kisses on each other. The passengers looked at them and smiled.

"Khaye-Etel! Is it really you? Oh I'm going to do myself some harm!"

"Auntie, what are you doing here?"

"What are *you* doing here? Where you going, Khaye-Etel, honey? To the hot springs?"

"Naturally to the hot springs. How about you, auntie?"

"To the hot springs, too. And this must be your husband, right? Oh I'm going to do myself some harm!"

And that's how we got to know one another—without actually speaking or introducing ourselves. I discovered that she was my wife's aunt Nekhame, who came from a little oddly-named village, Otseles. Which means that it was spelled Volotsegolovo, but the Jews, hating long names, shortened it to Otseles. And so she was known: Aunt Nekhame from Otseles.

"Which bath are you going to, auntie?" Khaye-Etel asked.

"The devil knows the name of the place. Actually, I once *did* know where I was going to, but I forgot. I just know it ends with *bad*."

"Could it be Marienbad?"

"Could be!"

"Or Carlsbad?"

"You hit the nail right on the head. Let it be Carlsbad!"

"Perhaps it's Francesenbad. Or the Baden-Baden baths?"

"Let it be that bath. What do I care? Hot baths, cold baths. So long as it's a bath. The doctor told me to bathe in hot springs and that's what I'm going to do. In his letter to the professor he probably mentions the place."

Aunt Nekhame deserves to be written up right and proper. So here's her life story in a nutshell. First of all, she was Khaye-Etel's aunt, my mother-in-law's sister. So any aunt of Khaye-Etel's was an aunt of mine. And, second of all, she's the sort of person it pays to get to know closely, believe me!

Evidently, she was quite beautiful in her youth and to this day she remained good-humored and fun-loving. Her first husband was a rich, but senile old fogey. She suffered along with him for a little while until he kicked the bucket. This made her a childless and well-loaded young widow. Now, these things are no drawbacks in finding the right man, marrying a second time, and starting anew. What sort of bird

this "right man" was, I don't know. I only know, he stayed
back there in Otseles and sent her abroad to the hot springs for
six weeks and told her to have a good time, spend freely, do
anything she wanted, and buy whatever she liked.

That's how Aunt Nekhame put it, and, as she spoke, I saw
the rest of the women turning green with envy at the carefree,
happy life she had with her husband. Even Khaye-Etel, I'm
ashamed to say, looked at her aunt, then at me as if to say:
Well, that's what I call a husband!

Auntie's tongue kept wagging without a break. Pint-sized,
white, and round all over was she, with a round, double-chin,
a nose like a little kidney-bean, gray eyes, and a hoarse voice.
She kept moving as she talked, dancing this way and that, doing a jig with her body and hands. She kept forgetting what
she was talking about, mixed the man in the moon with the
price of tea in China, and got so confused she didn't know
whether she was coming or going. Then, she'd slap her hefty
hips and say: "Oh I'm going to do myself some harm," and
laugh so lustily that everyone had to laugh along with her.

"Auntie," I asked, "which professor are you supposed to
see?"

"Ask me another!" said she. "My dandy doctor from
Otseles wrote it down on a slip of paper, but I don't know if
he's in Vienna or Berlin? Oh I'm going to do myself some
harm."

She started going through all her pockets and couldn't find
the note.

"Do you at least know what's wrong with you?" I asked,
out of curiosity.

"Here we go! Now I'll start rattling off my list of ailments,"
she said, and started laughing. All the other women giggled
too, as if I'd said something silly. Nevertheless, I was tickled
pink and thankful that she had come along just at the right
moment. I'll never forget her for getting me out of more than
one pickle, both while en route and while at the hot springs.
Actually, she was just what the doctor ordered for my wife's
nerves. She alone was able to bring Khaye-Etel around, mak-

ing her chatter when she was silent and laugh when she was blue.

If you're married, reader, and your wife has a nervous condition, and you have to take her to the hot springs, may God send you an Aunt Nekhame from Otseles. You'll be spared many of the headaches that can befall a married man.

6. The Big Scare in Vienna— Their Damn Language—We Starve

We stuck together until we got to Vienna, agreeing to get off at the same station and go to the same professor. In short, we couldn't separate. But the minute we got to Vienna, pandemonium broke loose. There was a general hodge-podge and things got entirely out of hand. The first blow came with the help of the railroad porters who swooped down on us from all sides like a bunch of devils. They talked queerly, didn't look you in the eye, grabbed your luggage, and then said in German: "Carry your bags, sir?"

But I didn't know what they were talking about. Khaye-Etel wanted to stop them and gave me the eye, as if to say: why don't you open your mouth? But these hoodlums paid no more attention to us than Haman does the noisemakers. They took our bags and started scampering to God knows where, we tailing after them.

"Why'd you let them?" Khaye-Etel hollered, chasing after them. "Why don't you ask them where they're taking us? You can talk German with them."

"They're probably going up the station. What are you worried about?"

"Is that so? What am I worried about, eh? You're looking for another jewelry box, huh?" Khaye-Etel was all set to let me have the talking-down I deserved. But then we saw Aunt Nekhame stretched out on the floor, her hands spread over her bundles, like a mother eagle protecting her young. One of the gangsters standing next to her wanted to take her bags. But she would not let him and yelled:

"Get your paws off the stuff! Oh I'm going to do myself some harm!"

That little scene looked so comical, even we couldn't help rolling with laughter.

"God be with you, auntie," Khaye-Etel said. "What are you afraid of? They're carrying our things too, and we're not worried."

In the midst of the tumult, we lost the Ekatrineslav woman, her daughter and sister. Thank God that at least Khaye-Etel, Aunt Nekhame, and I held on to one another. Aunt Nekhame took hold of my wife's dress and would not let go of it. Khaye-Etel grabbed me. And that's how we three managed to stick together.

After all that trouble, we finally unloaded our baggage. Then, one of the hoodlums, a red-head with a white apron, came up to us. He started spinning out a yarn in his mixed-up lingo, which couldn't be understood, since he talked not with his mouth but with his throat. Anyway, he swallowed his words so quickly, I could barely make them out. I did manage to snatch the words "hotel," "horses," and "wagon."

"What does he want? Oh I'm going to do myself some harm," Aunt Nekhame asked Khaye-Etel.

"Ask the porter what he wants," Khaye-Etel told me. "Ask him in German what he's saying."

"He wants to know if we want to use horses or the trolley to get to town."

"On horseback!" Aunt Nekhame shouted. We all laughed.

"Stop giggling," my wife told me. "Tell him in German to call a coachman."

I made a whipping motion with my hand and backed it up with a whistle. Just imagine! He understood me right away!

"*Jawohl*," he said, and in a flash we were all seated in a huge carriage hitched to such healthy horses, the likes of which we'd never seen. The brawny red-headed German also took care of our bags. After I'd slipped him a good-sized coin, he doffed his hat and started pouring on the thanks. Pipe in mouth, our full-sized cabbie slowly took the blankets off the horses.

(Here, all the horses were blanketed so that, heaven forbid, they would not catch a cold.) Then the cabbie sat down, turned around, and started jabbering. I couldn't make heads or tails of his guttural tone. Out here, they all used their throats instead of their mouths.

"What does he want?" asked Aunt Nekhame.

"Ask him what he wants," Khaye-Etel told me.

"What is it, German? What do you want?" I asked the cabbie, doing most of the talking with my hands.

Aunt Nekhame helped by asking in Yiddish: "Are you talking about a hotel?"

"Enough, auntie," Khaye-Etel said. "Let my husband say it in German."

These words pepped me up so much that I started talking German and French. "Un grande hotel die beste qualität frante fenetre!" To that, I added a French click of tongue. My cabbie understood me and said, "Jawohl, jawohl."

Before we knew it we were in front of a huge building with shining windows. Another pack of black-jacketed demons ran toward us, snatched the luggage out of our hands, and brought us inside. A man with two cheeksful of beard approached us. You could have sworn he was a duke or some such big-wig, but he turned out to be Swiss. He flicked off his hat and wished us a hearty good morning.

"How many rooms do you want?" he asked the ladies in German.

"What's he muttering about? Oh I'm going to do myself some harm," said Aunt Nekhame.

"He wants to know how many rooms you want?"

"Tell him two in German," said Khaye-Etel.

I stuck out two fingers then added in French: "Frante fenetre, bonjour."

"Jawohl," he said. "First floor," and led us into a suite of huge rooms.

"What's the rate per day?" Aunt Nekhame asked in Yiddish.

The poor German looked at her dumbstruck; he didn't know what was going on and threw a honeyed smiled my way. "I suggest that perhaps we continue speaking German."

"Tell him in German," Khaye-Etel told me. I rubbed my thumb and forefinger, as if to say: how much? He blinked, completely at a loss. Blast their language! Back home, we also spoke German, but it wasn't the German they spoke here. Sometimes in Yehupetz I had business dealings with Germans. I talked half-Yiddish, half-German and we got along swimmingly. But here, God save us, you could break your teeth talking to them.

Only at first, though. The longer we stayed, the more we got used to their language. Soon we understood one another with just a glance. In fact, the next day Khaye-Etel and Aunt Nekhame went shopping all by themselves. They bought all sorts of things and were royally cheated, like in the worst of dives.

"Well, how do you like Vienna, Khaye-Etel?" I asked my wife after we had washed, changed clothes, drunk tea, and seen the town.

"May it burn to a crisp!" she said. "Imagine not finding one place to eat in this whole town!"

What was wrong? We had looked for a Jewish restaurant and wandered all over Vienna for six hours without success. Whoever we approached, either didn't understand us, or we didn't understand them. When we *did* get directions—left, right, straight ahead—upon arriving, we found absolutely nothing! So for nourishment that day, we ate our hearts out, living on coffee, soft-boiled eggs, and Viennese butter-rolls which melted in your mouth like snow.

Finally, on the second day, we found a kosher restaurant. Not only kosher, but kosher to the nth degree. The owner of the place, although German-speaking, wore a skullcap; the customers washed themselves and said blessings before they ate. They greeted you and wanted to know how you were, where you were from, where you're going to and why? If on business—what sort? If for health—which doctor? In other words, quite Jewish-like, just like in Warsaw.

7. Home Among Jews—
The Restaurateur's Advice—
A Lamp Salesman Examines the Ladies

You know, there's a lot of truth to the saying: "Among Jews you never get lost." What would we have done, for instance, if we hadn't stumbled on to the Jewish restaurant where the owner himself was kind enough to suggest a doctor?

If we had stuck to the Germans and their jaw-breaking lingo, we'd still be wandering around Vienna. That Swiss hotelman didn't give a damn about what we did in Vienna. As far as he was concerned, we could have stayed until after *Rosh Hashana* and even *Sukkoth*. What did he care? So long as we stayed in his plush place, drinking his fine tea, which was served straight from the kettle, paying for each glass of water and for the elevator which we used twenty times a day. That elevator didn't please Khaye-Etel at all. She said it gave her dizzy spells. The first time Aunt Nekhame rode in it she had such a fit, we had to pinch ourselves to prevent an outburst of laughter.

But among Jews, it was entirely different. The owner of the restaurant started grilling us right away. Who were we? Where from? Where to? What's wrong with us? Which professor were we seeing?

Hearing that we were on our way to the hot springs and scenting lots of cash, he told us we'd have to see a professor first, for it would be too bad for us, God forbid, if we went to the hot springs without seeing one. The next problem was —which one? That could be answered only by the doctor. Which doctor? Only his brother-in-law could tell us. He had connections with all the doctors. If we wanted, we could wait for him.

Naturally, no one likes the looks of the whole business.

"Maybe it'd be a good idea if we headed straight for the professor," I said. "After all, we're not knocking at death's door, heaven forbid. We're pretty healthy, thank God. We only want to know which hot spring to go to."

"Where do you think you are, Russia?" the restaurateur said. "So you want to go straight to the professor, huh? Well, go right ahead. Only don't be sorry later."

"You always have to start something!" Khaye-Etel whispered.

"What do you care if we see a doctor first?" Aunt Nekhame chimed in.

The upshot was, we would first see the doctor. That is we'd wait for the brother-in-law. He would then bring us to the doctor, who would take us to the professor.

Look at how much pull you had to have in Vienna just to get to see a professor.

We spent an entire day in the hotel waiting for the brother-in-law. The sun was about to set and we three sat by a window watching the bustling city and its silly Germans, all of whom ran about wearing top-hats. Suddenly, there was a knock at the door. After the third rap, in walked a man looking like a diplomat. He wore a top-hat, gloves, morning coat, and carried a huge cane. Although it was pitch black outside, he said in a sing-song:

"Good da-a-ay!"

"May a bunch of dingy nightmares plague all my enemies! Oh I'm going to do myself some harm!" said Aunt Nekhame.

We couldn't restrain ourselves and burst out laughing. But the German didn't go for this at all. Our laughing made him mad as hell and he banged his cane on the table, shouting:

"Shameless curs . . . Russian swine!"

Pigs, in other words, eh? So, I got up and told him we weren't laughing at him, but at our aunt.

"Is she mentally ill?" he asked in German, then asked in Yiddish if she was *meshugge*. Hearing that Yiddish word, I knew he was Jewish. I learned he was the brother-in-law we'd been waiting for. Chances are he spoke Yiddish, too. We then went wild with joy, quickly ordered some tea, and got down to business.

"Well then, what's wrong with you?" he asked us.

How could we tell him if we didn't know ourselves? I sidestepped by saying that it was something we could only tell the professor. But he went on his own sweet way and said that there were as many professors in Vienna as stars up above. There was a different professor for each disease. (Knock wood; I thought.) I wondered what my next move was to be? What sort of malady should I dream up for him? I considered it—then made a complete about-face and told him the honest-to-goodness truth that I was as healthy as a horse. I pointed to my wife and aunt and said *they* were the sick ones.

"Did you get the sense of what I said?" I asked him.

"Yes," he said with a queer look, then turned to the women. "Would you mind telling me what's wrong with you?"

"Oh, I'm going to do myself some harm! Get him out of here," said Aunt Nekhame to Khaye-Etel. They kicked me out of the room for a few minutes. When they admitted me again, I found out that the professor's name was Roytnagel and the doctor's Zilbershtern.

"What do you do?" I asked the brother-in-law.

"I'm a lamp and lampshade salesman," he said, calmly.

"I knew it! I knew it! I could have told you so! Oh I'm going to do myself some harm," Aunt Nekhame burst out, clapping her hands. Khaye-Etel turned red as a beet, and I went into hysterics again. In order that the salesmen not feel insulted again, I thought up a phony excuse and told him I just remembered something that happened in Yehupetz the year before.

"You get the sense of it?" I asked.

"There's no doubt that *I* got the sense of it. But if you've got any sense at *all*—that's another matter!" he said in German, and picked up his cane, top-hat, and morning coat and left in a huff. I had the feeling that a bitter hatred had started between us.

8. The Professor Wants to Separate Us— Our Squabble with Vienna— Aunt Nekhame Shows Her Stuff

It's easier to get a son into a Russian high-school or out of the military service than it is to see Professor Roytnagel. Before seeing him, Doctor Zilbershtern did us all sorts of favors, gave us plenty of advice, and wrote prescriptions. All this for the sake of the lamp salesman who in turn was doing *his* brother-in-law, the restaurateur, a favor. It wasn't until the third day that we got to see the friendly Professor Roytnagel. He admitted us separately, and prescribed for each of us a different hot spring. He packed my wife off to Francesenbad, Aunt Nekhame to Marienbad, and me to Carlsbad.

Coming out of the professor's office, we all stopped in our tracks and stared at each other, not saying a word, but thinking: Well, what now? We decided to ask Dr. Zilbershtern's advice. But, since we didn't come during his office hours, we had to go back to the lamp salesman. Not knowing where he was, we ended up going to the restaurateur.

"Well, what's new?" he asked.

"Nothing new at all," we said. "Your brother-in-law just killed us. All three of us. He had each of us sent to a different bath."

"Oh, is that all? What's so bad about that?" he said quite calmly.

"You're some smartie," my wife told him. "You think I came way out here to be separated from my husband? Me go up north and him down south?"

"Take it easy, lady," he said, "it's not so far from Francesenbad to Carlsbad. A two or three hour trip at the most. Either he can come see you or you can go see him."

"Thanks for the tip," Khaye-Etel said, getting mad. "May you live to tell better news and give better advice . . ."

". . . to the noodles in the kitchen," Aunt Nekhame added, sarcastically.

"I have nothing to do with fishwives," the restaurateur said.

This peeved Khaye-Etel and she told him that that fishwife was none other than her own aunt and came of much nobler family than he, his whole restaurant, and even his fine, door-to-door lamp and lampshade pedlar of a brother-in-law.

"Come on," Khaye-Etel said to me, "let's go. I'd rather eat soft-boiled eggs than meet up with such hoodlums who give you German sweet-talk while they cheat you out of Russian rubles."

None of these insults bothered him until he heard the words "Russian rubles." He then flew into a wild rage. He got so hot under the collar that he sprang at us like a savage beast, ready to do us in. The long and short of it was that we barely got out of the restaurant alive. Adding insult to injury, they escorted us out into the street, waving their fists and hollering: "Russian swine, Russian swine."

But the best was yet to come. We had a little encore at the hotel with the brother-in-law. A bit later the lamp and lamp-shade salesman knocked at our door and came in with an-other German, also wearing a top-hat, but without the morn-ing coat.

"Why was I insulted behind my back?" he wanted to know. He kept banging his cane on the table, getting red in the face. We were sure he would start slugging us. Who knows what tricks the German was liable to pull?

But this didn't faze Aunt Nekhame from Otseles. That German didn't bother her at all. Jumping out of her chair, she ran right up to him, and hands on hips, she stuck her face up to his and let him have it and in plain Yiddish, too.

"Now you listen to me, you half-baked German, you wood-pecking nitwit, you broken-down lampshade. Oh I'm going to do myself some harm! You thought you'd scare us with that funeral outfit and that black chimney on top of your block? But all you've done is hold us up for a few rubles for abso-lutely nothing, you hoodwinking rascal. Think we don't know who you are, you seedy beggar, you down-and-out bum? Are you still here? In another minute I'm going to pluck out every last hair of your mangy beard, you hear? Because I've socked men who wouldn't even put you in their side pocket. Well, what do you say that crazy German with that noodle-pot on his head! Oh I'm going to do myself some harm! Take my ad-vice and beat it. You'll be better off!"

I don't know if he was frightened away by Aunt Nekhame, who at that instant looked like a mad hen ready to scratch his eyes out. Perhaps he just didn't want to start up with her. The German took his morning coat, his top-hat, and beat it as fast as his legs could carry him to the door. He slammed it with a bang. Once on the other side of the threshold, he called us Russian swine. But we'd gotten used to that greeting just like we'd gotten used to hello.

From that day on I began to respect Aunt Nekhame. Her stock shot up 99 per cent in our eyes, and we decided to remain together for the rest of our trip.

GLOSSARY

Baal Shem Tov: see *Hasidism*

bagel: a donut-shaped hard roll, whose dough is first boiled, then baked.

borscht: a soup made of beets or cabbage, of Russian origin.

Code of Law: (*Shulkhan Arukh*) published in 1565 and compiled by Joseph Caro, it contains all the laws observed by Orthodox Jews.

dredle: a child's top.

grieven: fried bits of skin and fat.

Hagada: the book of the Passover home service which recounts the Jewish exodus from Egypt. At the beginning of the service, the youngest child asks his father the *Four Questions*, the first of which is: "Why is this night different from all other nights?" The father answers by telling the story of Jewish slavery and liberation.

Hanuka: the Festival of Lights celebrated for eight days, starting the twenty-fifth of Kislev (December). It marks the struggle for religous freedom and the successful revolt of poorly armed Jews against the forces of Antiochus Epiphanes, who proscribed the practice of Judaism. In 165 B.C.E., the Jewish fighters, led by Judah Maccabeus, routed the Syrians and rededicated the Temple.

Hasidism: founded by Israel Baal Shem Tov, the Master of the Good Name (1700-60). The movement, a revolt against rabbinism and its intellectuality, accented good deeds and piety through joy of worship, songs, legends, and dance. It had a wide appeal with the masses and its followers were, and still are, called *Hasidim.*

Hoshana Rabba: the seventh day of *Sukkoth.* Tradition has it that on this day God's judgment of man, sealed on *Yom Kippur*, receives final confirmation.

knaidlach: matzoh-balls.

kugels: puddings.

Lag Ba-Omer: a day of festivity, especially for Jewish children, who are released from their studies and taken into the fields and woods. Tradition says that the plague which attacked the disciples of Rabbi Akiba, who fought and died in the revolt against Rome (132 C.E.), ceased on this day.

latkes: pancakes.

matzohs: the square, unleavened bread eaten during Passover.

meshugge: crazy.

mezuza: a rolled piece of parchment containing the verses from Deuteronomy, VI:4-9 and XI:13-17, and inserted in a wooden or metal case. It is affixed on the right-hand doorpost of Jewish homes and synagogues.

Mishna: the body of oral law redacted c. 200 C.E. by Rabbi Judah.

Ninth Day of Ab: a day of mourning and fasting (August). Tradition tells us that both the First Temple (586 B.C.E.) and the Second (70 C.E.) were destroyed on that day by Nebuchadnezzar and Titus, respectively.

Passover: the eight day festival starting the fourteenth of Nissan (April) and commemorating the Jews' freedom from Egyptian bondage. It was also an agricultural feast during which the Israelites offered up the first fruits of the winter barley.

Purim: the festival celebrating the Jews' deliverance from Haman's plan to exterminate them, as described in the Book of Esther. It is celebrated on the fourteenth day of Adar (March), and is noted for its gaiety. In the synagogues, where the Book of Esther is read from scrolls, children rattle noisemakers whenever Haman's name is mentioned.

Reb: Mister.

rebbe: the spiritual leader of a group of *Hasidim,* not necessarily the rabbi of a community. It was quite common for Jews to travel distances great and small to visit their *rebbe.*

ritual fringes: (*tsitsis, talith-kot'n*) a four-cornered, fringed garment worn underneath the shirt by male, Orthodox Jews, who observe the biblical commandment to wear a garment with fringes (Numbers, XV:37-41).

Rosh Hashana: the Jewish New Year, celebrated the first and second days of Tishri. Next to *Yom Kippur,* these are the the most solemn days of the year.

Seventeenth Day of Tammuz: a fast day (July), commemorating the day on which the city walls of Jerusalem were breached. This subsequently led to the razing of Jerusalem and the destruction of the Temple by Titus.

Simkhas-Torah: the festival immediately following *Sukkoth* on which the reading of the Torah is completed and begun anew. This joyous holiday is traditionally celebrated with singing and dancing.

Shevuoth: The Feast of Weeks celebrated on the sixth and seventh of Sivan (May-June), seven weeks after Passover. It marks the day on which the Torah was given to Israel on mount Sinai, and also the day on which the first fruits of the wheat harvest were offered to God.

Sukkoth: the Feast of Booths celebrated for seven days (nine, including *Shemini Atzereth* and *Simkhas Torah*), starting the fifteenth day of Tishri. It commemorates the Jews' living in booths or tents during their wanderings in the desert, and is, in addition, the harvest festival.

Torah: literally, the Teaching; the Pentateuch; the five books of Moses.

traif: not kosher.

Yom Kippur: the Day of Atonement, the tenth day of Tishri. This is the most solemn day of the year, wherein the Jews pray and fast all day long and communicate their sins directly to their Creator and beg for forgiveness.

www.ingramcontent.com/pod-product-compliance
Lightning Source LLC
Chambersburg PA
CBHW031923060726
47496CB00002BB/297